INTO THE DEADLANDS

BOOK 2 OF THE KARA MASON STORY

JILL N DAVIES

JILL N DAVIES BOOKS

INTO THE DEADLANDS

Book 2 of the Kara Mason Story

If you've ever thought "I'm not it,"
You're wrong.
And this book is for you

KARA MASON

MOE SIMONS

JOREY

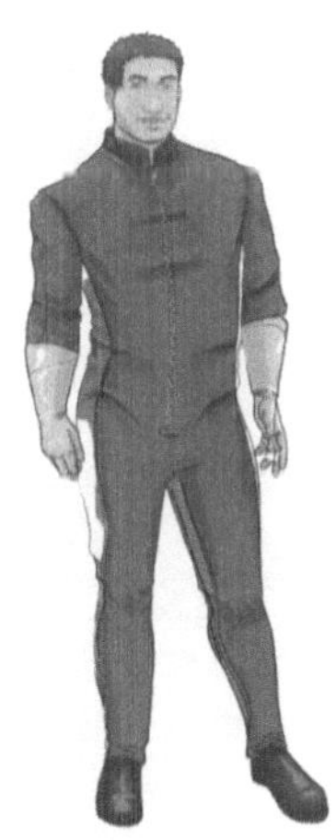

AUTHOR'S NOTE

Kara's story continues in the harrowing journey of Into the Deadlands. Please note the content warnings and read at your own discretion.

For everyone who waited literal years for this book release, I'm indebted to you, your support and your undying faith in my ability to get this written. As far as the contents of this book, I'm sorry, but I'm not sorry.

Content warning:
Depictions of PTSD and trauma, violence, gore, injury/injury detail, vomiting, character death, succumbing to a disease, sexual harassment, implied sexual assault, reference to abortion, use of alcohol, mild cruelty to animals, and fire.

CONTENTS

Part I   1
The Cure

Part II   109
Tunnels and Reactors

Part III   253
The Outskirts

Acknowledgments   363
About the Author   365
Also by Jill N Davies   367

PART ONE

THE CURE

CHAPTER
ONE

I STARE out the back of the transport vehicle at the ruins of the Northern Laboratories. Everything is gone—the dormitories, the cafeteria, the training room. The kill floors and cure labs. Black wisps of smoke reach upward with ashy fingertips, grasping at the wind, which draws them into the frozen nothingness surrounding us. That smoke carries the ashes of the dead like an ancient pyre. I imagine Shelby's remains getting swept up in the storm and scattered across the barren tundra along with the lost families. Our hopes are bitter and burnt, a bad taste carried on the wind.

Shelby sacrificed herself to save me.

She chose me over Hank, over Tucker, and now, over herself.

My mind spirals through the hall of tragedies that make up my life. Dad, Bruce and Hank, sacrificed in the clearing only half a day's walk from our exit point. Miller's vacant, staring eyes. The blood running down millions of fiber optic strands stuck into the ceiling of the training room. Simons' cry of agony at the sight of Trudy, transformed and hungry. The panicked expression of hopelessness on Altman's face as the hive surrounded him. Shelby leaping into Orman's shot. Death converges on me from all sides.

I close my eyes, trying to turn the images grey, but they remain vibrant, red-stained scars on the back of my eyelids. My breath catches in a choked sob. I give up trying to force the memories to fade, drawn to the present by a dull moan that transforms into a piercing cry of pain. The sound comes to me from far away.

The winter we turned thirteen, Hank broke his ankle falling on the frozen creek that flowed through our field.

"Hank! Wake up," I whisper too loud in the low morning light.

"No. Can't wake, need sleep," he mumbles into his pillow, rolling away from me.

I shake his hunched figure, trying to pry the cover from his grasping fingers.

"Busy growing!" he protests again as I yank even harder against the covers, revealing the top tuft of his mussed, reddish hair.

"Snow means a snowball fight," I prompt.

His head pops up, alert now. "Is it really that much snow?"

"See for yourself," I say, hopping off his bed and rushing to the closet to get dressed. Hank is right behind me as I pull on my warmest clothes, the challenge accepted. We race down the hall, taking care not to rouse Dad. In the mudroom, we throw on our thick canvas jackets and step into knee-high boots…

The engine roars effort, and someone cries out.

Hank is on his back, wailing in barely contained agony at the snap of bone where his fibula used to connect…

I shake my head to banish the converging memories. There's a commotion and heavy panting in the back of the vehicle. I look over my shoulder, past the empty cryogenic cylinder slots and passenger benches to where Richards is hunched over Dunn's gory frame.

"Don't bother, I'm finished!" Dunn pants.

"You're going to be okay," Richards sooths.

He moves a blood-drenched hand toward Simons, who produces a syringe. I think of Carmen, so calm as she sighed her last plea: *find her.* There was so much death in the Northern Laboratories. We had to burn it down. We had to leave. But Shelby was supposed to be here with us. This was her plan.

"One thing at a time," Shelby said. First we get the cure out of the Northern Laboratories, then we worry about dodging the DDC and getting through the Deadlands. She was going to explain all of it after the escape.

Instead, we're without a guide. The thought transports me back to wet ferns glancing across my pant legs as I follow Dad through the unmarked forest with the vague notion of our destination—*South.* Shelby was supposed to have this role—she was better suited and infinitely wiser. I know little more about the Deadlands now than I did all those years ago. Whatever happens next will have to be my plan.

"He was selfish. He destroyed more lives and saved none." The memory of Amos's proclamation about my father rings through as clearly as if it were her hand resting on my shoulder instead of Jorey's. I've taken on the same task he did, with his same reckless lack of foresight.

Hank was always good with electronics, but the months after he broke his ankle made all the difference. It was when we split into different people, still twins, still connected, but unique. If we'd taken the test before then, our scores would've been identical, and Hank wouldn't have built me a miniature moon.

"Help me!"

"We've almost got it."

There is no safety. No comfort or security. We're driving into a storm. The wind roars a pulsing beat through the frozen valley. Every gust causes the vehicle to slide on the icy road. My own inertia drags my body against the cold metal grating covering the floor as the vehicle accelerates to the left.

The darkening clouds heave ominous thunder as powdery snowflakes transform into sleet. Visibility is compromised with every passing second, and we haven't set our course yet. We have to get off the road and out of sight before someone finds us. *Before they send out their trail of near-dead to track us...* It won't be hard. There's nothing but road for hundreds of miles between civilization and the Northern Laboratories.

In a brilliant flash of clarity, I recognize my symptoms for what they are: shock. The lucid images, the inability to focus, the rapid thundering heartbeat and ragged breaths. I was expecting to not make it out of the Laboratories. I wasn't planning to run again, responsible for everyone's lives.

I swallow the brassy taste and breathe deeply, attempting once again to turn everything grey. Our situation rushes into focus, and I become vividly aware of the frantic activity behind me. Cain and Richards are hard at work trying to get Dunn's bleeding to stop. The entire side of Dunn's suit is ripped away, exposing a gaping wound.

"It's over. Just kill me—" Dunn's head flops against the side of the vehicle.

Richards lifts his hand to set aside the sedative, then returns to the work. "Put your hand there, just long enough so I can cauterize the artery," he instructs Cain.

Minutes pass until the job is done. Cain stands, holding his blood-drenched hands out in front of him. Richards offers him the ultraviolet wand—the only sterilization mechanism we have. It'll have to be enough. Cain uses it on himself, then the floor of the vehicle before returning it to Richards.

"We need to find shelter. Now," Simons says.

Cain turns toward him. "No, we have to get off the road."

"Are you crazy? Dunn won't make it if we don't do something," Simons protests. He shifts from his position next to me to face Cain, and I lose my view of him.

"He's infected, he's not going to make it! The roads aren't safe. We'll be too easy to find. Believe me, someone *will* be looking for us," Cain insists.

"There's no way anybody could have survived that blast," Simons objects.

"Somebody survived. We need to get underground," Cain presses.

"Underground?" Jorey asks, yelling over a new, violent gust of wind. His grip on my shoulder tightens as the vehicle sways.

"Just trust me, okay? How do you think I got up here?" Cain

growls. His voice is tense. I imagine his jaw clenched tight, making his strong face stern. I wonder if his fists are balled up.

I've never heard of anyone arriving at the Northern Laboratories any way besides a transport. It's supposed to be impossible. *Underground?* Does he mean figuratively? The question itches for my attention, probing me to dive in and explore. It whispers for me to ignore our situation, to pretend that our next decisions won't determine our fate. I force the notion down with the sharp flavors of shock. Questions can be answered in the dark, but right now, we have to act.

When I speak, it feels as though my voice is fighting to be heard through thick layers of viscous fluid, but the sound is strangely clear. "He's right. We might as well be dead if we can't find somewhere to hide."

Simons looks down at me. His broad forehead crinkles. I can see him make the decision before he shouts out to Frances, "We're going to crash the vehicle."

"What? No! We can't do that!" Frances shouts through the communication partition, surprise lacing her words.

"We have to make the truck disappear," I say, the confidence of my tone trickling down into my core and spreading into my appendages. My hands break free from the surface as though they've just thawed, and my fingers flex away the icy stiffness.

Cain offers me a brusque nod before moving to the front of the transport bed. His body rocks back and forth with the violent wind gusts. He puts his head nearly completely through the divide between the cargo area and the driver's compartment. "Turn off over here. We can wreck the vehicle by the river and force it under once it's unloaded."

Despite her misgivings, Frances complies, and the vehicle dips and shudders unsteadily as we leave the relative safety of the paved road for the permafrost-covered tundra floor.

CHAPTER
TWO

THE NORTHERN LABORATORIES were built in the harshest region of former Alaska, hundreds of miles from the nearest city and accessible only by road. We were told this was for safety reasons, but likely, it was to keep the government's secrets far from prying eyes—or to ensure there would only ever be one access point for their weapon. Regardless of the truth, it puts us in a difficult position when it comes to disappearing.

"I don't think we should destroy our only mode of transportation. Surveillance up here is difficult; we should be fine once we get off the main road," Frances argues through the partition as she struggles to keep traction on the semi-frozen, uneven ground. The wheels slip, and the vehicle slides to the side as it makes its way down an increasing grade leading toward the river.

"Difficult, yes, but not impossible. This is a large vehicle, and the first thing they'll look for when the search starts," Cain points out, using his forearm to hold the partition open.

"If we leave it wrecked by the river, they'll find it. It won't take them long to catch up if we're travelling on foot, which we'll have to do if we're abandoning our only form of—Look out!"

Frances turns the wheel sharply to the left, over-correcting the sliding rear wheels. The transport tilts precariously. Richards grabs at

Dunn's unconscious form to stop it from sliding across the floor. I brace myself for the upturn, headed for the hollow slot meant for a cryogenic cylinder, but before I make it, Simons and Jorey throw themselves full force against the opposite side. It's just enough to bring us back to level. Jorey groans from the impact. The vehicle continues to careen out of control through a maze of ice, mud, and standing water as we approach the icy buildup along the riverbank.

The vehicle jackknifes, our wheels unable to find traction. The truck hits more uneven terrain, and the right side loses contact with the ground, causing a spin that whips our bodies across the grated steel floor. I slam into Cain's legs. The force of the impact drives him forward, and his body folds over mine. For a second, we're pressed against each other before we join Simons and Jorey in a hard collision with the wall. Someone grabs my waist before I'm thrown the other way.

The vehicle moans and twists as it careens down the steep bank until we're nearly on top of the river. Our bodies roll and tumble against one another and into the walls, tangling with our scattered supplies. A burst of pain blurs my vision as someone's foot—or elbow or chin—digs into my knee. There's a loud boom like distant thunder as the back tires break through the still-frozen riverbed. They sink immediately into the rushing waters, halting our spin and forcing an abrupt, quaking stop. Someone slams against the opposite wall.

"Is everyone alright?" Simons asks through a pained grunt.

"That was worse than the trip up," Jorey moans, shifting under me as I scramble to climb off him.

Frances shifts gears, attempting to ease the vehicle back up the bank. The front tires spin uselessly in mud while the back tires churn at the broken ice below, causing the vehicle to shift and moan with the hollow tones of grinding metal. Suddenly the rear door buckles, and a rush of water gushes through the seams.

"Out now! We'll freeze to death in this river," Cain commands.

"Someone give me a hand!" Richards calls.

A sharp pain greets me when I turn my head to see Richards stooping over Dunn's motionless body, cradling his head and neck.

Cain springs forward to assist, his body lean and loose like a predatory thing. My joints groan their protest as I find my feet and scramble up the tilted floor, away from the gushing water. Jorey boosts me through the narrow barrier between the cargo hold and the front. I reach for Frances' hand so she can pull me onto the truck seat. It takes some doing, but we manage to maneuver Dunn's body out through the partition and onto the slick synthetic seats of the driver's cabinet before Cain and Richards join us.

The second I step out onto the frozen riverbank, the biting wind presses sleet against my face, reminding me how brutal the conditions this far north can be, even this late in the spring. A gust catches my braid and rips it from the collar of my uniform, whipping it across my eyes. I shove the braid back into my collar with numbing fingers and lean into the driver's compartment to lace my hands around Dunn's armpits. I glance into the back of the vehicle.

"What are Simons and Jorey doing?"

Cain slips past me, pressing his body against mine as he makes his way to the riverbank, boots sinking deep into the sucking mud. "Simons has the door braced so we can get the supplies out."

"I can still get the transport out. It will be easier with the back unloaded," Frances presses.

"Give it up, this thing needs to go. You've got it this far into the river. The job will be easy from here," Cain says, giving Dunn's body a heave. The weight of his unconscious form tugs at my arms until Richards joins us and the load is balanced.

"He's right. We're not going to be able to hold on to it," Richards says, waiting for Frances to join us. She gives him a desperate, pained look before sliding out of the driver's seat to stand next to him.

Together, we bring Dunn to the top of the slope. Cain and Richards take extra care to place his head gently onto a patch of thick grass, whose ice-tipped surfaces provide a cushioned, yet abrasive barrier to the frost packed ground. The frosty ground immediately stains red below him.

"That doesn't look good," I say.

Cain's jaw tenses. He looks up, searching for the right words. "You know, it might be better if—"

"I don't want to hear it," Richards snaps. His face is twisted with grief. Dunn is the only remaining symbol of what he lost—injured but not dead, infected but not gone.

"I'm just trying to say—he's infected. At least he's unconscious. No pain…" Cain continues.

"Cain! I need a hand," Simons calls from the river, holding the driver's side door open for Jorey to dump an armful of supplies into the mud. His timing is so perfect I wonder if he heard the argument over the commotion and interrupted on purpose.

Cain lets the matter drop, sidestepping and sliding back down the bank to help Simons pull supplies from the icy mud. Frances gives Richards' shoulder a squeeze before following him. I watch them go, then turn my attention back to the blood pooling under Dunn.

"I'll get a med kit and see what I can do," I say.

"It's alright, Mason, I've got this. Go secure the packages," Richards says.

I look back, unaccustomed to him taking charge. "Are you sure?"

"I'm sure. I'm—I'm actually a doctor." He stammers over the words as though he's just discovering a long-lost secret about himself.

Richards is a doctor? The concept is so strange I want to reject it. *A doctor?* He means before the Northern Laboratories. "Oh. I didn't know."

"Mason!" Cain's voice pulls at me from the vehicle, but I can't tear myself away from Richards—not the kindhearted volunteer I've known since arriving up north, but this new Richards who is stooped over Dunn, pressing gently against his blood-soaked temple.

Crisp grass crunches under heavy steps behind me. I recognize Jorey's presence before he speaks. "Mason, we need you."

Using a knuckle on his blood-streaked hand, Richards adjusts his glasses on the ridge of his thin nose. "I'm sorry I never shared that with you before, Mason. I didn't realize you didn't know. Maybe because it didn't matter in the Laboratories. But out here, it's going to be different."

"I…" I'm frozen in this new discovery, wondering what other revelations might lie in wait.

"It's alright. Go!" He offers me a reassuring, yet bashful grin, shooing me with his free hand.

Jorey grabs my hand. His firm, reassuring grip snaps my mind into focus. I study him. He still looks like himself.

"What's wrong?" The crunch of ice under our feet is drowned out by the sounds of the rushing water as we return to the river's edge.

"I can't find it," Simons answers, stepping down from the driver's cabinet. The vehicle bobs with the impulse, and the metal moans in protest.

"That's my pack, right there." I point at the battered canvas of the old pack containing my research.

"No. Shelby's. I can't find Shelby's pack," Simons says.

He means the cure—Shelby's cure—the reason we left the Northern Laboratories.

"It has to be here," I insist, stepping toward the pile of supplies. I sift through the packages, certain my hands will fall onto Shelby's small satchel with the red stripe. My fingers will wrap around it, and I'll feel the weight of the stacks of papers she used to meticulously outline the cure. A pile of supplies grows at my side as I push aside packs and parcels. I place each sack securely against the other until I'm staring at a scattering of items against the dirty white backdrop of ice.

"Impossible," I whisper, nauseous.

"It has to be on the truck," Jorey says.

"I cleared them all," Simons insists.

"Maybe it's jammed up against one of the cryo-platforms," Frances offers.

"We checked," Cain says, wedging his booted foot against the knobby wheel and resting his hand on his raised knee.

"We've got to check again," I snap, launching myself with the same apparent ease I'd credited to Cain earlier.

Frances holds the door for me as I push myself onto the seat, using the steering wheel for leverage. Jorey steps in behind to help me ease into the transport compartment. I grab his hand and position my body along the narrow slit, still scanning the compartment for signs of Shelby's pack.

My eyes settle on a shadow wedged between the bench and the bent-in door, just visible above the white froth of the water's surface. "Got it," I say.

I grip Jorey's wrists and drop my legs into the transport compartment. A sound like crackling campfire fills the air, punctuated by the wavering of a thickly coiled spring. A crack and then a shuddering burst like artillery surrounds us as the ice bank breaks and the vehicle moves with the section of freed surface. The transport compartment shifts, and water rushes in, pulling it downward.

The front cab moans and drags away from the bank. There's a floating sensation as my feet touch the freezing cold of the rushing water.

CHAPTER
THREE

THE FREEZING WATER steals my breath. I reach back up for Jorey's hand.

"You okay?" Jorey asks. He pulls me back toward the gap. My feet slip against the metal siding, dancing just above the rising water.

"Yeah, I'm fine. Just cold," I say, my words a wavering shiver that echoes in the half-filled transportation compartment.

I look back over my shoulder, scanning for the red stripe in the swelling darkness. The pack bobs just under the surface, about a foot below the roof, obviously hung up below. The vehicle rocks back and forth against the broken surface of the riverbed.

Jorey tries to hoist me through by my forearms. I pull away. "I've got to get the cure!"

"No way, the truck's going to go!" he shouts, refusing to let go of my arm.

I wrench my body away. The front cabinet breaks free from the bank, allowing the swift water to force the whole thing over on its side. My arm twists in Jorey's grasp as the rest of my body flails and splashes. We move with the current, the vehicle bouncing against the broken slabs of surface ice.

Before I can find my footing, Jorey forces me through the passageway. I land sprawled against his chest as his head hits the glass of the passenger door. Behind him, the cab is sinking. I push against him, my knees boring into his stomach as I scramble for the passageway before the vehicle is forever lost to the river and the mountains beyond.

"I'm not going to let you kill yourself!" Jorey yells, pulling me back.

"If we don't get the cure now, we'll lose it in the river. That's thousands of miles of flow with hundreds of passages and channels. We'll never find it!" I clench my teeth and pull against him.

Jorey wrestles my wrists out from under me, pulling me down until my chin smacks against his collarbone. His arms find my shoulders, and he shakes me hard. "I know!"

I snap my eyes up to his. He looks terrified. "We have to get it, Jorey," I plead.

"But not like this. Let's get out of here and make a plan. A good plan. Something that won't get us killed, maybe?" His voice is softer now, and a smile begs to surface onto his lips before it's chased off by a shivering gasp.

Jorey lifts his foot out of the cold water, and I shift so I'm not sitting on top of him. "Right," I say, coming to my senses.

I use the wheel to pull myself toward the door, which now acts as a ceiling to the sinking cab. The front windshield is cracked and splintered from our sideways impact. Spiderwebs of fractured glass obstruct our view, but errant splashes of water against the driver's window guarantee the front of the vehicle is still above the surface. Jorey hoists himself to stand next to me, and together we push the door open, allowing drifts of falling snow to waft against our exposed cheeks.

We climb out, taking turns holding the door as we straddle the opening. A gust of wind blows against it, forcing me into it while Jorey finds a better position. He pulls me toward him until we're both perched on the roof. The wind swirls around us, whipping loose strands of hair against my temple. I search the bank for the rest of the team. I don't see them.

"What's the plan?" Jorey asks.

I scan our surroundings, trying to pinpoint our location against my own mental map of the area surrounding the Northern Laboratories. "The ice builds up downstream from the impact," I say, trying to guess how far we are from the river's confluence. "It's only a matter of time before the truck gets wedged against the larger buildups. Once that happens, we should be able to access the back hatch from the outside."

"Works for me," he agrees.

"We have to get it and get out. If we go into the main river, we'll be cut off from the rest of the group by the mountain pass," I explain, pointing far ahead where the landscape disappears into a snowy haze.

Jorey gives the back of my hand a clumsy pat. "We'll get it."

The vehicle moans and shudders as it drags along the narrowing channel, never quite sinking low enough to fully submerge. Ahead of us, I can see the bottleneck where the ice accumulates at the surface, forcing the water below. As long as the blockage holds, the vehicle will remain in place. Once we have the cure, we should be able to escape to the bank. I point out our line of impact for Jorey as the narrow passageway squeezes in on us.

The front end makes contact with the barrier unenthusiastically, with a dull crunch of metal. The driver's compartment shifts and sinks, forcing the back end up from the swelling water. I set my sights on the back end of the transportation hull. "Let's go in from the back."

With carefully measured moves, I make my way across the roof to the back and wedge my fingers into the opening between the roof and the rear door, Jorey right behind me. We peer over the edge together to find the door flapping loosely in the swelling current.

"Something must have busted it loose," Jorey says.

"That makes our job easier," I reason, reaching out to pull the door open the rest of the way.

Jorey grabs my ankles and steadies us as I drop down into the opening. I allow my weight to hang from my midsection, searching the water for the telltale bob of the red-striped parcel. I have to squint to see into the dim compartment and darker waters. A flicker of red catches my eye about three feet below me and further into the trans-portation hold, just out of reach.

"A little lower!" I yell to be heard over the echoes of churning water.

Jorey shifts his weight, pushing my ankles further over the edge until I'm dangling in the passageway just above the water, blood rushing with thunderous pressure into my temples. If I let my hands fall, they'd plunge into the frigid swells of gathering water. I'll have to go into the water to get hold of it.

"You need to hurry!" Jorey calls. His words bring my attention to the hot friction where his hands grip at my ankles. His whole body must be supported by his elbows pressed against the edge.

"I'll hurry!" I promise, twisting myself backward.

The slip happens before I can get in position. Jorey's hands drop down along with the sound of something sliding against metal. I don't have time to register what happened before I plunge into the water, head first. The cold steals my breath and forces a shocked gasp. I close my eyes, and my body swirls in the biting water, feeling for the floor—for the surface—for anything. My hands brush against the rough ground. I bring my feet below me and point myself upward.

I burst through the surface with a gasp. The sound is ragged and short. I can only manage choked gasps as my muscles tense, threatening to seize. The sound echoes through the compartment, drowning out Jorey's shouts, but I catch him saying, "Hold on!"

I've only got minutes, maybe seconds, before I'm useless in the water. I shake my head and start paddling in the direction I saw the pack, grasping with numb fingers but retrieving nothing.

No—not nothing. I lift my hand up to see the thin red strip of fabric hanging there, limp and dripping. The edges are frayed where the pack ripped away from it. I stare in disbelief at the flayed thing, then ball it into a fist and plunge my hand back down, searching desperately for the pack.

"Mason!" Jorey's voice travels into the compartment.

I look up to see him holding the door, knee deep in the swelling water.

"It's gone," I tell him.

"The pack?" he asks.

I hold up the red strip of fabric. He stares at it, and I watch as the shock and disbelief take hold in his expression.

"It must have pulled free when the door went," I say, imagining the most likely scenario.

Suddenly I realize the water around my legs has changed direction. It flows out of the compartment with frightening speed.

"We need to get out of the river," I say, reaching for Jorey's hand.

Together we brace against the churning waters until we're scrambling through mud and ice onto the riverbed. The water chases us for another minute, rising and pressing against the river's blockage until it matches the forces of resistance. Ice and vehicle crunch and moan until they break free and tumble into the churning water again. We watch helplessly as the vehicle turns over, then disappears into the river's depths.

"HOT TEA."

"Extra blankets."

"Sun—sunshine."

"Warm breakfast."

I look over at Jorey, my teeth chattering as we make our way, one painful step at a time, back toward the rest of the group. We step over slicked ice, river-smooth stones and crushed rock. Much of the top ice has slowed its relentless thaw as the temperature plummets. The already-bloomed wildflowers freeze on their delicate stems. Harsh wind blows across the open land and straight through our clothes, rendering them virtually useless.

"Breakfast? That's the worst meal of the day!" I laugh. The sound comes out as a warble, broken by uneven gasps. Jorey's face is pale. His eyelashes and the collar of his suit are laced with ice crystals, but still, he smiles back at me.

"That's a matter of opinion, you know. I actually really liked the breakfasts," he says, offering me support as we scramble through the mud and branches littering the riverbank. Our situation is dire, but the danger feels far away.

"They're not even real eggs," I argue, offering support as he takes another step.

"It tasted like eggs, so does that really matter? How do you know the stuff we got before was real egg?" he continues.

"Let me see…" I lift my hand to my chin in mock-deep thought. "Maybe because they came in these breakable vessels that looked exactly like eggs?"

I cackle at my own joke, crazed by the notion that we're both very near death but arguing about breakfast. Our bodies have already begun to show signs of shutting down. My eyelids are heavy, begging me for rest, and my arms are numb. It takes great, conscious effort to keep my limbs moving.

"Exactly! They only *looked* like eggs. And if they were eggs—were they chickens? Sparrows? Maybe we were raised on baby lizards!" Jorey's foot catches, and he goes down on one knee, sinking deep into the freezing, sucking mud.

"Easy there," I say, stooping to help him. I'm no better off, but the only thing we can do is keep moving. Our only chance for survival is to get back to the rest of the group.

"I'm okay. I can't feel my feet anymore. Or—maybe I can. It's hard to tell." He pulls himself up.

I lean into him, and we stand huddled, dependent on one another for support. The moment creates the illusion of warmth, and I want to bask in it. "I feel exactly the same. That's why we've got to keep moving," I tell him.

"I know," he says.

My body jerks back. Our hands are still intertwined, and he hasn't started moving yet. He takes a step, and then another step, still not releasing my hand. We fall into motion again. "They were chicken eggs because lizards and sparrows were supposed to be extinct."

"I saw a lizard once. It was sunning itself on one of our supply crates outside the storage bay at the clinic," Jorey says, referencing his life in the city, before the labs.

"What was it like… living in the city?" I ask, suddenly taken by the notion that Jorey lived an entire life before becoming a volunteer—or at least part of one. I, on the other hand, never got a chance to experience the sort of life I supposedly dedicated myself to preserving as a scientist. Running away denied me even the ability to know what it's like to grow up.

"Oh, you know. I was a clinical tech, working my way to medic. I thought I was happy. Life was ordinary, or at least that's how it felt. I didn't know anything else," Jorey says.

"But I don't know. I left when I was fourteen, remember?" My words are starting to slur.

Jorey nods slowly. "I know, but on some level, it never sinks in. You seem so much older."

"That's just the crushing responsibility. It adds ten years." I laugh, unable to help myself as I consider the monumental task set before me. Regardless of what Shelby and Amos believed about me, it's too much.

"Ten years makes you the adult in this situation, so it's your call what we do next," Jorey says.

I should be anguishing over career options right now, not running from a malicious government in the middle of a frozen tundra chasing after a missing cure we have no hope of reclaiming. "We keep walking," I say. It's the only answer.

"I was afraid you'd say that."

The conversation falters. The storm clouds have cleared, at least temporarily, offering a dazzling view of the early-summer sky. The sun sits low on the horizon, blotted out by the white-grey mist and the errant, puffy cumulonimbus that threatens to settle overhead again. It will soon dip behind the western mountain range but won't sink low enough to darken the sky for hours yet. Instead, it will offer us a twilight to make our way back to the others.

"Hey, Mason, look! The moon…" Jorey's excited voice trails off as he takes in the midday spectacle of the glowing gibbous.

I stop to take it in, immersed in the awe of its presence. "I haven't seen it in so long," I whisper.

Jorey puts his arm around me, and I imagine the heat it should provide. I lean into him, hoping we'll find the strength to move on, but not ready to end the moment. My mind wanders to another moon from long ago. *Full, gibbous, crescent.* I'm safe in its glow. I rest my head against his chest, ignoring the crunch of his frozen suit. "I'm not going to let us die out here."

He brings his other arm around and pulls me into a clumsy embrace. "Me neither," he says.

"There you are!" Cain's loud voice bursts over the hill, filling the space with an otherworldly strangeness.

I pull myself upright and look away from the river, toward the sound. His big, goofy grin shines back at us, framed by the gathering fog. "Cain! It's so good to see you!"

I squeeze Jorey's hand and urge him forward. He squeezes back but takes another moment to get moving. By the time we're both working our way toward Cain, he's jogged down the hill, his body moving easily compared to ours.

"You guys look like hell!" Cain proclaims as he wedges himself between us.

"Mason went in after the cure, and I went in after Mason," Jorey explains as Cain slaps his back. His other hand makes an attempt to ruffle my hair, but the frozen mass resists disturbance.

"And to think I told everyone you'd be fine riding the river for a couple miles. I guess the joke's on me." Cain laughs.

"This hardly feels like a time to joke about much of anything," Jorey grumbles.

"It's a turn of phrase, brother. Easier for me than to admit I should have run down the river after you two," Cain says by way of apology. He guides us up the hill. "So did you get it?" he asks.

I pull out the crumpled ball of frozen red fabric and hold it with numb fingers for Cain to see. "We lost it in the river," I say.

"Well, that sucks," he says.

My mind races to come up with a retort, but nothing comes to me. Instead, I return the fabric to the pocket and zip it shut, unwilling to let go of the only piece of the cure we managed to retrieve.

"Where are we going?" Jorey asks as we make the last few graceless steps up the embankment and away from the river.

"Underground," Cain says simply.

"Another turn of phrase?" I ask. My lips crack.

"No, this time I mean it. We're going to go under the earth," Cain says. My sluggish mind can't figure how such a thing could be possible.

"How far away is *under the earth*?" Jorey asks with a moan.

"That's a good question," I chime in.

Cain looks down at me, and something in his smile changes, warming ever so slightly. "Oh, maybe a mile or so. With any luck, Simons and Frances will have gotten a heat source sorted by the time I get you there," Cain says, steering us southwest.

Jorey grunts, resolved to keep putting one foot in front of the other.

"There's a series of channels built under the ground all over the outskirts of the City States. It's how people survived during the first outbreak," Cain explains.

"There aren't any City States up here," I remind him.

"There used to be. It's where the early civilizations started to thrive after the first outbreak," Cain says.

"That's not in the history books," I say, more to myself than to him.

"Do you really believe the Endgal-filled junk the government spews into those texts?" he asks me with a sideways glance.

I bite my lower lip, unwilling to admit I believed everything in the history books, right up until the day we ran away. I wonder if Simons knows about the tunnels—if all dissenters know about them.

Ahead, a tall, dark figure stands out against the snow-spotted plains. Simons waves his hands over his head before setting out in our direction. My heart lifts at the sight of him and the promise of the shelter. The first order of business will be to recover, but after that, it's time to talk.

FIVE

IN MY MIND'S EYE, I can see Shelby sitting at her desk amidst stacks of notebooks and loose papers. In all the Northern Laboratories, Shelby was the only scientist to produce and keep work on paper, and she did so prolifically. She generated hard copies by the stack until her office was overcome by mountains of data. I only learned at the end that she did so to hide the cure in plain sight. The work of solving the indestructible virus was done in the Northern Laboratories. All I had to do was get that work out of the labs and into the hands of the dissenters. It wasn't an easy job, considering we're up against the DDC, but I never imagined I'd immediately lose it!

But that's what happened. The cure is gone. I repeat the thought as my fingers run across the tendrils of frayed string along the little red strip. I can't see it in the darkness, but I hold on as though it could offer me comfort. I know it's just a piece of fabric, but still I can't let go. I run my hands over it, along its edges and across the slick surface.

It's probably ruined anyway, I remind myself, thinking of the pack tumbling down the river and being torn apart by jagged rocks and the sharp fingers of gnarly branches. Or maybe it's hung up somewhere, water seeping into the fine openings—maybe the very openings created by this piece of torn fabric—and turning the papers inside into a mushy pulp.

I need to sleep. Now that the danger of hypothermia has passed, it's the best thing I could do in this darkness, swallowed by the earth, but my mind refuses. The time for talking—for figuring out our next step—can't come soon enough.

So many years ago, in another lifetime, someone decided to dig. They dug deep, blasting rock and earth from the depths and hauling the debris out until there were these holes, connecting waterways and building channels. This is not like the meticulously crafted passageways between city structures I know from my childhood. Rather, it is the rough work that marks the life and passing of the first survivors after the war—the ones who didn't make it into the history books. We're sitting within the jagged scars made by others who wouldn't die.

They wrote their stories on the walls so we could read them and understand. Their marks remain as if they knew they'd be written out of our world. *We were here. When you find our world, you will remember us.*

Somewhere above us, the waxing gibbous moon continues its arc in the sky, but down here, it's dark. If it weren't for the small blinking lights indicating the energy receiver on my glove, it would be pitch black—the total darkness that doesn't exist in reality. It reminds me of a simulation in the moment right before it begins or after it ends but before I can tear the helmet from my head and relieve myself of the terrible nothing. If it weren't for those blinking lights...

I count between each blip. *One... two... three... four... blink.* Over and over again to keep myself calm.

My mind wanders to campfires on cold nights—to hot soups and empty stomachs. I can't stop the memories. Huddling next to the fire with Hank, hopeless and helpless as Bruce yells at Dad about running away. The water-logged tablet that cut us off from the underworld of dissenters and the endless stream of near-dead plants that led to the clearing... It's all too familiar.

Once again, I'm running into a wild nothing, hoping to connect with the dissenters on the other side. This time, the coyote is running with me, and I know the names of the others I want to connect with. But Simons doesn't know any better than I do who our contacts should be, and Amos is buried deep in the belly of the Institute. Only Shelby had the key to bring it all together. Without her, the DDC will close in on us before we can make our next step. Without her, Orman is free to hunt us.

I swallow the lump that fills my throat and chest. The loss we experienced on the kill lab floor looms heavily in our presence. If it descends upon us, we may be lost, so we keep it at bay—knowing but not feeling. The tension it creates is palpable in every action, every moment of silence and shuffle in the darkness. On the outside, we're a cohesive team working toward one purpose, but inside, we're broken.

It started with Frances not wanting to sink the transport but spread quickly to Richards and Cain's disagreement about Dunn. Even Simons pushed back when Cain compelled them to move to the tunnels instead of chasing after Jorey and me. And though we're back and largely unharmed, he barely contains his unease. Trapped underground with nothing to hold us together besides our disagreements, we're a powder keg too close to a fuse. Or perhaps a virus replicating without end, given our circumstances…

Dunn is infected.

At some point, he'll become our biggest problem. He doesn't even know what he's in the middle of yet.

I think about what I'll say when he wakes up—*if* he wakes up. What happens next? It all depends on which strain of Zoribiatus he's contracted. The chances he's contracted one of the prevalent strains— one of the many we learned to identify on sight at the Institute—are low. He's probably got one of the emergent strains that mimic the primary ones.

If we're lucky, he's got one that will go dormant, but there's no way to determine what we're dealing with now that the Northern Laboratories are gone. The chances his wounds will heal are about as low as the chances I'll be able to reproduce Shelby's work. It's far more likely the disease will manifest quickly, and we'll lose him. No matter what the outcome, we need to be careful.

What would Shelby have done? What would her next step be? She and Amos had a plan. I was supposed to be a piece of *their* plan, not coming up with my own! They're the ones who argued for my life a dozen times over. And even they couldn't keep me safe without help.

Amos was able to save me because the DDC was interested in my test scores. She used the DDC's aspirations against them. Shelby saved me by sacrificing others. If I'm going to get everyone out of here, I need to be like them.

I force my eyes shut. Shelby was able to make the hard decisions. Now it's up to me.

CHAPTER
SIX

JOREY SHIFTS IN HIS SLEEP, his hand falling to his side and brushing against mine. I lift it from the cold ground and return it to his chest, then decide I also need to lift myself from the cold ground. My motion sends vibrations through the space, disrupting the quiet of so many resting bodies. Sitting upright, I tell myself I feel warmer.

A pinprick of light draws my attention away from the thin strip of torn fabric and my own thoughts. The white light pierces through the space, illuminating the shadowy silhouettes of the sleeping party. A barely visible figure rises from the shadows and extinguishes the glow. I listen as the lone figure rummages in the darkness. The shadow is much too small to be Simons, but too tall to be Frances and far too quiet to be Cain. It must be Richards. He switches on a dim light that glows like the sun, bringing color to the black space.

I watch him silently as he kneels over Dunn's body, checking his pulse and counting breaths. He holds the light up to Dunn's face and opens first one eye, then the other before checking the crude bandages. The work is silent and careful. If I were unaware how long he's been confined to the Northern Laboratories, I would think he hasn't been away from medicine for more than a day.

"How is he?" I whisper.

Richards looks up, swinging the light so it shines painfully in my direction. "Sorry, Mason, you startled me," he says, swinging the light back down.

"No, I'm sorry," I apologize, keeping my voice quiet so I don't disturb anyone else. "Are there any changes?"

Richards glances up toward me without lifting his head to shine the light at me again and offers me a reassuring smile. "His vitals are strong, and he's showing good responsiveness—unfortunately to pain, I think. But his injuries are severe."

"How much blood did he lose?" I ask, picturing the telltale glisten of his blood-soaked kill suit, the way the ground under him stained red.

"It was substantial, but I was able to close the torn arteries. It doesn't look as though he's got any major damage—beyond infection, that is," Richards corrects his line of thought.

"Yes, well, there's that," I agree.

Richards shakes his head. "We have to help him. It's the only right thing to do."

"Of course we do. What would make you think we wouldn't?" I ask, startled by his defensiveness. For Richards, Dunn has become the only one left to save. I watch his expression, deeply shadowed by the angle of his headlamp, and know why before he speaks. *Cain.*

"I understand the risk, but he isn't a liability—he's a life," Richards says.

"I don't think Cain meant to suggest we should let him die. I think he only meant to state an uncomfortable possibility," I suggest.

"I wouldn't be too certain of that, Mason. I wouldn't be too certain of anything when it comes to him," Richards warns.

"No. Not certain, but we need to trust each other—look at what he's done for us already, where he's brought us. Out here, we're all each other has," I say. I want to outright deny Richards' wariness, but I don't dare, given the volatility of the night. The ruthlessness Richards is suggesting goes against every impression I've had of Cain since he joined Simons' group. The first thing he did was save me in the simulations, and he hasn't stopped going out of his way to help since.

"I know." Richards sighs, casting his head downward so his eyes are lost to deep shadows. When he speaks again, it's barely a whisper.

"He didn't hesitate to help me save Dunn in the transport even though he knew what the injury was. But I have this feeling…"

"Your fast work probably saved Dunn's life," I say, steering the conversation as far away from Richards' feeling as it will go. "And the sedatives were a stroke of genius. Were they your idea?"

He shakes his head, the light glancing from side to side. "Simons. He got them from Shelby in case there was trouble."

"Between us all, we thought of everything… almost."

"I suppose it was inevitable things would go wrong somehow. We all knew the risks." He sits back, settling into the conversation, but keeps his head down so the light doesn't shine directly in my eyes.

"Yes, but… to lose Shelby and the cure…" My voice falters, knowing even with everything at stake, I'm missing the most critical loss. "And your families…"

Richards brings a hand up to wipe the tears from behind his glasses. It's quiet for a very long moment while he composes himself. He sighs twice. The first is jagged, as he forces his composure, but the second is smoother. His thin hands brush once more over his face and then he speaks. "What happened to our families was—it was unforgivable. It was cruel and pointless. But—that's exactly why we had to do it."

His hands continue to visit his face, wiping tears, fidgeting with his glasses, and running off the chill that bites his flesh.

"Are you saying it was worth destroying the Northern Laboratories even without the cure?" I ask.

"Yes, it had to be done. And no. I believe I'm saying I don't think the cure is entirely lost," he says.

I exhale a laugh, wiping an errant tear from my own cheek. "Believe me. It's gone." I offer up the red strip as proof.

He nods. "Yes. That one is gone, but you're still here."

I shake my head. "Oh no. I have no idea what Shelby's cure was. I wouldn't even know where to begin—that wasn't my specialty—"

"You'll figure it out," he interrupts me.

"No," I say. "I was supposed to get Shelby and her work out of the Laboratories. That was always my role—since the day Amos enrolled me in the Intern program. I was supposed to get the cure out of the

Northern Laboratories. I ruined whatever plan Shelby had for me in that regard."

"Did you ruin it or put it into motion?" Richards asks.

"We had no choice but to run. If we hadn't, Orman would have destroyed all of you. I wanted to save you, and I'm barely doing that! I mean—I was a mess back there. I can't seem to keep it together. I think something's wrong with me."

"What do you mean?" His light envelops me as he looks up.

"I can't think straight. It's like a panic, but worse," I admit.

Richards moves over to me and stoops down. I squint to make him out in the light.

"Has this happened before?" he asks.

"Sort of, but we learned control at the Institute," I explain.

"I'm not sure I understand," he admits, shaking his head and offering a sympathetic look.

"What sort of doctor were you? Before?"

"Obstetrics mostly, but you know how it is with medicine—by the time you're doing your job, you know the full gamut."

"The Northern Laboratories must have been a huge change."

"I moved from bringing life to extinguishing it." His face pales.

"You didn't kill anyone. The patients are already gone—you know that." I put my hand on his shoulder, trying to comfort him.

He places his thin hand over mine and pats it gently, then brings it up to situate his glasses again. With a heavy sigh, he says, "Unfortunately, that's not the only thing I did."

"What else is there?" I ask, suddenly chilled.

He looks down, ashamed. "Have you ever wondered how the Northern Laboratories could be so… sterile?"

"The procedure—they do it to all the Interns and volunteers before they travel north," I say. My heart is thundering in my chest. I know how imperfect the procedure is. My parents are proof of it.

"When the procedure is done in the cities, there are three repeat appointments because of the frequency of failure. At the Institute, it's only done once, before departure."

I nod. He's talking about me, about Miller, the volunteers and all of us.

"In the cities, once you have a reproductive license, there's a choice —a fundamental right. In the Northern Laboratories, they sent them to me. Some were grateful, but we're talking about people who already lost their families…"

I gasp.

Richards' body shudders at my reaction. His thin, trembling fingers cover his face. "They threatened my wife, the team. I had no choice but to comply. I couldn't… I couldn't put others at risk."

I watch him struggle through his guilt, helpless to guard him from his own conscience. His hand was forced by the government's decrees. He's a victim. His patients are the victims—just like our families and countless others before us.

I swallow hard, reaching out to place both of my hands on his shoulders. "You did what you had to do to survive—to save others. It wasn't your fault. And it's done now," I insist.

He straightens his shoulders and adjusts his glasses. "I'll never forgive myself."

"It's like you said, a place like that—one that uses innocent people to hurt others—it shouldn't exist," I remind him.

He nods again and this time offers a tentative attempt at a smile. "See what I mean then? It's about more than the cure."

He's right. Losing the cure doesn't change the necessity of what we've started. I went to the Institute to get answers, and I got them. I've never been more certain than in this moment that our job is only beginning. I can't rest until I've done everything in my power to stop the secrets—the infections, manipulations, and devastation that the institution of our government has brought. It's what Shelby wanted, and it's what the dissenters are fighting for.

"You're right," I say, bolstered by his perspective. "We'll figure this out. Between all of us, we can make a plan. And it's a good thing, too, because this is all that's left of Shelby's life's work," I add, placing the red fabric strip in his hands.

He holds it up in his light. It hangs stiffly in the yellow glow as an homage to what we might have accomplished if things had gone differently.

"I suppose there isn't really a use for crying over what we've lost.

Maybe, now that the Laboratories are gone, we can start again. I think you can do it, Mason. Simons told me Shelby said you were—"

I watch the fabric dance in the light, convinced my traitorous mind must be playing tricks on me. As it tilts back in its gravitational pendulum arc, I catch the glint again. I seize the strip from Richards' grasp and hold it close to my face, interrupting his musings. "Richards, can you turn up the light?"

He does without question. The warm yellow glow changes to a piercing white. Cain moans a protest to the light's infiltration before flipping his body around and covering his head with a pack. I ignore him, shifting the fabric in the light until I catch the glint again and locate the threaded pattern.

"What is it?" Richards asks in a voice too loud, having forgotten the night.

"I know how to recover the cure!"

CHAPTER
SEVEN

"YOU'RE STANDING IN MY LIGHT," I say, scowling at the shadow Cain casts over the exposed circuitry of the glove.

"I just want to see what you're up to!" The shadow moves so I can make out the microscopic workings of the communication panel. It's the same sort of conductive maze I once peered at with wonder as Hank did the magic work of repair.

"Would you like to use a light?" he offers, fidgeting impatiently while I work.

"I told you; we can't use any of the equipment that sources the energy grid until I get this done," I explain, rolling my eyes, then squinting at the network. A channel of gold, so thin it was likely painted with the precision of machinery, stands out over the other components. I bite my lip and carefully bring up the blade of the knife to scrape a disruption into the circuit.

"Richards' light is self-contained," Cain offers.

"Richards needs his light. That's why we're up here," I remind him, setting the knife aside to check my work.

"Why exactly did you need me, again?" Cain asks, plunking down and folding his legs. I can see his hands twisting around a pale blade of tundra grass.

"So you could hand me that piece of cloth," I say, still working. "And that knife again."

He sighs, then leans forward to grab the knife and the silken diode screen I once used as a remote workstation projector in the Laboratories.

"And the wire from that pack," I say.

"Jorey could have done this," Cain grumbles, following my commands and handing me each piece in turn.

"Jorey is helping Simons set up a perimeter."

"I'd be much better at that," Cain pipes in.

"You slept through that decision," I remind him.

"Because nobody woke me up!"

I can tell he's teasing, which makes me smile. "Quit your complaining. This is way more important."

"Equally important," he corrects me.

"Fine. This is equally important, so you shouldn't be complaining about it." The smile doesn't fade as I smear the copper surface of the wire against the panel, then use the knife to clean up the work.

"Sure—altering our grid signal is just as important. The problem is you're doing all the smart work, and I'm just your lackey. That's hardly glamorous!"

"Do you know how to rewire a personal receiver?"

"I've never tried. I could be a genius, but you won't let me try," he says. It's a game now.

"Yeah, well, I have." I tilt the glove so the sunlight hits the area I've been working on and nod in approval.

"You have?" he asks in mock-incredulity.

I lay out the diode screen, which flutters briefly on the breeze like the delicate fabric it is, then use the wire to attach it directly to the glove. "I have it on good authority that I'm a genius."

"I sure hope so because if you're wrong about this, then you're about to get us all definitively killed."

His warning makes my guts twist. I look over my work one more time to convince myself it's solid. Hank couldn't have done a better job himself, though he'd argue that point.

"Well, I suppose you're lucky I'm the one doing this and not some uneducated mercenary." I look up at him, proud of my comeback, then before I can talk myself out of it, I engage the system.

The screen flickers on, drawing the remaining energy stores from the receiver. I work quickly to cue up the grid settings before the power runs out and I have to ruin another glove to get the job done.

"How do you know I'm uneducated?" Cain asks, leaning forward to read the screen. "And what is all that?"

"It was a lucky guess. But you just gave yourself away. This is the programming for our power grid signal," I tell him. My fingers fly through the settings.

"So I didn't get a government education—that doesn't mean I'm not a genius," he argues.

I work for a moment longer, ignoring his statement until I feel guilty. "That's true. But not everything in the education system was conspiracy and propaganda. Some of it was technical—like this."

"Granted," he agrees, letting the matter drop.

I didn't learn all of it from school. There is so much Hank in my work that I could nearly ignore the private tutoring sessions with Amos that lasted through so much of my stay at the Institute— but only nearly. The screen flickers. There are only seconds of power left. I abandon all thought and race furiously toward completion.

"I got it!" I cry triumphantly.

"That's it?" he asks, sounding disappointed.

"What do you mean, that's it? We can now access the power grid without detection! We can track the cure, use high-powered weapons to defend ourselves, and anything else we might need to do!" I say.

"No—that's great, really! I suppose I just expected it would look a lot cooler. I mean, the screen didn't even change."

"Boy, you have high expectations." I sigh, looking up at him. He's wearing a crooked smile under his unkempt blond hair. His sharp, fiery eyes are filled with humor... and something else I can't quite place.

"Hmm. I suppose I do. I ought to give you more credit. You did it after all—and you only ruined one glove." He arches his brow, trying to look serious but failing.

"Thank you," I say, putting all the good-humored exasperation I can into the statement.

"Whose glove was it?" Cain asks.

"Dunn's. I figure he doesn't need access to anything that could get us in trouble."

"That's for sure. I mean—are you so sure we should keep him around? He's a big liability…" Cain drops his voice low.

My eyes widen. "You aren't suggesting we—"

"I don't know." He shakes his head, torn. "I'm saying it's dangerous to have him around—I mean, even if he's on board, does he really know what's at stake here?"

"Don't let Richards hear you talk like that," I warn, looking over long enough for him to catch my eye.

"Does he have a problem with me too?" Cain crosses his arms over his chest.

"Too?" I ask, forgetting momentarily to give my attention to the red strip of fabric that will connect us across miles of wilderness to what remains of Shelby's work and the dissenters' greatest hope. "Who else has a problem with you?"

"Seems like everybody. Frances is still sore about the transport, and Simons thinks I left you and Jorey out to freeze."

"I don't have a problem with you," I say. Then, taken by a streak of mischief, I add, "Yet…"

"Gee thanks, you're really making me feel like a hero."

"Maybe things would go better with everyone if you cut the hero act and just worked with the team. We're sort of in a crisis right now. It would help if you acted like it."

"Like pointing out that Dunn's situation might threaten our survival?" Cain asks.

"We can't make assumptions. He just woke up. He's injured and disoriented and coming to terms with everything that happened."

"And what happens when the disease progresses?" Cain's voice is stern.

"We don't even know which strain of Zoribiatus he contracted. What if it stays dormant until it can be cured?"

"Is that likely?"

"It's possible," I snap.

"Are you willing to risk everything for *possible*?"

I chew my lower lip, anguishing over the impossible decision. "We at least have until the first signs of manifestation. We owe him that much."

I turn toward the sound of approaching footsteps, eager to let the topic rest. Jorey waves to me as he and Simons approach. I lift my hand in return, waiting for them.

"The perimeter is secured. Everything is clear for now," Simons says, dropping down to sit on a rock, one hand unscrewing the lid to his canister.

"How did it go here?" Jorey asks, looking over the strewn equipment.

"Great! From now on, every time we access the power grid, a signal will manifest in one of fifty thousand possible locations, cuing one of the thirty energy management facilities as the nearest local power source to the incident. It's now functionally impossible to trace us," I say, folding my arms across my chest with an exaggeratedly smug smile.

"Have you pulled up the signal signature from the fabric strip yet?" Simons asks, bringing the canteen down and smacking his lips together, satisfied, before handing it to Jorey.

"That's our next step. We need to determine if the pack is still traveling down the river—or if it's hung up or dumped to shore. Once we know where it is, we'll know what we're up against. It could be as near as a few kilometers downriver…" My voice trails off as the other possibility—the more likely possibility—threatens to surface.

"What do we do if it's gone beyond the pass?" Simons asks, elbows resting on his knees as he faces me.

"It might not have gone that far. There's a lot of debris in the river," Jorey suggests.

"It might have," I say.

"We can't go straight overland; those mountains aren't passable," Cain says.

"Could we go around?" Jorey asks.

"That's a lot of miles. Wilderness travel isn't easy," Cain warns.

"We could keep heading south and come back for it once we've found help," Simons suggests.

"And hope it stays preserved in the river?" I scoff.

"Shelby knew what she was doing," he says, adjusting his position to reach for the canteen Jorey left between them.

"She wasn't planning to throw the cure into the third largest river on the continent!"

We stare at each other, unsure of the next right move. Simons takes another drink, emptying the canteen while Jorey peers out at the mountain range Cain called impassible. I can't see what Cain's doing because he's moved to look over my shoulder at the silken screen with its blinking cursor at the bottom. I place my hand over the destroyed glove, letting my fingers brush against the conductive fabric and knowing what our only option is.

"If the signal comes up, we get the cure—even if we have to go around," I say. "We need it."

The sharp groan of metal hinges disrupts the moment as Frances pokes her head through the hatch to the ancient tunnels. I watch as she blinks to adjust to the brightness of the reflected light in the snowy tundra. She calls out. "Mason, Dunn is asking for you."

I swallow, feeling guilty and not quite certain why. I've been dreading the impending conversation since I first set eyes on his wildly confused face in the back of the transport vehicle. It reminds me of Tucker and how I pushed him away until he was gone. I won't do that to Dunn. I vow to tell him everything.

"I'll be right there," I say, stooping to gather our supplies.

CHAPTER
EIGHT

ALTMAN AND DUNN were cure scientists. During my brief installation in the Northern Laboratories, both worked on a cellular level. Neither made big impressions. They blended in— black suits and white coats moving in the background of the cure labs, the din of conversation amongst colleagues in the dining hall.

They had the same scientist-short cropped hair and studious, yet detached look. They both wore glasses. Dunn always tried to be cheerful, companionable. The most striking thing about him was that he seemed like the sort of guy who *wished* he could say, "Just call me James."

Looking at him now, lying on the bare tunnel ground in the dim glow of Richards' light with more bandages than clothing, there's so much more to remark on James Dunn than I ever noticed. He's about one week late for a trim. His short brown hair looks to be the sort that would bleach to blond in the sunlight. His pale, bloodless face is speckled with freckles from a childhood long past in a place far removed from the Northern Laboratories. All of it together reminds me he is a whole person—with his own hopes and dreams—the way I've seen the volunteers, but never fellow scientists.

He licks at chapped lips, and Richards offers him a sip of water. He makes a short attempt to drink before turning away, either too tired or disgusted with what we have to offer. His eyes are bright blue, sharp but distant.

"It's good to see you up," I say, taking a seat in front of him so he doesn't have to strain to see me.

"I'm not so sure about that," Dunn says, shifting toward me and wincing.

"I am. That you're here with us at all is incredible," I say, dancing around the truth.

"I know what tore me open. I'm infected."

"Yes." His eyes widen in surprise at my admission.

"Will I go into cryo?" he asks.

It's my turn to be surprised. He doesn't remember—or he doesn't understand.

"A lot has happened since you were injured. Going into cryo isn't an option anymore."

"It's gone," Dunn says, his eyes suddenly clearing.

"It is." I wait to see if he wants to hear more about the destruction of the Northern Laboratories.

"Altman... Shelby... and Orman... The volunteers said you'd explain?" Dunn stammers, looking around for Richards.

"Altman was overcome by the hive. He didn't make it off the kill floor," I say.

Dunn blinks against glistening eyes. "Orman and Shelby?"

"Orman killed Shelby during the evacuation." I keep my voice even and measured, not taking my eyes off his.

"Why?" Dunn asks.

"He was trying to stop us from leaving," I explain.

"He was trying to shoot Mason," Jorey adds from somewhere in the background. Simons gives him a quiet admonishment.

"Orman killed Shelby. He tried to kill you..." Dunn repeats. His lips move wordlessly as he struggles to process it all.

"He was trying to kill all of us. That was the real purpose behind my experiment being pushed forward," I say, hoping this isn't too much.

Dunn's eyes clear again, focusing on me. He studies my face for a moment, as if he were seeing me for the first time in a new light.

"Why did you do it, Mason?"

I falter, unsure what he means. Why did I design the experiment? For so many reasons I wouldn't even begin to know how to explain. Why did I destroy the Northern Laboratories? To escape. To try and save the patients in the cryo halls. To stop the manufacture of weaponized Zoribiatus...

"It was the only way to get the cure out of the Northern Laboratories," I say, hoping this is enough.

He's quiet for a moment. His lids sag over tired, watery eyes, and I think he's going to sleep again.

"Orman developed family members for that hive. He developed pre-stage patients even though it's illegal," Dunn says, opening his eyes again. This time, he fixes his gaze on the team, on Simons and Jorey, Richards and Frances.

Frances quakes at the mention of her lost family. We've barely mentioned them. There hasn't been time to process in the midst of the chaos.

"He killed them. And he tried to destroy our only hope for a cure," I say, hoping Dunn can see the truth.

He nods. Shelby was right about him. We'll still need to be cautious, but Dunn will come to our side...

"We need to report him," Dunn says.

"Orman?" I blurt.

"Yes, we need to inform the DDC—the president," Dunn says, urgency raising his voice.

Somehow, after all this time, Dunn is still a true believer. Maybe most scientists figure out the real purpose of the Northern Laboratories, but Shelby was wrong about him. Dunn really believes.

"Orman was working on their behalf. The whole government signed our death warrant," I say.

He blinks again. He's done it several times throughout our conversation, and I realize it's because he doesn't have his glasses.

"No..." The word is almost a whisper, not meant for me. He shakes his head, forcing away his own thoughts. The movement brings on a wave of pain he barely manages to contain.

"I need to give you another dose for pain," Richards says, moving toward Dunn with a supply bag in hand.

Dunn lifts a hand. "No. Not yet," he gasps, breathing through the anguish. He turns his focus back to me, squinting.

"Dunn, we can talk more when you're feeling better. You need rest," I press.

"Kara Mason," he hisses through clenched teeth. It's a pained sound that isn't quite angry. He fights against the rising discomfort. I move toward him, placing a tentative hand on his. "I knew someone like you once," he says, panting now.

"Take the medicine," I beg.

"Let me say this!" he snarls. "If I die before I say it, you'll never know, and she'll be gone for good. If I succumb to infection, then so does her memory!"

He's delirious. The concussion is disorienting him. Still, I wait to hear what he has to say. Richards gives me an uncomfortable, urgent look.

"Tell me," I say.

"When we were kids… there was a raven—people on the outside."

He closes his hand on mine, his grasp weak.

"Outside the city?" I ask, hoping to hurry his nonsensical rant along.

"She left. Before I went to the Institute, she told me about the lies, but… I didn't believe her. I didn't want to believe her," Dunn says.

His eyes are dimming. With my free hand, I urge Richards over to administer the shot. He does so without hesitation. It only takes a moment for Dunn's entire body to relax into unconsciousness.

I assist Richards in checking his vitals while he tends to the bandages covering the considerable wound. We settle him back onto the ground, then take turns with the ultraviolet wand.

"What was he talking about?" Jorey asks.

"I don't know. I don't even think he knew," I say, turning away from him.

"Shelby said he wouldn't be much of a problem," Simons says.

Cain barks an incredulous laugh. "He's been more trouble than he's worth, and we haven't even gotten started."

"It's my fault he's infected," I snap. "If I'd trusted him, he would've understood what was coming."

"If you'd trusted him, he would've reported you. You heard him!" Cain says, pushing away from the eroded wall to stand at full height, pointing an accusing finger at the unconscious form on the ground.

"What's done is done," Simons says, rising to meet Cain.

"He'll report us at his first opportunity if he doesn't outright die before then—or worse, turn!" Cain says.

"Let's give him a chance," I say, standing to greet them both in the dim barely-light of the tunnel.

"A chance to what?" Cain asks. Jorey and Frances are on their feet now, too.

"To live. To understand what we're doing and believe in it," I say.

Cain shoots Dunn a derisive look. If he could, I suspect he'd take care of the problem right now.

"He thought Orman needed to be reported. That means he probably believes in the cure. If he wants a cure, then he's on our side," Frances chimes in.

"So what are we supposed to do? We can't just sit here and wait for him to get well enough to travel, can we?" Cain throws his hands up.

"We need time to track the cure and solidify our plan anyway," Simons says.

"I need to see if there's a way to get in contact with Amos," I add, knowing it's impossible but needing any excuse I can find.

Cain stares at us, unbelieving. "Why are government-trained people always idiots?"

Jorey starts toward Cain, but I beat him to it, landing a practiced blow to his kidney. Cain doubles over with a yelp, clearly not expecting the hit.

"What was that?" he grunts, grasping his side.

"I have two brothers and zero tolerance for your attitude," I say.

Cain's face is blank. He looks like a different person without his big, goofy grin.

"You have brothers?" he asks.

"Had brothers," I correct. It's the first time I've said it out loud. Something flashes across Frances' face.

"I guess that doesn't do much for your tolerance," Cain says, shrugging broad shoulders.

Frances' breath catches. A pale hand makes its way to her lips, where it shakes for a moment before falling. "Have some compassion, Cain," she scolds.

"For her tolerance?" Cain asks.

"She's talking about her family!" Jorey growls.

"I didn't see them in the hive," Cain quips.

"You don't know how to stop, do you?" Simons snaps, moving away from the wall.

Tension fills the tunnels. I consider hitting him again in his other kidney so he can have a matched set. Then I remember what Jorey said about wanting to hit Smith when we were traveling north…

If I hit him, then he knows he got to me…

I already hit him once, yet again revealing my impulsive nature and incompatibility with the role the dissenters gave me. The worst part of it is how badly I want to do it again, like I'm sitting alone at my data port deciding to select hive studies all over again—changing randomly selected frequencies to government-controlled channels. My annoyance with Cain's attitude grates on the same level as Orman's apathetic disinterest. I won't give him the pleasure of a second blow.

"It's too soon, Cain. For all of us," I say.

"Should we give it another 48 hours?" Cain asks.

It's the last straw. A guttural laugh escapes from inside of me. It comes out as a raw, animalistic caw that echoes through the stale tunnel air. The idea that the best I've done to grieve my family in the last four years is crack a poorly timed joke is too much to bear. A sob wells up from somewhere deep inside my chest, but it remains buried by the insane laughter. My whole body shakes with the soundless, agonized thing that threatens to shatter my sanity.

Simons stares at me, a look of terrified concern painted across his face. It only makes me laugh harder until my abdomen convulses, and it hurts. I put my arms across my midsection, making Cain jump back.

"I thought she was going to shoot me," he says when Jorey gives him a startled look.

"You'd deserve it," he says.

"That doesn't mean I want to be shot!" Cain protests.

"Then quit acting like it!" Jorey says, making Frances snort.

She looks startled by the sound, as if she, too, can't fathom the idea of laughter during such a time of grief. Jorey glances between her and me, bewildered. I reach out and grab his hand, still shaking with laughter. He offers a weak chuckle in return.

"I think everyone's lost it," Simons says, heaving out a disbelieving guffaw.

Slowly, as if pushed by some invisible force, we descend into temporary madness, allowing laughter to take the place of our grief.

CHAPTER
NINE

I DON'T KNOW how long Dad had been planning to run away. He must have entertained the fantasy for a long time because we started packing our bags and practicing evacuations years before we actually ran. But whatever carefully calculated plan he might have had went out the window the moment our test scores filled the display of our data port. I don't know if I can avoid making the same mistakes he made, but I can try.

Our first order of business is making our way to the other side of the pass to retrieve the cure. It's not going to be a short or easy trip, but without a means to reach dissenter help, it's our only option. Whatever state it's in after the trip down the river, it's a better starting point than from scratch. The fact that Shelby sewed a tracking device into the pack suggests she probably took care to create other redundancies to keep the cure safe. It might be completely intact. It could also be sending a signal to someone else to come get it—another failsafe perhaps. Another me.

It's possible that a signal could be traced, alerting the wrong people and dooming us all. That it's such a strong possibility makes me believe Shelby wouldn't use that sort of technology, but I still let myself hope. The idea of someone meeting us at the cure to usher us to safety is too powerful to let go. All I want is for someone besides me to work on the next steps.

For now, being able to track the cure is enough. We've been stagnant for two weeks, watching the signal as it lurches and halts its way deeper into the wilderness, mapping our course and planning. Having a direction gives me purpose and keeps the panic at bay.

The DDC will loose near-dead across the tundra in an attempt to narrow the search. If the technology existed, they'd cast a net across the whole of the northern range to catch us. I shudder at the idea of encountering Orman in the wild, soothed by the knowledge that it's not likely to happen unless he can trap us or pinpoint our location. Thanks to Cain, we have the tunnels, which the DDC doesn't know about. We have the signal-scrambling code and the signature from Shelby's pack, and we have Simons, whose former career was helping others disappear.

We don't have dissenter maps, but I managed to download a location grid that gives us an overview of the terrain. Jorey turned the grid into a sketch of the area that follows the river, and Cain added a rough approximation of the tunnel system. Their combined work reminds me of the map I gave Simons to leave in the shack before we went to the Institute. I wonder if someone else picked it up, if they used it to slip past the DDC's searching gaze and find safety. Perhaps this map will become like that one someday.

If Cain is right about the tunnel system, we can follow the channels a long way toward our destination—the blinking red sister signal to the woven microfibers of the red strip. I trace my finger along the winding line of river that cuts across the grid, wishing I could expand the map and pluck the blinking red light off the screen and be done.

Powering down, I fold my silken diode screen into a small square and place it over the other items I store in the pocket of my glove—the folded strip of red fabric and the faded picture of Carmen's daughter. Absently, I consider the words that accompanied this gift. *Find her*. The thought gives me a pang. I've done absolutely nothing to grant Carmen's final request. I haven't even mentioned it to Simons.

I don't know how leaving the Northern Laboratories has changed the odds of locating Madison Carmen, but I won't feel right until I've done something to address it. Once we get moving, I can talk to Simons about it. I can't imagine the two of them working side by side for so long without any mention of Carmen's missing daughter.

"All ready for transport, boss!" Cain disrupts my thoughts with his cheery salutation.

I stand, pulling my pack over my shoulder and tucking my braid into my suit collar. "Ready and raring to go?" I ask, cocking my eyebrow in his direction and letting him know I'm aware of his and Frances' dissenting opinions on our course of action.

"We'd be a lot better off waiting out the DDC's initial search under shelter and making a plan for offensive action," Cain responds, not for the first time. His recommendation to let go of the cure and head for a dissenter safehouse was hard to turn down.

"Let's get the cure, then I'll hear you out about your contact," I say.

"Frances is eager to get her hands on some more supplies," Cain prompts.

I glance toward the larger portion of the cavern, where the rest of the group is convened, catching Frances as she helps Richards fasten his pack. "She used to work in distribution analytics for the capitol," I say.

"Well, she's not wrong. We're going to need a lot more than a few pulsar guns to go up against Orman."

"Frances might agree with you about supplies, but you're the only one who wants to go head on with Orman and the DDC out here," I say, ending the conversation and joining the rest of the group.

Cain takes up the lead with Richards. Frances and Jorey follow close behind, holding their lights high enough to illuminate the area ahead, which is mostly made up of rock and darkness. Simons is taking the first shift dragging Dunn on the gurney we constructed. I walk just behind Simons so I can engage him. Though he's able to sit up on his own now, Dunn isn't strong enough to cover the distance ahead of us.

"How are you feeling today?" I ask as we begin our journey through the tunnels.

"Like a burden," he says in a toneless voice, avoiding eye contact.

"I feel more weight from the packs than I do from this carry system," Simons insists.

Dunn looks up, unable to see the carrier from his upright, rear facing position, his arms and legs bound. "I suppose I'll feel like a much heavier load once my mind goes. I doubt you'll be so positive then."

"That may not happen," I snap.

He glares at me, fear and anger swelling in his eyes. "It'll happen. Infection from direct contact is 100%. I'll be gone in three weeks—maybe sooner. I know about the lacerated artery. I know what's inside of me, and you do, too."

There's no use arguing with him. "You're right. But you said you studied cell cultures for dormancy. And you were on so many of Shelby's experiments. That means you also know there's a chance you'll recover—maybe even go months without disease expression."

"A very slim chance," he corrects.

"It's a chance I'm willing to take. Look around. It's a chance we're all willing to take—to save your life."

Dunn studies me. His glistening and bloodshot eyes sweep across our travel-ready group before settling on his restraints. He lets out a weak sigh. "And if you're wrong… at least I won't hurt anyone else."

"That's right," I assure him.

He deflates, the frustration and anger leaving him along with so much energy. "You studied infection science before you switched to hive, right?" he asks, proving I meant a great deal more to him than he ever did to me.

"Amos told me to choose it," I affirm, wishing I could go back and change everything.

"Do you know why?"

"I don't know anything for sure. I used to think it was because she wanted to keep me safe, but I know better now. Miller and Tucker thought I learned the Northern Laboratories primary code. For a very brief period, I thought they might be right, but now I know it had something to do with the cure," I explain.

"Do you really believe Shelby found the cure?"

"I told you; I've seen it with my own eyes—held the paper in my hands," I say.

"And it's lost now."

"Yes," I admit, purposefully leaving out the details of the first leg of our journey to unite with the dissenters waiting somewhere south of the cities.

I've been trying to reach them for years, I think, not knowing how to express this to Dunn or anyone else. Instead of trying, I say, "Shelby found the cure. If you question it was possible to do in the Northern Laboratories, then you must understand, at least on some level, that the government didn't want a cure."

It's Dunn's turn to be lost in a long silence. He looks stuck between two truths that can't exist on the same plane.

"I thought..."

His voice is very quiet.

"I thought there was no more risk to the cities. I thought the risk came from the outside—that all the patients came from the outside and we needed a dormant strain to infect them. I thought that was why the focus skewed away from the cure..."

I contemplate his explanation—people living outside of the cities who aren't dissenters. I don't know what to make of it, and from the expressions on my companions' faces, they don't either. I want to attribute his explanation to delirium, but that would be foolish. Dunn knows something about the world we don't, but it's impossible to make sense of it. Until he recovers, we're going to remain in the dark, which would be fine if the clock weren't ticking.

"Dunn..." I begin, treading carefully.

"James, please. Or... call me Jim," he says.

I nod assent, too awkward to take him up on it. "You've mentioned people living outside the cities several times. Is that something you've talked about before?"

"Not much at first because I didn't quite believe it myself, but after a couple of years—the constant influx of patients, the magnitude of the cryo halls, the paradox of the infection versus the safety protocols—it was the only explanation, wasn't it?" he says, still putting it together as he speaks.

This is why he was assigned to my experiment. He might've been wrong about the details, but he knows too much. He was meant to be a casualty, which makes me see him in a softer light, even if he's wrong.

"The threat of Zoribiatus is real, but it's not from people living on the outside, it's from the government—they've weaponized it," I say.

Dunn's eyes widen in grim understanding.

"Do you mean the hive?" he asks. A silent shudder moves through the group. I resist the urge to tune my attention to the tunnels, listening for the limping scrape of patients ambling in the darkness.

"I've seen it firsthand outside of the Laboratories. Simons has too, but it's more than the hive—it's about infection in the cities. Everyone here has lost someone who didn't set foot on the outside."

"Is that why you destroyed the Laboratories? To take their weapon from them?" Dunn asks.

"The Northern Laboratories isn't their only weapon. It was just a place created to control society," Cain breaks into the conversation. It startles me even though I knew everyone was listening.

"How do you know?" Dunn asks.

"Because I'm a dissenter. It's my job to expose the government's lies," Cain says. I cast him a skeptical glance, wondering if he's considered that someone like Dunn hasn't had an opportunity to know who the dissenters are.

"That's what they're called—dissenters," I rush to explain. "And they're everywhere—embedded in the cities, the Institute, the Northern Laboratories. Shelby was a dissenter, and Amos was, too. They're responsible for getting me into the Northern Laboratories. They might even be the people you think live outside of the City States in the Deadlands."

"Nothing can live in the Deadlands!" Dunn scoffs. Already, his head droops from fatigue.

"They live beyond the Deadlands, in the south," Cain says, throwing his arms up in exasperation. He glances around for someone to agree with him.

Frances shakes her head, bewildered. Cain looks at Richards, who responds by saying, "I've only heard stories!"

"Unbelievable! Jorey?" Cain says, turning to look at him.

Jorey shrugs. "Just stories."

"They're not *just stories*. It's a whole world," Cain says.

"No civilization could survive in such harsh conditions. They live in the woods, in ancient cities." Dunn shakes his head, struggling to fill it with such thoughts.

"There's a whole world outside of the structure of the City States. Even I've only seen part of it. You're a fool if you think everything you're taught is even close to the truth," Cain says, glancing first at Dunn, then me.

"I know about the South," I insist, ashamed of how much I don't know.

Cain continues his explanation for Dunn's sake, but we all take note. "The government doesn't want you to realize things are good on the outside. That's the reason for the Northern Laboratories. The world outside the City States is just as safe as the one on the inside—safer maybe."

"But your expeditions… you told us you made a career of taking researchers on expeditions to the south to gather soil samples and explore food solutions!" Jorey argues. His words bring forth another memory. *It's easy to believe the only thing we've ever been told…*

"It's true. But who approves those expeditions?"

"The government?" Richards asks, knowing he's right.

"Exactly! And if they want people to believe the land outside the cities is uninhabitable, they need people to prove it."

"If the land is alive, wouldn't an expedition prove it?" Jorey argues.

"There's still a desolate belt—the Deadlands. Expeditions don't travel below it. Ocean currents keep the land dry, and weapons specialists periodically target the area and keep the soil contaminated. There are always near-dead in the Deadlands, sometimes thousands of them."

"Where do they come from?"

"They have to be planted there," I speculate.

Cain nods.

I look over and note that Dunn is sleeping. I turn to Richards and ask, "How did his wound look this morning?"

"Still clean. There's no sign of manifestation," he assures me.

"Yet," Cain says under his breath.

I glare at him for not leaving it alone. "We all agreed. He stays with us."

"How far gone does he have to be before you're willing to pull the trigger?" Cain asks.

Richard casts a scathing glare in Cain's direction.

"We're not pulling the trigger while he's alive," Simons insists in the tone that normally ends all arguments.

"Who makes that decision?" Cain presses.

We're all silent. It's a question I've asked myself every night as the lights blink away the darkness. I don't know the answer.

"Mason. She's the scientist. She makes the call," Simons says. I knew the responsibility would fall to me but hate hearing it.

Cain looks at me expectantly. His piercing stare screams, *I told you so.*

I look away, uncomfortable, reiterating Simons' statement. "We don't kill the living."

"And when he develops?" Cain presses.

"We can handle one contained patient," I insist.

We walk on in silence, winding west at every opportunity to follow the path of the river. My words hang in the air, echoing in the darkest parts of my mind. *We don't kill the living.* I had my chance to kill Orman and didn't take it. How differently might things have gone if I'd been able to make the shot. Cain took the shot and missed.

I study him as we walk on, thinking about what else he's willing to do.

CAIN SCOFFS AT JOREY, his face plastered with his characteristic smile as we crest a hillside in brilliant daylight. "You miss dainty cakes? How about mountains? Fresh running water?"

"I didn't say I missed *dainty cakes*. I said the way Frances described them made them sound really good," Jorey pouts.

"Oh yeah. Lemons and sugar with intricate yellow icing put on display at the corner bakery!" Cain imitates Frances.

"I think I could eat twelve of them," Jorey repeats, unwilling to relent on the issue.

"How about you, Mason? In the mood for a *dainty lemon cake*?" Cain asks as we pause to take in the sweeping vista of summer tundra below.

"I've never had one," I admit, knowing this will get him off Jorey's case and onto mine.

Miles south of the Northern Laboratories, the landscape is vastly different. Acres of fuzzy grasses, sedges and shrubs span out ahead of us in a rolling terrain of color. Yellow bell-shaped flowers dot the pastures as they bask in the glow of late-night sun. To the east, a small cluster of caribou graze in a mass of mosses and lichen brought back from the brink by the thawing ground. An arctic beetle lumbers out onto the edge of a barren branch near Jorey, only to turn and scurry for cover as a speckled brown bird perches on the ground nearby. The entire expanse seems to breathe with the life that fills it—*extinct* life.

Kara brought back an entire ecosystem—quick, someone reinvent the Nobel Prize! Hank's voice echoes in my mind like a ghost that can't rest.

Yeah, and she can probably name every single one of those beetles, Bruce points out as Dad chuckles.

"This place is beautiful," Jorey observes, pulling me out of the past.

"Beautiful but dangerous," Cain corrects him as I take a knee and dig through my pack for supplies.

"Dangerous?" Jorey asks, leaning against a mossy rock, completely oblivious to the life burgeoning around us.

"That's right. It's totally wild up here. If the weather doesn't kill you, something else will," Cain says.

"Near-dead?" Jorey asks.

"Not up here—not usually, anyway. More likely wild dogs or a moose. Maybe even a bear," Cain continues.

"Bears are extinct," Jorey says, giving an uncomfortable glance at our immediate surroundings.

"I doubt that. Maybe they were nearly there, but once the people were gone… look how much has come back. Have you even seen this much wildlife?" Cain asks. His voice trails off as he watches a fox pounce into a burrow, a movement so subtle in the vastness of the area that it takes keen observation to detect.

"I've never been outside the city before," Jorey says, forlorn.

I glance up from my work. A fuzz of dark hair is growing atop Jorey's normally shaved head. It casts dark shadows over his already dark complexion, making him look more like the person I rode up with than he has in years. Cain is also studying him, his face plastered with amusement, likely at Jorey's naïveté. I return to my task, spreading the diode screen across the spiky tips of the ground cover next to Jorey's sketch so I can cross-reference our progress.

"How does it feel to be out now, brother?" Cain asks Jorey as I cue up the signal.

The screen blinks to life, displaying the scrambled connect code.

"It's not like I thought. I don't think anyone could imagine something like this," Jorey says.

Relief floods in when I'm able to connect with the sister signal of the cure pack. I pull up the terrain grid and superimpose it with the signal, all the while thinking about how similar Jorey's reaction to the outside world is to mine so many years ago.

"Is that what stopped you? A lack of imagination?" Cain persists.

"No. Not at all. You know how it is, right, Mason?" he implores.

I stop what I'm doing to look at him. "What do you mean?"

"In the cities. Everyone knew—if you leave, you get infected." There's an edge of pleading to Jorey's voice.

"And you believed that? Is everyone inside the barriers as gullible as you?" Cain laughs.

Jorey's mouth opens in protest, but he doesn't speak. Cain slaps him on his shoulder, cawing his delight again. He looks down at me, still laughing. "Mason, can you believe this guy? I mean—you didn't believe that kind of thing, did you?"

I look between the two—Cain's bright eyes squinting with tearful humor and Jorey's gloomy, pleading expression. "It was different for me. I lived outside of the city when I wasn't in school, so I sort of knew better." I look down.

I hurry to make a few calculations, marking them on the paper. My answer is a betrayal to Jorey. All the city kids believed it. It's why they wanted nothing to do with my brothers and me, but for some reason, I don't want to admit it to Cain. I want him to think better of me.

I cut the signal to the screen before standing.

"What's the verdict?" Cain asks, looking at the marks I made on our map.

"The good news is that it looks like the pack hasn't moved since the last time we checked," I say.

"What's the bad news?" Jorey asks in the quiet voice he only uses when he's hurting.

I point southwest across the tundra toward the mountains. "The most direct route still takes us right over the range."

Cain lets out a low whistle. "Yeah, that's not going to happen."

"Is there any chance the tunnels pass through?" I ask.

"None. They'll take us south if we keep at it." He points at the channel on the map that steers us away from the river.

"Yeah, that's what I was afraid of," I sigh, putting the screen back in its pocket before grabbing up the water canister. I take a long drink before handing it off to Jorey. I try to give him a look that imitates the guilt growing inside of me.

Jorey takes the canister, shrugging. After he hands it off to Cain, he leans over my shoulder to point at the grid. "We can follow the tunnels to this juncture. That should bring us to that first area where we thought we might be able to cross the range."

I study his proposal, comparing the markings on the map to the landscape laid out before us. "That might work." I turn to Cain. "What do you think?"

He puts a hand on his hip and exhales loudly as he mulls it over. "It'll take at least another week to make that trip."

"Yeah," I agree, the reality of our circumstances sinking in. Our supplies are rapidly dwindling, and with them I fear will go the group's support for prioritizing the cure. Dunn's words ring in the background of the wild quiet. *I'll be gone in three weeks—maybe sooner.* Even if the infection stays dormant, it will take weeks after we recover the cure before we can get him help… And the days before the government narrows their hunt for us are numbered.

"But I think it's our best option," he finishes.

I nod, folding the map and slipping it back into the pack along with the water canister. "Back to the tunnels, I guess," I say, taking one last look at the high north summer before we descend into darkness.

Cain takes the lead back down the hill. I follow behind him next to Jorey. Cain starts singing a song I don't recognize. His loud, atonal voice causes a small flock of birds to take flight in the red light of dusk.

Over the misty mountains
    Down the valley below…

I glance over at Jorey and use the mask of Cain's song to reach out. "You okay?"

"I'm fine," he answers as Cain belts out another line.

Where I bring my family…

"I didn't mean to—"

"You didn't do anything. I know you grew up on an energy management facility," Jorey insists in his quietest voice.

"Why do you let him get to you?" I ask.

Jorey shrugs and offers a hand toward Cain, whose own hands are outstretched as if to carry his note across the hillside. "I don't know. He's just…"

That's the place I call home

I smile, knowing the tension between us has gone. "Something else," I finish for him.

"I'll say," Jorey agrees.

Cain kicks a clump of dirt, scattering broken pieces of grass and a couple of flowers down the hill as he gears up for another verse. It's an old song, long lost to the City States and the safety of the new world, but there's something familiar about it too. If I concentrated, I could almost imagine my father humming something quite like it, as though the people who pined for a better place were all connected by the ancient tune.

Oh, I ain't from Mississippi
And long gone is Cincinnati…

"He's kind of a jerk," Jorey offers.

"I don't know about that," I say, watching Cain's lanky, free frame as he descends ahead of us.

Jorey raises an eyebrow at me. "Don't you?"

I raise my own eyebrow at him and don't answer.

Jorey acts as if he's going to say something but doesn't.

I sigh, wishing for the ease of the empty cafeteria. Cain stops dead in his tracks and throws his hands straight up for his finale with a grand last note.

And when we come together, there will be home

CHAPTER
ELEVEN

THE TUNNELS ARE wet and cold in comparison to the open tundra. *At least there's no wind down here*, I think as Cain secures the latch behind us. I turn on my headlamp and scan the entrance, grimly determined to do what it takes to retrieve the cure.

As I scan the tunnel walls, something catches my attention. Below a thick layer of dripping ice adhering to the tunnel's rock walls, an encrypted message is carved over other messages eroded by decades of ice and water. I walk up to it, running my fingers along the grooves that make out the symbols. "What is this?"

"That's code," Cain says as he steps up to the wall. His shoulder touches mine as he reaches out to trace the markings.

"What sort of code? And how come this is the first I've seen of it?" I ask, still absorbed in the strangeness of these markings in the middle of the frozen tundra.

"They're messages left by dissenters for anyone who needs direction, and most of them are hidden," he says.

"Out here?" I ask, turning my headlight so it illuminates him.

"Out here, and anywhere else the dissenters have been," he says, as if it were the most commonplace thing that could happen.

"Can you read it?" I ask.

"I learned it when I was young. Most of us on the outside can read it," he says.

My mind races back in time to my dad. I picture him walking the boundary of our property along the shimmer of the force field, holding his illicit tablet. Could he read it? Did he know about it?

"What does it say?"

"It's directions to the nearest dissenter-friendly safe haven," Cain says, pointing at two of the symbols. One is an image of the sun; the other looks like a bisected triangle. "These symbols are ideographic scripts. They represent the traveler in these tunnels and a type of safe-house—an energy management station."

"An active one?" Jorey asks, one hand on my shoulder as he peers over my head at the script.

"As far as I know, all the fusion stations are active." Cain indicates the script surrounding the two main symbols in a semi-circle. "This describes the channels we need to take to get there—in this case, we would have to follow the underground waterways." Then he points to the series of lines below the markings. "This is the key explaining the distance we have to travel for safety, and this blank space indicates there are no resources between us and the safe-house."

Cain moves his light away from the message and walks down the tunnel back toward the rest of the group. I take one last look at the carvings— a whole other language— before I turn to catch up with him, still looking for explanation. "Where did you learn to read it?" I ask.

Cain's light dips temporarily in my direction. "My mother taught me."

"Is your mother a dissenter?" I ask, a pang of regret twinging my midsection. There was so much I didn't get to learn. If we'd made it—or if we'd stayed—how different would things be? Dad thought he was protecting us, waiting for a life we would never have together...

"She was," he says without looking at me.

Jorey scuffles to catch up. His headlight swings over to Cain. "Is she—"

"Dead," Cain cuts him off flatly.

There's a temporary pause in conversation. The sound of water dripping from the ceiling echoes in the empty passageways as I formulate my next question, not wanting to admit the constant ache trying to consume me, but also not wanting to sound insensitive. "Was she always a dissenter?"

Cain shrugs. "No. Like most people, she came to it because she was tired of all the deceit. She could see right through what they were doing with the Northern Laboratories."

"She was government, then?" I ask.

Before Cain can answer, Jorey asks another question. "How did she find the dissenters?"

"Something like that. And she looked," Cain says, answering both of us.

I let the topic rest. For days, Cain has been giving nothing but half answers to every question. I'm getting more frustrated each time with the way he eludes full disclosure. I don't like that he's hiding something when we're completely dependent on him to guide us through the tunnels.

We turn the corner to find Simons and Frances rifling through the supply packs. Frances is studying the materials lined up along the cavern wall while Simons pulls more from the packs. They both look up at our arrival. Our lights create a white dome at the juncture of two caverns.

"Is everything alright?" I ask, disquieted by the scene.

"I can't find my glove," Frances says, returning her attention to the organized chaos of equipment.

"You weren't wearing it?" Cain asks.

She shakes her head. "No. It was bothering my wrist, so I took it off. I thought I put it in Richards' pack, but he insists it isn't there."

"Where is Richards?" I ask with growing apprehension.

"He's with Dunn. Bandage change," Simons says, emptying another pack.

I turn abruptly, leaving them to their pile to reassure myself that my anxiety is misplaced. We chose to stop here due to the high number of junctures. The possibility of an ambush has been heavy on my mind, despite Cain's insistence the existence of the far north tunnel system is a well-kept secret. If we didn't need to surface to read the signal from the pack, I might be more confident, but the signal is still too weak.

My stomach lurches as the light fills our little camp to reveal Richards, spread out face down on the ground. I rush over, the uneven ground boring into my knees as I turn him over to investigate. His face is clammy and cool. I watch his chest rise and fall with the steady breaths of a deep slumber. *He's drugged*, I realize, scanning the ground for the telltale syringe. I roll Richards' unconscious form until he's lying on his back before reaching out to the divot on the cavern floor to retrieve a small glass cylinder with a thin silver needle. I turn it over in my hand, piecing together the sequence of events. How long has Dunn been planning this?

The medical kit lays open. Richards hadn't even had a chance to start tending to Dunn's bandages before he went down—likely as soon as Simons and Frances took off to search their equipment. I close my mouth and listen for an indication of which direction Dunn headed. He couldn't have gotten far, and if he intends to use Frances' glove to make contact with someone, he's headed for the surface. I briefly consider heading back to inform the rest of the group of his escape, but there isn't enough time. I have to beat Dunn to the surface and stop whatever plan he's set on executing.

The echo of my footsteps drowns out the distant sounds of cheerful conversation as I race to find him.

CHAPTER
TWELVE

WE CAME through the only exit hatch to the tunnel system in this area no more than fifteen minutes ago. Unless Dunn was waiting in the shadows for us to pass through, I don't see how he could have left undetected. But if he did slip out after we came down, it might already be too late.

I jog around the second juncture, which loops back toward the exit. I have to turn my body sideways to squeeze through the narrow passage. My light shines on the solid earth, worn smooth by the erosion of repeated thawing and freezing. The stone face is rusted green from exposure and covered in a fine film of lichen. Deep grooves mark where the surface has been brushed clean, confirming Dunn came through this way.

Clear of the narrowed tunnel, I stand upright and push on toward the exit. The beam of light piercing the darkness tells me everything I need to know. Dunn reached the surface. The thought makes me want to vomit, but I swallow the bile and cautiously push the hatch open the rest of the way. The sky greets me in shades of dark blue fading to purples and pinks where the sun persists at the horizon. I swing my legs onto the frost-covered ground and pull myself upright, leaving the hatch open so Simons or anyone else who comes looking can follow my trail.

The cold air bites at my cheeks as the wind tears through the tundra, uninhibited. I wait for the gust to die down. Something screes in the distance, likely caught by a predatory bird—an owl or some other winged terror of the twilight. I turn off my headlight so I can search the perimeter. Wherever he is, Dunn can't have stepped out of our security perimeter without triggering an alarm. I scan impatiently, waiting for my eyes to discern the difference between a clump of shrubs and a hunched body.

I hear him before I see him, pulling the sound of muffled sniffling out from the chorus of nature. I follow the sound until his form comes into view. He's balled up, his arms wrapped around his knees and his head buried in the space between. I approach him silently, waiting until I'm within arm's reach.

"Dunn. It's time to head back underground," I say, keeping my voice soft and kind so the fear doesn't break through. It's easy to do —a costume I put on to protect from the dangers around every corner.

"What's the point?" he murmurs without looking up.

"We're going to need to talk about what you did," I say, trying to decide if I should reach out for him, trying to assess the risk.

"You should have killed me," he says, another sob bubbling up from inside of him.

"We're not going to do that. Not if there's even the smallest chance—"

"THERE ISN'T ANY CHANCE!" he screams, his head snapping up. His eyes are wild and bloodshot. Tears and snot smear his pale face. He turns to his side and brings himself upright to expose his unzipped lab suit. Beneath it, the bandages hang loose to expose the raw, half-healed wound. The jagged tear is held together with sutures that make his skin pucker like swollen red lips. Where the skin should be scabbed, a thin film of pus has started to ooze, dripping down across his greying flesh. "Only a little while until full expression now," he whispers.

The sight of the wound, unhealed and infected, begs me to look away. My mind works automatically to diagnose him—ZCD, rapid expression, patient prognosis less than two weeks. *Not patient,* I correct myself. *Dunn*. I direct my gaze into Dunn's tortured, wild-eyed stare. "Dunn… I'm so sorry. Does Richards know?"

"I w-wouldn't let him change them this morning. N-not before I had my chance to… to…" He breaks down into another sob, his hands flying up to cover his face.

The terror for what I know he's about to say grips me, making it difficult to breathe. I force myself to reach out and put a hand on his shoulder. "It's…" I struggle to find the right tone to comfort him. I take in a breath and try again. "It's awful. It's not right, and I'm so sorry. It shouldn't have happened like this."

His hands fall so that he's looking at me again. "But it could have happened. Even if things had gone the way you planned, it still might have happened."

The truth of his words stings. I ignore my natural desire to wince against the pain, channeling all my years of Institute training. It's too easy to keep my face neutral. It's imperative I discover what he did.

"You're right. I made a decision to gamble with your lives, and now I've lost you and Altman," I admit, realizing that even though I ache for what's happened, I would do it over again. It makes me so much more like Shelby than I ever realized, as much a monster as the Institute intended for me to be.

The image of Shelby's finger on the button is replaced by one of my own. After all, I initiated the detonation of the Northern Laboratories. *Am I any better? Does the end justify the means?*

"Don't forget you've lost Shelby, too," Dunn spits.

"She knew the risks." Simons' deep voice startles me.

Simons approaches, holding a pulsar gun in one hand and a lashing pole in the other. He stops right next to me, plunging the back end of the lashing pole into the ground before saying, "Besides. I'd like to remind you that if Mason hadn't put together that plan, we'd all be dead, not just you and Altman. Don't forget that experiment was put through specifically to kill us."

Dunn's lip quivers, and he hangs his head in shame. "I'm sorry, alright? You spend your whole life believing in something and then—"

I look over at Simons, grateful for his interjection but unsure what to say. Simons studies my expression before putting a strong hand around my shoulders. "Mason took a chance. Things might be a bit worse than a mess, but at least we've still got a chance of doing something good for the world because of it. I know that doesn't do a whole lot for you right now, but I'd like to believe you can step outside of yourself long enough to see it was the right decision."

I blink back the surge of emotion brought on by Simons' proclamation of faith in me.

"Come on back to the tunnels so we can talk about what's going to happen next," I offer.

"If you're going to kill me, you should do it up here, so you don't have to deal with the infected stink of my body down there," he whimpers.

"I said we don't kill the living. I meant that. But this does change things," I say, gesturing to the manifestation of the infection spreading across the wound.

"What if I asked you to?" Dunn asks.

"Is that what you want?" Simons retorts.

Dunn's face contorts as he struggles to find his answer. "It's what I deserve, but no. I'm too much of a coward to face my own death."

"Then that's that," Simons answers.

Dunn nods, his whole body trembling. He reaches out in surrender, offering up the stolen glove. I take it from him before Simons binds his hands with the magnetic lashing. I turn the small black power relay over, considering the trouble it may have just created for us.

"Did you use it?" I ask.

"I just wanted to say goodbye," he whispers through trembling lips.

"To your family?" I ask.

He nods, staring into the ground.

"Did you make contact?" I press.

He nods again, still unable to meet my gaze.

"Dunn. You know how important it is we stay hidden as long as possible. If the DDC doesn't know we're alive, then it might delay a search. I need you to tell me exactly what happened. What did you say?" Even as I speak, I know it's too late. If Dunn made contact, the government knows there were survivors, and the DDC is already gearing up to start the hunt.

"I told them goodbye. I said I was as good as dead, and the labs were gone." He breathes in an uneven shudder, pausing as he contemplates his next words. "You have to understand—they were devastated. I just wanted to give them some hope."

"You told them about the cure," I say, fear racing through me.

Dunn nods before collapsing to the ground, overwrought. "I didn't know they'd already gotten to them!"

Simons shakes his head as the weight of Dunn's mistake settles over us. He lets out a heavy sigh before holstering his pulsar gun underneath the thick canvas jacket he's wearing again since we left the Laboratories. Before I can formulate the words that describe the thoughts churning in my head, Simons speaks.

"It's going to be okay. They were going to find out one way or another. At least this way we know for certain they're going to be on our tracks."

Simons leads Dunn back into the tunnels. I follow, reality weighing me down like lead. Even if we get moving tonight, I can't muster the same level of certainty everything is going to be okay.

CHAPTER
THIRTEEN

DUNN'S CONDITION has deteriorated rapidly. The accelerated timeline of progression is a combination of the depths of infection along with the severity of his injuries and our complete inability to do more than treat his symptoms. A fever struck on the third night, and his mind hasn't been the same since. He wavers constantly between feverish rants about the cellular progression of each class of Zoribiatus from our early studies at the Institute to delusional stories from his childhood and back to himself, weak, exhausted, and terrified.

"You will note the total loss of dexterity of my right arm and lower appendages as the infected cells overtake the musculature surfaces," he says, tipping the grey flesh of his chin toward his right to indicate the condition. His ceaseless dialogue marks our slow progress as we navigate through dense brush and muddy gullies between steep, hilly climbs.

Frances glances helplessly in my direction, unable to follow the complexity of his descriptions but incapable of tearing herself away.

"ZCD is known for its particularly aggressive attack of muscle tissue," I offer, hoping to bring Dunn through his point.

"Nothing like the ZCZ strain though, so I suppose we can be grateful for that much. It's nice to have a frightfully predictable disease progression," he says.

This is the part where he usually dives deep into pathology. I'm not certain I can handle it today. In an attempt to steer him away from technical discussion, I ask him, "Did you want to be a scientist? I mean, before you went to the Institute."

Dunn's fevered eyes flick from me to the sky, then down across his deteriorating body, as if everything were too bright to look at for more than a second.

"I dreamed of it," he admits, his attention fixed temporarily on the movement of a windblown shrub.

"Was it the prestige? The job?" I ask, hoping to keep him on topic.

"It was my parents," he says, blinking until the haze of confusion dissipates from his expression. He licks at cracked lips before saying, "I wouldn't have admitted it then, but I know it's true. They wanted—no, needed me to go to the Institute. So they could be proud of me, so they'd be seen as right."

"No one could demand that of a child!" Frances interjects, her brow furrowed in consternation, her pale cheeks ruddy with the effort of our progress. In this moment, she is very much a mother, her energy focused on the wellbeing of the child despite the reality of the world we all grew up in.

"It's just how it was with them—with so many families. Everyone was so afraid. People were disappearing…"

A dreamy look crosses Dunn's face as he's transported back to childhood. I think he'll lapse again, but he stays with us. "It's why they disapproved of Mora," he says.

It's not the first time he's mentioned the name—an old friend who disappeared shortly before he went to the Institute. According to Dunn, she escaped the city to find people on the outside. Apparently, I remind him of her.

"Because she didn't want to go to the Institute?" Frances asks with practiced curiosity.

"Because she didn't even try," Dunn says, the dreamy look persisting.

"Did she tell you she was leaving?" I ask. I might remind Dunn of Mora, but his mythical friend reminds me of someone else. *Find her…*

"When I knew I couldn't talk her out of it, I helped her escape," Dunn says.

Treading as lightly as possible on the fragile state of his memories, I ask, "Do you remember if she ever mentioned anything about coyotes?"

"Yes. She thought they might come after Omen... if they existed," Dunn says.

I bite my lip, frustrated we're entering nonsensical territory again. I should be grateful we've gotten this far, but I can't help but want more answers.

"What's the omen?" I ask, biting back the edge in my voice. All I've been able to get out is that it has something to do with ancient texts—something from the world before the war and the first outbreak.

"She named him after a writer, but I can't remember which one. I used to remember... when my mind was whole..." he says, scowling.

"Do you remember what the writing was about?" I ask.

Dunn closes his eyes. He takes in a ragged breath that sounds somewhere between a gasp and a snore. A low whine makes its way out of him, wavering in pitch between a moan and a scream.

I take another step through the thick mud, waiting to see if Dunn will come back. A gurgled sucking sound accompanies my efforts to lift my foot out of the muck. Jorey offers me a hand to steady myself as my other foot sinks down to my ankle. "We need to find higher ground," I say.

"I think we better start setting a camp for the night," Simons retorts, shifting his grip on the front of the gurney so he can roll his shoulders.

"Yeah. I'm pretty sure my blisters have blisters," Cain agrees, balancing the back end of Dunn's gurney on his knee to wrap another strip of gauze around his hand.

"I'll take over for a while," I offer, stepping through the thick muck toward them.

"Me too," Jorey pipes in.

I stagger through the mud toward Cain, who offers me gauze to wrap my hands. "I'm alright," I say, waving to dismiss it.

"Suit yourself," he says, crumpling it up and shoving it in his pocket.

Simons raises his arms over his head in a stretch to relieve the built-up tension from hours of hoisting Dunn's carrier over the difficult terrain.

"Mason, why don't you come ahead with me and check out the coverage that way?" he asks without turning.

"Sure thing. I'm sure everybody could use a break," I say, suspecting there's something he wants to discuss with me.

Jorey eases up on his end of the gurney, standing. Cain gives the handles a hard stare, clearly tired of hauling Dunn like so much dead weight. There's plenty of light still, but Simons is right about making camp. We can't push on indefinitely if we don't know when help will come.

Simons drops his larger pack next to Jorey, transferring his pulsar gun from the chest holster to the one at his right. Frances and Richards drop their packs, sighing with relief. I mimic Simons' weapon transition, accepting the lashing pole from him before taking off from the group as they pass the canteen between themselves.

We march up the hill, making quick work of the shrubs and roots covering the ground like wild carpet. When we've moved far out of sight and well out of earshot, Simons speaks up.

"Richards says he doesn't have long."

"He's right," I agree.

"Exactly how long does he have?" Simons asks, holding back low-hanging branches for me.

"I can't say exactly, but days at most," I say, pausing to consider.

"We can't keep this pace with him going like he is," Simons says.

I've been thinking the same for a few days now but haven't wanted to admit it. The closer we get to the end, the harder it is to imagine following through with what's required.

Shelby killed the living, I remind myself, unsure if I'm goading myself or assuaging unease.

"I've been thinking the same thing, but I'm not sure what else to do," I admit.

"It's time to stop," he says.

The definitive nature of his proclamation removes some of the doubt I've carried, but it doesn't solve the fundamental problem.

"We can't stop. We need to get to the cure before the river changes again," I say.

Simons shifts his massive frame so he's facing me more completely. His look of authority has more of a conspiratorial air to it this evening, promising he has an idea.

"I've been thinking about that," he says. "Not all of us need to stop."

Immediately I understand what he's proposing. It's a risk we haven't been willing to consider up to this point, but the time has come to take a chance.

"You go on with Frances and Jorey to get the cure. Richards and I will stay with Dunn until it's time. Cain can choose which he'd like to do, but I think I know what his pick will be already," I say.

Richards will insist that he stays with me even though the end promises to be unpleasant. He won't leave his patient until it's over. Even though Cain will likely move on with the rest of the group to get the cure, the two of us are more than capable of handling Dunn's final moments.

"I'll be staying back with you," Simons corrects.

"You don't need to—" I protest. His leadership is far too important to be spent on death watch. With Frances and Cain on their last threads of patience—Cain with Dunn and Frances with the pursuit of the cure in the face of our dwindling supplies—I need Simons to hold them together.

"I don't feel right going on without you," he says, shaking his head. Blurred shadows dance across his sweat-streaked skin from the sun breaking through branches. He looks so much like he did the morning in the shack.

I argued with him then, certain I'd landed on the only correct solution. Now I know there's no certainty in anything. A gust of wind moves through the brush, stirring up a whisper of leaves and grass and sending a chill straight through my core.

"I don't like it, but it doesn't feel right to argue with you," I admit, suppressing a shiver.

"They'll have Jorey to keep things together. He'll make sure the job gets done," Simons says.

"We can move fast to catch up once it's done. It might not take more than a couple of days," I speculate, accepting the necessity of this division. "I'll make the announcement tonight after we set up camp."

CHAPTER
FOURTEEN

I KEEP MY EYES FORWARD, glancing quickly between the trail and Dunn's unconscious form as I move with Jorey, lost in my own thoughts. The weight of Dunn's gurney tugs at my arms, making them burn with the constant lift and jostle of our uphill scramble through the thick summer growth. Even with my mind set to the task, it's a struggle to stay within sight of the rest of the team as they climb ahead of us, choosing what they believe will be the easiest path forward.

Dunn is lost in deep but fitful sleep, whimpering and reflexively pushing against his restraints every time Jorey and I struggle to keep the gurney level. Though he looks ill, he's still very human—scared, frantic, and confused. There's enough of him left to witness the horror of inevitable demise. He'll be himself right up until the moment the disease takes his mind. When that happens, like a flash, he'll transform into the same sort of hungry monster that followed our trail so many years ago across the open field…

A sweat breaks out along my hairline as we make the last push to the top where the team waits for us. When we finally make it, we set Dunn's gurney down on a mostly-level section of ground. Jorey runs his hand over the scruff on the top of his head as Dunn begins to stir. I hold my breath, wondering which version will wake.

His eyes open, wide and innocent. He looks around, blinking

against the passing shadows cast by the overhead trees before settling his gaze on me. "Hey," he says, his voice soft and timid.

"Hi there," I respond, trying to sound casual.

"Did you know there are at least six species of rodent that aren't actually extinct?" he asks, offering me a brilliantly sweet smile.

I can't help but smile in return, but I know my smile is much sadder. "I did. And beetles and lizards and wild dogs and probably raptors too!" I say conspiratorially.

His eyes widen, full of childish wonder. He starts to say something, then is overtaken by a coughing fit. When he recovers, he glances down at his frame. "I'm really sick, aren't I?"

"Yes, you are," I agree.

He licks his lips again, his wide eyes darting around, lost. Just when I think the line of our conversation has been broken, he asks me, "Do you think I'll get better?"

"You're really sick, and we're a long way from help," I say.

I watch the hope flicker behind his glassy eyes before it dies. I look away from child-Dunn's confused and innocent face, desperate for some relief. This is so much harder than his crazed rants and delirious stories. Jorey steps to my side to offer my shoulder a sympathetic squeeze. I clear my throat, buying time to think of something to say.

Before I manage the task, Dunn asks, "Will you tell Mora I wanted to say goodbye?"

"I don't know where Mora is," I say. Frances and Richards hover close by, ready to help if the opportunity presents itself.

"She'll be on the roof with Omen. She promised she wouldn't leave before me," Dunn says. He blinks, heavy eyelids taking their time to open again.

I don't bother to correct him. He isn't actually here with us, but he isn't completely in his past either. It's more of a foggy middle ground where ghosts wander.

Richards steps between us, drawing Dunn's attention. "I'm going to give you something for the pain," he says, holding up a syringe. I wonder how many we have left.

"There isn't any pain," Dunn says, confused.

I slip away from them, eager to get camp set and the next set of instructions over with. I move toward the pile of eagerly dumped supplies, calling out to Simons, "Do—"

"Hush!" he snaps in a low growl of a whisper, throwing his arm back at me. The harshness of his growl joined with the abrupt gesture brings my attention into focus. I've been lost in my own thoughts—about Dunn, about the group's separation and the journey to the river. I haven't been focused on our surroundings.

I glance over to see Frances standing with her hand over her mouth. Richards turns away from Dunn, straightening his glasses before offering her a comforting hand. Cain appears frozen mid-motion. I follow their gaze through the pale alder trunks and around the thicker fir trees until I find it in the gully carved along the slope by runoff. It's making slow progress, tripping through thick mud and getting hung up in clumps of dogwood.

I watch the sorry creature stumble onto broken hands. Its emaciated legs scramble as it tries to right itself without working joints, all the while making an effort-driven grunting sound. It only takes a minute of watching to know the creature won't be able to right itself. It's fallen one too many times through the difficult terrain, and its body is too broken to manage anything more than a crawl.

The wind is in our favor, and it hasn't noticed us yet. There isn't much of a threat of it coming after us, but I don't want to have to deal with its shrieking cries as it pines for our flesh. I need time to think—or to get us out of here and set up camp somewhere else… if Dunn can make it, that is.

The click and whir of a charging pulsar gun draws my attention away from the sad spectacle. Cain is leaning, braced against the smooth bark of an alder for additional support while he makes his shot. I reach out to halt him, placing a hand on his tensed bicep to pull his focus. He lowers the weapon fractionally, looking over at me with an inquisitive expression.

"We can't kill it," I whisper.

"What? So now we're not killing the near-dead either? Why not?" he asks, shrugging my hand off his arm to resume his aim.

"You said there aren't ever any near-dead up here, right?" I hiss, keeping my voice low and quiet so as not to alert the thing to our presence.

"I did. But you can't argue with me that this one isn't here." He dismisses me, trying once again to take aim.

I pull hard against his arm again, annoyed. "Listen to me!" I snap, managing to turn his body toward me.

Finally, he lowers his weapon.

"Of course I'm not delusional! I know Dunn's almost gone, and I know that thing out there is real! You think you're the expert on all these things because you navigated your way up here, but you need to start listening to the rest of us because I know something you don't," I growl at him.

The creature lets out a frustrated wail before resuming its slow crawl. I let my eyes visit the thing as its hand tangles in the dogwood, then situate my gaze on Cain's furrowed brow. "If that thing is out here, it means we're already being hunted. There's a good chance the DDC doesn't know where we are right now. There could be near-dead planted everywhere within a hundred-mile radius of the Northern Laboratories."

"What's your point?" Cain asks impatiently.

"The only way they're going to find us is if we leave them a trail of dead to follow. That's how they found my family," I say, knowing this statement will require further explanation.

Cain blows out a frustrated breath, allowing his body to fall back against the alder. "You make a good point," he admits.

"Besides," I say, stepping back from him now that I'm confident he won't fire, "it's not much of a threat like that. It's only got another day or so before it's dead and the natural predators take it to pieces."

I catch Frances wince at my statement. Her reaction makes me regret my heartless words. Listening to Dunn's technical analysis of his own demise these last several days has made me realize I don't sound much different. I'm just as heartless and cold as he is.

I swore I wouldn't let the Institute change me, but it's obvious now I couldn't stop it. Little by little, I succumbed to the persistent mindset that made the Northern Laboratories thrive. Like a disease, it's made its way inside of me and spread without my notice. I move with no real purpose, intent on distracting myself from the terrible knowledge of what I've become.

I reach for our map, but before I can pull it out, Cain walks past me, a thick-bladed knife in his hand and a grim expression on his face. He sidesteps down the slick slope toward the crawling alarm. I drop my pack in frustration and raise my voice to call after him. "Cain! I said you can't—"

I wince, realizing my mistake immediately as my voice alerts the creature to our presence. It lets out a thick, mucous-y gurgle as a precursor to the high-pitched wail, but before the sound can rise, Cain grabs it by a scruff of hair and plunges the knife deep into its throat. Instead of dragging the blade across the neck to sever the larynx and jugular, he turns the knife over so he's dragging the dull edge, tearing flesh and tendon as he opens the thing up in a gruesome mess. I watch in horror as he drops the dead thing to the ground, then kicks it over so its chest is exposed. Frances buries her head in Richards' chest, stifling a sob.

"What the…" Jorcy whispers, as he stares at Cain's work with wide eyes.

"What are you doing?" I hiss, wondering if Cain's lost his mind.

Cain plunges the knife into the dead creature's gut, ripping once more with the dull end of his blade to spill the intestines. Without looking up, he says, "It was only a matter of time before it caught our scent and started wailing. We can't leave it to alert every predator. Besides, it's like you said, they can't prove a pack of wild dogs didn't do this. With this much stench in the air, they'll help themselves and cover our tracks just as soon as we've cleared out of here."

I watch him work, stunned, and consider his explanation. He has a point, but still, the work is despicable. When he finishes, his hands are stained red with blood. He scrambles back up to the group, approaching Richards.

"Hey doc, can I borrow the ultraviolet wand? I'm going to run to the creek and wash," he says, just as light-hearted as ever.

Richards digs the wand out of his pack with trembling hands and passes it over to Cain, who takes it with an easy smile. Cain turns to wash himself, but before he can take a step, Simons halts him.

"Cain. There's something we need to discuss," he says in a stern voice.

Cain rolls his eyes. "Is this another *We don't kill the living* talk?"

"No. This is a *We make decisions as a team* talk," Simons says, completely unmoved by Cain's humor.

"Well. As a *team*, I think we can all agree that what I did was a smart move." Cain dismisses him, turning again.

"Knock it off," Simons bellows.

Cain stops and turns slowly. His lips are pursed under a growing layer of facial hair speckled red with blood. "You know I'm right," he says without an ounce of humor.

"It doesn't matter if you're right. You're not out here on a solo mission. You're the only person here who can't seem to figure that out," Simons says, glaring at Cain. In the dim light of the low sun, Simons looks even more imposing than usual.

Cain doesn't speak.

"You got that?" Simons asks.

Cain's whole body is tense and rigid. My heart beats in my temples as I wait for Cain's response. He shakes his head, and his shoulders drop. "I got it."

Simons watches him. "Good. Go clean up."

Cain turns, walking quickly past Richards and Dunn's cot, toward the creek running down the backside of the tree-covered slope. I watch him go, conflicted about what just happened. I turn away from Cain, back toward the group, and catch Dunn's wide-eyed stare. I follow his gaze to the blood-strewn thing.

"Dunn?" I ask, not certain which version is behind the terrified stare.

"Is that what you're going to do to me?" he whispers.

CHAPTER
FIFTEEN

THE SIGNAL for the cure package is strong now that we're so close —maybe a couple days' travel unencumbered.

Unencumbered. I think about the word as I gather everything we'll need while the team finishes the trip without us. Not much, really—a pulsar gun, some lashing poles, the ultraviolet wand and a canteen. We should be able to catch up quickly once it's done.

"We'll come back once we have the cure… if it's not quick with Dunn," Jorey assures me as I entrust the red strip of fabric to him.

I stoop down to where Frances sits, wearing Richards' glove and going over the signal code on the diode screen. Her fingers trace the access port on the silken screen, pausing where the cursor blinks, waiting for the code. "Let me show you—"

"I think I've got it," Frances says, putting up her hand to stop me from explaining. She taps at the bottom of the screen and inputs the commands for entering new code before putting in the signal information I extracted from the fabric strip. She clearly doesn't need my guidance.

"You learned all of this for distribution analytics?" I ask, impressed.

"Not exactly…" Frances stalls, her cheeks flushing.

The signal pops up on the grid, a dotted line connecting us to it estimating the distance via satellite relay to be approximately 26.2 kilometers. It's a deceptively short distance. I read in one of the extinct species catalogues that this measurement would have been referred to by the idiom *as the crow flies*. If only we had a crow to fly that distance and retrieve it for us.

We look at it together in a bubble of contemplative silence as the others tend to their business around us. It's the last time I'll have to look at the cure this way.

"We used an interface sort of like this for inventory—not by code, of course, but the functionality was similar," she explains, marking our paper map almost directly over my last contribution.

"How did you figure out the coding?" I ask, not allowing her to hide behind humility.

Her lips tighten to a pale line as she busies herself with folding the map and handing me the screen. She clears her throat, still not meeting my gaze. "Hannah—my eldest—was interested in coding. Everything she did was novice, but she was so proud of it. She used to show me everything she did—explain it in excruciating detail."

Frances laughs, a cruel, mournful sound. "I only had to watch you do it a few times for it to make sense," she finishes.

"There's nothing novice about what you just did," I say, blurting out the first thing that comes to mind and feeling stupid for not saying something better—something meaningful.

Frances smiles at me anyway as Cain marches up, pack loaded and strapped across his shoulders. He places a hand on Frances' shoulder and gives it a friendly shake.

"Do you think we could make it tonight if we push through?" he asks.

Frances shakes her head. "No. And besides, we need to rest. I just don't want to do it here." She glances over at the stinking mass of bloody flesh.

For the last hour, the forest has been alive with the movement of wild dogs, drawn in by the smell of a kill. Cain was right about them not being deterred by infected flesh—one benefit of the cross-species inhibitor of the second outbreak. As the trees cast longer shadows across our little area, the combination of Dunn's fitful sleep and the increased activity creates an unsettling atmosphere, but the decision's been made.

"I don't blame you. Get as far away from here as you need. It won't be long now, and we'll be back together," I reassure her.

She blinks back tears, glancing over to where Richards kneels over Dunn's unconscious body. "I'm sorry we're abandoning you. I can't watch another night."

"Simons and I agree this is the best we can do for him. And for us," I promise.

She nods. Jorey walks over to her and puts a comforting arm around her.

"Are you sure you don't want another pulsar gun?" Cain asks, cinching his pack tight against his frame.

I shake my head. "It only takes one to get the job done. Besides, you guys need protection too."

Simons and Richards join us for the send-off. Simons puts one heavy hand on my shoulder and another on Jorey's so his arms spread across the gap separating us and his body fills the space. "It's just a quick aside. Dunn doesn't want a spectacle. We're going to make it quick and easy the second he goes, and then we'll be right behind you," he says.

"He isn't in pain anymore," Richards assures Frances, who wipes a tear away with a pale, freckled hand.

"The sooner we get the cure, the sooner we can head underground again," I agree, convincing myself this split is a good idea. In the distance, a dog howls, setting off a chorus that fills the dusky sky with a wild music.

"Alright then. We're off," Cain says cheerfully, knowing no one else is willing to make the break.

Jorey and Frances move to join him. Cain turns so he's walking backward and offers me a salute. When he turns back around, Jorey twists his body to offer one last wave. I lift my hand in return to both of them and watch until they disappear into the shadows, causing a scattering of yips and rustling in the underbrush.

I let out a heavy sigh.

"It can't be much longer. He's shutting down, don't you think, Mason?" Richards asks.

In the Northern Laboratories, I grew accustomed to measuring the progress of acceleration-assisted development from cryogenic freeze. It's been a long time since the days of meticulously tracking the natural progression of various strains of disease. It was a skill specific to the Institute setting with its donation program and constant influx of patients. *We don't neurologically develop patients at the Northern Laboratories…*

"I honestly don't know," I say, prompting a curious raised eyebrow from Simons.

"It's a little different each time," I explain, "and Dunn's progression has been curiously rapid for a ZCD strain."

"You don't think it's something new, do you?" he asks, settling down against a thick fir tree, his body facing the cot.

"It's possible, given everything happening in the Northern Laboratories at the end, but I don't think it's likely. They needed data on their weapon. It would have shown up in active experiments."

"That's a relief," he says. There's a distant rustle as some creature moves through the brush, driven off by the encroaching dogs. Dunn stirs restlessly, whimpering as if in response.

"What do we do now?" Richards asks, eyes flicking nervously between us and Dunn.

"We wait," Simons says.

Richards concedes, finding a tree near Simons. I settle in against a rotting log, aware of the beetles and grubs crawling at my back but not paying them any mind. The late sun makes the night more alive than it ought to be. My eyes settle on Dunn.

"I know I should be eager to get it over with now, but honestly, I'm dreading it," I admit, setting the pulsar gun on the ground at my side.

"Of course. How could you not be dreading it?" Richards asks, trying to find a comfortable position.

I laugh at his question. It comes out cold and distant. "I'm supposed to be above all that. I'm a scientist, after all. I've been trained to be completely unemotional—a distant and calculating weapon. Eliminating Dunn should be as simple as executing an experiment on a culture of cells. I should have been able to pull the trigger the second he was infected," I explain.

Richards looks at me as though I've said something unfathomable. "No one can be that distant. It doesn't matter how they've trained you or what they expect!"

"Is that right? Then how do you explain what they were doing in the Laboratories? How do you explain what they made you do?" I stop myself, glancing in Simons' direction. I'm not certain he knows Richards' secret.

Richards glances over at Simons, then back at me. "There are a lot of things I don't know, but I do know you can force a person to do terrible things, but you can't force them to not care while they're doing them."

"He's right. If they could have trained your heart out of you, they would have done it by now. The Institute and the Laboratories are too harsh of places to not take everything out of you they can. Your core is intact because that's who you are. The folks who survive this world—they're the ones who didn't die on the inside when the light was taken from them," Simons says, looking up into the cloud-streaked sky.

We fall into silence, content with our mutual presence. There isn't anything any of us want to say at the onset of our waiting. Dunn's transformation weighs too heavily on our minds for casual conversation, and we're too weary to talk about the things that really matter.

In the absence of our conversation, the howling starts up again. I catch rapid movement not far off from the corpse now. I think about Simons' and Richards' assessments of me as the night settles and wonder: *If they're right about my core still being intact, then why do I feel so broken?*

I search the sky for the tail end of the waxing crescent moon, but it's lost to me in the multitude of trees blotting out the horizon.

MY EYES FLY open as a fierce snarl rips through the relative quiet. In the twilight of the deep night, the silhouettes of hungry dogs converge on one another as they jostle for a better position at the carcass—a gift from the strangers traveling in their land. I reach up and brush a large, black beetle from its journey across my leg. It falls to the cold ground with a moss-dampened thud before moving on, unaffected by the relocation.

Another dog growls, inciting a scuffled dispute about their place at the dinner table. I lean forward, trying to make out their activity through the mist that's settled in the area.

Through the trees, the sky glows an eerie orangish-pink, casting long shadows that make the forest darker than a summer night should be. The hoot of an owl adds to the wild, disquieting atmosphere as the dogs settle back to their feast. With the dogs already drawn in by the other body, it's nearly guaranteed Dunn's remains will be cleared out before anyone can find him. Though unwelcome, I can't help but think it as we wait out his final hours.

I return my gaze to the sky, trying to determine how many hours have passed since I dozed. It's impossible to tell. The sun could be nearly set or an hour into its rise. I'd likely have better luck making my determination based on the state of the remains. How fast can a pack of wild dogs tear through a body?

Wolves eat the intestines first, just like the near-dead...

There are no dual-paned, vacuum-sealed windows out here.

It's easy to forget there are other causes of death besides Zoribiatus...

A dark shadow impedes my view. My eyes travel across it, and I wonder what trick of the light makes it look like it's moving toward me, reaching out as though it could nearly touch...

I'm suddenly all too alert. The shadow doesn't *appear* to be moving —it *is* moving. I glance down at the cot only to find it sitting flat against the ground, shreds of bindings strewn across the forest floor. My hand drops down to my side to grab the pulsar gun, trying to figure out how Dunn could have possibly managed to escape his bindings. The shadow takes another slow step toward me as I grope on the ground for the pulsar gun. I hesitate before looking down. It isn't there.

The shadow stops right in front of me, about three meters away, a hunched, human-like form, emaciated from illness and bent at odd angles. In the dim light, I can see Dunn's grey, blank eyes as he stares at me, there but not there. He's completely silent, setting off a multitude of alarm bells in my racing mind. Before I can act—before I can call out for Simons or Richards to grab lashing poles, or dive over the rotting log to put distance between us—the Dunn-patient opens its mouth as if to speak.

And then it does. "Kara Mason," it says in Orman's eerie, all-too-familiar voice.

"How are you doing this?"

The Dunn-thing tilts its head, ponderous, a sneering grin breaking out across its face. "Haven't you figured it out by now?" it asks.

"The simulations," I answer, suddenly understanding the purpose hidden just beneath the thin veneer of training. "The Northern Laboratories simulations create a shared experience through neural pathways. That's not possible anywhere else."

"You're a clever girl, aren't you?" the Dunn-thing speaks again.

"How did you survive the explosion?" I demand, trying to keep the creature talking long enough to figure out what to do.

The Dunn-thing laughs. It's a broken, strangely breathy sound, like the lungs are being forcefully expelled by an external machine and the sound is whining across the larynx. "Why should I give away all my secrets?"

A vicious snarl starts another scuffle at the corpse, this time erupting into an all-out brawl. The Dunn-thing jerks its head to the side to glance at the disturbance. I seize the distraction to stand, hoping to launch myself over the rotted log, but the Dunn-thing seems to have expected this. It lifts the pulsar gun, squaring its aim right between my eyes.

"Do you want to find out if I'm as good of a shot remotely as I am in person?" Dunn's body asks. If there was even the smallest doubt in my mind it was Orman controlling Dunn, this statement dismantles it.

There's movement between where the thing that used to be Dunn stands and where the dogs brawl over diminishing flesh. I keep my attention focused on the immediate threat as Richards and Simons flank Dunn, approaching slowly with lashing poles drawn.

I lift my hands out in front of me, meaning to keep Orman's attention. "How did you find him? How did you know he was infected?" I ask.

It laughs the strange laugh again, causing the gun to tremor in the diseased hand. "I watched it happen! Or should I say... I *made* it happen. I stopped the patient that attacked him long enough to allow an escape. I only had to wait for the disease to take hold."

The possibility of Orman having orchestrated this whole situation is too terrifying to consider.

No. He only wants me to believe he never lost any control.

Still, the possibility gnaws at the surface of my mind, tearing away rational thought. Orman uses Dunn's body to smile wide enough to show where the grey gums have receded, curling away from the now too-long teeth.

They eat the intestines first.

Simons is almost within reach.

"You should stop where you are now, Simons. *Doctor* Richards. I can fire much faster than you can wrap those lashing poles around this body," Orman sneers through his control of the Dunn-thing.

Simons curses under his breath but withdraws. "What exactly do you want?" he asks. His powerful voice causes the dogs to go momentarily silent.

"I want the cure," he says, looking back over at me. "And I want to know what's so special about *you*, Kara Mason. What did Shelby want you for?"

"The cure is gone," I say.

"Oh, now don't say such things!" he tsks. "What would you be doing out here if it weren't for the cure?"

"Why would I tell you what Shelby wanted me to do when there's nothing you can do to stop it?" I ask, scrambling for something to throw him off balance.

His eyes widen. I suppress the smirk begging to contort my lips, launching again into the story as Richards makes another quiet move toward the Dunn-thing's frame. "That's right. You thought you knew everything going on in the Northern Laboratories, but you had no idea. The cure was a diversion. Shelby knew you'd come after it."

"THE NORTHERN LABORATORIES IS MY KINGDOM! Nothing happens without my knowing!" he roars, slurring words through Dunn's uncoordinated mouth.

"So, you meant it to burn to the ground? How many of your lackies did you sacrifice to make that happen?" I spit, buying the last fraction of a second Richards needs to strike.

"Don't play games with me, Mason! You either, Richards. I've got the upper hand here."

"Are you so sure about that? Do you really think Dunn has the dexterity you need for a fast aim?" Richards demands, standing his ground.

The Dunn thing roars and turns, pulling the trigger again and again into the mist just over Richard's head. There's a series of yelps as the dogs scatter. Three bodies remain. Orman returns the gun to my temple. "Will that be all, doctor?"

Richards falls back, leaving me to face Dunn-Orman alone.

I close my eyes, frustrated. When I open them again, there's a blur of tears brought up by the thundering of my heart. Orman won't miss twice. "When he shoots, take him down and finish what we started," I tell Simons and Richards.

"No. They won't sacrifice you," he says.

"Do it," I tell them, ignoring the weapon in front of me and launching myself onto the creature.

I close the gap before the gun goes off. I collide with the creature with all my weight, knocking it off balance. We fall to the ground, and I wrestle for the pulsar gun. The Dunn-thing lets out its first beastly gurgle, making me wonder if Orman is losing his connection. It doesn't matter. The danger is the same either way.

I wrap my hand around the cool metal of the barrel as the Dunn-thing spits out an almost human moan. I snap my head up to watch its mouth, all too aware of the deadly proximity. I look into its grey, bloody eyes. They look forlorn and scared.

"Kara…" Dunn says in a childlike voice. He lets go of the weapon, a single bloody tear falling from the corner of his eye. "Make it quick."

I pull free of the struggling mass and aim. The shot hits directly though his temple, just in front of his ear, burning a thick hole that chars his whole head. His body falls back, lifeless. I sink to my knees, trembling, still holding the pulsar gun in its powered position, before turning my head to vomit into the dewy underbrush. I stay hunched forward, panting and afraid to turn my head back toward Dunn's lifeless body.

Simons approaches, his shadow blocking me from our fallen member. In the distance, a wild dog lets out a low, mournful howl. The sound pierces through the twilight, filling the night air as it rises and falls. Before the sound fades to nothingness, the others join in.

SEVENTEEN

"HE CLEARLY HAS knowledge of everyone's activity in the Northern Laboratories," I agree with Richards as we break out from the thickly wooded area into the grassy hills that lead us toward the river. Though the day has brought the sun high into the sky, it's done little to warm the chill of dread and anxiety that fills me.

"The volunteers weren't as invisible as we thought, I suppose," Richards concludes, reflecting on our remote encounter.

"Not all the volunteers. He knew who he was watching for. He knew about your services to the government, and I suspect I was on his radar for running errands for Shelby. I doubt he could've listed the whole team," Simons says.

"Yeah, well, we're lucky he only saw the three of us," I say, crouching down to run my fingers along the moss-covered stone marked with Cain's boot print. I smear it away as I pass, just in case.

"He can still make assumptions," Simons says, watching me pass around a muddy patch marked with moose tracks and bird droppings. If the others passed by here, nature has already covered their tracks for us.

"But that's all they'll be—assumptions. He can assume he knows where we were based on landscape, but there's an entire region with similar terrain, meaning he'd have to be lucky to flush us out straight away. He can assume our whole party is out here, but he can only be sure of the three of us. Right now, that's our only advantage," I say, holding onto the thin slice of hope the argument offers. I've already dismissed the notion he's managed to discern our location from his remote connection to Dunn. The simulations are powerful, but they can't do that. Besides, if he'd been able to pinpoint Dunn's location, we'd already be dead.

Simons nods. There isn't a point to debating the issue. We're doing everything we can to stall the inevitable encounter. Once we regroup with the others and the cure, we can do what Cain suggested and disappear. We'll make our way back to the tunnels and follow the ancient scripts to the dissenter shelter, avoiding the risk of communication until we know we're safe from Orman's imminent revenge.

"Do you suppose anyone else knows he can do that to a patient?" Richards asks, clearly unable to shake the strangeness of the previous night.

I consider his question, trying to account for everything I know about Orman and the hive technology. Too many pieces are missing from the picture to know anything for certain. The secrets begin at the Institute and run all the way up to the lead scientists at the Northern Laboratories and the government beyond. The DDC probably even keeps secrets from themselves.

"I suppose so. Maybe not everyone in power though. There's a reason the simulation technology is restricted outside of the Northern Laboratories. If that sort of power were available everywhere, it would be a small leap to suggest it could be used to control the signal through the semantic network of a neurologically inhibited patient," I speculate.

Richards nods thoughtfully. "The simulations work on everyone, but the disease creates the access for remote control."

"It's like erasing the base programming of human function to create a blank slate," I agree, pleased he understands the implications. "And I suspect not even the government knows the true power behind the hive."

"Endgal save us," Richards breathes. I've never heard him say it before. Behind him, Simons shakes his head, using his lashing pole to take an over-large step across a patch of muddy weeds, clearly disinterested in the technical descriptions. "I don't suppose it makes a difference understanding it unless you know how to stop the way Orman uses it," he says.

"I'm not sure how to do that," I admit.

"Yet," Richards corrects me.

I consider what he might believe, even after his experience in the Northern Laboratories. "Richards, you have too much faith in me. Scientists aren't what you think we are."

"I don't think you should have as little faith in yourself as you do," Simons suggests.

"The way I look at it, being a scientist makes me the only realist of the group," I say as the river comes into view.

"Oh! I think I see them," Richards calls.

I look in the direction he indicates, following his gaze across the shallow ravine where the river tears through, dark and fast with summer melt, toward the distant sea. If our plotting is correct, they should be further upstream still—at least, that's where the cure should be. I squint against the glare of midday sunlight to see the distant moving shapes of our compatriots.

"What on earth are they doing?" I ask, watching Frances secure a rope to the splintered stump of a tree whose corpse lies partially across the rushing body of water. Cain is already knee deep, wading through the current, holding the other end of the line in one hand and a lashing pole in the other, moving frantically.

Where's Jorey?

"Maybe the cure broke loose and came downstream?" Richards suggests, waving his hands in the air to catch their attention. Neither turns away from their task.

I stand, dazed for another second as Cain plunges himself headfirst into the swift depths of freezing water, then break into a sprint. Cain isn't going in after the cure. Shelby's pack is fastened securely across Frances' shoulders. He's going in after Jorey.

Blood surges as my heart thunders into action and my feet fly across the uneven terrain, paying no mind to caution. I force myself forward with more effort than any redline exercise could beg from me, my lungs burning with the efficient exchange of oxygen.

I burst onto the riverbank, unable to stop myself until I'm ankle deep in the icy water. The sound of my own gasps drowns out the splash of water as I run downstream toward Frances. I push on through the cold, waiting for something to happen, filled with useless knowledge.

The data runs across the screen in my mind. *Freezing temperatures. Rapid water flow. Time submerged at least three minutes and counting...* Cain's chances of fishing Jorey out of the water in time are slim. The lashing pole was a stroke of genius.

Frances looks up, startled as I converge on the rope. Her mouth is fixed in a pale line of suppressed panic as she wordlessly makes room for my hands. I grip the slick, braided surface, counting the seconds in my mind, unable to figure out how much time has passed. *It's been too long! They're lost. Both of them are gone now, dead in the water.*

My knuckles turn white as I stand there, gripping the line and reading the data.

Cain breaks the surface with a loud gasp as Simons and Richards make it to the bank. Cain's hands are high above his head, held in place by rigid, frozen arms. Using the little dexterity he has left, Cain holds the lashing pole, forcing Jorey's limp body to float on the surface of the rushing water. We pull them in, our hands turning over themselves as the coil at our feet grows.

Simons steps past us, plunging his body deep into the frozen rush and grabbing the lashing pole from Cain. Together they manage to get Jorey onto the shore.

"What happened?" Simons demands, falling to his knees in front of Jorey's lifeless form, searching for a pulse.

"We almost lost the cure again. Jorey dove for it and got caught up in the current. We thought we had him, but instead of reaching for us, he flung the pack into Cain's hand and got swept downstream. We were able to track him along the edge until he went under," Frances sobs as Simons turns Jorey's blue face toward the sky.

Wordlessly, Cain begins to apply force to Jorey's chest with a fast and steady rhythm. Jorey's body moves with each compression, stiff and heavy against the repeated assault. When Cain pauses so Simons can turn Jorey's head up, his eyes roll open, cold and dead, making me cover my mouth to stifle a sob as Cain resumes the violent compressions.

"Come on, Jorey!" Simons yells as Cain works, the terror clear in his plea.

Cain nods for Simons to give another breath, panting heavily with the effort of his work. The pause is brief but draws attention to Jorey's stillness. I step toward him, but Richards stops me. "Give them space," he implores in a pained whisper.

I swallow the scream welling up inside of my chest and hold my breath as if I could wait to breathe until Jorey does.

No one else was supposed to die!

"Any time now, brother." Cain pants at his next break, a look of serious concern crossing his face as Simons administers the breath that doesn't seem to reach deep enough.

There's a wet sputtering gasp, followed by choking and retching as Cain scrambles away from Jorey's body. Simons grabs him by the shoulders and turns him on his side as he heaves wave after wave, taking uneven, wet breaths between each round.

"Easy there, you're okay," Simons says before looking up with wide, relieved eyes.

"Alright there! Welcome back, brother," Cain pants, squeezing both of Jorey's shoulders in an exhausted, relieved embrace.

I let the air fill my lungs. The sounds of his broken gasps propel me forward. Falling to my knees next to Simons, I put a hand on Jorey's icy cheek, searching for the words swimming through my dazed mind to tell him how happy I am he's alright.

Suddenly I realize he's gone very still. I lift his face up toward me, calling out, "Jorey!"

His eyes are blank. I ease him back to the ground and look at Cain, who's supporting Jorey on his side. A grim expression paints his face.

"What's wrong with him?" I whisper.

"He came back for a second, but he's gone now." Cain sounds perplexed.

"What do you mean he's gone? Is he dead?" I shriek.

Cain's hands are running over Jorey's neck, searching for a pulse. I brush the moisture from Jorey's face, fighting with everything I've got to hold the sobs back.

"He's alive. He's in there," Cain says.

"Jorey?" I ask, as though he just needs to hear my voice and decide now is not the time to rest.

"He's in shock. We've got to get him warm. Now," I insist, helping Simons and Cain hoist him up to move him away from the riverbed.

Simons and Cain take over, moving quickly toward the tree line. I follow closely behind, telling myself Jorey will be fine once we get his body temperature back up and mentally running through everything I'll need to repeat the chemical reaction for fireless heat. The last thing we need now is an indication of our location. Even a flameless source of heat is a risk with Orman on our tracks.

"Is he going to be okay?" Frances asks Richards, pulling me out of my own thoughts. Richards has his hand around her shoulders as she clutches the pack against her chest. He's looking ahead at Simons and Cain.

"I don't know," he says, catching my glance. Blinking, he casts his eyes down and clears his throat. "I'm sorry, Mason."

I ignore him and hurry ahead to get to work.

EIGHTEEN

MY FINGER TREMBLES as I drag it through the white powder littering the bottom of the pack. The materials are gone, transformed into useless product of a reaction I can't perform to save Jorey's life. The wind tears across the valley, chilling the summer air, catching the dust from my hand and carrying it into the grey horizon. *How could I be so careless?* There should have been more than enough to dry Jorey's clothes and bring his core temperature up. I must have forgotten to seal the packet...

The simple oversight fills me with doubt. *How could I possibly get the cure to safety when I can't even remember to secure a few supplies?* It's a wonder I haven't gotten us all killed already.

"How's it going over there, Mason?" Richards calls out, forcing my eyes away from the wasted reactant.

"It's gone," I say, fighting the tightening in the back of my throat as panic wraps around my chest. "How's he doing?"

"His pulse is weak. I'm worried about his respiration," Richards says. His voice is soft and hesitant. He's holding back the worst of his diagnosis.

I curse under my breath, casting my eyes across the area, looking for fuel. "We have to start a fire," I insist.

"Everything around here is wet. Even if we could get a fire going, the smoke could give away our location," Simons protests.

"I don't care if Orman is on his way right now. We're going to lose him!" I snap back, holding onto the cracked fragments of my own failing calm. I stand, intent on finding anything dry enough to burn.

"Mason, we can't start a fire." Simons reaches out, seizing my arm before I can make my way past him. I whirl in his grasp, intent to spill the entirety of my frustration onto him but stop when I see his pained expression. "What if someone is scanning for contacts and manages a location off Cain's message? We're already taking a big risk."

"It's Jorey!" I beg.

Simons lets out a long breath through his nose, studying me. He rubs the back of his neck as he absorbs my rebuke. His forehead is scrunched and furrowed as he contemplates the impossible situation. He has to know we can't let Jorey die. "I know, Mason."

"We have to try everything," I whisper before he can suggest anything less.

"We do," he agrees. His face softens.

He releases my arm. Before I can resume my mission, Cain emerges from the brush with a glove in one hand and the diode screen in the other. My heart jumps into the back of my throat at his return, eager for news. "Well?" The question comes out as more of a high-pitched squeak.

"Five hours," he says with obvious cheer.

"Five hours?" I repeat.

"Yeah, it's not like we're close quarters up here," he says, shrugging off my incredulity as he tosses the supplies back into the pack.

"Jorey won't make it five hours. He's unconscious, his heart rate is slow, and his respiration is erratic," I object, listing his symptoms as if it could change the situation. Part of me knows that in reaching out to his contact, Cain has done better than anything we could have done, but the fear it won't be enough to save Jorey prevents me from accepting it.

"Oh, sure he will. Once you get him dry, he'll—"

"I can't. The alloy dust is spent. I must have spilled it," I tell him.

A flash of genuine concern alters his expression as he takes in my revelation, but it passes just as quickly as it appeared, replaced by his typical smirk. He slaps his hands together, rubbing them as if he were relishing Jorey's predicament. "Well then, let's get little brother warmed up the old-fashioned way!" he says, pulling at the collar of his volunteer suit so the zipper drops down.

"What on earth are you doing, Cain?" Frances asks, turning away from him as he undresses.

Cain ignores her protest, acting as though he weren't surrounded by dumbfounded stares as he steps out of the suit to stand at the edge of the open plain in nothing but his underwear. He rubs his hands across his bare arms. "Whew! It's a chilly day, isn't it? Where's the infrared sheet?"

"It's here," I say, gesturing to the pack with our cold weather supplies.

Cain saunters over, his movements quick and jerky as the air robs him of heat. He bends down to pick up the sheet, flipping it out so that it shimmers as it dances in the wind. "Alright. Hold it please." He hands it back to me, whistling to himself. I watch him, stunned into silence by the simplicity of his solution. He falls to his knees, unzipping Jorey's suit.

Simons scowls. "I don't see how undressing him is going to help. Wet or not, that suit is warmer than—"

Realization dawns for him at the same time it does for me—so simple we've forgotten in our panic.

Cain tugs until Jorey's suit is pooled at his feet, then reaches up for the infrared sheet again. He pulls it over Jorey, situating himself so his bare chest is pressed up against Jorey's back. He looks up at us, saying, "You know, this would work a lot better if someone else got in here with me."

"You want someone else to take off their clothes and get in there with you?" Frances scoffs.

"That's the idea. Come on in, Mason, it'll be nice and toasty after a while." He winks.

The wink, along with his stupid smile, makes something snap inside my head. Right or wrong, he can't help but make a joke of it. "What's wrong with you, Cain? Be serious for one second, if you can."

My fists clench at my sides as the heat creeps into my cheeks until my whole body trembles with resentment.

"I'm being serious. All of you are just standing there letting him freeze to death, and I'm the only one ready to do something. Forgive me if I want to have a little fun about it, but I'm trying to help him. I don't see how standing around being serious is going to do a damn thing," he shoots right back at me, his eyes flashing bright intensity in my direction.

I reel in the wake of his response, unable to act.

"Of course. How could we forget?" Richards marvels.

"Are you volunteering, doctor?" Cain asks, adjusting the sheet before returning his hand to Jorey's side.

"I wasn't, but—"

"I'll do it," I say. Cain's right, and admitting it, even if it means shedding some of my own modesty, is worth the chance to save Jorey.

"That's my girl, Mason! I knew you'd see reason," Cain says with a stupid oversized grin as he nuzzles against Jorey's chapped cheek.

Simons raises an eyebrow at me before turning away as I pull the zipper of my kill suit down. The cool air bites at my bare skin as I peel it off my body, bringing prickles of doubt to the surface. This is what he suggested Jorey and I do last time we fought off hypothermia. I thought he was joking. He's always joking, but not now—or at least not frivolously. Not when Jorey's dying. I resist the urge to shiver as I make my way under the thermal blanket.

"Have you done this before?" I ask, my hands brushing against Jorey's icy torso.

"Never in a life-saving scenario like this, but who hasn't huddled for warmth?" Cain says.

Once again, I wonder about the life he's lived. In all the weeks we've spent together since leaving the Laboratories, I haven't even gleaned the surface of Cain's past. There's always something more pressing in need of my attention. Or rather, it occurs to me as bare flesh converges in a medley of temperature extremes, Cain has a way of evading our inquiries. There's always a story, a lecture, or a lesson to be had while everyone else shares their lives.

"Remember, you want skin on skin contact," Cain adds as I settle, trying hard not to dwell on the glimpse of Jorey's blue-grey skin I caught before the blanket converged over us.

"I've got his front covered; you keep to his back. No funny business," I warn, pressing my back against Jorey's torso. The sheet crinkles with the movement.

"What makes you think I would joke at a time like this?"

He has to be teasing.

"You know this is how people treated hypothermia before fireless reactions and the rest of your fail-proof methods, which, might I add, happened to fail at this crucial moment?" Cain says.

"Alright, I got it, we're all idiots to have not thought of something so simple," I say, trying to forget I'm nearly naked in the middle of the wilderness.

Silence falls over us as we settle in. I press myself against Jorey, terrified of how cold he is and how I have to focus to detect his shallow breaths. I lay motionless, trying to feel him breathe. Cain reaches across Jorey's torso, his icy hand brushing against my stomach, making me screech.

"What are you doing? Your hands are freezing!"

"I was in the river too, you know. Did it occur to you that I could use some warming up?" Cain asks.

"You didn't hear Jorey or me complain when we went in. Instead, we went on a cross-tundra stroll," I say.

"Yeah, well, you're tougher than me," Cain mewls, winding frigid fingers against my flesh.

"Cut it out!" I snap, pushing his hand away.

"Unbelievable," Cain grumbles, his hand retreating over the boundary of Jorey's side.

I roll my eyes but allow myself to smile, knowing Cain can't see it.

Frances pulls her jacket up over her ears against the chill of tundra wind before settling next to Richards, who provides a small but significant windbreak. Simons shrugs off his massive canvas jacket, tossing it onto the ground so he can sit on it.

"Are there any more thermal blankets?" Frances asks.

Simons shakes his head. "I kept that one from before. Nothing like it in the labs."

"If we had more, they'd best be used on Jorey. The faster he gets warm, the better," Richards adds.

Frances sighs, resigned to wait in the cold, but before she can tuck her arms between her legs, Richards reaches out and wraps his own arm around her, tucking her against his side in a gesture of comfort and warmth. She leans her head against his shoulder, looking curiously comfortable.

She still has her clothes on, I think, not sure if I envy her state or her comfort. Things are already warming up under the blanket. Jorey's shoulder slumps against mine, drawing my focus to our nearness and the way heat seems to swell around rather than emanate from him. I pull his icy hand into mine, bending the fingers back and forth to stimulate blood flow as we wait for rescue.

CHAPTER
NINETEEN

HOURS PASS, marked by intermittent and insignificant conversation. Simons slips his jacket back on as the evening wind rips by, bending branches and flinging grasses with unforgiving gusts. My body aches from remaining in one position for so long atop the cold, hard ground, pressed flush against Jorey's bare skin.

It's quiet now. Whatever whispered conversation Richards and Frances were having has ended, and they appear to be dozing, leaning into one another for support. Simons rests with his head propped against the largest pack, his jacket collar pulled up against the wind. It's the first time we've rested since our encounter with Orman, and by the look of Frances, I suspect the same might be true for them.

I turn, pressing my hip into Jorey's stomach while resting the back of my neck on his bicep, wishing more than anything I could tell him everything that's happened since we parted ways. He would assuage my worst fears about the simulation technology, and I would castigate his decision to save the cure instead of himself.

"You would've done the same thing," he would argue.

"You wouldn't have let me," I'd say in return. We'd laugh about it before diverging to discussion of our next steps, no thermal blankets or skin contact required.

The sudden thought that I might never get to talk to Jorey again ends the imagined conversation.

"Hang in there, brother, it won't be long now," I whisper, using Cain's words in the absence of my own, lying still enough to feel him breathe and remembering how long he wasn't. I close my eyes and force the memory out, squeezing his hand. His still-cool hand squeezes back. His grip makes my heart race.

Cain was right, I think, unable to help myself as my mind wanders back to Dunn's final moments and our encounter with Orman. We never had a chance of saving Dunn, and his presence in the end probably jeopardized everything.

Cain's hand flops down from Jorey's arm, resting on my bare stomach. His fingers are warm. He snorts against Jorey's back, feigning sleep. His fingers bend, brushing against my skin, making it prickle.

"Hands to yourself," I whisper.

"You're absolutely no fun," he whispers back.

"And you're having way too much fun," I retort.

"Say what you will, but I guarantee we're warmer than the rest of them." The wind presses into the sheet, forcing air to rush out against my face. The moment the gust passes, cold air seeps into the cracks, proving Cain's point.

"So what other life-saving measures are you practiced in?" I ask.

"Too many to count. Being on the outside gives you a lot of opportunities to try out survival tips and tricks," Cain says, providing the perfect moment to inquire into his past and get some long-sought-after answers.

"I'm sorry," I say, choosing to let it pass.

"For what?" he asks.

"That I didn't trust you. You were right," I say, keeping my voice low so our conversation is private.

"Obviously, but which particular thing are you referring to?" I can't see it, but I can *hear* him smirk.

"Everything," I say, trying to impress my meaning upon him so maybe, just this once, he'll be serious enough to hear me.

"I said obviously," he repeats.

I push Jorey so his body will press against Cain's. It's the closest I can manage to smacking him.

As incorrigible as he can be, it's time to pay more attention to Cain. He certainly knows what he's doing out here. He's guided us through the tunnels and overland without detection, only to follow through by recovering the cure. *And he rescued Jorey.* From resuscitation to the thermal blankets and requesting help, Cain is singularly responsible for his life. Without Cain, we'd have nowhere to go.

"Did you use Jorey to hit me?" Cain asks.

"Yeah, I did." I stifle a giggle.

"That's an abuse of power. You can't use an unconscious man like that." Cain twists his body away from us in mock-hurt.

"You're not going to get too cold like that, are you?" I ask, twisting my body to try and see his face.

"I can't believe you'd use Jorey like a puppet," he whines.

"I'm pretty sure he'd be more than happy to oblige if he were conscious. Isn't that right, Jorey?" I ask, nudging his shoulder in jest. Cain ignores me.

"Umm. Mason," Jorey moans softly, nearly stopping my heart.

I squeeze his hand, looking excitedly at Simons, who's turned over in response to the commotion. "Did you hear that?"

Simons rises to his knees, beaming. "I sure did."

I roll over, my face nearly level with Jorey's, only inches away, tucking the infrared sheet under me to keep the heat trapped in. Jorey moans again, then coughs, before his eyes flutter open. I watch him blink, trying to determine how present he is. He lifts his head and looks down at the space between us, confused.

"Mason?" he asks.

"Hey, you're going to be alright," I say, reaching for his face, a big grin spreading across my own.

Cain's hand makes its way to Jorey's cheek before mine. The sheet crinkles as he nuzzles up against Jorey, pressing his lips flat against his forehead. "Mmm. Morning, sweetheart," Cain whispers in a breathy voice.

Jorey jerks away from Cain, nearly crushing me before he turns back, shaking his head, confused. "What's going on?" he rasps.

"We had to get you warm. We had to save you," I explain.

Jorey groans. The sound gets stuck in his chest, forcing him to cough. His lungs crackle with each forced exhalation until he flops to his side, exhausted.

Cain puts his hand against Jorey's forehead. "You'll be okay now, sweetie."

Jorey opens his eyes momentarily, shooting daggers in Cain's direction. "Please get away from me," he rasps before closing his eyes again, too tired to enforce his request.

I smack Cain's hands away from Jorey's head. "Leave him alone," I hiss.

In the distance, the low, choppy sound of a combustion engine releasing exhaust from its chamber draws my attention. It's not the sound any government-issued vehicle could make. It's a wild sound like everything else in this area, made from the combination of old-world parts and new-world technology. Without seeing the thing roaring in the distance, I know it could only be made by someone outside of the organized world, which means help has arrived.

"Listen, Jorey. Help is here," I say, turning to fish for my kill suit.

Simons offers me his jacket. I accept it, climbing out of the thermal blanket and wrapping myself in it until I can find my clothes, thankful the jacket falls below my knees.

In the distance, the low, growling machine makes its way toward us with a small figure perched on top. I watch it approach as I step back into the suit. The vehicle looks to be welded together from scraps of old-world vehicles. Huge, knobby rubber tires stick out on either side of the rider's legs, passing over the muddy terrain with noisy ease. The rider raises a hand in greeting as they approach, slowing the contraption and turning it to park. It's pulling some sort of sled behind it.

I pull the zipper up to my chin as the driver cuts the power to the engine, filling the area with silence. Cain pops up from the sheet to greet our rescue, unaffected by his lack of clothes. As the driver dismounts, his furred hood falls back from his face to reveal black hair streaked grey over a smiling, round face. The narrow man barely reaches up to Cain's chest.

"It's good to see you, Dó!" Cain says, reaching out to grab the man's hand and pull him into a warm embrace. When Cain said the dissenter running the next-nearest energy management facility was a *friend*, he meant it.

They release one another, and Dó looks him up and down as if taking in Cain's undressed state for the first time. "A bit chilly?"

"Did you bring what I asked?" Cain asks. I raise an eyebrow at his question.

He turns, reaching into a satchel strapped to the side of his vehicle and hands Cain the contents. Cain pulls the thick sweater and pants into his chest as if they were gifts from above before moving to dress. Dó shakes his head, letting out a high-pitched chuckle at Cain's antics before saying, "Alright, m'boy, let's get down to business. Who needs rescuing?"

His eyes fall on me, and he blinks twice to clear them. I reach out a hand in greeting, "Hi. I'm Mason—Kara Mason. We've got a man in need of aid."

He shakes my hand, taking me in, trying to place me. "Mason. Pleased to meet you. As I'm sure you heard Eli say, I'm Dó."

I nod. Dó looks over our group, settling his focus on Jorey, then asking Cain, "You said a near drowning?"

"I don't know if we can call it a near one. I'd say the river got the job done and we did some undoing after the fact," he says.

Dó watches for a moment longer before bouncing into action with a bright voice. "Right then, I suppose we shouldn't waste any time! Let's get this thing loaded up." He pats the handle of his transportation.

"What is that monstrosity?" Cain asks, pulling his head through the fuzzy knitted sweater, grimacing at the noisy metal contraption.

Dó looks at it proudly. "I made it myself. It runs on diesel I make from rendered fat."

"That's clever," I muse, taking a handful of supplies from Frances.

"I'm very proud of it," Dó agrees.

"You would be," Cain teases.

"I call it my Dó-mobile," he retorts, puffing his chest toward Cain, who remains unimpressed.

"You can't be serious," Cain groans.

Dó smacks him on the back in an all-too-familiar gesture and says, "Oh come on, Eli! You would have loved that back in the day!"

Cain shakes his head as Simons hoists Jorey off the ground, making their way toward the machine. Jorey moans before entering into another fit of coughing.

"Oh, I see we've got some signs of life! Let's get him situated in the passenger compartment. Then we can load you all up," Dó instructs, gesturing to the cracked leather square behind the driver's seat with foam sticking out from the center.

"There's no way he's going to be able to hold himself up for the trip," I say, looking at the precarious position.

"I can hold him," Simons offers.

"That won't work. You'll put out my suspension! I'm going to need you in the sled. Cain should be able to do it," Dó corrects as Simons hoists Jorey, helping him swing his leg over the center.

Cain leans against Jorey's shoulder. "I can't wait to spend another five hours wrapped up against you," he teases.

Jorey moans. "Please, no. Simons."

"I'm afraid that would be impossible," Dó apologizes.

"What are you trying to say?" Simons asks. His voice is deep and threatening, but I detect the edge of humor to it. I wonder if Dó can.

"Only that you are the singular largest man I've ever met," Dó says without a hint of a joke.

Simons bursts into brilliant laughter. His response to Dó's observation creates a sense of comfort and ease amidst our group. "I don't know that anyone has ever flat-out said it like that," he chuckles.

We load more supplies, allowing the relief of our rescue and Jorey's return to life to lighten us. When everything is situated, we pile onto the sled in a tangle of arms and legs. Cain climbs onto the vehicle, wedging Jorey's mass between himself and Dó before wrapping his arm around both of them. I don't miss the sway as Jorey resists Cain's teasing before they settle.

Dó fires up the engine, then turning back to us, he yells, "Hang on, everyone! We're about to head Dó-verland!"

Cain groans, unwilling to laugh at Dó's terrible joke as the vehicle jerks into action, towing the loaded sled with surprising ease.

PART TWO

TUNNELS AND REACTORS

CHAPTER
TWENTY

"ALL I CAN SAY IS you're lucky you didn't freeze to death!" Dó exclaims, pulling down his hood and kicking off his boots at the entrance to his private quarters on the energy management facility grounds. He opens the door wide so Frances and I can dump the last of the supplies before rejoining the others to check on Jorey.

I stumble forward on numb legs into the little mudroom, dropping an armful of packs on the floor. We've been off the Dó-mobile for nearly an hour, but my body still hums and vibrates with the rough motion of our long journey. Frances squeezes in behind me and mimics the action with weary arms.

"I can't thank you enough for coming to our aid," I say again, stalling in the mudroom. Five hours of transportation have given me enough time to consider Cain and his isolated dissenter friend, and I have questions.

"I'm always ready to help a fellow dissenter, and of course I'd do anything for Eli," Dó replies warmly.

"Are you and Cain close?" I ask.

Before he can answer, Cain bursts into the mudroom. "Whoa, Dó! You trying to cook us?" he exclaims, pulling off his coat and tossing it at Dó.

"Oh, quit your complaining, Eli! Give it a while and you'll fall in love with it all over again and never want to leave!" Dó takes Cain's coat along with the others and stacks them against the door.

"How do you know each other?" I ask again.

Dó smiles warmly, opening his mouth to answer, but before he does, Cain cuts him off. "Dó assisted me on my way in. I stayed with him for a few weeks recovering from the trek between facilities."

"Most recently," Dó says, moving out of the mudroom and into the kitchen, urging us forward.

I follow them through the open doorway, swallowing hard and wishing it looked different, but instead I'm greeted by more eerie familiarity. The whole property brings back long-suppressed memories —the basic structure and layout of the management facility and the private quarters are perfect copies of the home I grew up in. I take a deep breath as I move further into the kitchen, trying to not think about the last time I stood in this same position, the shattered data pod littering the floor. It doesn't do any good.

Inside the private quarters, a powerful heating unit blasts temperatures I haven't felt in what seems like a lifetime. It's amazing how the sudden presence of something that's been absent for so long can bring so much back with it.

In my mind's eye, I can see my father standing at the stove with an overloaded ceramic pan piping enough steam to obscure his face while my brothers and I pound our fists against the table, chanting, *Time to eat!*

The sound of laughter drifts from the living room, pulling me from my reverie. I tear myself away from the table and follow the sounds through the doorway to see Jorey sitting upright on the couch with Simons at his side and Richards kneeling in front of him, using a stethoscope from Dó's med-kit.

"It's good to hear you laugh," Simons says, gripping Jorey's bare shoulder.

Jorey's volunteer suit is pooled around his waist as he sits, shirtless and dazed. I think about how vulnerable he looks, sitting next to Simons with sunken eyes blinking back the haze.

"It's good to be back," he replies.

"Now, take another deep breath. As deep as you can manage."

Jorey breathes in, then immediately begins coughing again. The fit lasts nearly a whole minute before he gasps, "Sorry."

"It's alright. It's going to take a while for you to recover. That's enough for now," Richards says, pulling the stethoscope from his ears and setting it aside.

I move into the room, torn between the grief from the invading past and the relief of making it to a safe haven—something we didn't manage so many years ago.

"Hey Mason…" Jorey says, looking up as he pulls his arms into the sleeves of his suit. His voice is soft and raspy.

"Hey Jorey. How do you feel?" I ask as Simons stands to make room.

"I feel like somebody beat me half to death," he says, casually rubbing a hand across his sternum.

"Resuscitation will do that to a man," Richards acknowledges.

"Yeah, well, other than that… I feel groggy, like my head isn't all the way here," Jorey says.

"It's a miracle you're here at all!" Cain says, leaning over to slap him on the shoulder.

Jorey moves forward with the force of Cain's gesture, still weak from his brush with death. He straightens himself again, fixing his gaze on Cain. "I hear I have you to thank for that?"

Cain shifts uncomfortably. "C'mon, man. It was Frances and Mason that hauled your heavy butt out of the water. I had the easy job of fishing you out from the log."

"And the whole naked in the wilderness thing?" Jorey asks.

"Yeah, you're welcome for that. I'm going to take credit for Mason too," Cain smirks.

My cheeks flush with the mention of it. Jorey looks down before bending his legs and shifting his position. His movements are stiff, like he's forgotten how to handle his body. After a failed attempt, he readjusts, reaching out and saying, "Someone help me up?"

Simons grips Jorey's forearm and pulls him up. Jorey sways uneasily, then puts his hand out so he can lean against the wall.

"Take it easy, you'll get your legs back," Simons warns him.

"That's right. That's what you're here for. We'll get you all sorted out and ready for the next leg of your journey before you know it," Dó says in his quick, cheerful tone. I look to Cain for some indication of what Dó's talking about—how much he knows—but Cain isn't paying attention. He's watching Dó reach his hand out toward Jorey, who looks as though he's just realized the stranger amongst us. "I'm Dó. Happy to come to your rescue."

"Thank you," Jorey says, stifling a cough before attempting another step.

Simons steps into Jorey, offering support as he finds his feet. Jorey nods at him, staggering at his side.

"Why don't you all get cleaned up so you can get to resting?" Dó suggests. "I'll gather up a change of clothes and get something cooking for dinner."

"That's really kind of you," Frances says.

"It's nothing. It's what I do up here," Dó says. He casts a surreptitious wink in my direction and adds, "Other than keep the reactors running for the government, that is."

"Where are you going to get a change of clothes from?" I ask.

"I can supply you with just about everything you need to make it to your next check point," he says, moving into the kitchen. I follow him as he walks to the cupboard and begins rifling through its contents. He then adds, "I get donations from just about everywhere— every size, shape and stature I've seen come through here leaves something."

The implications of what he says aren't lost on me. It sounds as though his isolated energy management facility is a well-used bus station. Cain joins me, leaning over the kitchen table and watching Dó with curious humor, not seeming the least bit perplexed about what the purpose of so much traffic up north might be.

He continues as if what he's saying weren't so strange, pulling out a couple of unlabeled cans. "Of course, I've got synthetic undergarments for when you leave here, something to keep you warm enough until your next stop. That will likely be your longest trek—if you're headed south—which I assume you are. Cain, you didn't say when you were going to be back—and you didn't say you were bringing anyone with you."

I turn to Cain, perplexed by Dó's strange statements. "Did you plan to come back?"

"I didn't plan for much of anything," Cain says, sounding only partially honest.

I study Cain, then Dó, thinking about all the people he professes to come through his care. "Why do you get so much traffic?"

"Hmm?" Dó closes the cabinet and settles his attention on me.

"Your facility is located in the middle of nowhere—hundreds of miles from any City State."

"That is precisely why they come here," Dó explains. "The fact it makes absolutely no sense for anyone to come here makes it one of the last places the DDC would look."

"When people leave the City States, they come here?" I ask.

"Here or another place just like it. Until the DDC quits looking for them," Dó affirms, mimicking Cain's original proposed plan for us... minus the offensive action part.

"And all this time, I thought the energy management facilities were the loneliest places on earth," I muse.

"Was yours?" Dó asks.

"How did you—"

"You know, if you're going to surface once you move on from here, that suit *has* to go," he says, pointing his finger directly at me as though he's completely forgotten the previous conversation.

"What's wrong with these clothes?" I ask, touching my lab suit protectively. As my fingers pass across the synthetic fabric, I realize over the last several years I've come to associate my suits with safety.

"Those clothes are obviously government issued—you'll never blend in," Dó explains.

He's right.

"You shower. I'll go upstairs and get you some city clothes—something less conspicuous," Dó commands in his quick clip, his little body moving at the same speed as he abandons his kitchen preparations for the newest plan.

"Cain, you lead the way while I get you what you need. Then I'll cook for you all, so you have something warm when you get done," Dó says, heading toward the hallway.

"How about a popsicle?" Cain asks, wiping his brow in mock-distress.

Dó spins abruptly and hops up, managing to reach the top of Cain's head with a quick smack. "Enough of this, you! It will feel completely different once you're out of those clothes and cleaned up! Now go be a good host and show your guests the facilities!"

Dó shoos Cain off with the rest of us, waving his hands over his head in our direction before disappearing down the hallway to gather the promised clothes. I watch him go, slightly overwhelmed by his persistent energy and cheerfulness. Dó is exactly who I wished for during the long journey across tundra and mountain to retrieve the cure.

I give Cain a curious look as we start down the hallway. "Is he completely sane?"

Cain offers me a brilliant smile. "Mostly. I think the isolation gets to him."

"The way he puts it makes it sound like he's always got company," Simons points out.

"A blip on the radar of loneliness," Cain corrects him.

"That sounds so terribly sad," Richards says, pulling his glasses from his face and folding them.

"What are you talking about? Dó's the happiest person I know," Cain laughs.

"Second happiest person I know," I tease.

He smirks at my statement, clearing his throat to put on a show for us. "Is that right? Well then, follow me, ma'am!" He looks out at the rest of the group with a ridiculous smile on his face and continues, "Ladies and gentlemen, your luxury spa awaits! If you tip—there's a turn-down service in the evening. Ladies, you may use the facility to the right. Gentlemen, continue to follow me."

I stifle a smile, shaking my head and thinking Cain must think Dó is sane because he's half-crazy himself.

CHAPTER
TWENTY-ONE

STEAM FOGS the bathroom mirror as I peel my kill suit off for the last time, wondering what will become of it. Will Dó find a way to cycle it into his incredible stockpile of resources or will it molder away as a forgotten relic? I toss it aside, ready to envelop myself in the too-hot shower to wash away all thought. Then, at the last second, I stoop down and remove the golden scientist emblem pinned to the collar, tucking it into the glove on the counter, no surer why I'm keeping it now than when I removed Dunn's from his body before we left him to the dogs.

"I haven't felt this good in ages," Frances says once I exit the shower, wrapped in a thick towel.

"The showers in the Laboratories were at least as good," I observe, accepting one of the shirts Dó left for us from her outstretched hand.

"I couldn't say. That was a lifetime ago," she says, pulling her own towel from the mass of wet hair perched atop her head. It falls down her shoulders, leaving damp streaks on her shirt. She uses the towel to wipe the mirror before running her fingers through the tangles. I turn away from her to dress.

"Mason?" she starts, making me pull the towel back into my chest.

I turn to find her studying me in the mirror.

"What's wrong?" I ask, my cheeks hotter than the rest of me.

"I'm sorry for how I acted about the cure." She turns away from the mirror, leaning against the counter.

I scramble into the shirt, bashful from not having to share bathrooms for so long. "You weren't wrong about our supplies. But now that we have the cure, Dó has more than we could ask for."

Frances nods, turning back to the mirror and shaking her head until curls begin to form.

"It's strange, isn't it?" she asks, still watching me in the mirror as I tend to my own tangled hair. "That Dó has so much?"

I consider what she's suggesting. "It's not impossible if what he says about the dissenter network is true. I've seen some incredible things. And most energy management facilities are overstocked."

"Yes, but they're overstocked with the basics. We send them extra food, more socks, underwear, and blankets than they could ever use. What Dó says he has isn't possible—*can't* be possible," Frances presses, turning toward me and lowering her voice as though she were worried we might be overheard.

"Do you think Cain would walk us into a trap?" I ask.

She looks at me for a long moment. The hall on the other side of the door fills with sound as Cain and Richards make their way toward the kitchen.

Richards chuckles at something Cain said. "We'll see about that."

Frances waits until they've walked past before answering. "No. I trust him. Cain's done right by us."

"What is it, then?" I ask.

She sighs, shaking her head and reaching for my shoulder. "Maybe I'm only afraid it's too good to be true," she says.

She steps past me to the bathroom door. I leave her to join Cain and Richards at the dining table, intent on seeking out Jorey to assure myself everything is fine. I turn away from the enticing aroma of Dó's cooking in time to watch Jorey walk down the hallway under his own strength, Simons trailing behind him.

"You look a lot better," I say, noting his color has returned.

"I feel like I'm halfway there." His voice is still weak.

I slip my hand into his, giving it a quick squeeze before we enter the kitchen. I glance back at Simons, who offers me a reassuring smile.

"More than halfway," he assures me as we join the others to watch Dó scurry around the stove.

"Did you ask about your toes?" I ask Frances, pulling out a chair for Jorey before sitting between him and Cain.

"Frostbite?" Dó asks, walking over to the table with a steaming pot whose contents make my mouth water.

"Maybe, but not too bad, I think," Frances says.

Dó sets the pot on the table and stoops over to inspect her bare feet. He pulls one gently from the ground and inspects her toe tips. "I've got some antiseptic that should work on those," he says. I wonder if that's something specific to the supplies of a far-north energy management facility.

"What about you?" I ask Cain. He was the only other member of our group wearing civilian shoes.

"My toes are pink as a baby's bottom!" he says, rubbing his hands through the stubble on his unshaved face before tucking his hands behind his head.

I give him an incredulous look. "Are you sure about that? You jumped into the river with those boots on."

"See for yourself," he says, pushing his chair back and placing his feet onto the table to display his knobby, naked toes.

I look in amazement at his damage-free feet. Even the very tips of his toes where mine and surely everyone else's are still white from the cold are bright pink and vibrant. "Unbelievable! How?"

"Man, your legs are hairy…" Jorey jabs.

"You weren't complaining about that earlier," Cain shoots back, wiggling his feet in Jorey's direction. He tosses a sock at me. It smacks me on the side of my face before I realize what it is. "This is how." He balls the matched sock up and sends it directly between Jorey's eyes.

I investigate the sock, holding it away from my face. "Synthetics?" I ask.

"Here, here, look at this clean one," Dó insists, placing another large pot of something on the table. He takes Cain's dirty sock and hands me its clean twin before moving back to the stove.

"They're specially designed protective wear, similar to your lab-issued shoes, but better. My mom designed them," Cain brags.

"Valerie—Cain—used to make them for all the travelers," Dó says as he brings us dishes for dinner. Simons grabs one before Dó can set them on the table and begins to serve himself his usual extra-large portion of the thick, stew-like contents. The other pot contains government-issued rice. Dó brings a third to the table from which he serves us all hot tea of his own making. He continues with his story as he works. "Valerie was exceptionally talented. She practically built the network as we see it today. Communication channels like we've never had before—I can find out what's happening on the other side of the equator without the government picking up my signal. She was genius!"

"The only genius I want to give homage to right now is you, Dó. I haven't had food this good in... well, maybe never," Simons interjects heartily as he helps himself to more of the stew, piling the steaming rice over the top of it.

Dó chuckles at Simons' hefty appetite. "I love the company. Come back and join me any time. The days get long and terrible between travelers up here." He shudders, the terrible loneliness temporarily breaking through his cheer. "Sometimes I think I'll lose my sanity. When the storms roll through and the sun never rises..."

"You knew Cain's mother?" I ask, steering the conversation back to his earlier statement.

Dó looks over at Cain, surprised. "You didn't tell them?"

Cain shrugs. "Not yet."

"Impossible boy!" Dó shakes his head, bewildered, before turning his attention to me. "Valerie used to be a scientist in the Northern Laboratories before she made her break."

"A scientist?" I look at Cain, perplexed. "You said she worked for the government!"

Cain swallows a large mouthful. "Scientists work for the government."

"Why not just say it?" I demand.

He shrugs, dismissing me and taking another mouthful. "Same thing."

I look to Dó. "She came here?"

"She was my first visitor. I found her hiding in the tunnels," he says, suddenly adding, "Did you know they used to be part of an underground water transport system?"

I look at Cain again, amazed he could have kept so much from us. "Why didn't you tell me she was a scientist?"

He throws his fork down on the table, exasperated. "She was a scientist in the Northern Laboratories. Like everyone else up there, she figured out what was going on. But she made a break for it. Dó found her and helped her connect with dissenters in the south. There! You know the whole story now. I didn't realize my life needed to be an open book!"

He picks up the fork again and scoops up another heap of stew and rice, forcing it into his mouth.

"It's her story, not yours," Dó corrects him, joining us at the table.

Cain grumbles something incoherent.

The moment passes. After rehashing the nightmare of Dunn's passing, we move onto other topics, relaxing over Dó's generous meal. I eat until there's no more room for my stomach to stretch. Immobilized by the feast, I take a moment before waddling over to the couch in the living room. I plop down next to Frances and Richards and slowly sip my tea. Frances puts her feet on the table in front of the couch and buries her head in Richards' shoulder as Dó treats her frostbitten toes with a practiced hand.

"You won't be having any more of this problem now," Dó says as he cleans up his medic supplies. "You'll each get a pair of those socks. And—" He disappears momentarily to deposit his medic kit and returns with a pair of thick pants that look like over-developed overalls of some sort. "You'll each get a pair of these!"

The pants appear overall unremarkable but still compelling. "What are they?" I ask.

"Frontier pants!" Dó proclaims.

"That's what you call them," Cain corrects.

Dó gives him a reproachful look. "They're named for the founders of the Northern frontier who engineered the tunnel system," he says.

"I think everyone else calls them pants," Cain whispers loudly to Simons, giving me a wink.

Dó ignores him, expounding on the pants he so proudly named.

"They're suitable for a wide range of temperatures. Fitted, waterproof and—"

"We get it, you made a great pair of pants," Cain dismisses, wincing as he swallows too-hot tea.

"You'll all get a regular set of clothes too," Dó finishes, scowling at Cain as he tosses the pants onto our ever-growing pile of provisions.

He disappears down the hall again as we all sit, digesting and peering at our new clothing. Simons is stretched out on a chair that looks too small for his oversized frame. He rests his hand comfortably on his full stomach, holding his mug but not really tending to it. Frances hasn't fully emerged from Richards' arms yet. I watch her, curious as she rests her head on his shoulder, noting that Richards keeps his arm wrapped around her.

I'm curled into a tight ball next to them with my feet pointed in their direction and my own cup of tea resting on the arm of the couch. Jorey and Cain share the loveseat next to the couch, sitting uncomfortably close to one another and periodically shoving each other's legs as their bodies relax. Every now and then, Jorey coughs, but he looks miraculously better.

When Dó re-emerges from the hall, he's carrying an immense stack of blankets and pillows. He dumps them on the table where Frances' feet were resting just moments before. "You'll stay here for a while and rest—eat up and visit with me. Once the DDC shifts their search, you can move on. I've got to go check the power grid, then I'm going to turn in for the night. I cook early, so be ready for it."

We distribute the pillows and blankets amongst the team as Dó adorns himself in his thick parka and overdressed boots to journey into the cold and check the grid. Simons pulls the coffee table out of the living room, exposing the floor so he can make himself a comfortable bed. Jorey and Cain fight briefly over the loveseat until Jorey relents, retreating to the ground to set up his own sleeping quarters. Frances and Richards set up their pillows directly next to one another and pull a single blanket over themselves. Laying my head down on the soft pillow, I marvel at how incredibly comfortable it is and how eager I am to wrap myself in the blankets Dó delivered when I wanted to tear my clothes off only hours before.

Cain fluffs his pillow a few times before turning off the light and draping his lanky legs over the edge of the loveseat. I smile to myself, thinking that his bed might not be as comfortable as his victory was sweet. We begin dropping off to the gentle rhythm of each other's slumber.

CHAPTER
TWENTY-TWO

SOMEONE CRIES OUT in the darkness. I bolt upright, my heart racing, prepared to respond, but I reel with confusion as I take in my surroundings. *Home.* I'm home, but I'm sleeping on the couch in our living room instead of tucked away in bed.

Dad and Hank blew it up…

I blink back the panic as the moment passes and the memory of our journey to Dó's energy management facility—the carbon copy of my childhood home—returns, replacing the dreams.

"You okay?" Cain's shadowed figure appears next to me. I squint to make him out in the darkness.

"Someone screamed. Is Jorey alright?" I ask, suddenly terrified for him. *He was dead,* I think, not for the first time.

I move to check on him, but Cain puts his hand on my shoulder, sinking down to sit next to me. "Relax, he's fine. I can hear him snoring from here," he whispers.

I glance across the shadows of sleeping bodies strewn about the room, listening to each one. Sure enough, I detect his breath as it rises and falls from the ocean of slumber. Cain leans into me as I fall back into the couch, facing him. I let out a heavy sigh, trying to release the anxiety.

"Who screamed?" I ask.

"You did."

"What?" I ask, confused.

"That's what woke me up, anyway," he says, nudging me. I can see him smiling even in the darkness. "I think you were crying."

I bring my hands to my face self-consciously, suddenly aware of my flushed cheeks and swollen eyes. I bury my face in my hands, tucking my bare legs back into the blanket, embarrassed and fully aware of how childish I must seem.

"Are you being serious right now?" Cain asks, pulling my hands away from my face. I glance up at him, hot and exposed. His normal grin is tinged with concern.

"Seriously humiliated," I say, relenting my hand to him and using the other to pull my pillow to my chest. Cain drops my other hand across his legs, settling his hand on top of it in a comforting gesture.

"What's there to be humiliated about? Feeling a little overwhelmed? Having a bad dream? Those things seem normal, given the circumstances," he says, letting his fingers run across the back of my hand, then wrapping them around my palm.

"Maybe for you, but I'm a scientist. I'm not supposed to get overwhelmed... even though things have spiraled out of control," I hesitate before admitting, "And I know I shouldn't let it bother me, but this place reminds me of home."

"Did you grow up in an energy management facility?" Cain laughs quietly.

"I did," I say, keeping my voice soft enough not to travel beyond the couch.

"How unconventional of you," Cain says, giving my hand a shake.

"It's a long story."

"You know I hate being left out of things. Does everyone else know?" His eyes meet mine in the dark, searching.

"You love being the odd one," I tease. "But to answer your question, not everyone knows everything about me."

"Who knows what?" he asks, releasing my hand so his fingers can dance across my skin. My skin prickles, not unpleasantly, pulling my focus into the contact.

"Simons and Jorey know I grew up at an energy management

facility with my family. Simons knows I lost them before we went to the Institute. Jorey knows everything else about it," I say, looking out again onto the sleeping masses.

"So you're pretty close with Jorey, then?" Cain asks, his fingers trailing up my arm.

"Yes. I've known him since the trip north," I say.

"Romantically close?" he asks. The sensation of his fingers brushing against the flesh just below the sleeve of my shirt has a strange effect, making me want to pull away and lean in at the same time.

I crinkle my nose. "With Jorey?"

"Is it?" His body presses in against mine.

"No," I answer, letting the question sink in. "No. It's different with Jorey." I want to explain, but I don't have the words to describe what's different about Jorey. Not even to myself.

"Ah. Well, good then." He smiles, adjusting to drape his arm across my shoulders.

"Good?" I ask. My heart thuds.

"Good for me," he clarifies, confirming his intended meaning.

Realization dawns. I turn so his arm slides off my back and point my bare toes toward him, reclaiming my arm and tucking it across my knees. I don't know what to say, but I know I need to say something. "Cain, I…"

"Yes?" he asks, bending his elbow and propping his head against his hand, looking easy and amused.

"I'm not sure what you're thinking, but I'm not in a place where—"

"Hey! It's okay. You don't have to explain to me. I know exactly what you're going through," he says, pulling my hands into his again.

"You do?" I ask. His hands are so much warmer than mine. So much warmer than under the thermal cover…

"Yes. Remember? My mom was a scientist. She had the same training—and the same trouble when she left. I can help you," he says, letting his voice rise. Simons stirs.

I hold my breath, waiting for him to sink back into rest. I don't want to share this moment with anyone else until I figure out what it is.

"How do you know what I'm going through?" I whisper once I'm confident Simons has settled.

"I heard you talking to Richards after we left the Laboratories."

A rush of embarrassment surges through me before getting replaced with indignation. "You were listening to our conversation?"

"A little." He shrugs. I pull my hand away from his, upset he's betrayed some unspoken trust. He reaches back for me, whispering, "It wasn't on purpose! Honest. But that's how I know I can help."

I study his outline in the darkness. His shaggy hair is wild with sleep, and his lips are upturned under a growing beard, but his eyes are soft and kind, promising he isn't making a joke of it.

"Thank you," I whisper, accepting the offer.

"Hey, if I can get you to take your clothes off in the middle of nowhere, then getting you back to humanity should be a piece of cake!" Cain jests, nudging me with his shoulder. I nudge back playfully, and we're suddenly in a strong man nudge-off. We push back and forth until I stifle a laugh.

"Shhh! Someone is going to wake up," I scold, exhilarated.

Cain stops moving. I relax into him. The room is silent, save for the heavy breathing of the sleeping masses.

"Why did Dó think you were coming back with people?" I ask, turning to watch his response.

Cain breathes out, air rushing through his nose. "I wasn't sure what would happen when I went to the Laboratories."

"What did you expect to happen?"

"I thought I might stir things up a bit," he says dismissively. "Maybe rattle some cages, off some folks."

I look at him skeptically. "*Off some folks*?"

"Well, maybe just Orman. But I wasn't crazy about his toadies—Fisher and Hersh," Cain explains, deliberately flippant.

"How did you even know who Orman was before you got to the Northern Laboratories?"

He brushes his frazzled hair out of his face. The gesture doesn't completely mask the flash of anger darkening his features until he almost looks like someone else. The expression is gone before I can register the change. "Orman is a hunter for the DDC. He specializes in flushing out what the government would call *problem people*. It took a long time to figure out who he was, but once I was certain he was behind my mother's death, I wanted to do the deed myself. I've been on his trail for a couple of years, so when he moved back to the Laboratories, I followed."

"You want revenge?" I ask.

"No," he blurts, pulling back slightly. He lets out a heavy sigh. "Orman has killed a lot of dissenters. Taking him out doesn't break down the DDC, but it would hurt them. Revenge is just a side effect of a necessary task."

He isn't telling the whole truth, but what he says about Orman is true. Regardless of his motives and whatever other bits he's holding back, I want to trust him. With time, I can unravel the rest.

There's a long silence where the heat of his body pressed against mine is the most present thing in my mind.

"Are you moving back to the loveseat?" I ask.

"Nah, that thing was so uncomfortable," he says, settling into my blanket.

My stomach flips. "Do you want me to jump over to it then?"

"No, I don't want you to move over, dummy. I want you here. The last person I cozied up against was Jorey, and I think I deserve better." He puts his head down on my pillow and pats the couch next to him.

"I thought you and Jorey were getting along just fine," I say, trying to stretch out without completely compressing myself against him.

"Besides," he continues, his voice sleepier, "I don't want to couch jump if you start crying again."

I jab his ribs with my elbow. Instead of pushing back, he puts his hand over mine and holds it in place. "Don't be immature. Sleep," he scolds. The admonishment makes me want to recoil in embarrassment, but I don't dare move from his embrace. I don't want him to think of me as childish.

After a while, Cain's breath slows to the steady rhythm of sleep. I let it lull me into the thoughtless peace of slumber.

CHAPTER
TWENTY-THREE

THE GENTLE SOUNDS of cabinet doors opening and closing in the kitchen and of intermittent running water create an undeniable nostalgia. I lay with my eyes closed, warm and comfortable in my couch cocoon, and allow myself to remember. I pretend my father is in the kitchen and the rustling sounds of bodies stirring around me are my brothers. It's amazing how easily the memories come, when I used to struggle to hold onto each one.

Someone coughs loudly, and it pulls me out of my reverie, forcing my eyes open. Jorey's staring at me from his makeshift bed on the floor with a strange expression, making me remember Cain's arm is wrapped around me. He's awake, with yet another big grin plastered on his bearded face.

"Good morning," Cain teases with an exaggerated yawn. "Boy, did I sleep great!"

"You could have let me know the loveseat was available," Jorey grumbles, turning away. He tosses his blanket aside and grunts as he pulls himself from the floor.

Self-consciously, I push Cain's arm off and sit up. Cain moves his arm into a languid stretch as though he'd intended to right at that moment and yawns loudly again.

"Eh, I figured if that thing was too small for me, then it'd be nothing but punishment to offer it to you," Cain calls to Jorey's back.

Jorey ignores him and walks directly into the kitchen, where Simons' low voice is requesting coffee.

Cain calls after Jorey one more time, "Besides, somebody had to keep your buddy here from waking you lot up!"

I shoot Cain an angry look. I'm about to stand and head into the kitchen after Jorey when Cain nudges me with his elbow.

"Hey," I growl at him.

"Hey yourself, grumpy!" He swings his legs and sits up next to me.

"Are you going to tell everyone about last night?" I hiss under my breath as Frances and Richards stir.

Cain winces. "C'mon, Mason, I'm just giving Jorey a hard time. He's so serious."

I stand, leaving him to the couch. "I'm sure he'd be more than willing to lighten up if you could manage to be less of an asshole!"

Cain clambers after me into the kitchen as Simons pours hot water from a kettle into a ceramic mug. I ignore him and Jorey and observe Simons inhale the steam above the beverage.

"Are you only serving yourself?" I ask him.

"You can help yourself." He puts the kettle back on the stove, grabbing his mug. He carries it over to the table and sits down, crossing one massive leg over the other, smiling.

Jorey mimics Simons' actions, still not looking at me or Cain. I grab a mug and put two heaping spoons of the ground coffee beans into the mixture. In the Northern Laboratories, we had dehydrated coffee crystals that instantly dissolved into a rich beverage. What Dó has is very different—it's what my dad used to make. I pour the hot water over the granules and watch them float in the steaming mixture. The heat releases aromatic complexes bound within the solid structures, creating an intoxicating aroma.

Dó fills the kettle with more water and puts it back on the stove before returning to the counter where he's placed a variety of food-stuffs for preparation. I walk over and sit between Simons and Jorey. Jorey glances at me with one eyebrow raised.

"What?" I ask in a tone meant only for him.

He shrugs and takes a sip from his mug. I reach out and bump his hand with the back of mine, making him look at me again. "Don't be like that." I realize I'm scowling and replace the expression with the most pleasant smile I can muster. "Please?"

"Cain's an asshole," Jorey says to me in a low and quiet voice, still frowning.

"That's what I said," I reply, meeting his gaze with all the earnestness I can muster.

My expression breaks, and I giggle. Jorey smiles, and I know everything is fine.

"Are you talking about me?" Cain asks, bringing his own coffee to the table.

"Yeah, we both agree: you're kind of an asshole." I smile at him.

"That sounds about right," he agrees.

"So tell me, Dó, now that I'm awake, what are your thoughts about our situation?" Simons pulls us away from our inside joke and back into reality.

"Well, the first thing to do is cause a diversion to draw the DDC off your tracks," Dó explains as he fires up his stove. The roar of the cooking flames mixes with the hum of the heater resonating from the central hall.

"Don't be coy with us, Dó. What've you got planned?" Cain asks, popping a piece of something uncooked into his mouth.

"What is that?" Frances asks as she walks into the kitchen with Richards.

"That's potato. I grow them here. They get nice and sweet with the freeze," Dó says.

"Fresh potato..." Richards marvels, wiping his glasses against his shirt to clean them. It's a far cry from the reconstituted powders and pickles we've consumed our entire lives.

"Oh, that's not all. I've got onions too, and this is moose meat—lots of game up here in summer and fall," Dó brags. "There's plenty of food up here if you know where to look and how to keep it."

"As you were saying?" Simons asks, redirecting the conversation to our journey.

"Right, right," Dó continues as he greases a large pan. "Eli is right.

The dissenters already have a plan in the works. Most recent reports suggest the majority of near-dead sightings are to the east, along the main road, but there's been lot more activity in the last two days."

He means since the night of our encounter. I glance at Simons to see if he's caught the import of Dó's words. He grabs his coffee off the table. "You mean more tracking activity?"

Dó nods, adding onions and potatoes to the sizzling iron. "There's been some air activity in the area—transports dropping near-dead. But as I said, we're already on it. There's a group en route to cause a spectacle as we speak."

"What are they going to do, set fire to the tundra?" Cain asks, nabbing more food from Dó's cook station.

"Something way better than that," Dó says, pushing Cain's hand away. "They're going to blow up the fusion reactor outside the Laboratories tonight!"

"That ought to draw some attention," Jorey says, smirking as Dó again slaps Cain's sneaky fingers away from the now wonderfully fragrant pan.

"They're blowing up a reactor just to cause a scene?" Simons asks, taking a careful drink.

"Bold move, I know. If we're lucky, they'll be convinced Mason's behind it. That's the intent anyway," Dó says, turning only slightly away from the pan.

"Why would Mason want to blow up an energy management station? She's not a terrorist," Cain scoffs, waiting for Dó to turn his attention away from the meal preparations.

"Well, she blew up the Northern Laboratories—" Dó begins.

"Technically that was Shelby's plan," I remind him. A quizzical look crosses his face before he turns back to the stove.

"Destroying the Northern Laboratories was an aggressive move. If another government structure goes down, they're sure to believe you intend to attack them head on."

His explanation makes me think of the conversation with Orman through Dunn. He was so certain about the cure. Is it possible my suggestion of another objective could have been enough to throw him off? "It could work..." I say reflectively, hoping Dó's plan is the piece we need to complete the diversion.

"From what Cain's told me, it's exactly what you'll need to get far enough south to disappear for good," Dó agrees, giving the potatoes and onions a stir.

"Destroying a reactor will cause a massive surge in the power grid, won't it? It might affect energy in the cities," I say, still mulling over the proposal.

"It will definitely affect the city power supplies, but so long as we've got all hands on deck for every station from here to the Deadlands, no one should get hurt. We can keep the reactors from overheating in the surge," Dó says, suggesting the attack might be more serious than his casual attitude suggests.

"This is happening tonight?" Jorey asks.

"That's right. I got word this morning that our people are in place and waiting for the go-ahead." He adds the moose meat to his stovetop concoction.

"What about the Northern Laboratories cryogenic unit? Will it lose power?" I ask.

"That's not how the grid works. If we control the surge, there won't be any real damage to the other reactors or the power grid itself. Don't worry. This has been carefully calculated and well thought out."

"Is that level of attention even possible?"

"The dissenters have a strong presence on the grid, and most of the stations are more up to date than this one," he assures me.

"This place first generation?" I ask, taking a tentative sip from my cup. I'm surprised the floating grounds don't bother me.

"It is. But Cain told me you're familiar with the management stations, so you can help me, eh?" Dó turns from the cooking to slap my back and give me a shake.

"Well, yes. I suppose I can," I agree, confused. Last night he said something about the station I grew up on. That was before I told Cain about it.

"I don't need anything too technical from you. Only support." A tiny buzzer sounds for the oven. Dó opens it, exposing its glowing red belly to produce a large mound of freshly baked bread. He shuts the oven with a sense of finality and sets the loaf on a cooling rack.

The tantalizing smell of freshly baked bread becomes too much, and Simons can no longer contain himself. He reaches over Dó's shoulder and snatches up the scalding loaf.

"It has to rest!" Dó cries out in protest, horrified as Simons rips off the edge of the loaf and shakes his fingers as the hot crust releases steam.

I watch them bicker, mildly amused but reeling inside. The attack is an enormous undertaking—something that would've taken weeks to bring together. It must've been in the works from the moment the Laboratories went down—another measure to guard the cure and its transport. *Do they know the cure was lost?* I haven't even had time to fully examine it yet, and the dissenters are making a major move.

Dó is forced to turn away from the bread to stir his stovetop dish. Simons passes the bread to Jorey, who also tears a portion away before passing it along. Dó brings the pan to the table, causing Cain to drop the remainder of the loaf as he uses his piece to scoop a steaming mound of moose and potato. I grab up the bread and help myself to the dish. If I'm going to help keep another crisis at bay, I may as well do it on a full stomach.

CHAPTER
TWENTY-FOUR

I PULL Shelby's pack from where it sits atop the mound of our supplies. First thing after I knew Jorey was safe, I opened it, half expecting to see a destroyed mound of papers and half hoping for a miracle. The notebook appeared to be mostly intact, though damp. It's time to get a real idea of how much was lost to the river. Not wanting to face this task while others watch, I slip outside onto the front patio. I swing my body down onto the steps so the sun, already high in the sky and burning through the morning mist, can warm my skin.

Peeled paint crunches under my hand as I lean into the old wood. Though the steps are dry, they're spongy and loose from years of punishing weather. It's not surprising this is a first-generation facility, considering the age of the structure. I rest my boot-clad feet in the fuzzy growth of grasses below the porch step, thinking about how awkward and boxy they are compared to laboratory footwear. I haven't worn anything but government-issued suits and coats in so long that I'm uncomfortable dressed like this.

The wet leather of Shelby's pack is cold and heavy in my hands. I take in a deep breath, prolonging the moment. I pull the strings, allowing the folds to come undone and reveal their contents once more. In the bright morning light, I stare down at two notebooks. One of them is thicker than the other, its pages swollen with moisture. I pull it out with delicate fingers, treating it like an ancient tome that might turn to dust if I moved too quickly. Putting the pack aside, I set the notebook on my lap, balancing it on my knees as I look at the slick, black cover. Contained within the bindings is all that's left of a lifetime of work. Shelby's cure.

I open the cover with trembling fingers, terrified I might tear through damp paper and ruin a portion of something I have no chance of understanding. The sharp, slanted writing stares back at me in harsh contrast to the white background. Page after page of Shelby's writing reaches out to me, listing compounds and formulas in a language so clear she may as well be sitting across the way, describing it in real time. I absorb the information, turning pages faster and faster, starving for the explanation.

Mechanisms, synthesis, antigens, protein recovery… Everything I could possibly need flows out from the notebook with beautiful simplicity.

Relief floods my senses as I turn another page. The sensation is both soothing and stimulating. I blink back tears of gratitude as my heart thunders inside of my chest, giddy and energized. A pale white envelope sits atop the technical scrawls. I pick it up, my brain a moment behind the action as I process the new item, turning it over to reveal Shelby's signature scrawled black across the seal, guarding its inner contents. I leave the notebook balanced on my legs and break the seal, holding my breath as I unfold the message within.

Mason,

I don't suspect I'll be making it out of the Northern Laboratories. Orman's been interested in you since the Institute, and I don't intend on letting him have his way, which may cost me my life.

If it does, and you're reading this after my demise, I want to assure you I'm at peace with this decision. I'm too old to run. I don't want to spend my final days as a burden. I've made choices I'm not proud of, and I believe that I, like the Northern Laboratories, have reached my end.

You were always meant to bring the cure to the dissenters. Maybe not this way, but I'm not even certain about that anymore. We chose you for a reason.

I've attached detailed instructions for the synthesis and manufacture of the cure agent along with all my historical notes in case I've missed any detail. I achieved perfect cell death rate in the culture lab, and my entire history is attached so you can do what you need to do in the event of any further mutation. All you need is a place to manufacture.

The dissenters have waited a long time to get the cure out of the Northern Laboratories. Those who lived on the inside are responsible for your survival up to this point, but you need the ones who live outside now. Once you make it out of the frozen land, head to the energy management facility on the sixth line of divide. You'll have help from there on. Most energy management facilities are under the control of dissenters thanks to Amos' tireless work.

Your ultimate destination is the major power management facility outside the Institute, which is run by a talented woman named Green. Give her this correspondence. She'll know how to get in contact with Amos, who will get you where you need to go. Do not approach Amos directly. Orman has too many eyes at the Institute, and he won't be the only one hunting you, so I beg you not to feel safe even if you succeed in killing him. So long as the government's power remains, I'm afraid you'll never be safe.

You have become the key piece in a resistance that's been growing since before you were born. The government will do anything to stop the cure from reaching our people.

One final word of warning. After the loss of Carmen, Simons picked up a new man for his team—Eli Cain. Simons' sources confirmed that he works with the dissenters, but he's not who he purports to be. Though I cannot definitively say his actions are nefarious, I urge you to use caution where he's concerned. He is at best selfishly reckless and at worst a direct threat.

Stay alive, Mason, and you can end this.

—Shelby

My head spins. I read the last lines again, looking for anything more than the incomplete story scrawled out in bleeding ink. There are too many partial truths and too few explanations. I've known the dissenters chose to keep me alive since the Institute, but who made those decisions? Shelby was responsible for saving me from the hive, and Amos for getting me to the Northern Laboratories, but who are these others? And was I really chosen by chance? Because I was someone they could save? It's hard to imagine a random occurrence made me the cornerstone to the only chance to defeat the government's new weapon…

Knowing Shelby never expected to make it out of the Northern Laboratories leaves a hollow in the pit of my stomach that only fills with the terror of knowing everyone is relying on me to eradicate Zoribiatus. I've never felt less capable of anything in my life. Leaving the Northern Laboratories was a simple task by comparison. It was a safe bet under the security of Shelby's constant guidance and direction.

I believed Shelby could do it and I could help, but the intention has always been for me to do the heavy lifting.

I fight the swelling panic, reminding myself we haven't lost everything. I'm holding the cure in my hands. Jorey is alive and laughing in the other room, thanks to Cain, and we've reconnected with the dissenters. Dunn's death was an unavoidable tragedy. There's no way to know if we did the right thing keeping him with us.

A gentle breeze wafts across the open tundra. It blows through the fine woven material of my clothing, chilling me and rustling the papers of Shelby's notebook. A loose page breaks free from the binding, wafting away from the patio steps and dancing above the color-splattered expanse of wildflowers. I stand abruptly to chase after it, clutching the notebook and letter in one hand, too afraid of what might happen if I leave the precious tome unattended.

I maneuver through the poppies and fireweed, stepping around the thick clusters of white-petaled dogwood and furry paintbrush, waving the papers like a fan to brush aside the bees who are busy at work in the peak of the short summer, preparing for the inevitable storms. My boots sink into the gravelly topsoil, gripping against the loose pack as I whip around the accumulation of rapid summer growth. The quick movements send a family of ptarmigan scurrying for new cover.

I catch up to the paper as it blows against a bloom of fireweed just before the creek. I pull the sheet up, suppressing the curse that hangs at my lips. I don't think I could survive losing the cure again. Then I notice the state of the rescued page. The ink of Shelby's writing bleeds into the paper, spreading until the black stretches out into tendrils of pink and purple. Words bleed together into distorted images of complex molecules, forever illegible on the transformed page.

How many pages are like this? I reopen the notebook, careful not to test the limits of the distressed binding any further, flipping through page after page of information. About three quarters of the way in, the ink bleeds through. The two sides of each page compete for dominance as the water damage increases until I don't dare risk pulling still-wet paper apart.

It's not too terrible, I try to console myself, sinking into the sweet spears of pink fire. Once the pages dry, I'm certain that, with careful study, I can decipher the wreckage and recreate the work…

I blink away the sour disappointment stinging at the corners of my eyes, watching broken pieces of ice travel across the surface of the creek, which is likely only a narrow finger of the larger river. The ice glows in the bright summer sunlight as it melts into the water. I ponder the process—hydrogen and oxygen bound in position and vibrating with increasing energy until they are flowing freely, one at a time, millions at a time, transferring energy as they go. I wonder how many times an individual molecule is thawed and refrozen along its journey before the temperature is finally high enough to thaw all the surface ice.

The fireweeds wobble on their stems, bid into action by the perpetual breeze of the open land at the base of the forest. I watch them, noting that the blooms have reached the top of the stalks. There's an old saying that by the time the fireweed blooms reach the top, the summer is done, and the next snow is whispering its promise from the distance. Summer is already at its close, and the river's surface ice hasn't thawed. The bees hurry through their short lives in a frantic bid for survival, pulling pollen from the brief burst of growth to provide for the generations that will live in the next thaw.

I let out a breath, considering my own place in the larger dissenter movement. The Northern Laboratories burned bright, a brilliant summer flame before the return of a long winter. Perhaps I'm only meant to move in the sun, so the next generation survives.

My fingers brush across the edge of Shelby's letter again. *Only you have the ability to bring this cure…* Shelby intended for me to survive the winter and rise again.

If only she'd bothered to tell me how I'm supposed to do it! I shake my head, rising from the dancing stocks of flowers to return to the home-stead. The notebook needs to be dried before it can be restored. At least I know what our next steps should be. I need Amos. Once we're reunited, she can tell me the rest. I won't have to recreate Shelby's master work alone.

Once we make it to Green's management facility, I'll have my answers. Never mind that the task of getting that far south without being detected or captured is nearly impossible. We can make plans after I help Dó with the reactors.

I urge you to use caution where he is concerned… Shelby's words nag at me. She didn't trust Cain. But Cain's the only reason we've made it this far. He's the reason Jorey's alive. How can I possibly give him anything other than my allegiance?

I stop at the top of the stairs long enough to loosen my boot laces. I can hear the merry voices through the thick wooden siding, Cain obviously being the source of the laughter. Before opening the door, I tuck Shelby's letter of warning into the pocket of my glove with my other treasured items. There's no need for Cain to know he's been called into suspicion. I'll talk to Simons about it and find out what his sources know that Shelby's didn't. If nothing else, he can put my mind at ease. After all, he chose Cain for his team. He wouldn't have done that if there were any reason to be concerned.

I open the door to the sound of laughter, content with my decision.

CHAPTER
TWENTY-FIVE

"WE'LL LEAVE BEFORE full light. If we move quickly, we'll be long out of range before they realize we're gone," Simons says, looking over Shelby's message in the dim light of the back room.

"Are you sure that's what's best? It doesn't feel right. Just because there's some internal conflict doesn't make either of them our enemy," I say, leaning on the wall next to him.

"I don't think it's worth taking any chances. You've seen how Cain's been since we left—especially with Dunn," Simons says.

"But was he wrong?" I snap.

Simons watches me over the top of the note with a peculiar expression before letting out a long sigh. "Mason, I get where you're coming from, and I can't deny that Cain's been a big help getting us this far, but—"

"A big help? He *saved* Jorey's life. He's the reason we've made it this far. I don't want to throw all that away based on a letter that doesn't even say there's something wrong with him. What about your sources? They must've said something to make you choose him for the team." I press my hand against my forehead in exasperation.

Simons shrugs. "I only got word he's been among the dissenters for years. That's the only sort of information I get. Shelby's contacts are a lot higher up."

"And even she doesn't explicitly say he's up to something," I point out.

"What about the lies? What about this thing about his mother being a scientist? What about this reactor ruse Dó's putting on?" he presses.

I want to pull my hair out in frustration. Simons and I don't usually disagree like this. "I don't know yet, but I'm sure we can figure it out!"

The knock on the door sends a bolt of electricity through my whole body. I whip my head around in the same moment Simons makes Shelby's note disappear. Dó sticks his head through the door, a dark tuft of hair falling out of place over his dark eyes as he peers in. I can't help but feel as though I've been caught in something.

"It's time, Mason," Dó says.

I force a smile. *Act calm*, I admonish myself, standing to join Dó. He can't know I suspect anything. "Of course. Let's do this."

I look back to see Simons still leaning against the wall. He's watching me, deep in his own thoughts about our situation. He wants to break clean from Cain's questionable intentions and suspicious contacts. He wants to protect me—and the cure. I don't know why I can't give him that.

As I pass through the doorway to follow Dó to the mudroom, Simons calls after me. "Mason!"

I bite my lower lip before turning back to meet his gaze.

"You be careful in there tonight. It's been a long time since you were home," he says. I don't miss the true intention of his words.

"I promise I'll be careful," I tell him, then turn to catch up with Dó.

I pull the safety vest over my thick canvas jacket, uneasy with the fit of the heavy material. Dó isn't a particularly large man, but the vest still bulges around my arms and hangs below my torso after I tighten the straps, making movement awkward. I run my hands across the edge, making certain the pulsar gun doesn't show obviously through the layers and that I have quick access to it, just in case.

"Well, that looks like a near fit!" Dó nods cheerfully at me, pulling the thick hood of his jacket up over his ears.

"It probably fits about as well as the old ones did," I admit, brushing the front of it nervously. My hands fall to my sides, pausing. "Are we ready?"

"Yes, we better get to it," Dó agrees, opening the door.

As we walk around the back of the house, Dó's hand brushes absently along a thickly corded rope pinned between the cabin and the reactor facility. Every few meters, a rusted metal pole sticks out of the ground, propping the rope up.

"What this for?" I ask, mimicking his fingers as they trace the surface.

"It's a guide-line, for the stormy season. It's a very clever old trick —as old as settlement. Frontiersmen would put them up so they could get the livestock in the barns even during a blizzard. It's served me well more than a few times," he explains, clearly pleased with the usefulness of the ancient mechanism.

"That's clever," I agree, stepping aside so he can unlock the doors to the facility.

"I'll need you to man the secondary reactor—get the cooling sequence running before the strike, if you would," he says. The identification pad beeps, granting him entry.

I step into the concrete structure ahead of him, immediately affronted by the thickness of humid air, warmer than the house with the energy of the system. Dó secures the door behind us. As it locks, I'm filled with the sensation of being trapped inside the sweltering structure, the temperature making the walls loom far too close for comfort. I immediately wish I'd put the vest on under the jacket instead of the other way around, but I don't dare switch my layers and risk revealing the gun.

"Are you doing alright?" Dó asks, pulling my attention back to him. He's hung his parka on a metal pin next to the door, clearly versed in the conditions of the room.

"I'm adjusting. I'll be alright," I say.

"You have time to change while I open the system," he offers, accessing the identification panel to scan in like we used to do back at home. He inputs his code, and the database scans his hand. When the panel turns green, the station lights up so he can record measurements and make adjustments.

"No, I'm sure I'll be fine. It's a quick in and out anyway, right?" I ask, trying to shrug off my discomfort.

"It should be. You better get to it." He offers me the secondary screen in the back corner of the little room. I step around him, past the concrete slab that holds the hardware for the system's engines. I lift my hand so that it's suspended in front of the green-backed screen for the secondary system, noting the glow as it reflects off my skin, before calling up the system settings for the cooling vent procedure.

We work in tandem without speaking, tapping through the operations to send the parameters to record. When that's done, I pause, staring blankly at the screen, unable to remember the shortcut into the operations system. I never could, no matter how many times Bruce walked me through it. Unable to think of a better way, I pull up the schematics for the reactor to access the cooling protocol the same way I used to. The reactor blueprint is white with fine blue lines against the green background, simultaneously familiar and foreign. The system is state of the art compared to the operating software.

"Your reactor is only at 40%," I remark as the sweat drips down the sides of my face and my pulse picks up. I turn to watch Dó as he sets his vents into sequence.

"I told you the systems up here are older. They can't handle much more than that without leaking. I believe you had better coolant?" Dó looks over at me, then back at his station.

Better coolant. He's referring to Hank's invention. But how would he know about that? And why would he lie about the age of his reactors? "The schematics here are of a modern system," I say, gesturing at the screen.

"Oh, come now, that can't be right," he says, leaving his system to look at my screen.

Unease builds inside of me, amplified by the oppressive heat. I look at the blueprint one more time to assure myself I'm not wrong. The system is clearly up to date. I select the venting sequence on the screen as I force the words past my lips, "How do you know I used to live on an energy management facility?"

He's standing right behind me, so close his hot breath tickles at my hair. He's looking at the schematics of his up-to-date system, unable to deny their existence. There's no going back now. Dó is painfully aware that his absentminded statements about my past haven't gone unnoticed. I swallow, dizzy from the oppressive heat and growing alarm. It's too late to reach for the pulsar gun. My only chance to get out of this situation is to confront him head on.

CHAPTER
TWENTY-SIX

I WHIRL AROUND SO my body is positioned diagonally to his, making sure I'm not backed up against the screen. I glance down from Dó's stony expression to the old-world handgun with its barrel pointed straight at me. The sweat coating my body turns cold. My hands tingle, and my heart picks up speed.

"What is that thing?" I whisper, both curious and desperate to stall long enough to come up with a plan.

"It's a 357 Magnum pistol I restored from the wreckage of the old world. Fast, loud and just as deadly as the pulsar gun you've got stashed under your coat, so I wouldn't even try for it if I were you," he says, keeping his body square and his hand trained on me.

"I wasn't planning on it," I say, bringing my hands up so my elbows are bent close to my body in a position that could be mistaken for surrender.

"Then you're a smart girl, Kara Mason, maybe even as smart as everyone claims," he says. The corner of his mouth ticks up slightly in response to my hands, and he relaxes into his advantage.

"What do you want?" I ask, forcing my muscles to relax. I sink down to my knees, which are bent under my body. One foot points directly at Dó, while the other points at the wall to my left.

"Only to protect the cause. We've invested far too much to risk losing it to a careless interloper," he answers.

My heart sinks. He isn't a dissenter. It was right in front of me the whole time. Frances figured it out the moment we arrived and tried to warn me, but I didn't want to hear it any more than I wanted to believe Shelby's warning about Cain. I force myself not to react. At least now I don't have to feel badly for what I might have to do to him. I keep my eyes on his but don't lose sight of the barrel while I wait for the right moment.

"Is this the part where you shoot me and tell everyone I ran off?" I ask.

"Not until I get some answers," Dó corrects.

I raise my eyebrow, curious if Dó is stalling for time or if he actually wants information. If he wants something specific, it could be an opportunity to learn something.

"What do you want to know?"

"Who got to you?" Dó slides his foot toward me, intent on pushing me back.

"No one," I say. If he thinks he's going to get me to give up Amos that easily, he's nuts.

"Do you expect me to believe you decided to abandon Infection Science on a whim?" His eyes flash with anger. Small beads of sweat form on his brow, begging to be wiped away. I catch the slight motion of his hand—the dip in the barrel as the trickle of sweat makes its way around the corner of his eye.

I strike quickly, knowing this may be my only chance. The assault successfully catches him off guard. As my legs collide into him, my left hand flashes out, forcing the gun away. He manages to not lose his grip as we both fall to the ground. My knees smack against the concrete floor as Dó's body gives under me with a fast exhale. Even though I have the advantage, I know I have to get to my feet again. *A fight on the ground is a fight lost.*

I make one last attempt to force the gun out of Dó's hand. He uses the shift in balance from my outstretched hand to throw me off. My body makes impact with the wall, causing the straps on the vest to come loose. Before I can recover, Dó launches at me, bringing the weapon back to his center. I throw my foot out, making contact with his wrist and sending the gun flying across the room toward the bolted door. I'm on my knees when Dó sends out his own leg, knocking me back against the wall.

Get up! My mind screams as my arms tangle in the vest. Dó turns to retrieve the gun. I throw myself forward, grabbing his legs. He topples forward, his face barely missing the slab. Scrambling, I worm my way out of the vest and find my feet. Strands of soaked hair stick to my forehead and the sides of my face as I pant against the heavy air, positioning myself to keep Dó on the ground. I put one heavy boot on his shoulder on the inside of his collarbone at the crook of his neck. If I snapped the bone here, he would risk severing his carotid artery.

"Did Cain set you up to this?" I demand, ignoring the urge to grab the pulsar gun. I can't be distracted.

"Of course not!" Dó pants, keeping his body still against the pressure of my boot.

"Then who!" I demand.

"Nobody! I'm protecting the cause," he yelps against the pressure.

The green screens flicker with yellow and red light. A piercing buzz emanates from the center slab, where the grid bar surges into the red. The floors of the station shake as both systems vent superheated steam through the filters. The power surge tugs at my attention. Why would the power surge? Unless someone really did destroy a reactor—

Dó grabs my leg with both hands, turning his body away with all his strength. My knee impacts the ground with a burst of bright pain. A stifled groan escapes me as he continues his roll, pulling my leg until I lose the rest of my balance and pitch forward. I'm so distracted by the pain, I nearly miss breaking my fall. My arm flies out at the last second before my head makes impact, causing my cheek to glance against the rough concrete. Heat rakes across the side of my face where the sting of sweat mingles with fresh blood. Then he's on me. One knee pressed across my chest, forcing air from my lungs with crushing weight as he holds both of my hands over my head.

"Why did you abandon the original plan? A lot of good people put themselves on the line to get you in that position!" he yells.

His words blur in my mind as I struggle to fill my lungs in defiance of his crushing weight. I can't out-muscle him. He has the advantage, keeping his body centered and holding my arms and legs out of balance. Though he has me pinned, we're at a draw. He's lost his weapon and can't retrieve it without releasing me. All I can do is stall.

"I don't know what you think I did," I wheeze.

"I know who you betrayed," he says, shifting more of his weight against my wrists. I wait.

"More people than you realize," I hiss, thinking of Tucker and hoping to rile him up further.

"Then you burn down the Northern Laboratories and put the whole thing in danger. Who put you up to it?" he grunts, hands slipping against the thick canvas jacket.

I twist my arm free, thrusting my head forward until it impacts with his nose. He flies backwards, grimacing in pain, allowing me to throw his body the rest of the way off me. Instead of trying to overpower him, I jump to my feet, relying on the wisdom of higher ground.

"It was Shelby's idea to leave," I say, reaching into my coat to pull out the pulsar gun.

My vision turns white as a hot burst of pain erupts across my left hamstring and I fall backward. Dó's arms wrap around me like a vice, forcing the pulsar gun flush with my chest, rendering it useless as we roll across the floor.

"I don't believe you! She knew you backed out," Dó grumbles through the effort of his hold as I kick at the inside of his thigh, aiming for the tender place where the ligament attaches to the tibia.

I make contact, but my foot only glances across the spot, lacking the force needed to incapacitate him. I manage to get one hand free, thrusting it over my shoulder to gouge his eye.

"I didn't back out of anything. All I was supposed to do was keep my head down and stay safe," I say as my fingers rake across his face.

Dó throws me forward, his body slamming against mine. My hand lurches forward, away from his face, but still free of his unrelenting grasp.

"Amos gave you your assignment. You revealed yourself the moment you abandoned her for hive studies!"

His hands move, searching for a better grip. I force my body forward, grinding his hands into the concrete until he releases. I twist to the left, breaking free. I roll once more, choosing the gun instead of my feet. Dó rights himself only to find the pulsar gun pointed at his head.

He's beaten now, and he knows it. He lets his body fall back against the casing for the secondary system. His head rolls from side to side in distress as the ridge of his nose purples from the harsh impact. "Just tell me why. Who got to you?" He spits blood.

"No one! I did it on my own," I yell, wincing against the ache of my pummeled body as all the fury of the last few years pours into the sweltering room.

"Why?" he asks, his voice quieter now.

"I couldn't keep hiding while everyone else died. I needed to know who killed my family," I say. Absently, I wonder if this is the first time I've spoken those words out loud.

"*You* did," Dó moans, his head still lolling.

"I didn't! We didn't mean to pass the test!" I scream, flipping the switch so the gun cycles through its power.

"What happened to them? Why didn't you make it to the check point?" he asks, pitching forward onto his knees.

"I tried to save them but… but there were too many!" My hands shake against the gun as my head spins, threatening to let the past crash into the present.

"Too many?" he asks, confused. He rises to his feet.

"The hive…" I whisper, still frozen as he takes his first step toward me.

"Impossible. You couldn't have survived." He takes another step toward me.

"Don't move!" I say, pulling the pulsar gun into my body.

"No one survives a hive attack." He moves again, ignoring my warning.

I pull the trigger, sending a burst of energy into the concrete wall. The building shakes as the exterior splits, and dust rains down, filling the air with a chalky haze. "I said, don't move."

"You might as well tell me what really happened. You're going to kill me anyway, aren't you?"

"Shelby saved me. She should have let me die with them. No matter what she wanted to believe, it wasn't worth it," I admit, sick with the memory. Along with it comes the realization of the plan Dó thought I backed out of.

You were always meant to bring the cure out of the Northern Laboratories. Shelby's looping, meticulous handwriting taunts me.

Dó stops his progression to study me. My head feels too large in the stifling room. The pulsar gun shakes in my hand. I watch it quiver as I point it at Dó. Dó, who really is a member of the dissenters but thinks I'm the traitor.

I let the gun fall to my side, suddenly weak and overwhelmed. *We don't kill the living.* I won't kill him. Not over a misunderstanding.

Dó stands motionless in front of me. The purple has spread from the ridge of his nose to pool under his eyes like dark shadows. He extends his hand toward me. "Mason, I was wrong."

The gun clatters to the ground at my feet. I leave it there and peel off the canvas jacket, suddenly needing it gone. "I'm sorry, Dó. I thought you were working for Orman."

He lets out a high-pitched chuckle, taking the jacket from me. "What on earth made you think that?"

"Shelby. She said I shouldn't trust Cain—well, she wrote it anyway," I say.

Dó laughs again, hanging my canvas jacket next to his and stooping to pick up the old pistol. "That's ridiculous! His mother practically ran the dissenters. The boy might be a bit headstrong, but he's loyal."

He offers me a strip of cloth from his pocket. I accept it, watching as he uses another to wipe away the blood dripping from his nose. "Did I break it?" I ask.

"Probably." He shrugs, still chuckling to himself. "I can't believe I thought you were a spy."

"Not a spy, just an idiot," I say, dabbing the cloth against the scrapes on my face.

"Don't be so hard on yourself," he says, moving over to the massive crack in the concrete wall.

"I'm sorry about that," I say, my cheeks warming.

"We'll say it happened during the power surge." He winks over his smile as if our fight were nothing more than a child's scuffle.

"How many people are in trouble?" I ask, keenly aware their lives are as much my responsibility as the cracked concrete wall.

"Dissenters have always enjoyed a level of invisibility in the eyes of the government. Sure, they know we exist, but they've always believed us too small to pose any real risk. Not anymore. Now they know we're on the inside."

My stomach twists. Dó studies my reaction with knowing silence. He pats me on the shoulder. "Come on. Let's get patched up before someone comes looking for us and wonders what happened."

TWENTY-SEVEN

"I'M sure Amos had her reasons. And I'm sure she'll explain everything when you see her," Dó says, offering his hand so I can crawl through the window to his back room.

Standing on aching legs, I look around, amazed. The walls are lined with an astounding display of weapons. Just near the door, Dó has dozens of lashing poles lined up and organized by size and age. Beyond that, a case displaying a dizzying array of pulsar and energy laser guns—the most standard-issue weapons in the world. In addition to these, there are various energy cartridges and receivers, launchers, energy orbs—grenade-like balls that blast gamma radiation or heat the air to plasma. There's a technician station in the middle of the room with a computing unit and various tools. The last wall is covered with thin, metallic-looking hollow rings of various sizes.

I turn again to study the weaponry, distracted by the magnitude of the collection. I smirk, thinking about what Orman's reaction to this room might be—*Fury? Jealousy? Academic glee?* It's uplifting to know the dissenters are so well equipped.

"Why can't you tell me what the plan is?" I ask him.

"Because I don't know the whole plan. It's too dangerous to communicate that sort of thing," he says.

"That's not very helpful," I grumble, walking over to strange metallic rings glimmering against the bland white of the walls. "What are these for?"

Dó smiles broadly as he digs into his medic kit. I touch one of the rings, expecting it to be rigid. It buckles like a thin sheet of cloth. I pull my hand away, startled, but then try to grasp at the quivering foil.

"Impressive, isn't it?" Dó remarks, standing with an arm-full of aid, watching as I attempt to catch the ring. "One single layer of conductive metal—almost invisible—strong like diamond, but pliable. You can fold it into your sack so long as you're careful not to lose it."

"And it's for…?" I prod, still marveling at the shimmering ring of metal.

"Multiple uses. There's an input here where you can load a cartridge or an energy orb. Fling it out, and it will catch and conduct the hit in a very specific area, very highly concentrated. You can slice through granite with the right cartridge. Or you can load a receiver and generate a miniature force field. I haven't had a chance to test their maximum strength yet, but they're very powerful. Come here, I've got something for your face," he says, pulling me away from the rings.

My eyes water from the stringent salve, but it offers instant relief to the burning wounds. "Is this stuff going to cure your black eyes?" I ask with an apologetic smile.

"I'm afraid not, but it will take down the swelling," he says, blinking against the fumes as he spreads the ointment across his nose.

"How did you know I grew up on an energy management facility? Was that part of the dissenter information network?" I ask. He rubs another dose of the stuff into the back of his hands.

"Not exactly. But I did know your parents—remotely, that is," he explains.

"Were you his contact? Did you arrange the coyote—I mean, Simons?" I ask.

"No, I wasn't involved in your father's exodus, but I was in charge of getting them settled in their position at the facility."

"I thought Amos placed them," I say, confused. Dó gestures for me to roll up my pant leg. I follow his instruction, revealing my swollen knee.

"Amos was instrumental in their placement, but her involvement from there was limited by necessity." Dó rubs the ointment onto my knee, working from the outside in.

"Do you know who all the energy management dissenters are?" I ask.

"Not all of them, but a lot of them," he says, putting the ointment back into the med kit. He takes out a small tube, opening it so that little white pills tumble out into his palm. "Do you want one of these?"

"Sure." I take one, rolling it between my finger and thumb. "How many vital positions do the dissenters occupy?"

He opens his mouth to answer, but at that very moment, the hall light switches on. Dó shuts his mouth, bringing his finger to his lips. The whole point of sneaking through the back window was to avoid having to explain the mess we created. I hold my breath, waiting for the muffled sound of a door opening to signal the exit of the late-night visitor. The dark shadows of feet break apart the strip of light coming from the bottom of the door as someone approaches and stops.

"Is that you, Dó?" Cain asks, twisting the doorknob so the beam of light turns into an arc.

"It's me, Eli. We'll talk in the morning," Dó calls back. As he scrambles onto his feet to block the door, he knocks the med kit over, spilling the contents so they clatter across the floor. He presses against the door as Cain's bare foot appears.

"What are you doing? Let me in," Cain says in a too-loud voice, forcing the door the rest of the way.

"Not now, Eli, it's really not a good—"

Cain bursts through, knocking Dó to the ground. He grunts with the impact, and I wince, knowing how much it must hurt. Cain takes in the dried blood smeared on Dó's swollen face.

"Did Mason beat you up?" His eyes travel from Dó's battered face to mine before repeating the sequence as though he needed more visual input to process the situation. "Did you beat up Mason?" His voice is so loud it makes us both react with frantic shushing, afraid to create an even bigger spectacle.

"It's fine. There was a complication with the surge on the power grid that caused an incident with the reactors," he says.

"That's a load of crap! Tell me what really happened," he demands, helping Dó back onto his feet.

"It was just a misunderstanding," I say, rushing to close the door. Before I can get my hands on the door, Simons is in the entryway, swinging it the rest of the way into the room. I force a curse back from my lips by biting my tongue, preparing for the chaos that's about to ensue.

"I've been waiting half the night for you to come back—" He stops mid-sentence, taking in my bruises and scrapes. His eyes harden into dark, glistening specks, radiating anger. His palms rise up against his heaving frame, coiling into rigid weapons. "Where is he?"

Words fall from my mouth as I scramble toward him, desperate to ease his murderous intent. "Simons, it's fine. Everything is fine. There was a complica—"

He pushes me aside with gentle ease. Cain whirls to confront him, leaving Dó to temporarily sway without support.

"Easy there, brother!" Cain says, placing his hands against Simons' chest.

Simons shoves him. "Don't you dare tell me to be easy! You don't have the sort of sway around here you think you do, boy!"

"Simons! Please!" I yell, reaching out to pull him back.

"What did you do to Kara!" he yells, ignoring me. I haven't heard him use my given name since we first arrived at the Institute.

"What did we do? What did she do? Did you get a look at Dó's face?" Cain counters, stepping into Simons and blocking his path to Dó.

The commotion draws the rest of the group into the room. Frances stares, wide-eyed. "Mason. What happened to you?"

Richards steps past her, heading straight for Simons. His nose is scrunched up as he squints, glasses-less and sleepy, at the altercation. "Simons, come on, step back. Let's talk this through," he urges.

I turn to Jorey, desperate and frustrated. "Can you help Richards calm him down?"

Jorey looks from me to Cain and Dó, then at Simons. He returns his focus to me. "No. Simons has his reasons."

My mouth drops. Behind me, Simons is shouting, "She trusted you."

I leave Jorey without another word, inserting myself back into the situation as Richards loses his grip on Simons' arm. I wedge myself between Simons and Cain. They're standing so close I have to lean into Cain to look up at Simons' face. "Will you let me explain?" I ask, trying to keep my voice calm.

Cain relaxes against my back, signaling his confidence in my ability to diffuse the situation. He steps back to put his arm around Dó, who looks dazed and scared in the shadow of Simons' wrath.

"Who struck first?" Simons asks, finally stepping back. Richards attempts to place a calming hand against his arm, which Simons shrugs off.

"It's more complicated than that." I watch the tension build again and scramble to dispel it. "Technically I did. I struck Dó first."

"What the hell?" Cain asks, turning an angry stare toward me.

"Don't blame her, Eli. I pulled a gun on her," Dó implores.

"You what?" Simons raises his voice.

"It was a misunderstanding!" I snap before the situation can escalate again. "Dó thought I was working with the government."

Cain smacks Dó on the back of the head. "What were you thinking?"

"She went against Amos' direct instructions," Dó explains.

"It was an accident!" Simons defends me.

"We've been through this!" I raise my voice to silence them again. Simons pulls his lips in so his mouth is a small line, looking to me to finish. "When Dó pulled the gun on me, I thought the same about him, and I attacked."

"How could you be so stupid?" Cain looks down at Dó, shaking his head.

"We have very specific plans, and she went off of them," Dó says.

"And you didn't think to run it by me first?" Cain asks.

"I wasn't sure. You two looked…" He looks between us. "Close," he finishes.

A hot rush of embarrassment sweeps over me as I digest his words. I can feel everyone's eyes settle on me, and I rush to resolve the statement. "Cain's become indispensable to our cause. If it weren't for his knowledge of the tunnels, we couldn't have made it this far."

"What about Shelby?" Simons asks, raising his eyebrows as he stares at me.

"What about Shelby?" Cain responds, looking quizzically between us.

"She was wrong," I insist. Everyone is watching us now.

"How do you know?" Simons asks.

I glance at Cain. I could tell Simons why he went to the Northern Laboratories and end the argument now, but his secret isn't mine to tell. "I know," I insist. "You're just going to have to trust me."

"It's hard when you aren't giving me anything to go on," Simons says, rubbing the side of his head.

"You've done it before," I remind him.

He lets out a long, hard breath. "And Dó?" he asks after a long pause.

"We can trust him. He knew my parents," I tell Simons, deciding that this information is fine to share.

"That doesn't necessarily mean anything," he bites back.

"It proves he's a dissenter," I argue.

"Life isn't made up of dissenters and government agents. It's more complicated. Not that I expect you to understand. You're just a kid."

His eyes widen with realization as the words escape his lips. His mouth closes a moment too late. Frances catches her breath. It's the only sound in a shockingly silent, tension-filled room. I glare at him, hollow. His hands fall to his sides, and I pull away from the center of the confrontation.

Simons licks his lips, searching for the right thing to say. "Mason, I—"

"We're staying. We can trust them, and that's my final word on it." I cut him off, not ready to hear an apology. I brush past Jorey on my way out of the room without making eye contact.

CHAPTER
TWENTY-EIGHT

TWO DAYS after the fusion reactor incident, Dó received word the DDC officially moved the search into the cities after a *sighting* inside the west boundary. It's the last message received from dissenters inside the DDC.

"By the old management facility?" I ask, not quite daring to call it *home*.

"We thought it would be fitting," Dó agrees, adding, "If we can make it look like you're sticking to what you know, we hope they'll keep the focus on you rather than flushing out your accomplices."

It's a stern reminder of what the dissenters have lost. It's not just dissenters in the DDC. Communication from within government institutions has gone dark, leaving Dó and everyone else on the outside scrambling for alternative sources.

"How long do you suppose we have until they realize they've been had?" Richards asks, rising to help Dó clear the dishes from the cluttered table.

"They won't quit looking for us up here, no matter what they think is happening in the cities," Simons says, reaching across a stack of cartridges to correct Frances' count. He's apologized since calling me a child, and I believe he didn't mean it—or didn't *mean* to mean it. We're fine now, but things aren't the same.

"No," Dó agrees, precariously balancing mugs on a stack of plates. "But we've made them divide resources, which gives you a chance."

"That doesn't answer the question, Dó. How long before they realize Mason isn't taking a field trip home?" Cain presses, not looking up from his overstuffed pack.

"A week. Maybe less if we can't get communication from the inside back up," Dó says. The look on his face is uncharacteristically grim.

A week. It isn't much time for the one-hundred-sixty-kilometer trek south along the coast to our next checkpoint.

"Of course, none of that matters if we walk into a bad patch in the research zone," Cain says, giving up trying to fit one more meal kit into the front pocket. He tosses the packet toward Jorey, but Frances snatches it out of the air with a stern look.

"These are supplies, not toys," she scolds.

"Research zones?" I ask.

"An open area the government controls where natural resources are harvested. There are always near-dead," Dó explains.

"That's where the stories come from," Cain pipes in.

Dó waits a beat to make sure he's said his piece before continuing. "The research zone is a gigantic crater filled with volcanic vents. There's plenty of forest, but there are also large expanses of open area. The geothermal facility is just on the other side, and that's where you'll meet Max."

"Our savior's name is Max?" Cain muses, looking for something to do. He reaches for the stack of meal kits in front of Simons.

"Don't ask him for more. He'll deny ever having a surname—say the government couldn't label him if they tried," Dó confirms.

"At least we'll be prepared if we run into trouble," Richards says, taking in the multitude of weaponry we've yet to pack. We have access to every piece of technology and weaponry Dó's amassed in his time as a waystation for the dissenter network.

"It doesn't compare to keeping off the DDC's radar, but it's the best we can do," Dó says.

We finish organizing and packing our supplies, chatting idly until Dó makes his day-end journey to the reactors. We set up our sleeping quarters for the last time, our supplies laid out by the door for a departure at sunrise.

Simons switches the light off as the last of the conversation fades away. I try to convince myself sleep will come, but as minutes transform into hours, I begin to lose hope. Cain's description of the research zone worms its way through my thoughts, unwelcome. *"They'll flood an area with near-dead and watch as they tear everyone to shreds."*

His explanation is too familiar. A hive trickling in from the woods or over hilltops, scrambling in unison and leaving no path for escape… and behind it, Orman watching on a simulation screen, victorious in his hunt.

I toss and turn on the floor, unable to shut my mind off. Every time I close my eyes, Dunn approaches, laughing Orman's windy, wheezy laugh as he thrusts diseased hands toward me. I force the nightmare out, and it's replaced by a hive, waiting in ambush for us in the volcanic lands. It's hard to hide in the open.

I force myself to do mental inventory of our weaponry as though I'm counting sheep: *pulsar guns, rings, energy orbs, coded maps…* My mind is jarred by images of torn flesh and meaty pieces between teeth, wet and red—

I sigh, tossing my blanket aside. *I'll pace the hallway until dawn.* I maneuver quietly through the maze of sleeping bodies, trying not to disturb anyone's final night of rest. Someone whispers in the darkness. I turn, expecting to see Jorey.

"I didn't think I was snoring that loudly." Cain's quiet but distinctively sarcastic words shatter the anxious barrier I've built around myself.

"I can't sleep," I whisper.

"Aw. I miss you too," he taunts.

Warmth rushes to my cheeks as I recall our first night here—the last time we had a chance to be close—before Shelby's letter and the unending chain of distractions and disruptions.

I plop down next to him, thankful for the distraction. "I'm worried I'm about to get us all killed."

"Why would you do a thing like that? I thought we were all starting to get along," he says. I know he meant for it to be a joke, but he's right. Simons only just started looking at Cain in a way that doesn't make me think he's about to throw him up against a wall.

"I'm afraid I'll lead us into a hive and have to watch everyone get torn to shreds," I clarify.

"To shreds?" Cain asks in mock-concern. "Sounds like you're hungry to me."

He stands, offering his hand. I take it and we step over the last snoozing mass between us and the kitchen. Cain pulls the divide shut and flicks a switch, filling the kitchen with a soft yellow light. We're alone again for the first time. Releasing my hand, he moves over to the pantry and starts shuffling through the contents.

"What are you doing?" I ask.

"Whenever I'm having fantasies about near-dead," he explains, pulling out an unlabeled can and setting it on the counter, "it usually means I'm hungry. Simple connection—near-dead eat people because they're hungry. We think about near-dead eating people because *we're* hungry. Basic psychology."

I smirk, and he emerges from the pantry holding an onion and a potato. He dumps them with the can and moves over to the cold box to dig out more treasures. "Is this what you meant when you said you could help me?" I wrinkle my nose.

"No. You need way more than a solid meal to pull you out of the mind-scrambling mess the government created. But I've always been an expert when it comes to simple psychology," he brags, retrieving a tray of eggs. "Being good at stuff is sort of my thing."

He pulls something else out of the cold box—a white block. "For example," he narrates, "do you know what this is?"

"Agar?" I guess, thinking the milky-white block would look more at home in a lab.

"What? No—it's cheese."

"Authentic cheese? From *real* milk?" I ask, amazed such a thing still exists. I've never had anything but the salty, oil-pressed stuff that comes in orange stacks. "Where did the milk come from? Nobody manufactures cheese anymore."

"Dó does," Cain says as he pulls the cloth back from a corner of the block. "He domesticated a herd of wild goats. Incredible what a guy will do for a little bit of company."

Cain hands me a small chunk he sliced from the exposed corner of the block. I bring it to my nose and inhale its earthy, pungent odor. "It actually *smells* creamy," I exclaim.

"Don't just smell it," Cain urges as he prepares a slice for himself. "Taste it!" He tips his slice toward mine in a gesture like a toast.

I imitate the motion before taking a small bite. My senses are overwhelmed by the cheese—tangy and sharp, earthy and creamy and salty all at once—unlike anything I've ever had before. "Why hasn't Dó shared any with us?"

"He likes to keep it secret," Cain explains. "It takes months, or years, or something to make just one hunk like this."

"Don't you sound like quite the cheese expert?" I smile as I relish in another nibble. The fake stuff gets it completely wrong.

"I guess I'm better at people stuff," Cain says, putting the knife down and focusing his attention on me.

"People stuff, eh?" I chuckle. I reach for another piece of cheese, and he snatches it from me with a mischievous look.

I reach for it again, and he leans back, forcing me to step into him. "Yep. I mean, look at how I smoothed things over between Simons and Dó," he says.

I grab the cheese and dodge his attempt to grab me. He catches me as I move to his left, swinging me around so the counter is at my back and he's standing in front of me, smiling and wrapping his hands around my wrists.

"Oh, was it you that stopped Simons from killing anyone? I thought it was me." I pop the cheese in my mouth before he can take it again.

He grasps the counter on either side of me, boxing me in. Our bodies are nearly touching. "Okay, that was you, but the rest was me," he says.

I grab both of his hands, attempting to pry them from the counter. He twists free and grabs my waist, pulling me in close. I look up at him, heart pounding with the thrill of closeness. "Cain." I breathe his name.

"What was it you told him to set him off, anyway?" he asks in a quiet voice. He's holding me so tightly I can feel his pulse… It races like mine. He moves his head toward mine, and I'm certain he's about to kiss me. I hold my breath, wondering what it will be like.

The rustle of the divide being pulled back brings us both out of the trance. I whirl around to face the door, still very close to Cain, who hasn't taken his hand away from my waist. Jorey enters, sliding the divide closed behind him.

"What's going on in here?" Jorey asks, looking from me to Cain.

"We were hungry," I blurt, louder than I intended. I'm not even sure I was. My ears burn hot from being caught with Cain like this. I don't know what I'd say to Jorey—I don't even know what to think for myself!

"Hungry?" Jorey asks skeptically. He observes the food spread out over the counter and stares directly at Cain's hand, still resting on my waist. "You're *never* hungry, Mason."

I pull myself free of Cain's hand self-consciously and pick up the potato, trying to look enthusiastic. Cain plucks the onion from the counter and turns it over in his hands thoughtfully.

"Mason said she was having visions of near-dead tearing us up and munching on her flesh. I deduced that she was experiencing suppressed cravings for a late-night snack." He tosses the onion over to Jorey, who catches it reflexively. "You know, psychology."

"Ri-ight," Jorey says, replacing the onion onto the counter.

"Right," I insist, a little too emphatically.

Jorey leans into the counter, settling himself in for the duration. "So," he says in a challenging tone, looking directly at Cain. "What are we having?"

"Cheese. And this stuff," Cain says, waving his arms with a flourish, completely dismissing Jorey's suspicions. He grabs a second potato.

While Cain busies himself with food preparations, I snitch another piece of cheese, pinching it with my fingers. I nibble at it, trying to cool my thoughts. The kitchen remains silent save for Cain's rhythmic potato chopping. The awkward tension is exaggerated by the silence, making it impossible to think straight.

"Where'd you learn to cook, Cain?" I ask, breaking the silence.

"I didn't spend my life eating in a cafeteria like you guys," Cain says, grabbing another potato.

"You know, we didn't spend our whole lives in the Northern Laboratories. You're not the only one with real-world skills," Jorey says defensively.

Cain looks up, amused. "Oh, I'm sorry, I didn't know you were thusly skilled." He moves away from the counter and holds his arms out. "By all means."

Jorey accepts Cain's challenge without a smile. He walks over to the other side of the counter and holds his hand out. Cain gives him the knife, stepping back to stand next to me. He bumps me as he leans against the opposite counter—purposefully, I suspect. Jorey glances over his shoulder at us as he grabs the onion.

"We can all cook," I say, abandoning my perch. "You can teach me!"

"You can't cook?" Cain asks, looking at me from the corner of his eye, keeping his gaze on Jorey.

"Nope," I say, wondering why I sound so proud of this confession.

"I can teach you—it's a piece of cake," Jorey offers, urging me over with his knife-less hand.

"A dainty lemon cake?" Cain teases.

"Just get over here," Jorey says, rolling his eyes.

I stand in between the two as they explain and demonstrate the merits of chopping and dicing, bickering over personal opinions. Cain has me crack eggs into a large bowl, and Jorey instructs me in the art of salting *just right*. We get the stove fired up with a little pop and add some rendered lard to the hot iron skillet. The smell of sizzling fat fills the kitchen, and I decide I am, in fact, quite hungry.

The divider rustles again, and Simons appears in the kitchen entryway. "What's cooking?" he asks, licking his lips.

"You're just in time," I offer with a broad smile, "I'm cooking my first meal."

"Sounds good to me," Simons says, studying everyone carefully. I glance away, unable to meet his searching gaze. Cain drops the potato in the skillet.

The sounds and smells of the early-morning breakfast stir the rest of our team from the other room, and Dó emerges, still wearing his sleeping cap and slippers. The kitchen fills with conversation, and the last of the awkward tension fades away. I'm just about to present my first ever kitchen creation when Dó stumbles over and notices the unwrapped block on the counter.

He moves in to investigate and cries out, "Hey! Who's been in my cheese?"

I bite my lower lip and glance guiltily at Cain as Dó prods gently at the indent mark made by my fingers. Cain winks at me and hushes my confession. Instead, he says, "Who cares? It's breakfast time!"

CHAPTER
TWENTY-NINE

IT DOESN'T TAKE LONG for the plan to go wrong. South of Dó's facility, the tunnels become precarious as noxious fumes leech away at the exposed surfaces. In some areas, the gases are so potent we don't have any other option but to head above ground.

We make our way cautiously overland in the fading northern summer light. The rising geothermal energy has caused all the snow and ice to melt, forming a stream that we follow into the caldera. The air thickens with the sulfurous stench of mineral deposits as we make our way deeper. We climb down another series of rocky slopes and are met with a mostly flat expanse like the tundra but warmer and humid. Steam rises from pools of heated spring water, the swirling vapor making the area glimmer with refractive beauty.

"We're here!" Cain says, pointing out the obvious.

"No kidding," Jorey hits back, eyes rolling into the back of his skull.

Richards and Simons plop down on the crater floor, exhausted. Muddy sweat trickles down Simons' forehead, mingling with the dirt smeared across his checks and neck. We're filthy from our stint in the tunnels. Frances joins them on the ground, dropping the pack off her shoulders and groaning as she sits next to Richards, who puts his hand on her neck and rubs gently. Jorey's pack makes a loud clunk as he drops it from a standing position and sits on the new summer grass. I consider joining them, loosening the straps on my own pack.

"Come on, guys," Cain urges. "We can't stop here. There's a good shelter just to the east of here. We can camp there for the evening and take up again in the morning."

Frances groans. "I'm not sure I can!"

"It's not safe to camp in the open," Cain warns.

"How much further?" Richards asks.

"Maybe another kilometer—a mile at most," Cain says.

Simons stands, pulling his pack onto his shoulders again. "Might as well," he says, letting out an exaggerated sigh. "We've come this far."

"You drive a hard pace," Richards says, allowing Frances to boost herself up using his shoulder for support. It seems like they're always touching these days.

I re-tighten the straps on my pack, wondering why no one else has mentioned anything. We move on in silence, taking in the spectacle of green grasses and bubbling springs that reek of sulfur. Several rodents scamper across the grounds, braving exposure for a new location. In the distance, a bird of prey sounds a hunter's screech. We make our way through some shrubbery and a thin scattering of trees to a brushy area near a small spring which bubbles out to the east where it connects with several others.

The water rushes on, seeking lower ground. The area is well sheltered by the vegetation. I suspect this is the place Cain's been driving us toward. A boulder towers over a patch of soft ground. The boulder is streaked with soot, suggesting it's been a chimney for more than one fire.

"Very nice, Cain," I say.

"Thanks, I sure think it's cozy," Cain says, plunking down his pack, signaling to the group that they can finally rest. They do so in earnest, stripping off their packs and jackets.

Frances shakes her jacket in disgust, saying, "Oh Lord, I'm filthy!"

"Why don't you wash off in the springs?" Cain suggests. "Just do it downstream from where you want to pull drinking water."

"What a brilliant idea!" Frances says, searching the springs for an ideal entry point.

"We should hunt tonight and maybe make something fresh for dinner," Cain suggests, seemingly full of energy.

"You can hunt. I'm going to stick to the shelter," Simons says.

"Sure, I'll hunt!" Cain proclaims.

"You're not done-in after that cave-in? Something is wrong with you." Simons leans over the stream, bringing a handful of water up to wash the grime away.

"I can hunt," I offer, ignoring my own fatigue for the opportunity to spend some solo time with Cain.

"Great!" Cain smiles. "You can come with me. We'll stake out a hot spring and bring something in."

"I'll go too," Jorey adds.

"You need to rest, Jorey," Richards says.

"I'm fine. I haven't had any trouble," Jorey insists.

"It's better to be cautious. Without a full diagnosis, we can't just assume you're fine," Richards explains.

"You should stay, Jorey. We've still got a long way to travel, and it would kill me to think we were pushing you too hard," I urge him, not wanting a repeat of the ruined moment in the kitchen.

Jorey studies me, his crinkled forehead streaked with mud. "Alright, Mason," he agrees.

I smile at him before turning to Cain, who is picking through his pack for a pulsar gun. He pulls one out and tosses it to me. "Come on, Mason, let's go get some dinner."

I grab the gun and fall in step with him.

"Just don't be gone too long, Mason. This is the research zone," Jorey says before shifting his gaze to glare at Cain. I wonder if Simons told Jorey about Shelby's message.

"Let's see if you're any better at bringing in dinner than you are at taking out Orman," Cain jabs as we make our way off from camp, following the stream.

"I could have," I say defensively, not wanting to admit I had him in my sights and didn't fire. "If I hadn't been so worried about you," I add. The joke is strange, but Cain doesn't question it.

We walk until we come to a steep drop-off where the water tumbles down the cliff in a series of cascades. Cain directs me to a gentle path that follows the cliff down to where the water collects in a large pool. The waterfall sprays a warm mist as we climb down, wetting the dirt caked into my hair, skin, and clothes, turning it back to mud. Cain hops down off the last boulder and lands so softly I can't hear the impact over the rush of the water.

"Jump down. I'll catch you if you fall," he calls back up to me.

My feet hit the ground with a thud as he grasps at my hand, bracing my landing. "I don't need you to catch me," I admonish.

"Sure you don't, but I can if I want," he says, wiping a clump of mud from my eyebrow. "You're filthy!"

"Have you seen yourself?" I grab a clump of mud from his scraggly hair and toss it at his face.

"Let's jump in," Cain suggests.

I consider the crystal-clear water, its stillness interrupted only by the influx of water from above. There's nothing I want more right now than to rinse away the thick layers of muck. "Sounds good to me," I agree.

"Great!" Cain smiles, wiping the mud from his face, leaving streak marks exposing his skin and beard.

He tosses his gun into the grass next to the pool before tearing off his jacket, throwing it into the water. He unclips his belt and tosses it in the grass next to the gun before un-holstering his lashing pole, adding it to the pile. Next, he unhooks the clasps to his pants.

"Are you sure you want to spend the night in wet clothes?" I ask, incredulously.

"These clothes aren't going to get themselves clean. We can throw on some city clothes for one night. I promise I'll keep you warm!" He winks, tossing his shoes into the pile and his pants into the pool.

I follow suit, tossing my weapons, shoes and belt into the pile and throwing my own mud-caked clothes into the pool. I toss my jacket, shirt and pants into the stream and pull the tie out of my hair before joining Cain.

"Whoa there, Mason!" Cain calls out as I nearly trip in our floating pile of muck.

"Mind your business," I say, scrambling free of the tangle to bury myself in deeper waters. "You better not be looking."

"Why not? We've already snuggled in our underwear," he argues, splashing water in my direction.

"That was different. You've got mud in your hair." I submerge myself.

Cain plunges his head into the warm, sulfurous waters, brushing his fingers through his hair until the water surrounding him turns murky. He re-emerges, looking nearly as clean as he did at Dó's. I hold my breath and plunge deep into the water, running my fingers through my hair to lose the mud and undo my braid. I pop my head out of the water just long enough to take another breath and return to the business of ridding myself of filth until I can see my skin again. I swim over to shallower water and stand. Cain is floating in the middle of the pool on his back, spitting water into the air and letting it fall back onto his face.

"Don't get out yet!" he whines when he sees me standing in the shallows.

I grab our clothes and shake them into the water until they're clean, tossing them onto the bank as I work. "I'm not getting out," I correct. "I'm cleaning our clothes."

"How very homey of you. Let me help you!"

"Homey? Careful, or you'll be cleaning these clothes *and* hunting by yourself."

"Noted," he concedes, joining me in the shallows. Waist-deep in the water, I can't help but notice his bare chest and muscled arms. He's well-built, with a broad chest and wide rib cage. A thin strip of hair runs down his stomach, matching the sandy color of his beard. I continue to study Cain's form, noting the scar running from his hand all the way up to his shoulder, crossing back and forth with jagged edges across knots of muscle.

Cain catches my scrutinizing stare and says, "I noticed you've got a pretty awful one on your leg. Care to share?"

I drop my hand down to my thigh self-consciously. I often forget it's there. "It's from surgery."

"Surgery?" He leans in to try and get a better glimpse. "Surgery doesn't leave scars like that. What are you hiding?"

"I did have surgery," I say again, "to repair the damage."

"That the injury Simons saved you from?" he deduces.

"Yeah, that one. What about yours?"

"I got that the day my mother was killed," he says.

"How?" I ask.

"Mostly by being a dumb kid," Cain says, looking thoughtfully over his scar.

"What does that mean?" I toss another garment to shore.

"She took me on this mission to an abandoned energy facility. There was something there the dissenters really wanted, and she told me to wait and stay hidden while she got it," he explains.

"An energy facility? Do you know what she was looking for?" I ask, unable to stay my curiosity.

Cain shrugs. "I think it was some sort of medical building next to the energy facility—one of the old geothermal ones, you know? But I don't know what she was looking for."

"I didn't know there were any non-operational geothermal facilities."

"It was south of the Deadlands. The government doesn't reach that far. How could they explain functioning facilities south of the Deadlands? They aren't supposed to exist anymore," Cain explains.

"What happened?"

"I was screwing around on a roof, waiting for her to finish. At first, I thought there were just a few near-dead hanging around, like we used to see if we went into some of the areas between City States, but suddenly they were everywhere, and she was surrounded. I jumped from the roof to the fence to get down, but I missed. I panicked and looped my arm in some barbed wire. It ripped the skin off my arm from my shoulder down to my wrist like a giant glove. I saw them get her. I have no idea how long I was there after that." He tosses the last piece of clothing vigorously onto the shore.

"That's terrible," I whisper.

"That's not even the worst of it. Sometime late in the night, the near-dead all became alert, like they were responding to a signal. They walked into the woods, and someone came down from a hovercraft and incinerated them. That's when I knew it wasn't an accident." Hot rage fills his voice.

"Orman?"

"Yes."

"He didn't kill you?" I ask, awestruck.

"He doesn't even know I exist," he breathes, his tone darkening.

"What does that mean?"

Cain reaches for my hands, stepping into me. "I mean he wasn't hunting me. He thought she was traveling alone. She always traveled alone." He brings one hand up to the side of my face, tilting it up to his. I accept his advance eagerly, temporarily losing the thread of our conversation.

"How did you escape?"

He dips his head back to catch my expression. "Some folks from a local community came to investigate the fire."

"Dissenters?" I ask, stunned they might reside so far from the City States.

"No, local people."

"A community of local people?" I check, trying to wrap my mind around the possibility and what it might mean. If there are communities of people in the south, where else might there be civilization outside of the City States?

"Sure, Mason. But I don't want to talk about that," he says, pulling me back into him.

"But..." I protest as he wraps me in his arms. The warmth of his body so close to mine is intoxicating.

"Later," he promises, reaching out to touch the rough edges of the scar on my leg. The sensation sends chills down my spine. "Tell me yours. I told you mine," he says.

"It's not too different from your story. My family was attacked by a hive. My dad put me and my brother up on a boulder where they couldn't reach us."

"You said it was a surgery?" Cain asks, pulling me back into the depths of the water.

"Yeah, I'm not completely sure what was wrong with it. I was miles from the Institute when Simons found me," I explain, grateful he's asking about this part instead of about Bruce or the look on Dad's face as he fell. Or why, if Hank was safe on the boulder, he isn't with me now.

Cain pulls me closer, placing one hand around my waist while we float, listening to the sound of falling water. I bury my head in his chest, letting him brush his hand against the wet hair clinging to the sides of my face.

I tilt my head toward his, searching his face, hoping. His head dips down, and my breath catches as his lips find mine. I kiss him back, wrapping my arms around his shoulders. He pulls me closer, lifting me until my legs wrap around his middle. We move back into the deeper waters of the pool, still kissing. I forget about the clothes, the guns, and the rest of the team, lost in the moment. The rest of the world is drowned out by the roaring waters, and my mind swims in this deep embrace. We float out into the center of the pool, still holding each other. The spray of the waterfall pours down on us like a warm rain.

CHAPTER
THIRTY

"I'VE WANTED to kiss you since that first day on the track."

Even though it's what I hoped, his admission surprises me. Still holding me close, he uses his free hand to tuck a wet strand of hair behind my ear before kissing me again, this time more gently.

When he pulls away, I allow my head to rest on his chest, the water lapping at my arms as they dangle against his frame. I could remain like this forever.

"The surgery happened at the Institute?" Cain asks, his voice humming in his chest and rippling out into the water.

"Yeah. I think Amos set it up before I was admitted. I don't remember any of it, but the doctor that did it was a real piece of work," I tell him.

"But you don't know what they did to it?" he asks.

"They had to rebuild a lot of tissue," I say, propping myself up. He's watching me, looking thoughtful. "Why are you so curious about it?"

"No reason," he says, pulling me back toward him to kiss me again.

I pull away, a satisfied smile creeping across my lips as I consider what I'd like to say next. Before I can open my mouth, something in my periphery catches my attention. I look over, expecting to see a swarm of near-dead converging on our private pool to ruin the moment. Instead, a placid goose waddles over to the water's edge, oblivious to our presence. I shut my mouth and pull a hand free to point silently in its direction. Cain looks over his shoulder and nods. Turning back to me with a big smile, he kisses my forehead and releases me, moving as quietly as possible toward the pile of weapons we left on the shore. I follow him, doing everything I can to stay quiet.

Cain climbs out of the water and reaches into the pile to retrieve his gun. He takes his aim, and with a quiet pop, the goose goes down. Cain whoops joyously and lops over to scoop up his prize. Grabbing the goose by its limp neck, he cries, "Dinner is served!"

Behind the roaring of the waterfall, I hear a familiar, low gurgle. Instinctively, I reach into the weapons pile and retrieve a pulsar gun, aiming in the direction of the foreboding sound. The brush rustles violently, and a near-dead rushes, open mawed, toward Cain. I pull the trigger as Cain faces his attacker, dropping the goose in surprise. The thing falls to the ground, sizzling and limp. I recharge immediately and search the horizon for another attack, my heart racing at the base of my throat.

"Well, that was close," Cain says, stepping back from his attacker.

He walks over to the pile of clothes drying in the midnight sun and pulls his pants on. I grab my own pants, refusing to lower my gun as I search our surroundings.

"You going to fire again if another one shows up?" Cain asks, fastening his pants.

"We don't have a choice," I say, scrambling awkwardly into my own, nearly falling onto my face as I trip but keeping my finger on the trigger.

"What about the trail of dead?" Cain asks, cocking an eyebrow at me.

"You know how Orman used Dunn. Every single near-dead is a possible portal for him to get to us. We can't leave it to chance, no matter how many bodies we leave in our wake." My eyes flit nervously between the brush and the trail back to the top.

"You don't think he can do that with every single near-dead?" Cain asks, shaking his wet mop of overgrown hair.

I grab a boot and shove my foot into it, lowering my gun long enough to wedge my heel into place. "It's not likely, no, but it's not worth risking that he can."

We've just about got our shoes on when another one emerges from the brush. I hit it before it takes another step, cursing under my breath.

"What do you want to bet those aren't the only two in the area?" Cain asks, clicking his belt into place.

"I'm not willing to count on anything," I say, letting Cain clip my belt for me, still scanning the area for more near-dead.

I spy another one in the distance and take it out before it turns in our direction. "We need to get out of here before someone spots the dead. Orman won't hesitate to use them," I say. My whole body is wound into a tight coil. When Cain puts his hand on my shoulder, I practically jump out of my own skin.

"Easy. I know we need to be careful, but there are probably near-dead all up and down this area. Orman can't be monitoring all of them at once. How could he?" Cain asks, grabbing our remaining clothes and shoving them into his back pocket.

"It's related to the simulations. I don't know exactly how it works, but I've seen him turn a whole group like he did with Dunn."

"Hives are different. They're all in one place. And he knew Dunn was sick. He's not a magician; he's just got very powerful technology on his side," Cain points out.

"Yeah, well, he knows these guys are sick, too. And we don't know these aren't the only ones wandering around right now."

"He can't have a neurological map of every near-dead. No matter how much we've disrupted the government, they've still got to keep up appearances. I told you about this area. Just because these guys are here doesn't mean Orman's closing in on us," he argues.

"I'm not willing to count on that. I'm guessing we don't even know the half of how powerful the simulation technology is," I say, turning to check the area on the other side of the waterfall.

I try to shrug Cain's hand off my shoulder, but he resists, instead pulling me in to him. He plants a firm kiss on my forehead. "I get it," he says, forcing me to meet his gaze. "Let's not leave anything to chance, yeah?"

I nod my head in agreement before letting my lips find his for a brief yet satisfying second. We move quickly to the granite cliff. Cain hops onto the first ledge, reaching down to hoist me up so I don't have to lower my gun. Raised up reasonably safe from the ground, I lower the gun and clip it into the holster so both hands are free to climb. We make our way up the cliffside as the last rays of the late-night sun fade in the distance. I strain in the dark to see if any more near-dead are gathering down below. Almost a full body length ahead, Cain reaches the edge and cautiously peers over.

"It's clear. The cluster must have come from below."

Cain climbs onto the shelf above before taking my hand. We move quietly but hastily back to the group as the sun casts of the last of its fiery light for the night.

We spot the flickering glow of a small fire where the group waits for our return. I ache for its warmth as the cool air bites at my damp hair and wet clothes. The small fire casts over-sized shadows on the boulders behind our waiting group. Cain puts his arm around my shoulder, our jackets flap against his leg, brushing against my side as we walk.

"Can I get my shirt from you?" I ask, suddenly self-conscious and very cold.

"Hmmm? Sure," Cain says, stopping to pull the clothes free of his pocket. I grab my shirt from him and pull it hurriedly over my head.

"Don't you want to put on dry clothes back at camp?" Cain asks, pinching the jackets between his knees so he can pull his own shirt on.

"You want to march into camp half dressed?"

Cain shrugs, tossing the jackets over his shoulder and strolling forward. The initial urgency in his pace has faded. I press forward, annoyed. Someone stands up in camp to watch our approach. Judging by the size of the shadow I'm guessing it's Simons. Another figure pops up in the light—Jorey. I wave my hand over my head as we move forward.

As soon as we're in earshot Jorey calls out, "What, no dinner?"

"I had a goose…"

"We've got a problem," I interrupt. "Near-dead. Down below."

"Near-dead?" Simons asks, touching the gun at his hip. "How many?"

"Three," I answer. "But there might be more. I shot them, so we need to get out of here before they can track us."

My report sobers the group. They pack up camp without further discussion, ignoring their obvious fatigue. Jorey stomps out the fire while Frances and Richards gather our gear. I grab my pack. Someone scraped the mud from it, leaving it virtually clean. I look around to see most everyone else's pack is still filthy. In the moonlight, I can see that everyone is reasonably clean, having washed off in the springs. I'm about to ask who cleaned my pack when Jorey interrupts my thoughts.

"Take a bath?" he asks.

"Down below," I say, my cheeks warming with the memory. "I was disgusting."

"I know what you mean," Frances chimes in. "Those springs are amazing. It's a shame we have to move."

We point ourselves southward and make a wide berth around the cliffside leading down to where Cain and I had our encounter. The idea of packing through the night makes my heart sink. The collective silence of the team tells the story of our fatigue. I pull my gun up against my hip as we walk past a thick, brushy area, listening for the telltale gurgle.

"Any chance you know of another safe camp along our way?" I ask, hoping Cain has another plan.

"We probably need to cross the caldera. Maybe find a craggy area to set up camp… something a hive couldn't get to very quickly."

We keep a quick pace through the night, keeping our weapons at the ready as we travel. In the last hours of darkness, the area transforms from a featureless valley with pockets of swirling fog into craggy hillsides. Further ahead, dark shadows indicate a promising landscape.

We march on, our bodies begrudging in their compliance as we put distance between us and the corpses. As the sun makes its first show of early light, we reach the foot of a boulder field.

"Maybe we can find something here," I suggest.

"Worth a shot," Simons says.

The early sunrise makes it easier to spot a good camp. Several large boulders tower above the rest. Some appear to have relatively flat surfaces. We select the most ideal of these and, after a few passes around the perimeter of the behemoth, decide it's suitable.

"Perfect," Cain says, taking a knee and holding his hands out in a locked position. "Ladies first!" he directs at me.

"What's that supposed to mean?" I scowl.

"It's an old saying. Something somebody says when they're trying to impress a woman," Frances offers.

Cain's mouth opens in protest as Jorey lets out an amused huff. Frances offers a sly wink in my direction as I step into Cain's hands. He remembers his original intention and propels me upward until I can grab an edge on the boulder's face. I hoist myself the rest of the way, scrambling the last several meters on my own to the top. I ditch my pack and turn back around to reach for Frances' hand with a quippy "my lady" that makes Cain's face turn bright red. Before the sun makes its way above the horizon we're settling in for rest on the boulder's hard surface, more tightly packed than we ever were in the tunnels.

Sandwiched between Frances and Cain, I shift my weight to lean against Cain's shoulder. He snakes his arm behind me and rests his hand over mine, making my stomach twist and dance. Though it seems impossible that I might shut my mind off, I fall asleep with my head against Cain and my hand on my gun.

CHAPTER
THIRTY-ONE

I WAKE up from a black hole of exhausted sleep to the zap of a pulsar gun. I snap my head up so violently I nearly pitch myself off the edge of the boulder. I'm not certain what I thought I might find on the other side of my eyelids, but as my body teeters on the edge, a terrible thought strikes me.

This is a mistake. It's too similar—too familiar. The only possible outcome is ambush.

There's another pop and a zap of energy as someone steadies me, pulling me back onto the hard granite surface.

"Easy there," Cain says, one hand wrapped around my belt, the other squeezing down on his trigger. Somewhere in the boulder field, a body thuds to the ground.

"I forgot where we were," I say, thankful for his quick reflexes.

"They sure didn't," Simons says over his shoulder.

I shake the stunned panic from my mind, still reeling from my near trip over the edge of the boulder. Peering over Simons' shoulder, I make out the shambling frame of a near-dead. Simons sites it, but Jorey takes it out. Frances and Richards sit side by side, facing the opposite direction. She lifts her arm to indicate she's spotted another, then waits for it to clear the tree line before taking it down.

"They're coming from every direction?" I ask, the sick dread pouring into my limbs with the icy numbness of adrenaline.

"So far only from the north and the east," Cain says.

"How many?" I ask, searching the southwest for signs we're surrounded. It's difficult to tell for certain beyond the jagged, rocky landscape. In the distance, a creature reacts to our discourse.

"That's five," Richards answers, taking Frances' gun while she rummages through her pack.

"There," Simons says, pointing toward the tree line. "They're coming at a steady trickle—not even two at a time."

"They're probably attracted by the smell of fresh meat," Cain says.

"Or someone's sending them our way a little at a time," I say, dismissing Cain's flippant suggestion.

I scan the field, counting the corpses for myself as Simons adds a sixth. "There are too many bodies," I say, still holding back the growing dread. Everyone's too casual. The high vantage point is giving them a false sense of security. The slow trickle of near-dead makes them too easy to pick off. The entire situation screams set-up. If we haven't already been spotted, the bodies will give us away.

We wait a moment longer, huddled together in the silent morning before the roar of a distant geyser shatters the stillness. The steaming mist sprays up from a mound of mineral deposits. It burbles and churns for several minutes, releasing pressure until the valley returns to its previous stillness. Even after the geyser settles, the silence remains. The trickle of near-dead seems to have stopped. I loosen the grip on my gun and rest my cheek on Cain's shoulder. He responds silently by leaning back into me.

"Maybe those bodies are a coincidence, but I'm not going to count on it," I say, considering the situation.

"What should we do about it?" Frances asks, a slight edge to her voice giving away the apprehension beneath her cool exterior.

"If there are any more out there, we can't leave them walking, but the more bodies we leave, the easier it will be to close in on us," I explain, still searching for a reasonable exit plan—wishing for a river to erase our trail like it did for my family when we ran from the mounting onslaught of near-dead.

"Why can't we leave them be and sneak around this area?" she presses.

"She thinks that Orman can use them like Dunn," Cain says in a tone that clearly indicates he doesn't agree.

"He can't have a neurological map of all of them—that only happens in the labs," Simons objects, his head swinging back and forth.

"That's what I said," Cain laments.

"Well, I'm so glad you're all in agreement." I roll my eyes. "But if we don't disappear now, it's only a matter of time before they've got us."

"What's the plan? Do we try and make it into the hills?" Jorey asks, checking the power cylinder on his pulsar gun.

"It might already be too late. They might just release a hive and be done with it the second we step off this rock," I say. Frances' face pales. Richards' lips draw tight as Jorey looks away, fumbling with a cartridge.

"I'm sorry. I shouldn't have said that."

"I don't think the situation is so straightforward. We're in a fairly safe location right now. I think we could handle a moderate hive from up here. They might not bother," Cain suggests.

"So what would they be doing then? If they aren't pinpointing our location, then why bother setting out patients at all?" I ask, exasperated.

The gurgle of another attacker draws our attention. In unison, we fire at the approaching menace—a thoroughly developed specimen, wet with decay and stumbling on maladroit limbs. It hits the ground with an uneventful thud. I ponder this creature—the first that I've had a good look at since I woke up—and assess its fitness. It was not the exceptionally dangerous patient type. It was slow and decaying, with a high potential to lose body parts while moving over the boulder field. If we've been flushed out, then Orman could be trying to tempt us off the boulder.

The risk of letting too much time pass weighs heavily on my mind. Where the near-dead are concerned, every single incident involves the DDC, and Orman by extension. Every second matters. Wordlessly, I rummage through my pack until I find what I want—the thin sack that holds one of the metallic rings from Dó's weapons room. I reach into the sack and carefully grab the ring, pulling it out and flicking it in front of me so it expands, shimmering in the sunlight. I grab two different receiver cartridges and spring wordlessly into action.

I swing down from our granite stronghold, landing soundlessly on my feet. I ignore the protests from above and pop myself up onto a much lower boulder. There's enough height to keep something from catching me by surprise, but I'm low enough that it would be worth sending a hive.

"Mason! What do you think you're doing?" Cain cries, his voice mixed with exasperation and worry.

"Get back up here! What are you going to do if it's a hive?" Simons commands in a voice that leaves no uncertainty that he expects me to comply.

"Yeah, come on, Mason, are you crazy?" Jorey leans over the rock with his hand out to encourage my return.

I quiet them all, holding my hand out to silence their protests. The menacing chorus of gurgles confirms my suspicion—these are not random wanderers. The sound makes its way through the boulder field, bounding from rock to rock and obscuring the source. I estimate the direction of origin as I tune my receiver and load one of the two cartridges into the ring. My heart moves to my throat. I keep vigilant scan of the horizon, but a cacophony of sounds from our camp assures me the team is readying themselves for what's about to happen.

They come all at once—maybe a few hundred. This hive is made up of freshly developed specimens, not the sad messes of flesh and bones that made their way inward up to this point. Their appearance and uniform state of health suggests specificity in their development. I shudder to think of this sort of ambush as a war tactic. I watch their approach, waiting patiently, albeit anxiously, for them to get close enough. A series of shots make their way into the hive from the boulder as the team does what they can to thin it out. I stand still, rigid with determination, clutching the loaded ring.

The pack makes its way closer, staying tight as it moves through the field, scrambling over rocks and land masses with an awkward, unnatural determination. I count to the third boulder out and wait for the lead to reach it. My hand trembles.

"Mason, you better move!" Cain pleads, still picking off the leads as fast as he can. The others call out similar warnings with increasing urgency.

The instant the hive leads reach the third boulder, I flick the cartridge on and launch the now-glowing ring out into the mass. The energy of the orb—typically too powerful to use in close proximity— radiates out from the ring, moving through the hive and tearing down near-dead with such intense radiation that there's no need for preci- sion. The shrieks of dying bodies echo through the field in ear-piercing waves. When the glow finally subsides, there are only a few straggling near-dead left to be taken down. The team does so efficiently, and we're left in silence.

"That was incredible!" Jorey proclaims.

"I'll say," Cain agrees, nodding his head and whooping, clearly impressed.

"Not bad," I agree, relieved the ring worked as remarkably as promised. I try not to slump in relief, intent to pretend I was completely confident the whole time.

I engage the magnetic pull of my glove-receiver, and the now-limp and unassuming ring flies through the air back into my hand. I catch it in a tangled mass over my head and immediately begin to untangle it. The team is slapping each other on the backs and calling out jovially as I manipulate the thin ring back into a coherent geometric structure. Finally, I succeed and hold it out over my head to display it to the group in triumph.

Cain's face transforms from amusement to horror, and he calls out, "Mason—behind you!"

CHAPTER
THIRTY-TWO

I TURN TOO late and see the second hive approaching in total silence. It's enormous, maybe four times the size of the first and moving fast. Where the first hive moved with an awkward collectedness, this one is completely synchronized—almost as if it were following a different program—a different simulation. I'm frozen in a mixture of curious awe and terror, simultaneously panicking as I transform what I see to the simulation that makes it possible. The knowledge I'm about to be overwhelmed is lost somewhere in the distance as I imagine the code for the neural map that must make up a hive…

Cain and Jorey fire first, stirring the others into action. The shots whiz past me, close enough that I feel their heat. The nearness stuns me into action. I take the second cartridge and jam it into the ring, this time laying it on the rock below and stepping into the center of the ring. As fast as I dare, I tune my receiver and engage both it and the ring. The buzz of energy emanates upward from the ring, and I thrust my hand high so the signal will arc the force field over my head.

The hive descends upon my personal bubble of defense as shots rain down from the boulder, some bouncing off the force field and into the hive. The faces of near-dead press up against the force field, melting from the intensity of the energy. Again, their shrieks and cries fill the air. There's nothing to do but sit helplessly, holding my hand over my head to keep the field intact. The hive continues its attack, some of the members now badly charred from multiple encounters with the force field. The sounds of their gurgles and cries, mixed with the repeated discharges of pulsar guns, are deafening.

Bodies push upon bodies as the hive descends on my energized haven. The rock shakes beneath me, moved by their collective force. It's only a matter of time before they manage to uproot it and tip me into their midst. If I'm not incinerated by the ring's energy, they'll rip apart my flesh, leaving me strewn and soaking into the dirt before turning to attack the others.

Knowing is the worst part of it. It's the same thing Dad must have felt when the hive started to push at the tree. I force my eyes shut so I don't have to see the burning, contorted faces surrounding me. Hot tears run down the sides of my face as I plead for my life to be enough, and that no one else jumps down from the boulder.

The ground shakes below me, and a bright flash of light pierces the blackness of my shut eyes as a wave of heat and energy sweeps out from beyond the hive. I brace myself, arm stretched out over my head, holding my position. Someone must have discharged an orb. I spread my legs against the grit of the shuddering boulder, keeping my arm bent so my hand doesn't drop down below my head. When the burning light subsides, I look out to see the last straggling survivors of the hive scrambling aimlessly on broken bodies. The hive connection was broken by the explosion, likely disrupted by the surge of energy and definitely exacerbated by the total neural collapse of so many dying patients.

I watch the remaining near-dead, contemplating the reality of the hive technology. I hope it hurt like hell when the program was disrupted. The thought of Orman wriggling and writhing in the absolute blackness of an interrupted simulation brings the shadow of a smile to my lips. I could take care of the remaining bodies with a couple quick shots, but I keep my hand up, not ready to take down the force field.

My heart thuds too fast in my chest and ears, mingling with the high-pitched scream of soundlessness. I know it's over, but I can't stop the racing panic that keeps me in the orb. After several minutes, I coax myself to disengage the force field. I grab the ring from the crumbled remnants of the boulder and extinguish the last survivors without removing the gun from my hip. I turn back to the boulder, squinting through the fine silt of dust hanging in the air to see that it's been split in two by the force of the blast.

Bile rises in my throat as I envision my entire team incinerated, leaving me once again the sole survivor of a hive attack. I step off my own miniature boulder with numb feet, somehow able to control my body even though my mind is far away. I open my mouth to call out, hoping despite the futility of it that someone will respond.

I run my hand absently along the grainy surface as I move around the boulder and finally see them, huddled in their own rings with their force fields engaged. Relief floods my senses, making the world sharp again. Cain sees me first and immediately disengages his force field, rushing toward me. The others are quick to disengage their own force fields, and the air fills with the bluster of their exclamations and inter-jections.

Relieved tears stream unbridled down my cheeks. "You're alive! You're alive! I thought I'd lost you all!" I stammer over the gush of words that flow out of me, racing and shuddering like my over-wrought body.

Cain scoops me up into his arms and kisses me without waiting for my rambling to stop. My words are stifled by the warmth of his mouth. He breaks away from me long enough to scold, "Mason, that was just stupid. Please don't ever do that again."

My hands rest against the base of his neck. His whole body is tensed and vibrating. Sound is muffled by the persistent ring in my ears, which only adds to the tilted unreality of the moment. Adrenaline pulses through my body, making my limbs numb and buzzy despite knowing everyone is alright. Cain's hand brushes across my face, wiping a tear into the film of dust settled on my cheeks. The touch brings me back to reality. I look up from Cain's embrace and realize everyone is staring at us. I tap Cain's shoulder with the hand clasping the ring and draw his attention to our audience. He looks up at the group, smiling broadly, pulling me against him.

"Looks like everybody made it!" he exclaims jovially.

"I can see that," Simons says slowly and thoughtfully. "I can see."

I release Cain and rush toward Simons, who envelops me in an overdone embrace. "I thought I'd lost you," I say into his chest.

"The feeling seems to be going around this morning," he says.

"I didn't—I couldn't—" I stammer, unable to express the thing trying to get out. "It was just like before."

"I know. It was like I was watching all over again," Simons says, understanding what I'm trying to say. His body trembles despite his restraint.

"That blast saved us. Which orb was it?" I ask, desperate to move away from my own emotional spiral.

"That was the high-powered plasma blaster," Jorey says. I turn my head, pulling away from Simons to where Jorey stands, still several paces away from everyone else, rigid.

"Cain set it off," he adds with unmasked fury.

"Somebody had to do something," Cain protests. "The hive was closing in too fast, and I wasn't sure how strong the ring force field was—if they'd broken through…"

"If you weren't sure how strong the ring force field was, you shouldn't have set off the highest energy orb! What if you'd killed her?" Jorey nearly shouts. "You could have killed us all!"

"What did you want me to do?" Cain asks, raising his voice and stepping toward Jorey. "Was I supposed to sit back and watch the hive break through the force field? You weren't going to do anything!"

"That's not true! I'm just not a reckless fool. You got lucky, Cain!" Jorey bursts into motion, raising his arm toward Cain.

Simons grabs Jorey by the shoulder, jerking him back and stepping between them, exerting his authority without words and towering above both men. Jorey flashes him a drawn, angry look.

"We all got lucky," I say, desperate to help. Desperate to feel anything besides the quivery, sick upset churning inside me.

"That's right," Simons agrees. "Nobody knew if any of it would work the way it was supposed to. This isn't a simulation; it's real life. Mason didn't know if the rings would work, and they did. We didn't know if the force fields were strong enough, and they were. Cain didn't know if the orb would save us or kill us, but here we are. We're all just that—lucky."

Simons' words hit home with heart-wrenching truth. Even before the Northern Laboratories, he depended more on luck than anything else. All the careful planning in the world wasn't enough to keep coyotes safe from the DDC. There's a moment of silence that heightens the tension in our stretched and overtired team. I search for words.

"I know what I did was rash, but if I hadn't done it, we would still be trapped. Everything we do out here is rash."

Frances, who's been silently observing in the background, chimes in. "If we think we can get through this without taking risks, we're fooling ourselves."

Richards nods eagerly. Frances breaks away from him and walks toward me, pulling me into an emphatic embrace, which I return clumsily. She looks me straight in the eye and says, "Mason, I'm so glad you're alright." Then she turns to Jorey and Cain, adding, "We're *all* glad that Mason's alright."

Jorey slumps his shoulders as he turns away from us to grab a pack. "Let's get on with it then. We better get out of here and to the next shelter point before they can develop another hive."

"That's probably the only thing saving us right now. There's no doubt they know we're here. We need to get to the trees before they send scouts," I agree, all urgency returning.

We exchange cartridges in the weapons clipped into our holsters and load our packs onto our backs. I stuff the ring back into its little pouch, tucking it into my pocket instead of my pack. As we head out, I catch Simons' eye. I hold his gaze for a moment before moving, headed toward the tree line. I have the sense that something significant passed between us in the moment before Jorey and Cain's altercation. But it passed too quickly, and there isn't time to explore it now.

THIRTY-THREE

I SPOT the first hovercraft less than an hour after we clear the attack area. It's a large craft—likely the same one that brought the hive. It tears through the sky with a deep roar, dropping vertically into the clearing. We watch from the cover of thick brush, too scared to move, until the scouts complete their search.

"It doesn't look like anyone could have survived that blast. Maybe they'll think we're dead," Frances suggests with a hope that doesn't manage to touch down.

"They won't stop looking so easily," I say.

"Orman needs proof. We won't give it to him." Cain says what I can't. I squeeze his hand, hating the truth in his words but drawing from his resolve anyway.

We fall silent as the craft passes by close enough to rustle the leaves of the overhead trees, tilting on its axis before pivoting and crossing the clearing again. Several long minutes later, it makes a final turn before ascending into the clouds and disappearing.

"We better clear out of here. The next craft won't stay airborne. There will be an on-ground search party," Simons says.

I use the tree to hoist myself back onto my feet, stunned at how tired my legs are. It doesn't matter. As a former coyote, Simons knows more about government searches than everybody besides the DDC themselves. Except for maybe Cain. I reach out and grasp his hand, giving it a little shake. "Is there a tunnel access point on this side of the crater?"

"There's no guarantee it will be accessible," Cain says, his thumb dancing across my knuckles. His brow furrows.

"It's worth checking. Out here, we're too exposed," Jorey says, stepping to my other side.

I nod, searching for Simons' consent. He tips his chin down, turning his head toward Richards and Frances, who also nod. "Can you take us there?" he asks Cain.

"I can, if that's the vote," Cain says. His tone is easy, but his grip on my hand is tight, as if he were only acting the role of a team player. I lift an inquisitive eyebrow in his direction, but he shakes his head and puts his arm around my shoulder. "Let's get to it."

We make good time despite the difficult terrain, descending back into the tunnel system before the sun crosses to the west. We navigate past several rockslides, choosing to take the time to break through rather than risk returning to the surface. It's slow, hard work. At Frances' request, Simons describes his experience with on-ground search parties, suggesting this one could remain in the area for several days.

"Won't they find the tunnels?" Frances asks, pressing herself against the wall to squeeze through the small opening we cleared.

"Maybe, but they can't get in," Cain says.

"Surely they could force their way through," Richards suggests, taking Frances' hand to help her through.

"Not without causing a cave-in. The entrances are rigged—to protect against near-dead attacks. If they broke through, they'd have to clear out a mess worse than this to move forward. By then we'll be long gone," Cain says.

"Unless they detect the mechanism and disable it," I say.

"They probably won't even try. Most of the tunnels along the coast and south of here are built from the original aqueducts that were sealed off during the war. Ancient history. If they can't get in, then neither can anyone else. That's government thinking for you," Cain adds.

I doubt his assessment. Destroying the Northern Laboratories changed things. Even Dó understands that much. Now the DDC knows they're dealing with something bigger than a couple of fringe rebels. I look back at the weary group, searching their dirt-streaked faces.

"We need to rest," I say, then realize we're missing someone. "Where's Jorey?"

"He was just here," Frances says, looking back past the rock pile the way only a mother could.

"He was keeping up just fine," Richards agrees, concern taking over.

"He stopped a few minutes back. Said he needed to check something. I told him we'd wait up for him here," Simons interjects, setting everyone's minds at ease.

"Go ahead and start setting up camp. I'm going back to check on Jorey," I say, dropping my larger pack.

"I'll come with in case somebody needs to carry our brother back," Cain pipes in with good cheer masking his fatigue.

Simons puts a heavy hand on his shoulder. "I think Mason can handle a check-in on her own."

Cain shrugs Simons' hand off, scooping up my pack in the same motion. "Does this thing have any food in it?" he asks, reminding me of Hank and the soups.

"A few meal packs. Frances has the rest," I say, trying to discern Simons' intent from the subtext of the redirection. He must know how badly I want to talk to Jorey. Either that or Jorey wants to talk to me. I'm not sure which I prefer.

I hoist myself up onto a rock and squeeze through the opening. Once I reach the other side, I spot the glow of Jorey's headlight in the distance. I make my way toward him, my footsteps echoing through the damp tunnel, muting the receding sound of conversation as the group sets up camp. The passage brightens with Jorey's light as I approach, and the babble of running water dominates other sounds.

Jorey is stooped over the underground spring, totally consumed with the task of filling water bladders.

My heart thuds. Everything about our friendship is off-kilter lately. I get the impression that my and Cain's momentary display of affection hasn't helped, seeing as Cain's infiltration of the group hasn't settled well with him. His reaction makes we want to second-guess my own judgment. I can dismiss Simons' reticence as over-protectiveness, but it's different with Jorey. We're equals.

I watch him work, unaware of my approach. He pulls the sterilizer from his pack, dipping it into the water and stirring, murmuring a countdown under his breath. I can't remember the last time we talked. The thought is striking considering how frequently we used to discuss nothing and everything. Suddenly I ache with how much I miss him.

"Hey there," I say, crouching down next to him, the tips of my boots barely touching the water's edge.

"Hey Mason," Jorey says, tipping his head in my direction with a tired smile before refocusing on his task. "Twenty-three, twenty-four…"

"How long have you been out of water?" I ask, wishing I'd brought my own bladder to fill.

Jorey finishes his count and pulls the wand, setting it back into his pack and sealing the full bladder. "Only just. Simons said we'd be stopping soon, and I saw this little stream. It barely smells like sulfur," he says.

"You're a pretty smart guy," I say, giving his arm an off-balance nudge.

"You say that, but you're only being nice. You're the scientist," Jorey says, nudging me back so that I lose my balance and land on my butt with a soft thud.

"Sorry," he says, plunking down next to me.

"My fault." I settle into a sit my body's been craving for hours.

Jorey lets out a heavy sigh. We remain for a while, listening to the trickle and rush of water echo off the rock surrounding us.

"Do you think it ever makes its way back to the surface?" Jorey asks, watching the stream flow back the way we came on a gentle downward slope.

"Maybe if any of the old pumps still work. More likely it flows into a water table." I tap my toes in the water to make a small splash. I didn't come here to talk about water, and Simons didn't hold Cain back so I could help Jorey fill his pack.

"Hey, Jorey?" I begin, still not knowing where I want the conversation to go.

"Yeah?" he asks, his eyes trained on his hands, which are folded across his knees in front of him.

I pause, struggling to find the ease I used to take for granted. "I was just thinking it's been a long time since we talked like we used to. That's my fault. I've been so busy with... with this disaster I've created." I sweep my arms in a broad arc.

"I know, Mason. I don't blame you for any of this," he says.

"Is there anything going on? With you? That maybe you want to talk about?"

"Do you want to talk about Cain?" Jorey asks.

"Yeah, Cain." Apparently, he doesn't have as hard of a time bringing it up as I do.

"I don't like him," Jorey says flatly. "I mean, he's fine, probably. But I hate his attitude. He's trying to run the show like he's been in on it since the beginning, and he barely joined our group."

"He's been a dissenter his whole life."

"He didn't have a clue what was happening in the Northern Laboratories—what you or Shelby or anyone else was doing," Jorey objects.

"True, but he knows what he's doing out here. He's helping us." I look up so that our eyes meet in the near-darkness. I want to tell him what Cain said about killing Orman, but I don't want to betray privileged information.

"He's an arrogant prick." His voice rises, dripping with vitriol.

"He saved your life."

"Yeah, there's that, but he's mostly a headstrong and reckless jerk. And you—" he stops himself suddenly, looking away, back into the blackness of running water.

My face flushes, knowing I can't deny what Jorey's saying. "Yeah..." I say quietly.

"You and him."

"Yeah," I repeat, not knowing what else to say. I came here to talk about Cain, but now that I have my opportunity, I'm at a loss.

"You like him?" Jorey says, grabbing his pack and shoving the water bladder and all the other contents back inside and zipping it shut.

"What do you mean?" I ask, stalling an answer.

Jorey stands, pulling his pack onto his shoulders. I pull my legs back and stand with him, wishing for my own pack as if it were another layer of protection from my feelings.

"Obviously, you do," he answers for me. "And he's clearly made his claim."

He turns the dial on his headlamp up so that the path is illuminated and steps away from the water's edge.

"Made his claim?" I demand, reaching for his arm and swinging myself into his path so I'm facing him, forcing him to look at me. This isn't how I thought things would go.

"You know what I mean." He tries to step past me, and I block his progress again. He rolls his eyes, clearly exasperated. "I don't want to talk about it."

"Jorey!" I exclaim, frustrated. "Give me a break... I've never... this has never happened before. It's all new to me! I thought you would understand."

"I don't understand, Mason. I have no idea what you see in him."

"Well, it's not your call," I snap. His disapproval hurts more than I thought it could. I turn and walk away from him, back toward our camp.

Jorey follows me. I listen as each of his footsteps causes the frustration to build up inside of me and pour over. "Who said you could have an opinion?"

"Sorry," Jorey says, sounding hurt. We walk for a moment in silence before he says, "That's not how I want to be with you."

I won't look at him. "Maybe you should keep your judgment to yourself then."

"I'm not judging you! I just—" There's a hint of desperation in his voice as he searches for words. "Never mind. I'm sorry I said anything. I just want you to be happy." He gives up.

We walk the rest of the way back to the group in silence, and I have a sinking feeling that I've just lost something from my friendship with him that I never really knew I had.

CHAPTER
THIRTY-FOUR

WE DARE to surface sometime in the early hours of a morning that is, by my estimation, early on the fourth day after the hive attack.

"You know your estimation is right. Why won't you admit it?" Cain complains as we trudge through the thick foliage of the almost-coastal woods.

"Because even a good estimation is still an estimation," I say, watching the distant ground where it meets the brush. Though it'll be some time before the sun breaks over the horizon, the combination of a full moon and light scatter from cloud cover is more than enough to light our way.

"If she's half as good at keeping time as she is at tracking the exact phase of the moon, then she's correct within a tolerance of several seconds," Jorey adds.

I glance back long enough to see Cain roll his eyes. Jorey catches my look and winks. Smirking, I turn my attention back to our surroundings, still searching.

"Fine. Have it your way. So long as Cain is half as good at directions as I am at the moon, then we're very close," I say.

"And if we're not?" Richards asks, stifling a yawn. He reaches into the side pocket of his pack to grab his water bladder and takes a long drink.

"Then we're in trouble," Simons concludes, voicing the truth we're all too well acquainted with.

At this point, we won't make it very long in the open before we're located, no matter what precautions we take. After the hive attack, the DDC is well aware we're still in the northern territory and has surely abandoned any searches in the city. They're likely aware we're traveling on foot, and if they suspect otherwise, they've already taken appropriate precautions to thwart other means of transportation.

"We can't be careful enough. Even if we're close, there's likely danger," I say, spotting the first signs of a force field.

"You mean a hive?" Cain asks, kicking a rotted branch out of his path.

"At this point, I might expect armed agents," I correct.

"Like Orman," Jorey clarifies.

"Oh," Cain says, almost as if he were relieved by the idea. "Then we can shoot him ourselves."

"If only it were that easy. Orman would never let us get the drop on him," I argue. The third tree to the west waivers again, making me certain of what I'm seeing.

"Unless you have a death wish, you better hope we don't run into Orman out here," Simons says.

"When are you going to quit underestimating me?" Cain scoffs.

I let their conversation fade into the background as I approach the edge of the force field, taking care to identify the energy boundary. Cain, Simons, and Jorey continue their bickering, their voices becoming a din in the back of my mind. Breeching a force field from the inside might be simple, but from the outside, a wrong move might be as deadly as the DDC hunters.

Placing one hand on the grooved surface of the giant hemlock to my left, I reach my other hand toward the open space in front of me. The fine hairs on my arm rise as a tingling sensation travels all the way to the back of my neck. I move my hand forward a millimeter at a time until the tingling sensation changes to a burning one and the nerves on my fingertips sing with the sensation of a thousand needle tips. Any further and I might not get my hand back.

I retrieve it, shaking out the burning ache. Cain raises his voice in protest to something Jorey says, but I can tell by his tone that the discourse is still innocuous.

"Is that the force field for the geothermal facility?" Frances asks, peering over my shoulder.

"I'm trying to pinpoint the depth of the field," I confirm.

"We can't pass through like we did at Dó's?" she asks, startled.

"Dó was carrying a signal canceler," I say, doing a few mental calculations.

"Isn't that what we have?" Frances glances down at my pack, where I'm rummaging for what I need to break through the energy barrier.

"What Dó used was a specific signal repeater, programmed to the frequency of his facility. What we have is a pinpoint blocker." I retrieve the small, rounded device. I haven't seen one since the night I left my own management facility.

What was once a mystery is now a matter of simple mechanics. The hard part is setting everything up correctly. If I trigger the magnetic field too far from the field's core, the signal won't hold long enough for us to make it through. Too deep and I'll lose my hand—or at least part of it.

"Better standing shot doesn't mean you're a better shot overall. You can't make a moving shot to save your life," Cain scoffs.

"Not every statement requires critical feedback," Jorey retorts.

"Because you can't take criticism," Cain snaps back.

"Are you going to stop them?" Richards asks Simons, who's abandoned the arguing duo in the interest of the force field.

"Nah, they sleep better when they're worn out." Simons looks my way. "Isn't that right?"

"So long as they don't ruin my concentration," I reply.

Simons turns back to the squabble. "Knock it off or we're leaving you behind."

Cain springs to his feet, abandoning the argument as if he were only engaging to pass the time. "Mason would never!"

I turn back toward the force field, smiling because I know he can't see me. "Keep it up and you might be surprised."

Jorey breathes a satisfied harrumph, making it to my side in three swift strides. He puts his hand up against the edge of the force field, shuddering at the sensation. "Will it breech the other side?" he asks.

"If it doesn't, we're at the end of the line," I say. We don't dare attempt to make contact with the DDC so close on our tracks, and we can't go back. The tunnels aren't safe anymore. No matter what Cain says, the search must have gone underground by now.

He nods as the group falls silent. I turn on the receiver to the signal blocker so the first light blinks green. My finger hovers over the single black button covering the bulk of the device's face. I take in a slow, deep breath, then another one. At the last second, I close my eyes, channeling all my focus into the changes in sensation running from my fingers up to the back of my neck.

Fine hairs tickle at my collar as heat radiates and pulses along my nervous system. At the first instance of the sharp needles, I engage the button. There's a momentary pause as my finger, overwhelmed by the sensation of near-discombobulation, receives the signal. The buzzing, burning sensations disappear at once, leaving me feeling like a broken circuit. I open my eyes to see the body-sized circle with my hand at its center.

I grab one of the packs and toss it through the opening. It lands with an uneventful thud on the opposite side. I let out a breath I didn't realize I was holding. Frances tosses her pack through, then reaches for Richards'. Jorey, Cain and Simons do the same until all of our supplies wait on the other side.

"Simons, you should go first," Cain says amidst our collective silence.

"Why?" he asks, giving Cain a suspicious glare.

"Because if you fit, the rest of us can rest easy knowing we do too."

Simons lets out a single, breathy caw of laughter, slapping Cain on the back. "Your sense of immortality is going to get you killed one day!"

We chuckle at this exchange as Simons steps forward. He doesn't have to grope around to sense the limits of the portal. He tucks his head and puts his arms forward as if he were using the limits of the signal breaker to brace himself before ducking through the portal. He lifts each leg to pass through and, without much ceremony, finds himself on the other side, looking back at us.

Cain nods his head in simple admiration. "Proof is proof."

He tucks down and follows Simons to the other side. He turns, putting his hand out obviously toward me, but before I can act, Jorey grabs it.

"Thank you," he says, clamping down on Cain's hand. He steps through the portal with a self-satisfied smirk.

I give way for Frances to pass through next, then Richards insists I take my turn. He brings up the rear of our team, taking my hand as the others rummage through our packs, re-fastening them in the relative safety of the facility boundaries.

"That was simple enough, given the comparative stress it put us through," Richards observes on the facility side, peering back through the portal.

"It's nice to have something work so well after all we've been through," I agree, disengaging the energy receiver so the field-breaker falls at my feet.

"This place is gorgeous," Frances breathes, taking in our newest safe haven.

Tucking the blocker back into my pack, I turn to see what has Frances so affected. I gaze upon the sweeping fields of flowers, bright in the early-morning light. Given what we just passed through, I'm certain the flowers are cultivated by hours of painstaking work.

Just like before, the grounds bear a striking resemblance to my old home, right down to the gentle brook that wanders through the far side of the field.

"Who could believe all of this was hiding on the other side of the force field," Richards marvels, returning to Frances' side.

"There's the residence," Jorey says, turning toward the small building beyond the generator facility.

I follow his gaze, my eyes settling on something—some *things* moving fast. Enormous silhouettes split the tall grasses as they make haste toward the facility boundaries—as they make their way toward *us*.

"Wild dogs!"

THIRTY-FIVE

I REMAIN frozen in place by a mix of fascination and terror. These dogs are so much larger than the ones that infiltrated our camp. Their hulking frames peek easily out from the flower bushes and tall grasses. Worse than their size, though, is the fact that they've managed to breech the facility grounds. It can only mean something terrible has happened.

"Get back!" Simons cries, casting a protective hand in our direction as he steps into the path of the approaching beasts.

In an instant, our pulsar guns are ready, aimed at our attackers. Any one of us could take the dogs out. A spark of regret kindles inside me as I watch the dogs close the last bit of space separating us. That we should extinguish such magnificent creatures in the name of self-preservation seems shameful, regardless of its practicality.

"You're such a bleeding heart," Hank would say. Concepts such as sparing the living would fall on deaf ears where he was concerned. Bruce was the one who would understand—who would still himself long enough to hear my reasons.

"Don't shoot them!"

A cry from the distant residence pulls me from my reverie, stilling my hand and breaking my aim. I don't need to look to know the others have followed suit. A man as massive as the beasts he's calling after emerges from the building. His red beard and hair stream after him, seeming to glow in bright contrast to the still-grey morning as he screams.

"Friendly! I swear they're friendly. For the love of all that's good, don't shoot my dogs!"

The black dog lets out a deep, bellowing call—something between a bark and a howl—as it lopes the last hundred meters toward us. The tan-and-white twin bounds after it, barely a length behind after turning toward their master's cries.

"If they're friendly, then I'm dinner," Cain says, keeping a cautious hand on the butt of his pulsar gun.

The big black dog runs straight into Simons with hardly any effort to slow. They collide with a grunt, the dog offering up an apologetic yelp. The tan-and-white dog bypasses Simons and makes a run for Jorey, yipping and prancing around him as though they were long-lost friends. Jorey puts out a timid hand, and the dog throws its body into it, forcing the physical greeting with gusto.

"I guess you're dinner, Cain," I laugh, watching the assertive greeting between Simons and the other dog. He puts his hand out like Jorey, and the dog rears up onto its back legs, letting its front paws flail in the air. By the time their greetings are complete, the red-haired man has made his way to us, gasping and heaving.

"They're my dogs," he puffs. "Don't be afraid."

"We've figured as much," Simons says, letting his hand run across the ridged back of the white-and-tan dog as it returns to its master.

"I'm Max," the man says, still winded from his sprint across the field.

"Max," I repeat, thankful to have his name confirmed.

He stands before us, nursing a stitch in his right side, one arm around the tan-and-white beast whose head comes all the way up to his chest. His face is sunburnt red and painted with too many freckles to count. When Simons steps forward to greet him, I realize Max is nearly his equal.

"It's good to see a friendly face—or three," Simons says, embracing Max's hand in his own.

Max returns the greeting, taking us all in with wild exuberance.

"You made it," he murmurs under his breath, more for himself than for our benefit. "I was starting to lose an edge of hope, but here you are…"

"You must know about the hive," I say.

He locks eyes with me, his disheveled eyebrows giving him a comical expression of surprise. "Know about it? Isn't that an under-statement. You don't just drop a thousand-strong hive without every-body knowing about it." He nudges my shoulder and lowers his voice conspiratorially. "Dissenters, I mean. Folks in the city don't know anything. They don't even know how to tap into the government's encrypted relays."

"If you knew about the hive, then you must have realized we escaped," Cain says.

Max grabs a pack from Frances, urging Richards to give up another. He slings both over his shoulder, gesturing toward mine.

"I've got this one," I say, hesitant to relinquish it.

Max's eyes brighten with knowing. "Of course. I wouldn't dream of overstepping my role in the cause."

He urges us forward toward the residence, taking us along a cobbled path I hadn't noticed before. It splits the flower field with a purposeful, delicate curve, running around the generator building. I'm struck by the cultivated beauty of this facility in contrast to the man responsible.

"We knew they hadn't recovered you, but there was some question as to whether you survived. You know how hard it is to get informa-tion from the inside now. If the search didn't force remote communica-tion, we wouldn't know as much as we do," Max explains. "I knew you must have survived if they were still looking—you must have known they were still looking."

The dogs trot dutifully ahead of us, calm now with the intruders properly vetted. I split my attention between their graceful gait and Max's report.

"We went back into the tunnels," Jorey explains.

"It's what we figured," Max confirms. "But we didn't want to take any risks they'd go in after you. We sent an aerial to the east to draw the search away."

"An aerial?" I ask. Frances stops to admire the lupine sprouting vibrant purple amongst the fireweed.

"Grab some of those. I need to freshen the pots inside," Max instructs her.

She hesitates long enough for Max to pluck a demonstrative handful of flowers, then does the same. Max hands the freshly picked bunch to me. "A hovercraft. We had a pilot take one out close enough to look like a pickup. Took some skilled piloting to get in and out without casualty."

"Such a big risk," I breathe.

"Some risks are worth it. It'd be different if we were loading you onto the craft—that's a level of risk we aren't willing to take," Max insists.

He ushers us into the living quarters, which are the cozy twin of those in every other energy management facility. His quarters are filled with over-sized, overstuffed furniture that he likely upholstered himself. It's clear to see Max has come up with his own way to deal with the crushing loneliness of energy management work. The flower fields and giant dogs are only a part of Max's thousands of hours of isolation.

His dining table—an exact duplicate of Dó's and mine—is decorated with an over-sized vase filled with wilting flowers. As we deposit our packs, Max refills the vase with the fresh flowers.

"You know where the showers are," Max says, placing the vase back in the center of the table. "I'll start cooking so you have something warm to put on your bones before you rest."

We go through the same routines we went through at our first station, taking turns to shower and change into clean clothing before rejoining Max in the kitchen, sitting at the large table to await the feast he's busy preparing.

"Communication has been nearly impossible since the Northern Laboratories went down," Max explains as he worries over a large frying pan.

"Dó explained about the disappearances," I concede, stifling the pang of guilt at my role in the trouble.

"It's worse than that," Max says. "There's been a total collapse in the internal network. It's as if government communication's completely shut down. We've lost access to our people. Nothing in, nothing out. Even dead drops are blocked."

"How many dissenters are in direct danger?" I ask.

"It's not just about the dissenters. There's a war brewing." He stirs vigorously, his enthusiasm causing some of the contents to spill over the edges.

"What do you mean, war?" Frances asks before I can get the same question out.

"It was never about the dissenters. It would be easier if it were, but the government is worried about losing control of the City States," Max says.

"To whom?" I ask, stunned.

Max gives me an incredulous look. "To the people on the outside," he says in a low voice. I wonder, not entirely seriously, if these are the same outsiders Dunn rambled on about in his last days.

The kettle on the stove whistles. Max removes it from the heat, handing it over to Simons, who promptly fills the mugs Max placed on the table for us while we were showering. As the hot water penetrates the herbs and leaves within, the kitchen fills with their floral notes. Simons pushes the first mug toward me. Cain takes the next, bringing it to his face and inhaling with a satisfied sigh.

"That's an old one, Max. Don't tell me you're into conspiracy theories," he says, taking a cautious sip.

"Don't be so sure you know better, boy. Plenty of folks dismissed evidence Endgal had the cure before the first outbreak, and we know the truth about that now, don't we?" Max points his spatula at Cain. He's talking about the old Henry Endgal stories we all used to believe in—that I used to believe in.

"It's not as straightforward as all that," I argue, drawing the intensity of Max's stare away from Cain.

He studies me, assessing how much time he wants to invest in educating me in the world of conspiracies and cover-ups. Something falls from his outstretched spatula, and Cain swoops in to catch it. The large black dog stirs from its resting place to give him a reproachful glare. Clearly, they're accustomed to a certain level of cleanup privileges.

Max shrugs off his former intensity. "Now's not the time for this sort of talk. Once you've rested, I've got some documents you'd be very interested in."

Cain leans over behind Max's back and plucks something from the smoking pan, tossing the steaming morsel between his hands to keep from burning himself. Dog tails thump against the floor as they watch with fixed interest.

"I would be," I agree, trying not to laugh at Cain's antics.

Max turns to tend the pan, causing the dog tails to thump double-time. Without looking away from the food, he cuffs Cain in the back of the head, snatching the food out of his hand and tossing it back into the mix.

"I already have two miserable thieves in my house. I don't need a third," he says. Cain rubs at the back of his head, nursing his wounded pride.

Chuckling to himself, Simons turns to the maps strewn across the table, considering the plotted course. Cain abandons the pan, now fastidiously guarded by Max, to join the rest of us.

"With the DDC hot on our trail, we can't travel through the cities," Cain observes.

"Ayah," Max agrees, glancing over the counter toward the map. "And I promise we won't be risking it."

"Then we're stuck?" Jorey asks.

"Nah. We've worked things out. We're going to send you around," Max says. He reaches over the stove to points with a thick finger at the deep bay. He sweeps it out and around the peninsula, then south to the next landmark.

"The only ships that run the bay are government operated," Cain protests.

"Ayah," Max agrees again, as if this were the least concerning feature of the plan. "We're working on that too. We've got enough folks working in transportation to organize safe passage, so long as we take the time to do it right and flush out any spies. The crew needs to be indisputably loyal to the cause. Once we work that out, we're going to stow you on a cargo ship."

"How long will it take to organize our passage?" I ask, admiring the simplicity of the plan. We'll be hiding in plain sight, just like Amos did for me back at the Institute.

"A couple weeks if we can break back into the government network and restore communication from inside," he says.

"And if communication isn't restored?" I ask.

"A month? Maybe two. It depends on who the DDC flushes out from their inner workings." Max pulls the pan off the stove, plunking it onto a heavy wooden stand at the edge of the table.

"Once you reach the next landmark, it'll be one final stretch up the coast to the management facility outside the Institute. Folks are already working on the plan for that," Max promises. He gathers the maps off the table, replacing them with plates.

"And Amos has the plan from there?" I prompt, needing him to confirm.

"Right," he says. "But enough for now. Eat."

Cain rubs his hands together in eager compliance as Simons grabs a plate.

Max's meal is not as elaborate as Dó's, but his jovial personality fills our spirits. We stuff ourselves full of rich, greasy meats and preserved vegetables. When the meal is complete, he brings out two containers of distilled liquor flavored with rose, elderberry and honey from his own kept hives. We toast to our persistent survival and to the cure. Max sings us a song that sounds eerily familiar before launching into a series of stories that carry us past the afternoon and late into the night.

CHAPTER
THIRTY-SIX

SOMETIME AFTER MIDNIGHT, after the sun disappears for its few hours of slumber, I stumble through the piles of sleeping bodies toward the restroom, my stomach churning from rich food and strong liquor. I barely make it through the doors toward the toilet to empty the contents of my turbulent gut.

The world spins around an axis of me as I relive the spoiled scents and tastes of our extended feast. The conversations that filled the living space move in and out of my consciousness as I heave and moan, waiting for the sickness to pass, and my heart thunders warning at the base of my neck and temples. The sensation is similar to the stifling panic of the hive converging on the bubble force field.

I vomit again, remembering the grit of decomposed granite digging into my knees, the ache of forcing my arm rigid above my head, the split boulder that once stood as our temporary safe haven. I'm filled with the knowledge that I can't do anything to save them even if I open the bubble that keeps me safe from the converging hoard.

"They'll kill you too!" Hank screams from deep inside my memories as Dad disappears into the mangled, reaching hands with a bright spurt of blood.

Only it's not Dad, it's Simons and Jorey disappearing into the manipulative precision of the hive weapon as Cain breaks free to take refuge on the broken boulder. He lifts his pulsar gun and takes aim, pointing the weapon straight at my heart. When he fires, the shot crawls slowly from the weapon as a smoldering ball of energy that grows large enough to envelop the attacking hive.

"I knew I could count on you to understand the magnitude of this accomplishment," Orman taunts in a laughing echo. His face flashes angry from the darkness as he snarls, *"Be careful, Mason!"*

"I am being careful." The words get stuck in my throat as I survey the bloody field that used to be my family's refuge. Blood trails across the tall grasses, pooling at the base of a metallic floor—the training room where Smith's remains paint a gory mess for all to see.

No one was supposed to die…

"You can't save everyone," Amos says, shoving me into a room where Trudy thrashes against medical restraints while a team of interns gazes upon her.

"Obviously, you like him, and he's clearly made his claim," Jorey jeers from the harness suspended over the swarming hive. Richards reaches his hand toward him, firing into the mass of disease.

Jorey misses his grip, disappearing into the icy depths as Simons begs, *"Come on, breathe!"*

"You can't save everyone," Shelby says before collapsing in a heap of death in the dark tunnel leading toward our escape. Orman steps over her corpse, pressing his face directly against mine, the cold, hard surface jarring in its reality.

"Off limits until further notice."

I lurch backward, smashing my head against the wall as I pull away from the porcelain bowl. The bathroom crashes back into existence around me, and the swirling world grinds to a halt. I let out a sharp exhale as my hands fly to my head.

Those were dreams. I was asleep.

I sit for a moment, assessing myself for damage.

The nausea has passed, and even if it hadn't, there's nothing more to expel. The drunkenness seems to have passed along with the nausea, leaving me sweaty and chilled.

I flush the toilet's contents away and pull myself to the sink, where I rinse my mouth out for several minutes until the taste of spoiled liquor is gone. I look up at my reflection in the dim glow of semi-darkness. It's only then I notice the small light sitting at the back of the counter.

Its familiarity is so striking that it hits me in the guts—a sphere, small enough to fit in the palm of my hand, radiating soft, pink light. I'm certain if I reached for it, I would be grasping at the almost-nothingness of electrically repulsed fiber optics. I could flip it over and find the little black dot that controls the energy…

My fingers contact a solid surface, smooth and warm. The orb rests on a conical silver stand. When I lift it, the glass rises from the stand, revealing a glowing filament energized by a spinning magnet. Perpetual motion—or at least as close as we get given our gravitational conditions. The light is nothing like the one that Hank made, and yet…

"He would have loved you," I whisper, replacing the glass cover. He would have loved all of this—the adventure, the defiance, the high stakes work of bringing the cure… Hank was built for it. The thought sends a jolt down my spine.

What about me?

Eager to evade the question, I wash my face with cool water, then clean my mouth again with a fresh toothbrush from Max's mini-stockpile in the cabinet, which goes a long way toward making me feel better. Before I turn away from the counter, I brush my fingers across the light a final time, remembering what I used to say when Hank bragged about being the better twin.

"Anything you can do I'll do better by the time you've moved on to the next thing."

Hank left his night-light behind so many years ago, but I'm still holding on to it. The glow is haunted by all the ghosts in my wake, and I wonder if I could ever leave Hank behind—if I could let go of any of them.

A quiet tap on the door makes me jump, knocking the light-ball off the stand. A small cry escapes me. I scramble to catch the glass before it shatters. The door cracks open, releasing an arc of light as I cradle the orb in my open palms, my heart racing in my throat.

I tear my eyes away from the near-tragedy long enough to see Cain's face in the comparatively blinding light from the hall. I replace the orb on its stand, and the door opens the rest of the way. Cain has one hand propped on the sill to hold himself up as he sways. I wipe my hands and face on a hanging towel, smiling to mask the sea of pain and uncertainty.

He catches my shoulder and pulls me in, whispering, "You okay, Mason?"

"Yeah," I whisper, letting him hold me and willing his drunken embrace to wash away the dread and stifle the sadness welling inside of me. "Too much liquor and grease, that's all."

"It's that nourishment infliction coming back to haunt you!" Cain chuckles, oblivious to my turmoil.

I keep the cringe internal as Cain recalls the nightmare of our last days in the Northern Laboratories. I dismiss the idea of admitting my nightmare to him. His mind is far off from that sort of thing, and I want to join him there.

"Very funny," I say.

His hand travels down my shoulder until it finds mine. He steps away from me and gives it a gentle tug. I follow as he guides me deeper into the hallway.

"Come on, Mason." He pulls me closer in the narrow passageway, resting against the wall. "Lighten up."

"That was far from serious," I protest, squaring my body against his. The wanting is turning into being. The closer I get to Cain, the further the nightmares fade into the background.

Cain smirks dismissively at my argument before dipping down to kiss me. I turn my head away in protest before his lips find mine.

"I've been sick…"

"And I've been drunk," he retorts. "I don't care, Mason. Let me kiss you. It's torture when you ignore me," he pleads.

"I haven't been ignoring you," I balk, genuinely perplexed.

"Ever since the hive," Cain says, kissing the top of my head, urging me to turn back into him. His eyes are warm pools of desire that make me squirm. I blink to break the tension, reminding myself to breathe. I don't know how to respond, how to reconcile deep dread at the mention of the hive with my own mounting desire.

"You mean when we narrowly escaped a horrible death and kissed in front of a gaping audience?" I ask.

"Maybe you're not much for kissing in front of everyone. That's fine. I know where we can hide," Cain says, still trying to nudge my mouth toward his.

His statement piques my curiosity, and I let myself forget the hive. It's surprisingly easy to do. I brush my lips lightly down the side of his neck. "Show me," I whisper into the space between his clavicle and shirt.

His chest vibrates with a low moan. His hands travel down my arms, brushing lightly over my skin, raising gooseflesh. He pauses briefly at my waist, long enough that I try to grasp his wrists, before he moves them to my back and pulls me up and into him. I wrap my legs around him, and our mouths meet with barely contained desperation.

His hot breath is dressed with the taste of alcohol. The coarse hair of his beard tickles the top of my lip, and—for at least this moment—thoughts of all the looming dangers are gone.

Keeping one arm around my waist and without interrupting his kiss, Cain turns the handle to a door in the hall and leads us into the back room. At Dó's, this room was a treasure trove of high-tech weaponry, but here there's only a bed and a desk with a squat lamp sitting atop a knit, flowered doily. The door closes silently behind us, and Cain's other hand returns to my body, moving us toward the bed.

My stomach turns excited knots as Cain's tongue moves across my lips. I break away from his kiss, breathlessly clinging to his shoulders. His mouth finds the skin below my earlobe, making me shiver. I bury my hands in his too-long hair, cupping the base of his skull as I shudder against his touch. "What are we doing?"

"Isn't it obvious?" His lips brush across my cheek. "After so many nights huddled next to everyone's stinking bodies, I finally get you all to myself."

"We don't stink anymore," I point out. I expect the statement to disrupt the spell and bring reality crashing back in, but it doesn't. All it does is brings a mischievous grin to my swollen lips.

Cain exhales a laugh through his nose, his lips still tracing a path of kisses across the landscape of my tingling face. "I'm not going to let you ruin this," he says, lowering me onto the quilted surface of the bed. His body hovers over mine, framed in silver moonlight.

"Then what are you waiting for?" I ask.

His lips find mine, and the question is nearly lost to the moment. His fingers brush my skin where my shirt meets my bare thigh. My breath catches as his hand travels up my waist, pulling my shirt with it. I let a quiet moan escape as he pants against my cheek.

I grip the waistband of his pants, dizzied by the feel of him pressed against me. "Do I need to give you permission or something?" I ask.

"Something like that."

His hands move the rest of the way up, pulling my shirt along with them. He tosses it aside, pausing long enough to pull his own shirt off. Our bodies meet again, skin against skin, entwining. I move urgently, all thought lost to the pressing, numbing need pulsing so violently inside of me that I think I might burst.

Cain's hands move with silent knowledge, meeting that need. I grasp for the quilt, trying to pull it away from the bed. The pillows fall from the bed, and Cain pulls away, shedding the remaining barrier. Our mouths meet again as he returns to me. My back arches, pressing myself against him as he moves, and the rest of the moment turns to oblivion.

CAIN'S ARM is draped across the quilt, which I pulled across our entwined frames as the night's chill crept into the room. I look past his relaxed, nearly sleeping frame to the setting moon that fills the bedroom window. I stare at it, admiring its irradiated terrain, wondering at the silence that's taken the place of my normally racing thoughts.

A small, satisfied smile graces my lips. I chew my lower lip, pondering the gravitational effect of the moon on the earth's surface. I lift a hand to the side of Cain's face, letting it rest against the stiff bristles that have transformed into a full beard. I shift toward him so our bodies are parallel, our feet touching.

"Hey you, everything good?" he asks, proving he's still awake.

I could tell him about the doubt and worry threatening to make their way back in. I could admit I'm terrified to even look at the ruined pages of the cure, but that's not what he's asking about. "Yes, everything is good," I confirm.

Cain dips in to kiss the tip of my nose. "Good. I don't know if I could handle it if you'd said anything else."

"You know, if there were a problem right now, there are two responsible parties involved," I remind him.

Cain shakes his head, moving my hand along with it until it slips down to his neck. I let it rest there, feeling the strong, steady beat of his pulse.

"The only problem with your proposal is that it can't be you because you're perfect," he says.

I snicker. "That sounds like drunken ramblings to me. Eli Cain, are you still drunk?"

"I might be. But if I am drunk, it only means I'm telling the truth." His face is awash with wide-eyed earnestness. The expression is so ridiculous I genuinely can't tell if he's being serious.

"You can't use your romantic gibberish on me. I'm impervious to the ways of the outside world," I admonish, a grin creeping back to my lips.

"If you tell me scientists are above romantic entanglement, I'm going to call you a liar," Cain says, wiggling his intertwined leg against mine as proof.

"I didn't say that. I said *I'm* above romantic wiles," I correct, adding, "usually" as an afterthought that makes me giggle.

"I refuse to believe you've never been wrapped up in the passion of human desires before this very moment. From the way I hear it, the Institute is notorious for that sort of thing."

"What do you know about the Institute?" I give the quilt a gentle tug and pull myself up onto my elbows.

Cain brushes his beard across my fingers until he gets a smile out of me. "I'm no expert, but I know they throw a bunch of seventeen- and eighteen-year-olds together with nothing but each other..." He waggles his eyebrows suggestively.

"Well, I hate to disappoint, but my personal experience begs to differ with your *sources*." I trail my hand down his arm and grasp his fingers.

"Was it your leg?" Cain asks as if it's the only possible explanation.

"No. The surgery happened first thing when I arrived, and I was well into recovery by the time I joined the interns," I explain.

"What do you mean—*joined the interns*?" he asks, sitting up so our faces are level.

"Because I was there when I shouldn't have been—Amos didn't know where to put me, and she had to come up with a plan that would make the DDC think they were in charge." I know this explanation is insufficient, but it's a good enough start.

Cain's curiosity intensifies. "The DDC was involved in your placement with the interns?"

"Yes, they were very interested in my test scores. But it was Amos' decision to send me to the Northern Laboratories," I confirm.

"So you could bring the cure out of the Laboratories," Cain finishes.

"Exactly. I only messed that up completely," I sigh, thinking about the lost communication and the people on the inside.

"You show up at the Institute, get a leg-saving surgery—"

"Life-saving," I correct.

"Life-saving," Cain corrects, his thoughts distant. "And immediately afterward, the DDC gives the green light for you to join the intern program."

"Pretty much." I shrug, not sure where the conversation goes from here or why he's so interested.

"But why was it even an issue for you to join the interns in the first place? Isn't that what was supposed to happen?" His eyes meet mine, bright and curious, though his body sways subtly.

"Well, yeah, eventually," I say.

"What does that mean?" His intensity puts me on edge, unearthing some yet-unknown insecurity.

"It's just... I got there a few years too early. That's why I never... I was so much younger than everyone else," I say, trying not to sound defensive.

What I'm admitting to him is something I haven't even broached with Jorey yet.

"I lied about my age—well, Amos and the DDC lied about it—to get me into the intern program."

He's quiet for a long time, as if he's trying to work something out. His lips move wordlessly; his fingers brush absently across the raised surface of the scar. I resist the urge to pull away from his touch. The scar is just as much a part of me as the rest of my body.

"Early by how much?" he asks.

"Three years." My cheeks flush, knowing that in the wake of Simons' accusation, this is going to become a matter of my age.

Cain breathes a silent curse. I can't tell if it's anger or shock, but it sucks the wind from my lungs. "Don't make this weird. I'm not a child."

"Technically, no," Cain agrees, sitting up so the quilt pools at his waist.

"Technically, that's what matters. If I'm old enough for Shelby to trust with the cure, I'm old enough to make any number of other decisions, including this one, so don't make this about age," I blurt, scooting toward him so my legs dangle over the edge of the bed.

"I wasn't going to," he says, giving my shoulder a nudge.

I grab the shirt dangling precariously on the edge of the bed, not sure whose it is. I pull it over my head, and it falls loosely to cover my torso. "I saw you calculating," I say, not wanting to let him off the hook.

"I wasn't calculating your age."

"Well, if you'd bothered, you'd know for certain I'm an adult, but since you weren't, what exactly were you calculating?"

"I was retracing Orman's path before he went to the Northern Laboratories," Cain explains.

"You were already on his trail?" I ask, surprised.

"By the time he was wiping out your family, I'd already been following him for years," Cain says.

I consider this explanation. Cain's life is stained by Orman's brutality. He's spent years traveling in his wake, converging on one orchestrated disaster after another, narrowly missing his target. It sounds like an awful way to live.

"Does he always use hives?" I ask.

"Usually hives, but as you're well aware, Orman has an entire arsenal of weaponry." Cain's voice darkens. His body, formerly warm and pliable, is rigid and cold.

"I thought you said you didn't know it was him at first. It couldn't have been him every time," I protest. There must be too many incidents for Orman to partake in.

Cain tips his head toward me. "At first, no. But the DDC has specific patterns. If they're dealing with something near the City States, it's always agents. Agents and infected. They need to keep up appearances. But when it comes to dissenters—when it comes to the *real* threats, they send Orman."

Hearing Cain recount his own experiences and knowing he crossed the grounds stained in my family's blood turns something inside of me cold.

Cain grasps my hand, tugging me toward him until our bodies are touching again. He places a hand against my cheek, wiping away a tear I didn't realize was there. "You've survived a lot. You're going to be able to survive everything else. I know it. And when we face him again, I'm going to be ready."

My heart is broken and full at the same time. "How do you even know we'll face him again? There are too many ways for the DDC to get to us to be sure. Orman may have moved on."

"Orman doesn't move on," Cain promises. "I know how he works. He'll come to us when the time is right."

"You make it sound like you want him to find us," I say, dismissing the idea with a nervous laugh.

His laugh sounds forced. Cain kisses the top of my head, leaning back until he's lying on the bed, cradling me in the crook of his arm with my head resting on his chest. "I'm only preparing for the inevitable."

"Do you think you could teach me how to do that while you're at it?" I ask.

He's quiet for a moment, lost in a faraway thought. "You don't have to worry. I'm going to take care of you," he says. Behind him, the moon sinks into the mountains, leaving its glow spread across the cloud-covered sky.

THE SUN BAKES through the window, warming our bodies as we lay entwined in blissful rest. Cain's hand is draped across my stomach, just under my bunched-up shirt, as warm as the sunshine. He's still sleeping. His steady breath comes in deep snores that puff out, tickling the loose hairs from my braid against my neck. Even his breath is warm. It takes a moment in my sleep-addled state to realize it's coming from the wrong side of the bed.

Startled by the realization, I reach my hand toward the source. Before it even connects with the hulking body, I both hear and feel the thump-thump whip of a massive tail. I run my fingers through the short, silky hair on the heaving chest as the tail ramps up. A second later, the bed shifts as something else moves in, searching for my hand, wet nose first. Cain stirs, his hand curling around me as he nuzzles into my neck.

"Morning," he mumbles into a layer of blankets.

"Cain?" I prompt.

He responds with a careless hum, not bothering to open his eyes.

"We aren't alone anymore," I say as one of the dogs nuzzles its nose between Cain's hand and my stomach. The other dog squirms its way toward my face, flicking its tongue across my cheek.

Cain sits up, suddenly too awake. He runs a hand through his wavy hair, scratching at the wiry mass of his fresh beard. The black dog—Hector, Max called him—steps over me to put his face directly in front of Cain's in a space-invading greeting. "What the—"

He pushes gently at the dog's face to send the giant beast on its way. Luckily for him, the brown and white dog—Alto—chooses the same moment to offer me her belly, forcing Hector to flip off the bed. I give her the requisite treatment, sitting up to look around the room.

"The door must not have latched," I say, noting its half-open position.

"Or Max let them in to wreak havoc," Cain observes, thrusting his arms over his head in an exaggerated stretch.

"Why would he do that?" I ask, giving Cain the side-eye.

"To make sure you're still here," Cain says, tossing the covers aside.

"Why? The cure's in the front room next to Simons," I say.

"I didn't say *the cure*, I said you—the scientist." He ruffles my loose hair, then pulls me into his arms, kissing my forehead. "As far as I'm aware, you're the only one left."

He's teasing me, referring to my formal title rather than my training. But it reminds me of what Shelby said about the role of the Northern Laboratories in keeping the disease rampant. *You can't stop human progress, so the government seeks to control it...* They collected everyone with the potential to make a difference and locked them away. Now the Northern Laboratories and the scientists within are gone.

"I'm safe here. Who's he protecting me from, you?" I scrunch my nose at the thought.

Cain steps over to the door and holds it open for the dogs, who oblige by sauntering out. "You never know." He offers me a conspiratorial wink.

"I know," I insist, tossing the quilt and pillows back onto the bed.

"Max doesn't. And there's only one of you," he says, reaching for my hand to escort me from the room.

In the kitchen, Max bellows something at the dogs, soliciting a bright burst of laughter from Simons. Richards and Jorey are talking, but their words are lost to the sounds of morning. Cain and I will be joining them, for the second time, in an obviously coupled situation. The thought makes my stomach twist in ways I can't quite sort. I take Cain's hand and paint a smile onto my own face as we leave the back room.

We zip past the kitchen, trying and failing to pass without notice. As I plunge my legs into a pair of clean pants from the pile next to the sofa, Max calls out, "Do you do eggs or no?"

"Eggs for me," Cain calls back, forcing large bare feet through the tight cuffs of a pair of pants meant for someone smaller.

"Mason doesn't like eggs," Jorey says.

"Naw," Max responds incredulously. The interjection is followed by a series of loud bangs and a string of harmless words intended to replace foul language. "You can't survive up here without eggs."

"Are they real?" I ask, looping the string at the waist of the pants so they won't slip. Cain's pair is so snug that he can't even make a single knot. I stifle a snicker.

"Of course they're real!" Max says as I enter the kitchen, slipping away from Cain as he rummages through the clothing for a better fit. Max is shaking his head, my suggestion the government egg powder is a fabrication too unbelievable to fathom.

"Real dehydrated egg protein," Simons says, tipping the ceramic mug toward his lips. My spirit lifts at the notion of coffee, but then I realize the kitchen smells of aromatic spices. It's not the same as the night before, but it's still tea.

"Mornin', Mason," Simons says, setting his cup on the table and reaching for the kettle to refill it. "I see you survived the night, more or less."

"A little more in some ways, less in others," Cain says, entering the kitchen behind me, now wearing a second pair of much better-fitting pants. He comes up behind me, wrapping an arm around my shoulder. Frances glances my way, making my cheeks warm.

"I suppose you know the finer details of all that to speak for her about it," Jorey says dryly. He slides a mug in my direction without looking up.

"You know about the eggs; I know about last night," Cain retorts, reaching around me to claim the mug as his own. I dodge past him, swatting his hand away and taking a seat next to Jorey.

"No one needs to speak for me while I'm here," I say before they can take their quarrel to a new level. I grab the mug. It warms my hands, filling my senses with the most delectable mixture I can imagine. Suddenly I'm less discouraged by the absence of coffee. "Eggs are fine, Max," I add with a reassuring nod.

"Do you think there will be any time to tour the facility grounds?" Frances asks, handing a steaming mug to Cain and diffusing the situation with parental expertise.

"Sure! Until we get things situated, you've got nothing but time," Max says, pouring egg into a smoking pan and stirring vigorously.

The sulfuric smell of protein concentrate cooking too fast hits me like a sickening wave. I bury my face in my mug as Jorey gives me a knowing glance. I shrug at his sympathetic expression while Cain eases himself into the chair next to me.

"I've got to do some work after breakfast, but then I'll give you a tour. We'll grab some gear and fish the creek—fresh protein would probably do you all some good," Max says, taking the pan off the burner.

He opens the warmer under his oven to retrieve a behemoth loaf of seeded, aromatic bread. The smell is so tantalizing that it nearly erases the burnt eggs. The loaf takes center stage on the table, sitting beside a bowl of bulbous red berries and the jar of honey. Max places the eggs next to these before sitting across from Simons.

"I can imagine enjoying fishing," Richards says, serving himself from the bowl of berries before passing it to Frances. Max scoops a large portion of egg onto his plate, passing it to Cain as Simons slices into the bread.

"All right, then. I'm hoping to get some communication later this morning. I've got to change some battery cells on the backup generator, do some routine maintenance. I'll get you after that," Max says between slathering honey on a slice of bread and shoveling mouthfuls of egg.

"As nice as it sounds, I think I'll pass. I need to get to work," I say, warding off the spoon full of egg Cain tries to shove in my face. I put my hand over his and force the eggs out of the spoon onto my plate before he manages to get them to my face again, ruining his childish game.

"What are you up to then?" Max asks, peering suspiciously at me over the top of his mug.

"The cure," I explain. "It was partially damaged in the river during our escape."

"And you're going to restore it?" he asks.

Jorey slides a thick slice of bread onto my plate as I accept the berries from Frances. "I'm going to do what I can. Or see what I can do, anyway."

Concern flashes across Max's face, masked by another mouthful.

"She's being modest," Simons interjects. "Mason is more than capable."

Max accepts this without question. His faith leaves me unsettled, as if the entire dissenter movement hinged on my abilities.

"Most of Shelby's work was spared. I believe I'll be able to recreate it without a laboratory," I explain, much the same way I did to the others when it came up at Dó's.

"And the rest you'll fit together in our labs," Max says, settling the matter for himself.

"Are there labs ready for the cure?" I ask, taking my first bite. The bread is earthy and rich, completely contrasting with the bright jam's sweetness in an entirely pleasant way.

"We have a lab. Once we have you and the cure, the rest will come together," Max insists.

It's not the answer I want, but given our experience with dissenters on the outside, I have to believe he's right. I bypass the eggs, popping two of the berries into my mouth. The vibrant flavors are everything the food in the Northern Laboratories was missing.

"These berries are incredible. I don't think I've had their equal," Frances says, reading my mind.

"Well, of course you wouldn't," Max says, brimming with pride. "They don't send food like this to the cities."

Cain raises a knowing eyebrow. He abandons his mostly cleaned plate, propping his elbows on the wooden table and popping the last bite of toast into his mouth. I expect him to say something, but he's shockingly quiet.

"What about what's grown in the cities?" Richards asks.

It's only after he speaks that I realize what Cain's waiting for. He looks from Max to Richards, with a quick, sweeping glance at the rest of us before fixing his attention on Max again.

"You know better than to think food is produced in the cities, don't you?" Max asks, knowing full well Richards (and likely the rest of us) don't.

"The entire agriculture sector… the processing factories—the entire infrastructure of the cities is built around food," Richards protests.

"I used to work in distribution for the capitol. I saw the production reports," Frances adds, as if this were all the further proof anyone would need.

"Do you really think the cities—any of them on their own or combined—can produce enough food for the entire population? In factory buildings?" Max asks, balling his hands into fists on the table and leaning back into his chair. The wood groans under his shifting weight.

"Greenhouses," Jorey corrects. "They're factory greenhouses."

I want to jump in, to verify what Richards, Frances and Jorey are saying, but Simons is conspicuously silent. The City States are full of enormous buildings. Everyone knows them by their purpose—agriculture, production, processing and distribution. We learn about them so early in life that we never have to question, never have to wonder where our food comes from or why it comes in the forms that it does. It's integral to the way our world works.

"What one City State needs, the other makes," I say, utterly unconvinced for the first time in my life.

"A good lie is infinitely believable. But I'll ask you one question. If you can answer it, I'll let the whole thing go. If all the food is made in the cities, what's in all the shipments?" Max asks, leaving us dumbstruck.

CHAPTER
THIRTY-NINE

IT'S NOT that food isn't grown or processed in the cities. The problem is that it's logistically impossible to grow *enough* food within the confines of the City States. The government's own production reports are enough to prove the impossibility of their own design—if anyone were allowed to investigate the matter. In-house food production is a front meant to paint the picture of perfect balance and total control. Sure, the government could admit that agriculture and food production had to be expanded outside the safety of city limits, but that opens up too many opportunities for questions. It would expose a vulnerability.

All of this, according to Max, is so obvious that citizens are being willfully blind to not see it. I'm conflicted about his theory. It makes too much sense to not be founded in some nugget of truth, just like Dunn's outsiders, but his explanation is off-kilter.

"If the food isn't manufactured in the cities, then where is it being produced? Where is *safe enough* for it to be produced?" Max asks the stunned breakfasters as Cain looks on, amused.

"They couldn't get away with something like that without being found out. If not by regular folks, the ones in distribution…" Richards argues, looking to Frances, who returns his gaze, baffled. Max brings up the production reports again.

"We all know how easy it is for the DDC to eliminate folks looking into the wrong things," Simons says, nodding along to the conversation while slathering honey on a second slice of bread.

"I can get behind that, but if they're hiding it, they're doing it well. Why bother with the ruse at all?" Frances asks, trying to make sense of it.

"If food comes from the outside, it gets people thinking about the outside. What else might be on the other side of those safe walls?" Max asks, intentionally leading us to his conclusion.

"Force fields," I correct, still thinking it through for myself.

"What she said," Max says, waving a dismissive hand. "The point is, if people know food comes from the outside, the government's got a lot of explaining to do—about the outbreak, about the state of the world..."

I allow my focus to turn to the problem at hand. Shipments from the outside—from the *other cities*—are regular enough to keep the capitol in supply but sporadic due to alternating production schedules. Everyone knows the city's infrastructure can't provide continuous supplies. There aren't enough resources. The days of dedicated factories and streamlined production are ancient history. In the new world, resources are limited, and labor is scarce. The cities rely on one another and on the scavengers of the old world. Aside from the Northern Laboratories, it's the whole reason for the government. It's why their role is so vital to our survival. So why, in the context of our indisputable reality, did we never question the food?

It has to be more than soil that comes from the outside. The only question is, "Who grows it?"

The conversation, which has veered wildly from the egg production of domesticated fowl to the raw acreage required to grow carrots, stutters, then stalls. Max fixes his intense stare on me, eyes bright with the thrill of conspiracy. "The carrots?" he asks.

"All of it! Who grows the food?" I snap, stunned he took my question so literally.

"Carrots are a very common meal piece—from a commodity perspective," Frances says, having completely lost the thread.

"It's a good question," Jorey says. "Even if the rest of it makes sense, you can't grow that volume of food without a comparable workforce."

"It's not the production people; they're almost always family workers. The scavengers? Researchers?" Frances asks.

"There aren't enough of them," Simons says, leaning into his hands in his familiar thoughtful position. "And besides, it can't be anyone that goes in and out of the cities. The risk of that sort of thing getting leaked would be too great."

"Boy, that's an understatement. This thing getting leaked could topple the whole system," Max says, slapping the table. Hector and Alto turn their heads at the noise, but their lack of urgency suggests it's a frequent enough occurrence.

"So it's not anyone from inside the cities. Who does that leave?" Jorey asks.

The expectant smile nearly cracks Max's face in two as we push for the reveal he's kept from us until this moment.

"The rest of the world," he says in an urgent, hushed voice.

His statement conjures a thousand memories. The businessman with the leaking hole in his chest. Endless rows of frozen bodies in patient storage. Dunn's insistent, rambling stories of omens from the outside. Cain's face as he tells me about a community of people from the outside that he doesn't want to talk about…

"The rest of the—" Frances starts, but she trails off, as if the notion of the world is too complex to put into words.

"You mean other cities. Other government structures that have come up across the globe since everything was destroyed," Richards says after a pause.

"You could imagine it that way," Max says, nodding in Richards' direction as he takes a sip of tea. "Or you might imagine a world that never fell apart in the first place."

No matter how many times Max takes us through the idea, no matter how much evidence supports established life right outside the cities, his explanation doesn't quite work. There are people, but not where he says. The cities can't support themselves, but someone is. He's onto something, but the food can't come from a hidden, established world just on the other side of the force fields. Even if that supposed world is being held ransom by our control of the disease... I don't know what the truth is, but Cain knows more than he's letting on.

After breakfast, Max heads off to tend to his facility, leaving the rest of us to grapple with his revelation. I abandon the discussion, which isn't going anywhere, to dig up Shelby's work. Cain scrambles after me, leaving Jorey calling, "You can't just sit there with that stupid smile on your face!"

I raise my eyebrow at him in good humor and unwrap the first of the notebooks. "Jorey's a smart guy, but he's not the best at reading people."

Cain runs his fingers up the side of my arm, sending a thrill through me. "What's that supposed to mean?"

I set the pack aside and stand, giving him a playful peck on his cheek. "It means he's underestimating your ability to sit quietly and look stupid," I say.

Cain blocks the door, wrapping his arms around my waist with the clear intention of stalling my exit.

"Are you mad at me?" he asks, smiling in a way that makes it obvious he doesn't think he's done anything wrong.

"Why didn't you say anything?" I demand.

Cain's face turns blank. "About Max?"

"About the people on the outside!"

"Because Max is delusional!" Cain laughs.

"But what about the things Dunn said? And your story! You *know* about the people on the outside!" I snap, stepping back from him and crossing my arms over the notebook, holding it against my chest.

Cain drops his shoulders and dips his chin in thought. He shakes his head. "Yes, there are people on the outside. Small communities that have been surviving for a long time, but not in Old America. It would be impossible to keep hidden with all the outside activity. Remember what I told you last night? About the DDC controlling those areas?"

I nod, remembering our conversation along with the rest of the night. "Fine, but why didn't you say anything?" I press, taking a half step toward him.

"Because they aren't like Max thinks—they aren't old-world civilizations. They're like the City States. They're from now."

I let that sink in. It makes sense. Of course there are other communities across the world, building security and starting life over again.

"You don't agree with him, then?" I ask.

"Max has big ideas. He's not the only one. There's truth in them, but it's mixed with a bunch of conspiracy," Cain says, cupping his hand around my face.

"Promise to talk about the communities on the outside more?" I ask, resting my head against his chest.

His body stiffens. He wraps his arms around me. "To you?"

"To everyone," I say.

"I don't want to talk to everyone about my mom."

A pang of guilt strikes me as I realize what I'm asking. "Of course not. But maybe there's another way to talk about the communities— about how you followed Orman and how the DDC keeps control of the areas. I think it's important."

"Let me think about it."

I step back and give him another peck on his cheek. "I have work to do."

"Right now? From the looks of it, you're going to have plenty of time to get it done. Max said it could be months until we've got a passage to the south," Cain says.

"What am I supposed to do with that time, spend all of it arguing with your stupid smile?"

"My smile is brilliant. I have no idea what Jorey's talking about." Cain bends down and kisses me, lingering until I use Shelby's notebook to create space between us.

Flushed and vaguely giddy, we exit the room together to join the others in the living room. Frances offers me another cup of tea, and I take a seat on the overstuffed chair. I take it, settling with the intent to work while the others chat. I flip through the first of Shelby's notes as if they were a foreign language instead of annotated chemical pathways. I need to put the matters of food and the outside world aside and think like a scientist, but it doesn't do any good.

Up here, Max can believe what he wants, but the land outside the cities isn't populated by old-world civilizations. It's empty, so full of wilderness that it encroaches on our new-world infrastructure. If there is a world outside our cities, it's far from here...

I try with all my might to dismiss Max's hypothesis, but I keep coming back to the patients. There are too many of them. There isn't enough disease in the cities—or population outside the cities, for that matter—to explain the sheer magnitude of patients... unless Max is right.

ONCE I MANAGE to get going, I lose myself to Shelby's cure, retracing each note, each chemical pathway and cellular interface until they're burnt into my mind as I copy it for myself. I need to know her work as intimately as if I were the one to have created it. Only then will I be able to recreate the missing pages.

For the last several weeks, I've allowed myself the luxury of the brilliant mornings to soak in sunshine, walking the dwindling garden of wildflowers as the brief northern summer fades into fall. Morning frost drives the remaining blooms shut while others retreat to their buds. When I first started walking the garden, cool mornings warmed rapidly into the radiance of late summer, but as fall progresses, the cool air has begun to bite, and my breath leaves trailing puffs in my wake. After each walk, I warm my hands against ceramic mugs of honey-sweetened tea while Max cooks eggs and dips into his pantry for berry preserves.

I sit at the breakfast table with the team while Max describes the winterizing procedures for his garden and everyone discusses their plans for the day. Max will be ready for the first freeze far in advance with all the help he's getting. Most days, Simons looks like he'll jump out of his own skin without something to do. The long wait has that effect on everyone. Thankfully, with Max's help, he, Jorey, and

Richards are using their time to learn the dissenter communication systems while Frances delves into the historical archives.

Government communication systems are still dark except for some remote reports from the DDC. Since the status of communication from within remains unchanged, dissenters on the outside have abandoned satellite relay communication in favor of long-range radio relay. With the rebirth of radio communication comes the need for ciphers, which it turns out Frances and Richards both have a knack for. Though Frances is especially gifted at translating messages from their code-source, Simons pushes her to focus on Max's documents. Given the link between the shipments and the government's secrets, he believes she's the best suited to identify discrepancies in the supply chains.

Cain has become reclusive. Even when he's hanging around, his thoughts are distant, as though he were trying to solve a mystery of which only he's aware. I'm not the only one to notice, but no one else seems to mind as much.

He masks his reticence with a new affinity for fishing. When the rest of us pile into the living room to work, he excuses himself to the front porch to make lures in the bright afternoon sunlight. He stands at the bank for each sunrise and sunset, casting and pulling in fish as they migrate up the channels. Each night, he prepares his catches for Max to smoke so we can take them on our journey south.

Our activities are accompanied by Max's giant lumbering dogs, who invade our space, panting heavily and drooling over everything and everyone. Somehow no one seems to mind. Their persistent, too-close presence creates a sense of comfort. It's easy to understand why Max keeps them despite the drain on his resources. In the evenings, when my eyes burn and my mind is too full to be of further use, I venture out again into the expansive gardens with the dogs as company, losing myself as they chase errant rodents. When he's not fishing, Cain joins me on these walks, but more often it's Jorey or Simons.

"How's the progress on the cure going?" Jorey asks, turning his body to sidestep an overgrown branch.

"It's slow, but that's the nature of this sort of thing," I say, ducking down to bypass the branch Jorey holds out of my way. Hector uses the opportunity to brush past me and lope ahead on the path, nose planted firmly to the ground.

"You'll get it taken care of in time," Simons says, taking the branch from Jorey.

"More like I'll have it memorized before I've put the missing pieces back together." I laugh, shaking my weary head.

"That doesn't seem like such a bad thing," Jorey offers. Ahead, the air shimmers with the force field boundary. We turn left toward the creek. I squint into the sinking sun at the dogs sprinting toward Cain's silhouette as he casts his line out over the water. My mind wanders to our shared nights, and my face turns hot.

"You're right, Jorey. I think I'm tired," I say, knowing full well that tired isn't the right word. The long layover waiting for confirmed passage has provided ample opportunity to do everything we need to prepare for the next leg of the journey. We're more rested than ever.

"You can take a break," Simons says, eying me with obvious concern.

"It's not so simple." I turn my head away from him, afraid he'll see right through me to the heart of the matter—about the cure and about Cain. Cain is the easier one to explain away. The cure, on the other hand, has me in knots. Everyone expects that, as a scientist, I'll put it together with ease, but so far, it's taking everything I've got just to understand it.

"Mason, there's only one of you. It takes as long as you need it to take. There's help on the other side of this," he says.

I don't respond immediately. I'm too busy worrying he's wrong about what's waiting for us on the other side of our journey. Too much can still go wrong.

Our path meanders through thick grasses, the creek temporarily dropping out of view as we approach. From the other side of the bank, Cain cries out in surprise as the dogs descend upon him, causing him to lose his footing and the fish on his line.

"We can't act like we have more time than we do. Regardless of what Max has to say about the matter, I'm certain there's something going on in or around the City States. I don't think we have to worry about a mysterious old-world establishment trying to rise up against the government, but something is happening. The hive technology has a purpose," I say.

"They could be coming for the dissenters," Jorey suggests.

"They will be, but according to Dó, their concern about the dissenters was sparked by our actions in the Laboratories. I'd like to know what they were worried about before. What scared them enough to spend years developing the virus and hive technology? The possibilities are too many, and the consequences of getting it wrong could be devastating," I muse.

"Frances has been going through Max's records, looking for anything that might let us know what's going on," Simons says.

"If she's looking at Max's stuff, she's going to end up with Max's conclusion," Jorey says with obvious ridicule.

"Max isn't a fool. He has a lot of insight into some pretty damning information. His ideas are just a little off," I say.

"It's not Max's information. It's copies of government documents he's collected over time. Like Cain said before, a lot of the dissenters have similar collections. Some have come to the same conclusions, and others believe something different or suspend their beliefs entirely," Simons says. The bank comes into view. Cain gathers his gear, fending the dogs off his string of fish as we approach.

"You mean that Max is smart but quirky," Jorey concludes.

"I mean that a different set of eyes on the same information might see something new," Simons says.

Jorey accedes to Simons' point with a quick nod as Cain joins us, wrapping his arm around my waist so his pole rests on my opposite shoulder. Hector and Alto abandon the fish to examine the brush, naturally ushering us back toward the residence.

"Nice catch," Jorey says, gesturing to the string of fish strung from the holster of Cain's pants.

"They'll taste a lot better than the meal-kit protein we had to choke down on our last trek," Cain says, shrugging off Jorey's compliment. He dips his head down and kisses me. I thrill momentarily at the touch of his lips to mine, still not used to his displays of affection. "Where have you been?" he mumbles low into my ear.

"Working," I say, giving him a nudge down the path.

"We've all been working. Frances found an old file of literature and used it to create a twenty-six-row cipher code based on some old-world book," Jorey says, falling in next to Simons.

"It's only a matter of time before someone breaks it. Government has coders too, you know," Cain says.

"Do government coders read old-world literature? Does their equipment even pick up low-frequency signals?" Jorey protests.

"We don't know what they can do, remember? All anyone is doing now is scrambling in the dark," Cain says. The dissenters are being cautious, and we're all doing what we can to follow DDC activity and predict their technology, but Cain's right.

"It's a good code. She used Mason's program to encrypt it," Jorey says.

Cain rolls his eyes. "All anyone but Mason is doing is wasting time until our transport is ready."

Before Jorey can offer a retort, Simons pipes in. "Sometimes there's more happening than what you see on the surface. I don't know how you've made it this far in life without realizing that, but it'd do you a world of good to be less certain of yourself."

Cain opens his mouth in surprise. I can feel the sharp intake of breath from where our bodies connect. I don't want another quarrel. I give Cain's side a sharp squeeze, forcing him to look at me. *"Please,"* I mouth.

To my surprise, he relents. Ahead of us, Alto lets out a bellowing bark before bolting ahead with Hector. Instead of adding fuel to the fire, Cain says, "Is it supposed to freeze tonight?"

"Not yet, but we're close," I say, grateful for peace.

"Then why is Max starting such a big fire?" Cain asks.

His question is so nonchalant that my brain doesn't register the huge plume of smoke as anything other than what he suggested—a large fire. It's not until Jorey gasps, "The smokehouse!" that I realize anything is wrong.

I grab at Cain's wrist and squeeze as my heart leaps into my throat.

"What?" he asks, his mouth a second behind his mind as realization strikes.

CHAPTER
FORTY-ONE

WE BOLT toward the plumes of smoke billowing up from the smoke shack behind the residence building. I can't help but think the dark clouds of spent carbon and ash rising toward the sky may as well be a beacon for the DDC. We know they're nearby, searching for any sign of our passage, but not how close. Could this be enough to draw them in?

The wooden structure comes into view, smoke pouring from the roof slats. It's only upon further inspection that I see flames licking up the back frame. Just as I spot the fire, Max bursts through the door, his arms loaded with strips of partially smoked fish, smoke billowing around him like an enveloping fog. He throws the fish to the ground, heaving raspy coughs that wrack his whole body, then turns back toward the shed.

"Max, don't!" I shout as he disappears into the black hole once more. Hector barks after him, excited and confused, before descending upon the pile of charred fish.

Bright flames spread across the back end of the smokehouse, nearly invisible in the glare of the setting sun. Simons reaches the smokehouse one stride ahead of Jorey. Together they begin throwing off pieces of the rustic structure, working fast to extinguish the worst of it. Cain heads toward the back, kicking at a single flaming log that acts as the rear support. I don't even pause before running into the shed, intent to drag Max out before the whole thing collapses.

The smoke is thick, hot, and blinding. It burns at my unseeing eyes, trying to choke its way out of my lungs. I find Max by feel, wrapping my hand around a thick arm and pulling with all my might.

"Max!" His name gets caught in my throat, smothered by hot smoke. Coughing, I yank the collar of my shirt up over my mouth and try again.

"Max!"

He turns, ramming into me and spilling handfuls of fish at our feet. His body hits with surprising force, and we both tumble sideways through the now-open side of the smokehouse into a smoky twilight. A moment later, the building collapses. Simons and Jorey spread the boards, stomping out what flames they can as they go.

I collapse next to Max on the cool grass, coughing and retching as my lungs struggle to fill with clean air. We were only in the building for a moment—less than thirty seconds, but it may as well have been an eternity. I'm weak and nauseous and can't catch my breath. Cain abandons the flaming structure when he sees us.

Max raises shakily onto hands and knees, trying to scramble forward. "The fish," he gasps in a voice as dry and broken as ash. He lunges toward the dogs, trying to scatter them from the rapidly dwindling supply, pseudo-cursing in hoarse barks.

"Forget it, it's not important," I rasp.

Max lunges at the dogs. "Get on, you beasts," he scolds, giving Hector a firm push in the rump as he waves a threatening hand at Alto. The dogs step back reluctantly but dutifully, settling on the grass close enough to keep an eye on the remaining fish.

Cain drops down beside us, placing a hand on my shoulder and pulling me around to face him. The light in his eyes is bright and wild.

"What do you think you were doing?" he demands.

"What?" I rasp, stunned.

"The smokehouse could've fallen on you. It nearly did!" His voice is nearest panic I've ever heard. Possibly because he's the one who made the structure collapse.

"Max—"

My speech is broken by another wave of hoarse coughs. Cain runs his hand down the back of my leg, checking for burns.

"Mason, you're so stubborn sometimes. Don't you know you're everything? You can't take risks like that," he hisses.

"I'm not going to sacrifice anyone else. Not for a bunch of fish, or a burning building or even the cure," I choke through a broken voice.

"You don't have to be the one to take all the risks," he argues.

"You think I can avoid it? You said it yourself! It's only a matter of time before we're facing Orman again—before we're making decisions on who's going to take what risks!"

"You think I don't know that?" He uses his grip to pull me in. My body flies into his, and our lips meet. He drops my wrists, his hands traveling up my arms and wrapping around either side of my face. He kisses me deeply, urgently. When he finally pulls away, I'm breathless.

"Don't be stupid, Mason," he whispers.

"I'm fine," I insist, pushing him away. "Is the fire under control?"

"Those pieces will burn, but we can dig a barrier and smother the worst of it," he says.

As if responding to Cain's proclamation, Simons appears at Max's side. "Do you have shovels?"

Max tries to get onto his feet and staggers. He settles for sitting with his legs splayed out in front of him and gestures toward the mudroom. "Two," he croaks.

"You rest. We're going to take care of this," Simons says, leaving Jorey to tend the remaining flames.

I shift away from Cain, whose hand has found my leg again and is gripping it possessively, as if he were afraid I might lunge back toward the burning remains of the smokehouse.

"Max, what happened?" I ask, fighting the urge to cough again.

"I was around back, working on the damn storage batteries again, when I heard a whoosh. I came round, and the whole thing was up in flames. Door must've come loose," he explains in a voice barely above a whisper. "I had to get the fish. It's all I have to send you on with."

"We can take meal kits. It's not a big deal," I say.

He shakes his head, defeated. "I don't have any."

"What about the over-supply?" I ask, jarred.

Max retches into the grass between his legs, breathless and over-wrought. "Haven't had a supply drop-in… since…" he pants.

I look to Cain, stunned. He returns my gaze with a grim expression. "Since the Northern Laboratories went down?" he asks.

Max nods, wiping his brow. His admission reminds me of the real danger the smokehouse fire presents. The government is aware of the management facility and the man running it, but how close might they be to us now?

"Where are Frances and Richards?" I ask, scanning the garden area near the front window, alarmed they haven't responded to the fire and smoke.

"Inside, I think. Napping," Max says before succumbing to another round of coughs.

I find my feet, telling myself there's a perfectly reasonable explana-tion for their absence and not believing it.

"Where are you going?" Cain asks, scrambling after me.

"To find them," I say, dread building the more I ponder their absence. *Something isn't right.*

"I'm going too. Max needs a med-kit," Cain says.

In the dwindling light, I note his blackened palms. Max gives them a cursory glance, shrugging. "It's mostly char. They're fine."

"Stay here with Simons and Jorey, and don't touch the fish," I instruct. "I'll get Frances and Richards, and we'll take care of you."

Cain grabs my hand, and I use it to drag him around to the front of the house. He tries to say something as we pass Simons on his way back to the small disaster with a shovel in each hand, but I ignore him. My mind is too full of terrible possibilities to hear whatever light-hearted suggestion he has.

Inside, the house is quiet.

"Richards? Frances?" I call as we enter the empty living room.

"Maybe we should just grab the med-kit," Cain suggests as I stop at our packs to grab a pulsar gun, imagining that somehow Orman has made his way here undetected and is hiding somewhere, waiting.

"That fire should have had them running," I say, dismissing his suggestion.

"Max said they were napping. The fire probably smells the same as the smokehouse usually does." Cain shrugs, trying to sway me from my course.

"I need to see for myself," I say, forcing the second pulsar gun into Cain's hand. Reluctantly, he takes it.

The low glow of yellow light stretches our shadows long along the bare wooden walls. I move silently, checking the restroom where the glowing orb casts its light, unobstructed. The silence of the house presses in all around me. I listen to the distant scrape of shovels from outside, straining to hear the sounds of ambush within the safety of the facility's force field boundary.

I approach the back room, trying not to imagine Orman towering over Frances' and Richards' smoldering remains. My heart pounds in my throat as I cycle the power supply on the pulsar gun, placing my hand on the doorknob and checking to confirm Cain is ready.

"You should knock," he warns, giving me a concerned look.

I shake my head, pulling the gun up and turning the handle. The door swings wide, and I freeze. Immediately, my eyes are drawn to Frances' red hair. She's draped across Richards. They're alone, sound asleep in the low bed, Richards' arm across her bare chest. All thoughts of ambush flee my mind, replaced with the fierce burn of embarrassment.

"I told you we should have knocked," Cain whispers, trying to pull me back from the doorway.

"I thought..." I trail off, no longer sure what I must've been thinking to make such a rash decision. My mind reels.

Cain tugs at my arm again, and I step back. The second I do, Frances stirs, and I'm sure we've been caught.

She curls into Richards' side as he brings his hands over his head in a stretch. "I smell smoke," she breathes, pressing her body into him.

Cain yanks a final time, pulling me back into the hall. He knocks on the open door. Richards freezes mid-yawn. Frances' eyes fly open as she scrambles for the quilt.

Cain makes a big show of putting his hands over his face as he steps into the room. "Sorry to bother you, but there's been a bit of an accident," he says.

Frances clings to the quilt, looking past Cain with wide eyes.

"Mason, what's happened?" she gasps, taking in our guns as Richards reaches across the bed for his shirt.

"There was a fire in the smokehouse. When you didn't come out, I got worried," I say, releasing the power on the pulsar gun and wishing I'd heeded Cain's advice to either knock or leave them be.

"I'm so sorry… we were, um… napping," Richards stammers.

"As is your right, brother, but when you have a chance, we could use a hand," Cain says, a bright twinkle in his eye.

"Is anyone injured?" he asks.

"Jorey is out there breathing in smoke and dust. Max burned his hands, and you should probably check on Mason. She ran straight into the fire," Cain says, as if to prove I'm not off the hook.

"We'll be right out," Frances says, trying to dress beneath the quilt.

"Take your time," I say, pushing Cain with my body so I can close the door.

FORTY-TWO

THE DANGER of the smokehouse fire has passed. While nowhere is truly safe, my visions of imminent capture have subsided. The geothermal output indicator measured the concentration of exhaust particulates in the air outside the force field at *moderate*. In other words, no worse than when Max's backup generator first malfunctioned. In the meantime, notice of our departure came through, putting an end date to our extended sojourn by way of a dissenter-run salvage truck. It's ironic that the government's need to recover goods from the destruction we caused created the means for our escape. I should be thinking about the rest of our journey, and I am, but I'm also thinking about Richards and Frances.

"I knew they were close by the time we made it to Dó's, but I think their relationship might have started before we left the Laboratories," I speculate, remembering how even then, they were always together.

Cain reaches for my hand as we turn along the force field perimeter and head back toward the residence. I relish the warmth of his skin against the crisp morning air, and my face flushes with the memory of his body moving against mine.

"Probably," he agrees. "For all constructive purposes, they'd already lost their families. They're only human, after all."

I stop, the charred husk of the smokehouse just in view. The shadow of a black bird passing overhead catches my attention. I turn to face Cain, my brow wrinkling with dismay. "That's not what I mean. I mean their *relationship*. The way they came together," I say, unable to convey my feelings.

"Oh," Cain says, bringing my hand to his lips in a gentle kiss. "That too."

I let the matter drop, suspecting this is the best I'm going to get from him on the subject. Instead, I say, "Can you believe we're leaving?"

"Given that Max was able to give us the names of the ship's entire crew, I think it must be true. But it's a bit of a shame to leave all this behind," he says, steering us back toward the house.

I sweep my gaze across the dewy morning field, taking in the way the rising sun gives everything an almost force-field shimmer. The energy management buildings sitting amidst the field make me ache with a mixture of grief and nostalgia. "I could probably stay here forever…" I say. My eyes focus on the burnt husk of the smokehouse. "If it weren't for all the loss and ruin," I conclude.

"The smokehouse?" Cain asks.

I glance at him without turning my head. "You know I mean more than that."

"Right."

"I have to do more than recreate the cure on paper," I remind him.

He squeezes my hand. "You're right. We have unfinished business."

We remove our boots at the entrance to the cabin and hang our jackets. The cabin feels warmer as the weather gets colder. I savor the warmth, wondering what the remainder of our journey holds. The sounds of Max cooking breakfast and the others' conversations make their way through the partially opened door. I can almost suspend reality enough to believe they're the sounds of my past.

"Let's go before they miss us," Cain urges, wrapping his arm around my shoulder and planting a kiss on my forehead.

"If everyone's up, they already miss us."

"Okay, fine. Let's go before Simons eats everything," Cain jests.

"I hope you're hungry," Max greets us as we enter. There's a peculiar, anticipatory sparkle in his eye.

"What's going on?" I ask, taking in the tension of the rest of the group sitting at the table.

"They've been into the post-war documents," Max breathes, as if he were revealing a big secret.

I wait for him to say more, and when he doesn't, I turn to Frances. "What have you found?"

"Do you remember the Endgal stories? The ones from the beginning of the outbreak?" she asks.

Max snorts in disapproval at their mention. Of course I know the stories—everyone knows the legend of Henry Endgal and the first cure. It's the foundation of our government.

"We used to tell the stories when we camped in the backyard," I say, neglecting to mention the last time we turned to them.

"Everyone knows them," Jorey agrees.

"Not everyone believes them, though," Cain scoffs.

"I did," Jorey says with a hint of sorrow.

"My dad didn't," I add.

"Smart man." Max places a parchment with smoked fish on the table along with a fragrant loaf of crusty bread and some honey-covered berries.

"He used to say the war started before the supply chain failed. He said there was plenty of food still, and the war was started by the *threat* of famine," I explain, racking my memory for the other pertinent details.

"It's likely enough," Richards muses.

"How many seasons of failed growth before the food supply is in crisis?" Jorey asks.

Frances brings a hand to her chin. "It wouldn't even take a total crop failure to create a supply issue in one season."

Max hefts himself into the chair next to her with a theatric exhale. The legs screech across the floor as he moves close enough to grab a slice of bread. "The trouble is, you're basing your judgment on our *current* system. If that's what things used to be like, you'd be right. But the old-world governments had years of food stockpiled. They would've had a lot of warning before the food was gone," he says.

"But it's food," Jorey protests, passing the berries to Simons, who replaces the knife in the butter dish to accept them.

"They would've needed preserved food—and a sophisticated system to manage the surplus," Simons says.

It strikes me how similar this system sounds to the one used to transport food between the City States and the Northern Laboratories.

"Cheese, pickled vegetables, preserved food, refined grain…" Cain lists.

"That's not so different than what we have now," Jorey points out.

"It's not the types of food that are different," Max says between bites. "It's the scale of the operation."

"Okay, so it's plausible, maybe probable. But what difference does that make?" I ask.

"Well," Francis says, glancing from Max to the rest of us, "if the governments from across the globe knew there were going to be supply issues, they'd have time to prepare."

I immediately know where she's going with it. "They would have time to take offensive action," I say.

"Exactly." Max points at me.

Jorey looks stunned.

"But is there proof that the original outbreak was a product of biological warfare?" I ask.

"It's not exactly proof so much as the logical conclusion from the data. Without more wartime records, that's the best we can do," Frances says.

"Those records might exist, but we won't know until someone makes contact with the old world," Max says.

"If the old world exists," Cain corrects.

"When we find it," Max argues, pointing his fork at Cain.

I shake my head. "That's not the important part."

"What is?" Richards asks.

"Who was in control of the disease once the war was over," I say.

"Isn't it obvious?" Cain asks.

"Yes," I say, knowing full well we wouldn't be where we are now if things had ended differently.

"Henry Endgal is an imaginary character in a fantastical story with no enemies," Max says.

"History is written by the victors," Cain agrees, helping himself to another slice of bread before Simons can snatch it.

Max makes eye contact with him. "You got that right. And the government is willing to kill anybody they think threatens that fantasy."

His statement causes another thought to occur. "Based on these documents, we can conclude that the government used Zoribiatus as population control and to win the war. We know they've been using it to control the populations outside the cities... but what about within the cities? What about residents?"

"What do you mean?" Richards asks, leaning into the table.

I turn to face Frances, ignoring my empty plate. "You said that your husband was infected during a trip?"

"Right," she agrees.

"Well, what if his infection wasn't an accident?" I ask. "What if he found something he wasn't supposed to find?"

"Like an old-world establishment," Max interjects.

"It could have been anything," I agree, glossing over the unlikelihood of Max's theory. "Whatever it was, maybe the DDC decided to eliminate him?"

"I don't see how," Frances argues. She rubs her chin before bringing her hands together. "He made it through post-travel debriefing without issue. He picked up the girls on his way home. We spoke to one another after the trip—they wouldn't have let that happen if they were worried he knew something he shouldn't. He would have told me..."

"He might not have realized. In the cities we're taught about the old ways the disease is spread. What if they've changed how infection happens? I mean—they'd have to in order to infect people living outside the City States," I explain, heart racing.

I watch Frances' face, waiting for her to accept it. Max nods. She lets out a heavy sigh. "It's possible..."

Simons sits in silent contemplation, having abandoned his meal only half-eaten. He crosses one foot over his opposite knee. "The DDC isn't afraid to use a hive when they need to contain a situation. And I'm sure they weren't too worried about Trudy being a casualty," he says.

I wince. Though the attack happened so many years ago, Simons' loss is fresh. It's fresh for everyone.

"But people don't get sick in the cities," Jorey objects. His face is pale, as if the loss of his family were about to suffocate him.

"They do," I say, reaching across the table to grab his wrist. I give it a gentle squeeze that draws his eyes to mine. They glisten with grief. He closes them briefly, as if he might reverse time by keeping the memory away.

"The day Hank and I took the test, we saw a transport of patients leaving a city clinic," I say.

"We had a few patients in our practice. We did testing with routine care—it used to be best practice," Richards says, his voice apologetic.

"If that's true, it explains a lot," Jorey says, turning his wrist to take my hand in his. He lets out a heavy sigh before explaining. "There was a job—something for the DDC. My dad was really riled up about it. He and my brothers were recruited to look into some credit balances. They were supposed to travel to the main DDC offices, but they never made it. It was weeks before I got notice about their status…"

"It sounds like they were targeted," Cain says, leaning over the table and grabbing the edge of the loaf.

"But what on earth for?" Richards asks.

"It could have been anything." Cain shrugs.

"My dad was very interested in fraud—that was his specialty, so it probably had something to do with that," Jorey says.

"Janet wasn't into anything mysterious or criminal," Richards objects before anyone has a chance to ask.

"Are you certain? That was a long time ago," Cain says. He's referring to the age difference between Richards and his wife, a painful reminder of how long he waited to see her again.

"Yes, I'm certain! She was pregnant! She went in for a few extra tests and a blood draw, and there was a contamination error. I told you, it happened sometimes." Richards slams his fist against the table and raises his voice. It's so uncharacteristic of him that I start.

His cheeks are flushed, and his muscles are tensed, as if he's about to pounce on Cain. It occurs to me that Jorey might not be the only one who doesn't care for Cain. I wonder if it's the nonchalant way he referred to Janet's stasis and cruel death or if, like Jorey, it's been building over time.

Frances grabs Richards' hand. "She might not have known," she says.

Richards' face flushes. His mouth moves wordlessly, repeating the shape of the words he spoke before squeezing the trigger to end her life.

I love you.

Cain swallows hard, forcing the bread down his throat before saying, "Sorry, brother."

Richards sits again, and Frances leans into him. Simons places his hands on the table, making it clear he's had enough for the morning. "Maybe there are still accidents. We don't have to solve it all at the breakfast table."

We don't have to, but I'm certain we're on the cusp of the answer. Somewhere within the multitude of death and disappearances lies the government's true intent. I let out a heavy sigh, pushing my chair back from the breakfast table. "I better get to work."

"Don't you want to eat something first?" Jorey calls after me.

"I'm not hungry," I say without turning around.

PART THREE

THE OUTSKIRTS

FORTY-THREE

I STAND on the cargo ship's deck, absorbed by the early darkness of a late fall night, taking a much-needed break from Shelby's papers. The crisp ocean wind bites at my cheeks, bringing clarity that can't be found by lamplight in the ship's belly. The vastness of the sea brings perspective to my mounting concerns.

Shelby promised I would have everything I needed, but there are so many variables. The deeper I delve into her work, the more questions I have. *Where will I get so many antigens? How can I mass-produce such a tenuous mixture? Can it be done with ancient equipment?*

I think of the magnitude of what we're trying to do—even if the Zoribiatus cure is synthesized and manufactured, how will we distribute it to the City States?

I was more confident at Max's, but time moves too quickly. The fields succumbed to frost, and the long hiatus between the far north and civilization is over. I promised Max I would come back after the cure was ready and the threat of the government extinguished. But even if the cure is successfully circulated around the world, there's no certainty we'll be the ones to get the job done.

The dissenters are so much bigger than our journey, or even Shelby's cure. Once I figure out the answers and deliver the cure to the manufacturing site, our survival will become inconsequential. If our lives are unimportant, it's less likely any of us will make it back.

The immensity of everything piled up in my head is matched only by the magnitude of the ocean waters surrounding the ship as it makes its passage southward. Like all government vessels, the ship is nearly silent as it makes its way, running on freshly charged fuel cells from Max's station.

I let my mind dwell, sinking into the ocean depths where the matter of what life exists is both inconsequential and completely out of my control. I could live in this place indefinitely.

A humpback whale breaches the ocean surface for a breath—the sound of its gasp gives life to the arc of water spraying from its blowhole. It appears singular in the vastness of the sea, yet I'm aware that just as I stand alone on the ship's deck with others close at hand, this whale is merely seeking its own solace. The shudder of its new breath is largely unnoticed, and it sinks back into the depths.

Whales are supposed to have gone extinct before the war. I think about how few people venture outside of the cities, and how even fewer of them have made it to the ocean. How many people know whales are still around? I remember how many species of birds and insects we sighted when we left our home and how wild the northern tundra is. What other parts of the land have recovered since the days of war and disease? Was any of it dead to begin with?

I think about heading back down into the hull but decide I don't want to. I have no desire to spend another second poring over the cure. I don't have the capacity for it. Likewise, I'm not up for anybody's company lately.

"Alone again?" Jorey's voice catches me off guard. Usually, if anybody flushes me out on the ship, it's Cain.

"Hey, Jorey," I say without looking. Instead, I watch for the sign of another whale.

"Needed some air?" he asks, joining me at the railing.

"I like to come up here to think."

"I know. You've been up here almost every night."

"Did Cain tell you?" I ask, figuring Cain's been complaining about how often I sneak away to spend time on my own when I break from my research.

"Nah. He just comes to ask me where you are every time you disappear," Jorey says. A quick smile crosses his face.

"Oh?" I ask, turning from the ocean to study him more closely. He looks scruffy, like we all do now that we're traveling again.

"I only tell him where you are *sometimes*—enough to keep him from thinking I'm hiding it from him," Jorey explains.

"How do you know where I am? Are you spying on me?" I ask, incredulous.

Jorey laughs. It's a hearty sound that blends well with the waves. "You're an easy read, Mason. Back in the Northern Laboratories, any time you needed to think, you'd always sneak into the dining hall and stare out the window. You like to think in nature—of course you'd be up on the deck."

"Fair," I say, admiring his logic. "But how did you know where on the deck I'd be?"

"You follow the moon, and you like to watch for the creatures in the wake—you look out to sea, not in to shore," Jorey says, suggesting he knows me better than I know myself.

I smile, conceding to his expert observation skills. "You've got me figured out. I can't hide anything from you, I guess."

"No worries. I won't blow your cover." Jorey leans over enough to nudge me.

Our conversation is almost normal—like it used to be in the Northern Laboratories. We watch the wake in silence for a while before another whale breaks the surface. It exhales water and air, and I listen for its next breath.

"Do you think they come up to the surface for a few moments alone too? Like, maybe taking a breath is just an excuse?" Jorey asks.

"You're reading my mind, and it's almost creepy."

"You left your notes out when you came up. When I put them away, I read the last thing you wrote—*I need to breathe*." He leans against the railing so he's both looking out to sea and facing me. "Is that about the work, or something else?"

I let out a heavy sigh. "I don't know. Probably both. I actually think I've got most of what was lost handled, but it seems impossible."

"If Shelby says it'll work, then it's probably going to work," Jorey says.

"That's true. That's all that really matters—that we get the cure in the right hands. Maybe I'm anguishing over the details too much."

The ship groans as it sways with the deep ocean currents. A crisp gust of wind makes me shiver. I pull my jacket tight and close the collar before shoving my hands into the pockets and leaning against the railing.

After another moment of quietly taking in the salty night, Jorey ventures, "You're wondering if we'll live to see any of it happen?"

"Like I said, it's almost creepy how well you know my thoughts." I turn to face him.

"It's what I'm thinking, too. Look at what the dissenters have already done to keep us safe—they destroyed a management facility, sent hovercrafts as a diversion, and took over an entire ship's roster. Max practically burned his hands off to make sure we'd have fish for the trip! But how much effort will there be to keep us safe once they have what they need?" Jorey says.

"Maybe it doesn't matter beyond that. Isn't that why we went north in the first place? We were willing to die to end it?"

"Sure… yeah." Jorey thinks carefully before he speaks again. "But that doesn't mean we want to die."

"True," I say, appreciating Jorey's thoughtfulness. "It feels like I just started living. It's too soon to die."

"You're not going to die, Mason. No matter what the dissenters' plan is, everybody here's going to keep you alive."

His statement catches me off guard. I study his face for an explanation. I'm about to ask him what he means when I hear Cain calling from the opposite side of the deck.

"Looks like you're busted," Jorey says, nudging me with his elbow.

"Yeah, I think he noticed a pattern." I wink at Jorey.

"Eh, we make port tomorrow. You can find a new place to think alone."

"It's not so bad to think with company either," I offer. Cain sees us and jogs across the deck.

"I'll leave you two," Jorey says, stepping away from the railing.

"It was nice to talk—like old times," I say as he leaves. Cain wraps his arms around my shoulders and gives me a squeeze.

"Sure thing, Mason," Jorey says, looking me directly in the eyes. "Anytime."

"Later, Jorey. Thanks for the help tracking her down," Cain calls after him before turning to me. "You're slippery these days."

"I don't mean to be." I slide into his embrace, stand on the tips of my toes to kiss his chin. He responds by eagerly returning the affection.

"So what are you doing up here all alone anyway?" he asks, stroking my hair.

I sigh and turn to face the sea again. "Looking at the ocean. Thinking."

"There's a whole lot more interesting things to look at in the cargo area than a bunch of water," Cain says.

"From the Northern Laboratories? Is any of it functional?"

"There are some crates marked *destroyed*. But there are a bunch of electronics and some tech stuff you might be interested in," he suggests.

"You're not messing with any of it, are you? We can't let them know we were here." I tip my head back toward him, earnest.

He kisses my wind-chapped cheek. "No. I'm not stupid."

"If you tamper with anything, it could give away our location," I press, not letting the matter drop.

"I told you, I'm not stupid," Cain whines, satisfying my paranoia enough that I relax into his chest again. My eyes are just readjusting to the ocean's darkness when he says, "I'd read the manuals first."

"Cain!" I moan. He squeezes my midsection, bunching my jacket so the cool ocean breeze nips at my bare skin.

"I'm kidding," he growls into the base of my neck until I'm giggling. I squirm away from him, pulling my jacket back down to shut out the cold. He brushes a loose strand of hair back, mischief dancing in his lively eyes. "What are you so worried about anyway? You heard the captain; things are going great."

I let out a heavy sigh, all levity gone from the moment. "Are you worried at all about what's going to happen once we get the cure to the dissenters?"

Cain scrunches his face. A gust of wind blows his hair loose, whipping long strands across his face. "What do you mean?"

"What happens when we aren't important anymore? What happens when they stop protecting us?"

Cain looks down at me with a frown. He reaches out and pulls me back into his warm embrace. "They aren't going to stop protecting you."

"Once they have the cure," I say.

He shakes his head, his shoulders swaying with the bow and dip of the ship. "They're still going to need you. The cure is more than a stack of papers."

"Right, but they have Amos, and probably others," I argue, staring out into the ocean, my braid whipping against the side of my face as the wind blows, unobstructed. The ocean mist sprays my face, broken from the surface after being pulled across the face of the earth by the unseen force of the moon.

"The only person on this earth who wants you more than the dissenters is Orman, and he's not going to be able to reach you once we make headquarters." Cain continues to hold me, lost in his own ocean of thoughts.

In the distance, another whale surfaces from the depths. I strain to spot it in the moonlight. Then all at once, the whole pod breaks the surface, each with their own unique gasps and shudders. I listen carefully to their breaths, each a separate puff blended to make a cacophony of sound before disappearing into the depths. "We're never completely alone," I whisper.

FORTY-FOUR

THE DECK of the cargo ship vibrates as the engines cycle down. The harbor is in view now. I turn away from it, trying to absorb the ocean one last time before heading to the cargo area to be sealed into one of the cargo crates along with the rest of the team. Getting into the north port was tricky enough, but nothing compared to this next step. We'll be trapped, unloaded with the rest of the supplies, then loaded onto one of the freight trucks headed toward the cities. A transport worker will unload our crate along the route so that we're *"lost goods."* A lot has to go right for this to work.

"It's time, Mason," Simons calls from the entrance to the hold.

"I'll be right there," I say, turning to take in the sea one more time.

I try to stain my memory with the vast expanse of swelling waters before I turn away. Simons squeezes my shoulder as we both descend to the hold area where workers are using large equipment to move giant crates for unloading at port. A ship hand is gesturing for us to follow him to the back of the hull, where the crate we'll travel in has been prepared. I marvel at the small crew—maybe a dozen strong—all dissenters working against the government right under its nose.

"How did you get so many dissenters into position?" I ask the captain, who's overseeing our concealment.

He laughs before responding, "Gettin' bodies into these sorts of positions is the easy part of what we do. Not many educated government loyalists are wanting jobs like thisun, so it's more a matter of figurin' out who's already a dissenter and who's waiting to become one."

The crate we'll be sealed into looks exactly like the others—large, red and nondescript. Each vessel has its own unique number markings so we can be identified by the transport worker and correctly disposed of. Inside the crate, the walls are heavily padded and weighted so the contents—us—will go undetected. There are about two days' worth of supplies that will be packed along with us for the long wait.

"Are you worried about infiltration?" I ask, considering their operation systems.

"Ayuh." The captain nods. "We have our ways of flushing them guys out—and there's a bunch of 'em. It's why it took so long to secure a safe passage for you."

There's not much I can do but trust that he has the situation handled. He gives us a few pointers for surviving in the crate overnight until the dump. Mostly, he just tells us to be patient and not rush to break out once we think we're in the clear. Though I'd rather be traveling under my own strength, walking past the point of exhaustion, we're going to have to sit and wait this part of the trip out.

Simons ushers me toward the padded interior where Jorey, Richards and Frances wait. I glance back at the captain, then past him into the busy, noise-filled hull. "Where's Cain?"

"He was just here. Damn kid can't keep his nose out of the cargo," Simons laments, shaking his head.

"Said he was goina hit the latrine one more time before we locked him in," the captain says. Before he can finish the statement, Cain appears from behind a stack of smaller crates, his pack slung over one shoulder.

"I hope the rest of you did your due diligence," he admonishes, dipping down to kiss the side of my face before slinging his pack down into the pile of supplies and dropping to a sit on the padded floor of the crate.

"It's always a line with you, isn't it?" Jorey muses, shaking his head.

"What's the matter? You get backed up at the crucial moment?" Cain jabs.

"Don't start! I'm not going to listen to you two moan in the dark for the next two days," Simons snaps.

"I didn't start anything," Jorey protests.

I plop down between him and Cain, grabbing his hand and giving it a quick squeeze. "Please. Can we drop it? I think we've got enough to make us crazy between now and the next stop."

The crate falls silent. The crew welds the crate shut so we're swallowed by the shroud of complete darkness. Frances turns on one of our small, spherical lights. It has enough power to illuminate the space for twenty-four hours. We have three of them, just in case. We share a frugal meal and small rations of water while we wait out the night. The ship comes into port, and the unloading process begins. Our crate moves, and we brace ourselves. The sensation of weightlessness reminds me of falling in a simulation. The whole situation is like a simulation. Some hours after we're sealed in, I finally drift off to sleep in the dim light of our glowing beacon.

I awaken to my world once again being set into motion. The muffled screech of metal scraping on metal penetrates us as someone on the outside frees our crate from the rest. We're about to be dumped.

The light has dimmed nearly to the point of burning out. Frances' hand casts a shadow across what little light remains as she grasps it—likely for comfort. Once again, I think of Hank's night-light, and suddenly, my hand itches to embrace the glow.

"Here we go," Cain says, sitting up and reaching for my hand.

I grasp it and squeeze, trying to ease the mounting tension. "Have you done this before?" I ask him.

"Nope, I went north through the cities," he says. He sounds as nervous as I feel.

There's a low, shuddering groan, and the crate dips. It's supposed to hit the side of the road and right itself, but that doesn't happen. We slide as the ground shifts below us, piling onto one another while the crate falls away from the cargo transport. We impact with a loud, screeching grind, and the crate turns on its side. We fall over one another again before settling on what used to be the roof of our transportation prison.

We settle somewhere along a basin of earth. When it's clear we've stopped moving, we extract ourselves from the human pile of comfort we made during our bumpy ride.

"My body's going to ache for weeks," Jorey says as he stands and stretches. His hands brush against the crate floor as he lifts his legs.

Frances extinguishes the first light and pulls out a second.

"Should we wait a little longer before we switch lights?" I ask, startling at the nervous waver of my voice.

"Do you want to wait until the light goes out?" Frances asks, concerned.

"No," I say, more quickly than needed. "I only think we should be careful about our light source until we're out of here."

Frances turns the light over in her hand contemplatively. "It's only twenty-four more hours before we join the outside world again, and we have an extra light."

"I know it's not rational, but being in here is like starting a simulation. It's too blank," I explain.

"What are you talking about?" Cain asks.

"There's a pause at the beginning of the simulations where there's nothing. At the end too, if you don't take your helmet off in time," I explain. "Maybe you didn't go through enough of them to notice."

"I don't think I ever noticed either," Richards admits.

"I know what you're talking about," Jorey says. "But this is different because even if we didn't have the light, we could still hear each other."

I realize he's right, and it eases my anxiety. Not only can we hear each other, but I can hear myself—the swift intake of air and whoosh of each exhale and the steady beat of my heart. "Go ahead and switch lights, Frances," I say.

In the renewed light, Frances and Richards collect our supplies, returning them to a partially coherent pile. I join them, and the task takes less than a minute.

"What now?" Richards asks.

"We wait," I say, digging into our rations.

FORTY-FIVE

THE HOURS TICK BY SLOWLY. I try to doze as much as possible but can't quiet my racing mind. It's too dark to work. It's too quiet to listen. None of us can keep a conversation going for very long, so we wait, largely in silence.

When the light finally fades to nothing, we dig away at the thick padding against the metal walls with stout steel knives. Simons dons a pair of over-sized blue gloves and gets out the thick, clay-like substance we were given to eat through the metal. We don the masks meant to protect us from the fumes, and he sets to work, creating an arch that will become our exit.

As we wait, the temperature rises. I know it's the byproduct of the reaction between the melting agent and the metal, but I envision bright sunshine on the outside. Instead, when the metal falls away, we're greeted by the darkness of pre-dawn. The air smells fresh and earthy compared to the stale smell of sweat and stink of adrenaline that filled the crate. It's not as quiet as before. We're surrounded by the sounds of night—a gentle breeze, the hoot of an owl, and the low drone of insects. I step out cautiously, holding my pulsar gun in one hand as I scan our surroundings for obvious danger.

I note the steep embankment. Above, the road turns away from us and then east, toward the cities. The embankment has landed us in a marshy field—low land close enough to entrap the sea air in a thick mist. The world around us smells like wet grass and mud, suggesting our trek out will be slow and laborious.

Cain and Simons don their headlamps and begin spreading out the map the captain gave us. It looks like so many others we've used to make it to this point, but the coordinates are encrypted. Simons pulls out the tiny receiver that will detect our location and give us the code once it's turned on. We've been warned to turn it off as soon as we have the signal, since this is a dead zone, and we might risk the high-frequency signal getting picked up by government scanners.

Simons charges the unit and clicks it on, holding it in his open palm so we can all read the screen. The small black cylinder blinks with one red light, then two. I hold my breath as the seconds tick by. Three red lights. Suddenly, the light blinks white, and there's a beep as small green numbers appear on the smooth surface.

"Got it!" Cain says, and Simons responds by shutting the receiver off and replacing it in his pack. I look over his shoulder to see where his finger rests on the map. We're approximately 90 kilometers inland and hundreds of kilometers south of the Institute.

"It's so much further than I thought," I lament, struck by how completely this journey mirrors my last trek to the Institute. I knew we couldn't be certain of our route or drop point, but I wasn't expecting to end up so far from the Institute.

"Why here? This is the middle of nowhere," Jorey says, tracing the distance between us and our destination.

Frances studies the map along with the rest of us. "We're not in the middle of nowhere. I know this region!"

"What do you mean?" Richards asks, leaning against her to try and see whatever she sees.

"There are pre-war city structures not far from here." She points west of our location. Sure enough, there are markings on the map that indicate man-made structure. "It used to be an important metropolis!" The excitement is clear in her voice.

"Cain? Is she right?" I ask.

He looks thoughtfully at the map before saying, "Maybe, but I don't see how that's going to help us. Unless you believe Max and are expecting a glowing metropolis..."

"That's not what I'm saying. Maybe there's something in the city we could use—transportation or maps or weapons..." Frances argues.

"Or outsiders," Simons adds with foreboding solemnity.

"Not likely. Abandoned cities are too obvious of areas for re-settlement. They've been swept clean of people. There hasn't been anyone in the abandoned cities for a long time. People on the outside live in the free communities—south of the Deadlands," Cain says, ending the discussion before it begins. This wasn't what I meant when I said I wanted him to share what he knew about the outside communities.

"Alright then, back to the idea of transport," Richards says, trying to steer us toward Frances' original idea.

"If we use an old-world transport, we'll be spotted for sure," Simons says.

"What about Dó's overland transport?" Frances asks, clearly desperate.

"The far north doesn't have the same surveillance—it can't because of the storms," I say. I study our surroundings again. This area is very open, filled with tall grasses, low shrubbery, and sparse oak. There aren't many places to take shelter. We could be easily spotted by passing surveillance, and there isn't much to help us if another hive attacks.

"We should head to the city," I say, making up my mind. They all look to me, and I elaborate. "Cain, you said that most of the tunnels were built around city outskirts, right?"

"The tunnel system isn't the same here as up north," Cain says.

"We've all studied the maps," Jorey says, placing his finger along the coast. "There's supposed to be a tunnel system making its way up from our drop zone to the Institute. Does it matter what type it is?" Jorey asks.

Cain turns to him, hand resting on the pulsar gun at his hip. "Seeing as I've never been out this way, I can't say how much the tunnel type matters. What I'm trying to say is, I don't know how well guarded they are."

"We made it before," Richards says.

"Everything is different in the north," Cain says.

"We need to find an entrance," I press. "Even if the government can get underground. We're too exposed out here. The city is our only option. We can take shelter in the structures until we find the tunnels."

"It's decided then," Simons says, grabbing up his pack. We all do the same. Cain folds the map and tucks it into his pack.

The ground is as muddy and unforgiving as I predicted, making our progress slow and messy. Cain walks up beside me and catches my arm. "Hey you."

"Hey you, too." I return his greeting, taking another muddy step.

"I know the tunnels are a gamble, but I still think it's a good call," he says.

"I hope so. This would be a terrible place to get ambushed."

"We're better off taking Orman out when we can see him coming," he agrees.

"You make it sound like we're going to have a choice in the matter."

"You never know," he says, wrapping his arm around my shoulder. "I've got a feeling we're going to have our chance."

I glance at him. His face is sun-kissed from our time at Max's facility, and it makes me smile.

"What?" he asks.

"Nothing," I say, knowing this answer will drive him crazy.

"Don't be like that." He pouts.

"I was just wondering if I look as travel-weary as you."

He gasps so convincingly I almost believe he's serious. "You don't think I'm pretty anymore!"

"That's not what I said," I protest, but I know he's having fun.

I reach for him, but he brushes off my grasp, calling out to the others, "Mason doesn't think I'm pretty. She's going to leave me for someone else!"

"You're pretty!" I insist, finally catching his hand. "Okay?"

Cain looks at me, a wry smile plastered on his face. "After that long trip? And sweating for forty-eight hours in that stinky crate? Your standards must be pretty low!"

I smack him, laughing as we make our way out of the swampy field, trying to pretend my finger isn't resting against the trigger of my pulsar gun as we head into new and dangerous territory.

CHAPTER
FORTY-SIX

THE CITY IS an ancient ruin of crumbled concrete and overgrown structures. Sun-bleached grass grows through thick cracks in the roadways and walking paths. Yellow wildflowers dot the ground along with other weeds and vines. The area is just as much nature as it is structure. Most of the buildings have crumbled faces held up by partially collapsed walls. Beneath the natural growth that covers what remains of the fallen civilization lies something more dreadful—lost human remains.

I notice them first on the overgrown steps to what looks like an old town center—skulls and bones turning to dust as time washes them away. They're everywhere. They fill the roadways and litter the alleyways where youthful trees stretch their branches through the rubble toward the skies, lining the entrances to many of the buildings. These are the ruins of a city overrun by the first outbreak.

"First came the bombs, then came the disease..."

Seeing the ruins of this city up close, it's easy to believe it might have happened simultaneously, the way Dad described.

We make our way in silence through the eerie scenery, as if we were walking through a museum of human history. That's exactly what we're doing.

"Anybody still wondering if the old world is still up and running?"

Cain asks, his boots crunching over eroded debris that's equal parts structure and remains.

No one responds. There's no point to arguing Max's ideas in this grim reality. We're like ghosts visiting the scene of what once was. It takes incredible imagination to envision what it might have been like fully alive, but it isn't hard to imagine those last days. The chaos of war and panic is written in the ruins.

Most of the main roadways are littered with the rusting remains of abandoned vehicles, their windows broken out, their glass turned to sand. We navigate around collapsed buildings and the twisted metal of wrecks by turning onto side streets. In school, we learned about the scavengers who made their livings journeying to remote city ruins like these. They mined useful materials from the wreckage so the cities could assimilate old into new. But it doesn't look like anyone's been to this city since it fell.

"Does anyone else get the feeling like someone's watching us?" Jorey asks as we circumvent yet another collapsed building.

"I do," Richards says, giving the punched-out holes of a nearby high-rise a suspicious glance.

"Every time I look up, I expect to see someone looking back at me." Frances shudders at the thought, turning away from the towering structures.

"It's the buildings. No matter how empty they are, we recognize our own civilization. We don't like seeing buildings without people," Cain speculates.

"There are too many places someone could hide. Someone could be sitting up there watching us right now," Jorey argues, gesturing toward the third floor of a marketplace hidden in the shadow of a taller building. The windows are still intact but impossibly dirty.

"Maybe, but I don't see any evidence. You can't move through a place like this without leaving a trace." Simons points back down our path. Even though we've been careful, I can see the signs of our passage—a handprint smeared in the dust of a rusted truck bed, a broken branch, trampled tufts of weeds, and the scuffs of our boot tracks through the debris.

"Should we be worried about that?" Richards asks, studying our trail.

"Not yet, but the faster we move out of here, the better," Simons says.

"I don't think we can be so sure we're the only ones here. Creepy buildings or not, it feels like we're being watched," Jorey says, resting his hand against the pulsar gun clipped to his pants.

I want to agree with Simons. I want to believe Cain when he says the sensation of watchful eyes is, in fact, the empty buildings staring down at us. I can remember a similar sensation when passing the empty buildings with my brothers on our way to the tunnels. I've always known buildings could have eyes, but I can't convince myself Jorey isn't onto something…

"It's the birds," I say, suddenly realizing what we've all been seeing but not really seeing.

The others follow my gaze to the row of corvids lining the rooftops. They gaze down at us from their high perches, brilliant intelligence apparent even from afar. I watch as they track the swivel of my head. When I step away from the rest of the group, their heads follow.

"Is that normal?" Frances asks, clearly unsettled.

"They're ravens… or crows. I think crows were the ones that travel in groups," I say, still watching the curious birds follow my every move.

"Were?" Richards asks.

"They're supposed to be extinct." I take another step backward to hide beneath the sagging awning of a building. The birds on the opposite building keep me in their sights. A flutter of motion indicates some of the birds overhead have taken flight.

"That's a laugh. Crows are everywhere," Cain scoffs, glancing first at us, then at the birds, as if he can't figure what we're so fascinated by.

"I'm starting to think that nothing actually went extinct," Frances says as she watches a small group move through the air.

"Some things, maybe, but nothing near the scale we're taught," I agree.

One of the birds descends to a metal post jutting upward from the concrete not far from us, letting out a caw as it settles. Frances looks over her shoulder and shrieks at the bird's nearness. Her call doesn't startle the bird from its perch. It continues to watch us from eye level.

"They aren't scared of us," Jorey observes.

"Why would they be? People are rare in their territory. We're probably nothing more than a passing curiosity," Cain says.

Jorey lifts a hand toward the bird, who watches his gesture intently until Jorey steps toward it, closing the bird's gap of safety. The bird staggers backward, spreading its wings and returning to the sky. As it flies over us, something small pings against the cement. I scan the ground, trying to isolate the source.

"Did it just drop something?" Frances asks, curiosity surpassing trepidation.

Simons stoops down and retrieves the offending object—a small copper coin.

"Looks like it left us a present," Cain chuckles.

"I think they do that," Jorey says.

"Do what?" Richards asks, peering at the coin in Simons' hand, perplexed.

"Leave gifts," Jorey says.

"I was joking," Cain says, jostling Jorey's shoulder.

"I'm being serious," Jorey retorts, reigniting the flame of their eternal bickering.

"He's right. The extinct species catalog said corvids are intelligent and social. It suggested people could train them with food, and the crows might reciprocate with gifts," I say, hoping this will be enough to keep Cain from starting a more serious argument.

"Where do you guys get this stuff?" Cain shakes his head, bemused.

I take the coin from Simons and study it. There's a texture to the surface, as if something used to be stamped onto it. Whatever it was is long gone, washed smooth by decades of rain and silt. "I used to read a lot about extinct species when I was a kid. It was sort of a hobby."

"That explains you, but what's Jorey's excuse?" Cain jabs.

"Stories," Jorey says.

I glance at him, wishing he could elaborate, but knowing he won't if he wants Cain to drop the matter. I'm not sure Cain will let it go regardless.

"It's getting late," Simons says, drawing our attention away from the coin, birds, and bickering.

"Do you think we should push through to the city's edge or make camp?" Richards asks.

"I don't want to try and navigate this place in the dark," Frances protests.

"We should make camp and look for the tunnel entrance first thing tomorrow," I say, searching the team for their agreement.

"I'm not sure I want to make camp here, with them." Jorey nods at the birds, who continue to gather on the rooftops. There might be as many as a hundred now, if not more.

"We can make camp in one of the buildings, out of the elements," Simons suggests.

We find such a place on the second floor of a mostly whole building, not far from where the birds congregate. We skip the fire and split rations. I count out how much smoked fish we have left and compare it to the journey ahead. Averaging one meal per day, we have about a week's worth of mostly unburnt filets. I count them again and close the pack. As I set it amidst the others, I'm overwhelmed with the same sensation that's plagued us all day. Someone is watching me.

I stand, trying to look nonchalant as I reach my arms out in front of me in a stretch, then back to my body, where one hand brushes against my gun. I scan our surroundings again, certain that someone else is here—if not a person, then one of the birds nesting in the eaves. We've made camp on the second floor of a multiple-story building whose top floor has partially caved in. I can see the stars through the hole. I search the perimeter, looking for signs of life—eyes peering back at me or the movement of a shadow—but there's nothing.

I glance at the stairway, which we confirmed was the only entrance, and am greeted by the same nothingness. I do my best to dismiss the sensation, joining Cain against our piled supplies and letting out a heavy sigh.

"What's got you spun up, boss?" Cain asks.

"It still feels like we're being watched," I murmur, keeping my voice low.

"Me too, and not just by those creepy birds," Jorey concedes as he munches the smoked fish that's sustained us since we left the geothermal area.

"I know we set up the perimeter alarm, but I think we should take shifts through the night," I say.

"That's not a bad idea," Simons agrees.

"It won't hurt anything," Cain concedes. Frances and Richards nod.

"Great. I'll take first shift," I say, sitting up against the wall at my back and grabbing up a thin filet.

"I'll join you," Jorey offers.

"No, I'll do it." Cain glares at Jorey.

I roll my eyes, tired of their petty competition. "Okay, you two take it then. I'll take second shift with Simons."

Cain and Jorey look at me, mouths agape, and Simons smirks. "Works for me," he agrees, taking the final piece of meat and stretching out. "If you don't mind, I think I'm gonna sleep a bit before my shift."

"Wake us up when you and Simons need rest, and we'll take the early shift," Richards offers of himself and Frances. I nod and settle in to try and rest. It doesn't come easy.

CHAPTER
FORTY-SEVEN

A SUDDEN COMMOTION pulls me from a restless sleep. I blink into the darkness with no idea how much time has passed.

"Behind you!" Jorey shouts from the dark.

There's a considerable amount of scuffling before something scrapes across the ground, and then there's a heavy thud.

"Gotcha!" Cain yells in triumph. His proclamation is greeted with a shrill cry of frustration and terror.

I strain to make sense of the dim scene. The starry sky is obscured by thick cloud cover. The high walls and stacks of debris cast long shadows across the room. Keeping one hand on my pulsar gun, I scramble to find my headlamp. Before I get hold of mine, Simons has his on. It casts a hazy yellow light in the dust-filled air, illuminating Jorey at the stairs pointing his pulsar gun at the ground where Cain has his arms wrapped tightly around a struggling figure.

"Hold still," he growls, using his weight to leverage his captive into a sitting position.

His prisoner protests, grunting and thrashing his head backward, trying to hit Cain's face. He's much smaller than Cain. As he thrashes and moans, he yells frantically, "Lemme go! Lemme go!"

"It's a child!" Richards cries.

"He could be a spy, or bait," Cain snarls, struggling to better his hold on the wiry figure.

Simons is on his feet. In two strides, he makes his way to Cain and his struggling prisoner. He grabs both the boy's hands, pulling them over his head. With Simons' grip established, Cain releases the boy and grabs his pulsar gun from the holster, taking a step back to join Jorey at the stairs. He levels the sights with the boy's head and says in a firm, commanding voice, "I'm going to tell him to let go of you, but listen to me! You've got two very powerful weapons pointed right at your head, and I can guarantee we're both excellent shots. If you so much as *think* about moving once he lets go, we're both going to pull the trigger, and that'll be the end, do you understand me?"

This might be the only time Cain will ever compliment Jorey's marksmanship, and he doesn't even notice. Instead, he steadies his hands against the handrail, completely focused on the pint-sized threat.

The boy stops struggling and looks up at Simons through his stretched arms. "I don't have to listen to you!" He spits at his feet.

I'm overwhelmed with the impossibility of the situation—of being confronted by someone, an outsider, in this dead city—of the threat the child presents. More than anything, I ache with the reality that he's just a boy—a child whose innocence is indisputable, despite what someone might use him for.

"I don't think he's a spy," Frances says, finding her feet. One hand is on her gun, but the other reaches toward the boy. "Are you?"

"Orman put your families into the hive so you wouldn't shoot. Do you think he wouldn't use a child?" Cain demands.

The boy stares wide-eyed at Frances. "I won't struggle."

Simons addresses Cain. "I'm gonna let him go now, slow and easy."

"If he runs, we'll shoot," Cain promises, glancing nervously around the room.

"Cain! He's only a child," Frances snaps.

Jorey lowers his pulsar gun, casting an incredulous look that Cain doesn't see.

Simons looks at the boy, urging him to comply. He lets go, and the kid slumps to the ground. Slowly, he lifts his hands up in surrender. "You got me. Now what?"

"Who are you?" Simons asks, kneeling in front of the kid. He unclips his pulsar gun and rests the weapon on his knee so the boy stares directly at it.

"He can lie," Cain snaps, steadying the weapon.

"I'm aware of that, but it's where we're gonna start," he barks, then repeats, "Who are you?"

"Julio." The boy's voice is small.

"Okay, Julio. Where'd you come from?" Cain doesn't move his gun.

"I come from here."

"Julio from here," Simons repeats. "I need you to understand you've put us in a tough position. Like my friend says, you might be lying, and I don't know if I can trust you, so you're going to have to give us a little more to go on."

Julio starts to shake, sweat collecting at his brow. He closes his eyes and licks his lips. "We came here from the communities."

"You mean the City States?" Cain asks with an edge of hostility. He glances nervously into the darkness. In the background, Richards gives Frances a concerned look.

Julio looks up from Cain's gun, keeping his wide-eyed stare on Simons, as if the big man could protect him. "Don't you know about the communities?"

I recognize the value of what Julio is about to share. Before Cain can intimidate him out of speech, I step between the boy and Cain's line of sight, kneeling next to Simons. "Can you tell me about the communities? Are they *next to* the City States?" I ask.

Julio nods emphatically. "That's right! The fields are always by the force fields. You have to be careful during harvest."

Julio's explanation clicks into place—the missing piece in Max's conspiracy. The food isn't produced by ancient communities held hostage by disease—it's produced by people right outside the cities, kept out by the very force fields that promise to keep the cities safe.

"Mason, you have no idea if he's telling the truth," Cain warns, trying to shift around me. Jorey steps forward, blocking him.

I ignore them and ask, "How many people live in the communities?"

Julio's eyes move rapidly between me and Cain, trying to decide who he should focus on. Simons gives Cain a stern look, intending to make him back off. He doesn't, but he quits trying to get around Jorey. Julio settles his attention on me and shrugs. "I don't know. Lots."

"And the communities produce food for the cities?" Simons asks.

"That's right. We grow it, and they take it inside the force fields," Julio agrees, more relaxed now.

"All of it?" Richards chimes in. He looks like he wants to move forward, but he stays by Frances' side.

"Most of it. We get what's left—after *quotas*." He pronounces it *coat-ahs*.

"Is that enough?" Frances asks.

"If we keep more, we get in trouble," Julio says.

"The DDC?" I ask.

"Is that the government?" Julio asks.

"Basically," Jorey says.

Julio nods, as though he'd suspected as much. "If we don't make *quotas*, people get sick."

He doesn't need to clarify what he means when he says *sick*. Another piece of the government's control slides into place, this one at least as terrible as everything else.

"There's a problem with your story, kid," Cain says, interrupting my train of thought. He walks right up to me, placing a hand on my shoulder and raising his gun up to point at Julio's forehead. "If you live in the *communities*, how did you get here?"

I want to push the gun away from the boy, but Cain keeps a tight grip on my shoulder. To him, the boy is just as much a danger as the near-dead. He could be right, but the fundamental difference between situations is indefensible. Orman could be behind the boy's presence, but I refuse to believe Cain would actually pull the trigger. It's a bluff. He's trying to draw Orman out, like I drew the hive in the boulder field. Julio stares down the barrel of Cain's pulsar gun, the color draining from his face.

"Cain, don't!" Frances pleads, pulling away from Richards.

"There's no way the DDC is letting growers leave the communities. If he's here, they are, too," Cain says, the power cycling on his pulsar gun.

Simons puts his hand out to halt Frances and Richards from getting involved. "He has a point, even if he's going about it the wrong way."

Cain drops the gun down to Julio's torso, cutting the power-up cycle short. "How did you end up here?" he demands.

"We followed the ravens, like in the story," Julio says, clearly expecting us to understand.

"*The ravens*?" Jorey whispers.

"Growers, ravens and quotas…" Frances shakes her head, baffled.

"Tell me about the ravens," I say, my pulse quickening as something tugs at my memory—trapped behind the shimmer of that perfect creek and sweet, tall grass, glinting in the reflective light of my old data port. Whatever that thing is, it's the link between Dunn's story and this child.

"In the story, the ravens are messengers for a free world. If you see them, it's a sign. But the word is different," Julio starts, his voice shaking. There's a rustling above him. Jorey lifts his gun toward the noise, and a spread of dark feathers becomes apparent below prehistoric feet in the dim light. Another crow—or *raven*, if Julio's right. Alarm bells ring in the back of my mind.

"You skipped the part where you tell me who you're with, kid. Who's the *we*?" Cain demands.

"The season was dry, and the harvest was bad. The foremen said lots of people were going to get sick—an outbreak. So we left—all the growers," Julio says, a thin line of sweat trickling down his brow.

"They didn't just let you walk away," Cain says.

"No," Julio pants, clearly terrified. I can't tell if he's more afraid of Cain or the memory. "They came from everywhere."

"A hive?" Frances asks.

"Near-dead. So many of them," Julio confirms.

"Let me guess, they killed everyone and you're the sole survivor?" Cain demands.

"There were others who got out, but I don't know where they are," Julio says, a little too eagerly. He's hiding something.

A sign, but the word is different. When I first saw the black birds, I was sure they were crows because crows travel in groups. Ravens are solitary birds. I read their profiles in the *Extinct Species Archives* along with so many others, but that's only part of it. The rest of it I'd mistaken for fevered ramblings about a lost love and ancient texts… an *omen.*

"I want to believe your story, kid, but I keep coming up against the same problem," Cain says, his dark eyes intensely focused on the cowering child. Overhead, the number of birds has increased, much as it did when we were outside, from one to two and now five inside the rings of light cast from Jorey's headlamp. Cain's gun is only inches away from Julio's chest. "You're lying about being alone, and that's a big problem for both of us."

"I'm telling the truth!" Julio wails.

"I need to know who you're with, and if I've got to shoot you to find out, that's what I'm going to do." Cain's retort turns my stomach. This whole time, I was certain he was bluffing, but I don't know anymore.

Julio's eyes dart around the room. He sees the birds, and a moment of relief registers on his face. Before I can alert the others, the room is flooded with brilliant light. It pours in from the stairwell, casting Jorey's shadow long across Julio's face. It seeps in from the broken-out windows and the cracked floorboards under our feet. It's blinding.

"Drop your weapons," a cool voice says.

FORTY-EIGHT

A FIGURE STEPS into the room, squeezing past Jorey, whose hands are raised in surrender as another of the intruders digs the barrel of a gun deep into his ribs.

More people enter, settling their weapons on our team. The intensity of the light suggests there are more people just outside, waiting. Cold steel presses into my temple. Frances and Richards are likewise surrounded, leaving only Simons without a weapon aimed at him.

"Who threatens to shoot a child to draw out his people?" the woman scolds.

"It worked, didn't it?" Cain asks, swinging his pulsar gun away from Julio as she approaches.

"Shoot me and we drop everyone in your party before the gun can cycle power. I don't expect you'd like that very much," she taunts.

Cain knows he's beaten, but I don't miss the flash of anger that brightens his eyes.

Pointing her gun at Cain, she addresses Simons. "Let the boy go."

"He's free to go," Simons says, keeping hands back from the gun in his lap.

Julio's hands drop to his sides with an audible sigh of relief. Without further prompting, he slips behind Jorey and disappears down the stairs. The woman gives a low whistle, and all but one of the ravens take their leave, following the boy like a team of feathered escorts. The final raven soars gracefully down, perching on the woman's shoulder and giving me an idea who we're talking to.

"Alright, you've got your kid back. How about you drop your weapons?" Cain says, keeping his gun raised over his head.

"How about you drop that technological monstrosity you call a gun?" the woman replies. Her statement is odd. Pulsar guns are ubiquitous in our society. Anything else is considered old world.

"Not on your life," Cain barks, the subtlest of movements flexing the fine muscles along his fingertips. He thinks we can outgun these folks, and for a horrifying moment, I think he's going to fire on the woman, ruining any chance we might have of getting out of this mess.

"Cain, don't be an idiot," I snap, mindful of the body pressed against my side, blocking any retaliation.

"Listen to your girlfriend. Women always have more sense than men," the woman says. To show her fearlessness, she lifts her gun to caress the side of Cain's face. Her hood falls back just enough to reveal a tuft of dark hair and the sharp lines of her face.

"He's not in charge," Jorey spits. The raven tilts its head toward its mistress, settling its intelligent gaze on Jorey.

"Well, that's the problem, isn't it? You can never tell who's boss from the outside looking in," the woman says, giving Cain's cheek a patronizing pat. She leans in until her face is right against his and whispers, "Sort of like how you thought you knew who sent the boy in after you."

"Quit messing around, Emm. Let's get the goods and get out of here," the man at Jorey's side urges. I catch my breath, certain this is the final bit of confirmation I need. If I'm right, these people aren't dangerous—to us, anyway. Without drawing attention to myself, I bring my hand over my glove.

"We'll get what we came for," the woman—*Emm*—retorts without looking at him.

"What do you want from us?" Simons asks.

She settles her gaze on him, raising a critical eyebrow. "Who's asking?"

"I am, but that's not what you want to know," Simons says.

She turns her back on Cain as I retrieve what I need, running my fingers over it to be certain I have the right one. Before he can react, another member of their ambushing hoard takes her place, settling a gun against Cain's ribs. She approaches Simons with her gun at her side, settling directly in front of him, unaffected by his bulk. "You might be in charge. You've got the look about you—the confidence of a government man. And I didn't miss the way these guys look at you." She glances back at Frances and Richards with a wink.

"If I am?" Simons asks, still calm in the face of her inquisition.

"Then you get to be the one to tell me what you're doing in our city so I don't have to tear your little crew apart in front of you." She places her hand on his chin, cupping it and pressing his cheeks up as she shakes his head back and forth. It could be an empty threat—the sort that would make a government man faint—but if it's not and I'm wrong about her, we're in serious trouble.

"We aren't DDC," I blurt.

The woman turns her head in my direction, as if noticing my presence for the first time. "It's like you said to our boy. *You're lying*. Everything about you is government," she says, ready to do another of her investigative circles around me.

"I didn't say we aren't government. I said we aren't DDC." I urge her toward me. The others won't like my taking another risk, but I need her close.

"Are you suggesting the government and the DDC aren't the same?" She closes the distance between us. Her headlamp hides much of her countenance, but what I can make out fits with the rest of Dunn's story. All the way down to the black bird with a misleading name.

"I only meant it's hard to work in disease containment when the Northern Laboratories are in the business of propagating it," I say.

"Who are you?" she asks in a voice meant only for me. Her face is so close now the light no longer obstructs my view. She studies me with dark, fiery eyes.

"A friend of a friend, from before you got away," I whisper, opening my hand to reveal the golden scientist emblem with Dunn's name inscribed across the surface.

She stares at it, wheels turning frantically in her head as she calculates the likelihood of what I'm suggesting. I lift my hand over hers, releasing the emblem into her palm. She reads the name before her hand closes over it, exposing dirty fingernails.

I look into her eyes, now glistening with restrained tears, and whisper, "Jim told us about a girl who escaped the city."

I'm certain I've gotten through to her when the man at Jorey's back urges, "Come on, Mora, is it them or not? We're wasting time."

She swallows hard, banishing what emotion managed to surface back behind her wall of cool control. It makes me think of my days at the Institute. "This doesn't prove anything," she says. Then, loud enough for everyone to hear, "Warwick, search their gear." On her command, the man whose gun was previously jammed between Jorey's ribs moves toward our supplies. My heart lurches.

Mora's hand drops to her side, but Dunn's emblem doesn't fall to the ground. She takes a step toward Warwick's invasion of our supplies, her foot nearly touching the pack containing the cure.

"His name was James Dunn, but I didn't bother to know he preferred to be called Jim until it was too late. He said I reminded him of you—"

Mora stops as Warwick opens the first of our packs, making the bird on her shoulder open its wings for balance. She angles her body back toward me, looking past her companion.

"The bird's name is Omen, right?" I ask.

"This is Annabel," she corrects, giving the raven's breast an affectionate stroke. Annabel coos in response. Warwick replaces the wrapped fish, tossing the bag aside with its mouth still open. "She's Omen's first."

"Ravens can live for fifteen years," I protest, inexplicably hung up on this long-memorized fact. Warwick finishes his search through a second pack, and I curse myself for not wearing the cure through the night.

"Not around the near-dead," she says flatly.

"When you rescued the growers," I say, connecting the unbelievable pieces of Julio's story with reality. The growers wouldn't stand a chance against a hive on their own, but a surprise attack from the outside could change things—depending on the program controlling them.

"We've seen them like that before—moving together, acting like they can think, killing but not eating…" She trails off, lost in memory.

"The hive is their weapon, but we can fight back," I say, starting to move forward.

Mora steps in front of me, blocking my view of the rest of the group and Warwick's progress. She's angry now. "You can't fight something like that!"

"You did," I say.

"That was an ambush. And we still lost too many people. I'd be dead too!" She strokes the raven again before casting her hand toward the sky and commanding, "Search!" The raven takes to the sky, disappearing into the night.

Warwick is holding my pack. If he weren't distracted by our conversation, the cure would be in his hands—not that he'd necessarily understand what he was looking at. I'd still rather not take that risk. "Ever since I lost my family to a hive, I've heard the same thing, over and over—*no one survives a hive attack*. But I did. And then we all did again up north—two of them, more than a thousand strong. Now we know you fought one off. It's starting to sound like the government's most powerful weapon isn't as strong as they thought," I say. All eyes are on me now, eager to hear more. "Nothing scares powerful people more than the reality they aren't as powerful as they believed. And we're proof of that."

Mora considers this, her fingers playing with Dunn's emblem as she chews her lower lip. I recognize for the first time why Dunn thought we were alike. I don't wait for her response. Instead, I lay it all out.

"We can manufacture the cure. There's someone at the Institute. If we can make it that far, we'll have everything we need." I omit the details of what Warwick is holding and the yet-unknown journey below the Deadlands.

"The cure." Mora's voice is flat. The corners of her lips tug downward, twisting her expression. Her eyes flit back and forth between our supplies and me. "The *cure?*" she asks, registering what I said.

"If we can make it to the Institute," I repeat.

"We're so close, but it all has to come together," Simons presses. Behind him, Jorey nods.

"Once we've got it, we can come back," I urge, keeping an unobtrusive eye on Warwick.

"It won't do any good," she says.

I tear my gaze away from our supplies and focus on her. "Why?"

She walks over to Warwick and grabs the pack from him. Though her gun is no longer trained on us, my heart skips a beat as she swings the pack in my direction. "Cure or no cure, you're being hunted. The DDC won't let you live. Best-case scenario, they're onto you but haven't caught up. Worst case, we're all dead."

"That's not necessarily true—"

"Let's assume best-case scenario," she interrupts Jorey. Cain raises a dubious eyebrow. She continues as if she weren't interrupted. "We let you go, and you manage to escape. They'll know you were here. The DDC will flatten this city and scorch the earth it was built on just to be certain no one survives. Best-case scenario, you live to be caught another day, and we're homeless."

She opens the pack and peers inside at the stacks of bound paper. I can't tell if she understands what she's looking at.

"Are you willing to gamble on a best case?" I ask.

"For a *cure*?" she repeats.

I nod in silent promise, forcing myself not to look at the pack. "And for Dunn. He believed the cure would come out of the Northern Laboratories. He was only wrong about how it would happen."

"He used to call me the dreamer," she says, letting out a long, heavy breath. She tosses the pack back to Warwick, who lets it fall to the ground. My insides lurch at the impact, but I don't let it show.

"Can you help us?" Simons prompts.

Mora turns her focus to her people, chewing her lower lip again. "We're going to have to abandon this city one way or another…" Warwick resumes his search, pulling out one of the metal rings from Simons' pack. He holds it up to Mora, who raises her eyebrow, and he sets it aside before removing cartridges.

"We'll only take half of what you have," she says. One of her men opens his mouth to protest, and she shoves her gun at his chest. "I don't want to hear it! I'm in charge for a reason." She returns her focus to me. "If we get killed, it's a big problem, but if you get killed, we're all dead. I assume you have access to the tunnels?"

CHAPTER
FORTY-NINE

MY PACK IS LIGHTER.

It's lighter. Warwick and Mora's team ransacked supplies, dutifully taking one of everything. I tried to track what was taken but couldn't follow all the activity. Technically, there are two copies of the cure—Shelby's original notebooks and my transcriptions. If they took one of them, all I can do is hope they took mine because it's not quite done yet. I don't ask. If I ask, they'll know for certain what we have, which is dangerous no matter how things go.

"There's a railway onboarding station at the city's center," Mora says. "We'll take you that far before we make our evacuation south."

We make our way silently through the ruined city streets, led by Mora and followed by Warwick and three others from the ambush. We're no longer held at gunpoint, but they don't trust us enough to let their leader take us alone. The morning sun casts long shadows across the dust-covered remains of civilization. Though summer is long past, it's already warm. Mora's worst-case scenario hangs heavy on my mind. We've known since the hive encounter in the volcanic lands that the DDC is getting closer, but the seamless transfer from the cargo ship into the container gave us false security.

We turn at a city corner from a narrow, cluttered street into a square where several roads converge. Unlike other intersections, this one is open and clear of wreckage. Each intersecting road is blocked by the crumbling remains of large cement blockades meant to keep traffic away. It must have been a gathering place.

At the center of the open area, a twisted gate marks a stairwell of dusty, cracked tile. It leads downward into an underground area—the onboarding station that will lead us to the tunnels.

"Why are the roads blocked off?" Jorey asks.

"Markets, maybe, based on what's left," Mora explains, guiding us into this open space. Once we've made it into the center, she addresses the rear guard. "Prepare the team for egress. I have a feeling we'll need to move fast."

The men offer complacent nods, satisfied enough to leave Mora with us at this stage. As they depart, she summons a raven from one of the nearby rooftops with a low clicking noise. The bird soars down to her raised arm. She shushes it, pulls a slip of paper from her pocket, rolls it, and tucks it into a leather strap around the bird's leg. She moves her arm away from her body, arcing it upward. The raven lifts from it with a smooth motion, disappearing into the horizon.

"Don't you worry the messages will be intercepted?" I ask, watching the raven disappear.

Mora laughs as we reach stairs that descend into the earth. "That would require them admitting how far out of hand things have gotten out here." She steps aside to make way for us.

Cain takes the lead, peering down the stairs with Simons and Jorey close at his back, hands on their pulsar guns. Richards and Frances hang back, as if they had an unspoken agreement to keep me positioned in the middle of the group. I square myself with Mora, who waits for us to depart, making her look at me.

"I don't think you should use them anymore. Things have changed now that the Northern Laboratories are gone."

Mora scrunches her nose, averting her eyes. She lets out a breath, running one hand through her short, dark hair as she digests my warning. "Look, I get that things have changed for you since you jumped headfirst into this mess, but this war has been going on longer than you've been alive, and if you don't get into those tunnels, it's going to go on a long while after you're gone, too."

"Why don't you use the tunnels?" I ask, a creeping unease sinking in with the morning heat.

"We've got our mission, and you've got yours. So long as the government controls the food supply, they've got the people. If we want to end things, we've got to free the growers," she says.

"How will you get out of here?" I ask. Frances moves close, placing a supportive hand on my shoulder.

"Divide and conquer, right? If we don't say, they can't pry it out of you if you get caught," Mora says, stepping away from the stairway as Jorey comes back up, hand still on his gun.

"It's clear down there. Cain went ahead with Simons to check the opening."

As Jorey speaks, a shadow lifts into the northern horizon. We watch the birds as they move over the city. Mora's face hardens, masking the anxiety roiling below the surface. "You need to go."

Our time is up.

"Come on, Mason," Richards prompts, taking his place next to Frances. Between them, there's enough strength to drag me into the tunnels if they need to.

Mora pulls one of our lashing poles from her pack, holding it at her waist, ready to depart. "We're happy to have you on our side if that's where you are. Get out of here and make that cure. You'll find us again when you're ready," she says.

She doesn't wait for more questions or for us to descend into the onboarding station. She takes three long strides into the open square before turning back to look at me. "I was the only one who called him Jim," she says before turning and breaking into an earnest jog, heading in the same direction as the birds.

"Come on, Mason," Frances says, pulling my attention away from Mora and her flock of ravens. How many are descendants of the first?

"They don't stand a chance if a hive is coming," I say.

"If a hive is coming, we need to move now," Richards says.

"You heard what she said—we'll find them again when the time is right. For now, we need to focus on the cure," Frances urges.

She gives my shoulder a gentle squeeze, and we turn together to the stairs. I take Jorey's hand as we descend into the darkness.

Richards has his light on before we reach the bottom. It illuminates the underground space.

The onboarding station is made up of cracked grey tiles that might have once been any number of vibrant colors. Empty light fixtures house the dusty remains of glass tubes that long ago lit the open space. Busted machines that once sold entry to the transit line the wall next to the stairs. Ahead of us, the turnstiles that collect the transit tickets separate us from the single track the transport rail once ran on.

"If we can't find the tunnel system in time, those turnstiles might slow a hive down some," I suggest.

"Cain and Simons followed the track to the north, looking for a waterway entrance," Jorey says.

The muffled sound of an explosion draws our attention. The ground rolls beneath us as dust and broken tile rain from the ceiling. I brace myself against Jorey's arm as the percussive force moves through the earth.

"I don't think that was a hive," Richards says.

We launch into the darkness as the world above us shudders. Images of what terrible weapon might be at work flash through my mind, and I envision a hive larger than any we've seen pouring down the stairwell. Ahead of us, a bright light appears from around the corner, illuminating Simons.

"He's got it," he calls, urging us forward.

We run into him, not slowing to turn the corner for fear of what might be moving into the city above.

"What's going on up there?" Simons asks, ushering us toward the back wall.

"Something's coming," Jorey breathes.

"That doesn't sound like a hive," Simons says.

"At this rate, we'll be lucky if it's a hive," Richards agrees. His statement reminds me of Cain's ball of energy from my dream—*only it wasn't Cain's, it was Orman's.* The creeping plasma from his demo weapon. *Could he make it large enough to destroy an entire city?*

Cain appears from the tunnel's blackness. He reaches out and pulls me into him as Simons corrals the rest of the group. All around us, there's a whooshing roar, as if some great beast were sucking the air from the underground space.

"The entrance is going to collapse," Cain shouts into my ear. My body is pressed so close to his that I can feel his heart beating against my chest.

"We've got to get this door closed before it does," Simons yells.

Jorey is quick to help him seal the entrance, moving two thick metal doors until they're flush with the wall. He turns the wheel that seals them. There's a hiss as the old hydraulics do their work and then nothing. We're sealed in.

"That was close," Frances says.

"Explosions… was it fire?" Richards speculates, stroking Frances' hair as she rests her head against his chest.

"And I thought a hive would be bad," Jorey chuckles bitterly.

We listen as something tears through the city ruins. My heart sinks for the infinite possibilities this ancient city and its mysterious people brought. Another blast vibrates through the tunnels.

"We should move out. These tunnels can only withstand so much," Cain urges, not waiting for the earth to settle.

We move toward the city's edge, our own safety tenuous at best. Whatever is destroying the city, it's not a hive, but that doesn't mean that one isn't coming. Cain puts his arm around my shoulder, sensing my unhappiness.

"We'll stop to take inventory once we've put some distance between us and this disaster," he says.

I nod, unable to express my despair at the thought we might be the only ones to have escaped.

CHAPTER
FIFTY

SEVERAL HOURS north of the disaster site that used to be an ancient city, we break to rest and take inventory. We stop in a wide, open section of the tunnel system where several paths come together. In that wide space, under the scrutinizing glow of our headlights, we confirm the loss of six pulsar guns, three energy rings, half of our rations, jackets, socks, tools and lashing poles. It's what we expected but doesn't do much to soften the blow. Worst of all, my notes on Shelby's cure are gone. I knew they were, but the proof is devastating. What will a group of refugees do with an incomplete copy of the cure?

After facing the damage, we settle in to eat, choosing to distribute half-rations until we have a better sense of how long this last leg of our journey will take. I settle in at Cain's side, trying to make sense of my own twisted thoughts. Jorey sits across from us with Frances and Richards at his side making light conversation.

Simons finishes his meal fast, uninterested. The second the last morsel is in his mouth, he excuses himself to search for water. Richards offers to join him, but Simons waves him off, saying he wants some time to himself to think. We give him leave and try to rest, but no one manages. Too much has happened. Instead, we revisit the jagged pieces and half-truths that make up the last twenty-four hours.

"You can do it again. You said you practically had it memorized," Jorey encourages.

"Why did they even want it?" Richards asks, shaking his head as he picks at the remains of his dinner.

"Spite," Cain says through a full mouth.

"It's more than that. Mora and Dunn had some sort of a relationship. She was interested in the Northern Laboratories even if no one else was," I point out.

"They aren't scientists; what are they going to do with a pile of notes?" Jorey asks, using the last of his bread to pick up loose crumbs.

"Burn them. Wipe their asses," Cain suggests.

I reach over my head and smack him in the ribs for being crude. "They weren't villains."

The fish is dry and almost too salty. My piece is blackened on one side and tastes heavily of smoke from the fire at Max's. The dense bread cuts through the strong flavors. I wash it down with a mouthful of stale water.

"Mason's right. We were moving through their space," Jorey says.

"Says you, brother. You'd absolve the DDC to take Mason's part," Cain jabs.

"Not true. I just happen to agree with her in this matter." Jorey crumples the wrapper that held his fish.

"This and every other matter," Cain snorts.

I shift uncomfortably, knowing they're about to start another mindless argument. A glance in Frances and Richards' direction reveals their similar discomfort.

"I'm not an idiot, but you might be if you can't acknowledge that Mason's probably right about almost everything," Jorey says.

I stand, not wanting to referee their spat. "I need to talk to Simons."

"Do you want some help?" Frances offers, just as much for her and Richards' sake as mine, I'm sure.

"Of course."

Jorey and Cain barely notice our departure. I don't waste energy worrying I should scold them for using me as a game piece in their stupid squabble. If not me, they'd find something else. They always do.

On our way out, before their voices are drowned out by the echo of our footsteps and the whistle of wind through the complex ventilation system, I catch Jorey saying, "Good judgment, right. Does that include killing kids?"

His words make my stomach twist as I recall the way Cain held his pulsar gun level with the little boy's eyes. It wasn't that he threatened the boy, or the way he pressed him for information. It was the look in his eyes…

"Did you see which way Simons headed?" Frances asks, sensing my unease.

"He said he was looking for water, so he's likely headed toward the river," I suggest, trying to pull up a mental image of the blue lines running up the map.

"This seems right, then," Frances says.

We move ahead, listening for the sound of running water. Every now and then, Jorey and Cain's voices rise above the underground din, their words indiscernible but obviously hostile. Cain shouts something, and Jorey's reply is drowned out by a new sound—something grinding or churning. It's a solid sound, like metal against metal.

"Do you hear that?" Frances asks, head cocked as she strains to make sense of what she's hearing.

"They're certainly mad," Richards sighs, casting me a sideways glance.

Frances gives Richards' arm a sharp shake. "Not that. Listen!"

The grinding sound grows in intensity before stuttering into silence. There's a long pause where there's nothing but the wind, then a loud bang, the whine of a rusted hinge, and the grinding starts again.

The three of us rush forward, cautious in our anticipation until we round the corner and find Simons leaning into a massive, ancient vehicle. Its top is framed by thick, padded bars in roughly the shape a vehicle would take but is otherwise open. The wheels are as enormous as the ones on the massive transport vehicles, comically juxtaposed against the size of the rest of the vehicle. The sides are matte grey, or maybe green in better light. The front has two seats, and the back is open.

Frances catches her breath, too stunned to form words. Richards lets out a surprised "oh" as the grinding sound transforms into a roar and the vehicle shudders to life.

"Simons," I say, just loud enough to draw his attention.

He turns his head, a satisfied grin on his face. "I think we're going to make up some time tomorrow," he says.

A sharp odor fills the tunnels, something between the chemical smell of weapons and the astringent smell of burning oil. Simons catches a whiff of the odor and leans forward to turn a lever inside the vehicle, extinguishing the engine.

"Does it have enough fuel to make it the rest of the way?" I ask, noting a pile of red and green canisters stacked up against the rear of the vehicle.

"Depends on what it burns, but I'm guessing so. Three of those were completely full." Simons points at the canisters.

I suspect he's right. Dó's vehicle ran nearly six hours on two similar canisters of homemade fuel. Simons was taken by the machine and spent a long time discussing it with Dó, going over the construction once they'd finally made peace with one another.

"Do you think you can drive it?" I ask, embarrassed by my complete ignorance about transportation. I don't understand the differences between modern and ancient vehicles, or even the big transport ones versus the city buses.

"It doesn't look any different from the transport vehicles as far as function goes. It might be a little rough, but the indicator suggests it gets up quite a bit of speed." He points at the driver's dashboard, and I have to agree, in my limited knowledge and experience, that it looks exactly like the other vehicles.

"This is fantastic." I beam. "Is there any way for it to be traced if we drive it down here?"

"I can't see how, considering it's an old-world vehicle. It's probably down here exactly because someone needed to travel undetected," Simons says.

A thought strikes me, so impossible it might be the only explanation. "Do you think someone put it here for us?"

"It could be, if the dissenters are as organized as you and Cain say," Frances muses.

Simons rubs his hands along the open frame of the vehicle. "It's not something I'm intimately familiar with, but definitely a possibility. For all we know, there could be vehicles like this hidden across the coast for us to intercept."

The vehicle does more than cut our travel time in half. It quarters it —maybe slicing it all the way down to a tenth if the tunnels are clear the whole way. We might even make it to the energy management facility outside the Institute in as little as a day.

"I'm going to get Cain and Jorey. This ought to shut them up for the rest of the trip." An enormous smile spreads across my otherwise travel-weary face.

Simons laughs. Until then, I didn't realize how long it had been. "Let's all go. The sooner we get out of here, the better."

I take off ahead of them, leading the way with good news lightening my heart. I'm so happy that even the ancient city and its lost people seem distant. As I near our camp, Jorey and Cain's voices return, clearly escalated.

"You have no right to say that," Jorey growls.

I can't see their faces, but I know things have taken a turn for the worse.

"You can't hide in Simons' shadow forever. You're in the real world now, brother," Cain snaps back with equal malice.

"The real world?" Jorey sneers. "Everything you say is stories and deflection. You might have the others fooled, but I see right through your bluster."

I stop in my tracks, afraid to go any further. I can't see them, but I can imagine the scene in vivid detail. This isn't the sort of argument that will fizzle into the next urgent moment.

"Because you would have been just fine without me, right? Remind me, how close to death were you when you rode the transport vehicle down the ice flows? Or how about how actually dead in the river you were before I risked my own life to get you out from under that log? Do you think Mason would have stripped to her underwear without my suggesting it?" Cain scoffs.

"She would have." Jorey's voice is weak, trembling with self-conscious fury.

"Then what? I saved your life," Cain concludes, his voice dripping with satisfaction.

"You underestimate everyone but yourself. Mason could have gotten us through just fine without you, probably better," Jorey counters.

I sneak forward, dreadful fascination pulling me toward the epicenter of their quarrel.

"Mason needs me," Cain says smugly.

"You don't know what Mason needs," Jorey says. His calm tone doesn't mask his disdain.

"You can't understand. We love each other."

Cain's words hit me square in the chest. *Love?* All at once, the wind in the ventilation system ceases, leaving a dull ringing that vibrates through my whole body. I barely notice Frances move in beside me.

Jorey laughs bitterly. "You don't love her. You don't even know her, and I guarantee she doesn't love you."

"What do you know?" Cain says dismissively.

"What do I know?" Jorey keeps his voice at a low rumble that resonates with the ringing vibration in my limbs. "I know she worries about doing the right thing, that she's willing to sacrifice herself for literally anyone else. I know she cataloged every living thing on her family's management facility and that she and Hank used to torment Bruce for fun. I don't have to ask her what life was like before she came to the labs because she already told me. She's afraid of the dark, but she could tell you without looking where the moon is in its cycle. She's the only scientist to ever stand up to Orman, and she did it for a bunch of volunteers. So don't tell me what I know. I know Kara Mason, and I know that I love her, and you just love being the guy that got her."

I'm too stunned to move, reeling in the wake of Jorey's words—not in his admission, but in the extent to which he's gone to use our relationship as a weapon against Cain's provocation. I move away from Frances, creeping around the corner until I can see them facing each other under the yellow glow of their headlamps. Jorey doesn't look like himself. Cain's face is stained with a vicious sneer. He crosses his arms across his chest triumphantly and says, "Too bad knowing all that didn't do a damn thing. Mason is *mine*."

JOREY DOESN'T RETORT. Cain breathes a self-satisfied huff, turning away and not seeing his fingers curl into his palms. I know Jorey is going to hit him before he does, but it still happens too fast. He explodes toward Cain, landing a solid blow to the side of his face, fist raking across his nose. Cain's head whips to the side with a bright spurt of blood before he staggers backward, falling into a pile of supplies.

Cain struggles for a moment, arms flailing as he tries to untangle from the packs before Jorey can land another blow. When Jorey leans down to grab him by the front of his jacket, Cain's ready with a hit that connects under his chin, whipping Jorey's head back and forcing him to lose his grip but not his footing. Cain is fast, but Jorey is bigger. That, along with his training in the Northern Laboratories, gives him an advantage. Cain is still on the ground when he moves in for another blow.

Our light pours onto them unnoticed, illuminating the culmination of a dispute that's been gaining ground our entire trip. I stand in their midst, wanting to stop the altercation but muted by the rage seething just under the surface of my own understanding. Jorey launches himself at Cain as Simons steps into my line of sight to grab him. Then everything stops.

"Are you going to shoot me? Is that your solution to everything?" Jorey roars as Simons wedges himself between them. Simons grasps Jorey's shoulder, his other hand outstretched toward Cain, who's still on the ground a with pulsar gun aimed at Jorey, the power cycling up.

"Enough of this!" Simons voice booms over the commotion, resonating in the ventilation system like thunder.

I watch them through my own barely contained fury as they set all their focus on Simons, not even acknowledging my presence. Jorey takes a half step back, panting heavily, rage still pulsing through him. He wipes at the blood trickling from the side of his mouth with the back of his sleeve. Cain looks up at him from the ground, sputtering as blood gushes from his nose, still holding the gun.

"Put that thing down," Simons commands.

Cain cuts the power cycle short, expelling the cartridge and letting the pieces clatter to the uneven ground. "I wasn't going to fire," he says.

"You sure about that?" Jorey pants.

"This is shameful," Simons admonishes. "After everything we've been through, you can't resolve your differences like grown men?"

Cain brings his hand to his eye, which is rapidly swelling shut. His gaze meets mine, and he curses softly under his breath. Jorey looks in the same direction, freezing when he sees me. My fists clench against my sides as all the anger collides with unfathomable frustration, pulsing through my mind like a blinding wave. "I heard what you said about me."

Cain looks away, but Jorey lifts his gaze. I lock in on it. "I thought I was more. I thought we were friends. I thought you understood me, but I was wrong."

Jorey swallows hard, as if he's keeping something bitter back. Looking at him hurts.

"I don't belong to anyone but myself," I say as Cain turns his head back, licking at his split lip. "You may not claim or possess or *own* me any more than I'd allow Orman to collect me. I am *mine*." I channel the anger that's pulsed inside my veins since the blood-stained morning I lost everything. I carry that rage through the Northern Laboratories and let it pour onto them.

"Mason, I'm sorry," Cain mumbles, his voice thick.

"I don't want to hear it! Simons is right—you should be ashamed of yourselves," I scold.

Jorey opens his mouth to speak, but I cut him off. "I didn't pour my heart out to you all those times for you to turn around and use that for your own benefit. I didn't give those pieces of myself for you to flaunt."

Jorey flinches but doesn't protest. I turn away from the three men in the center of the room to find my pack and see Frances moving toward me. Richards stops her, putting an arm around her shoulders and pulling her gently into him. He brushes his lips across her forehead before whispering something in her ear. She nods, closing her eyes and wrapping her arms around his neck. The comfort and support they offer one another makes me feel empty.

I retrieve my pack, ensuring everything is still there.

"Love isn't supposed to be about winning or knowing more. It's about being there when things are terrible. It's supposed to lift you up, not tear everyone else down. Honestly, they're the only ones in this room who know what love is." I gesture toward Richards and Frances as I make my exit, unable to leave fast enough.

The tears come unbidden, rushing down my flushed cheeks as I crawl into the back of the vehicle. My pack makes a dull thud when it connects with the grooved interior. I sink down next to it, burying my face in my lap to let the sorrow and rage overtake me. All the grief, loss and anxiety wash over me like a tidal wave. I cry until I'm exhausted and there's nothing left to give.

I've lost track of time when there's a gentle tap against the hollow metal siding of the vehicle.

"Mason?" Cain's voice is gentle, tentative.

"What do you want, Cain?" I say, trying to force exasperation to mask my distress.

He takes my response as an invitation and hoists himself into the back of the vehicle, crossing his legs so he can sit directly across from me. I wipe at my eyes, trying to clear my face as I meet his gaze.

"I want to apologize. I want to make things right," he says, reaching for my hand.

I hold it back from him. "Do you really want to apologize? Are you actually sorry?"

"Mason... I..."

When nothing immediately comes out, I interrupt, "What's gotten into you? You pulled a gun on Jorey!"

"I wasn't going to fire," Cain says, leaning toward me.

"I want to believe you. I *need* to believe you, but after the city—after the boy?" I heave out a breath, willing myself not to cry again. "I just don't know."

"You know me." Cain looks at me, sadness etched across his face.

I want it to be true. "Look, I know with Jorey—it's not like it's just your fault," I say, searching for a way to come together again.

"What am I supposed to do with a guy that's going after my girl?" he says defensively.

"*Your* girl?" I quote, the sweltering fury rising again.

"Well?" he offers plainly.

"That's right," I seethe. "I need you, don't I?"

"You know what I mean," Cain tries, clearly seeing his words and actions as forgivable.

I cross my arms tightly over my chest, pulling my legs closer into my body. "The thing is, we all need each other. That shouldn't be the defining feature of our relationship, or whatever this thing between us is."

"Is?" Cain asks, lifting his chin in a tentatively hopeful gesture.

"Is... was... I don't know. I can't wrap my mind around this right now," I say.

"I really do love you," he says, reaching for me.

I pull back, surprised even though I've heard it once already. "How can you even know that? With everything else that's happening... there hasn't been time for love."

"I'm not going to let you walk away from this," he says, searching my face. "Unless you want me to?"

I let his question hang in the air for a long time. Above the whining vents, the waning crescent moon races across a late morning sky. Beneath it all, I can hear the murmur of voices as Simons, Richards and Frances have their own conference with Jorey.

"I don't know. I need more time," I admit, studying the space between his and my shoes.

Cain lets out an exasperated breath. "I know I messed up tonight."

"Messed up?" I repeat, bristling. I could explain Julio or Jorey on their own away, but together Cain's actions are damning.

"Yes. Pointing a gun at Jorey was a mistake," he insists.

"But threatening to shoot a child wasn't?" I venture.

Cain shakes his head, frustrated. "I needed to know if Orman was using him."

"But you didn't know, and you did it anyway!"

"I didn't shoot him," Cain insists, pushing off the vehicle to settle next to me. He takes my hand in his before I can protest. "What Jorey said about Orman—about you standing up to him…"

The memory of Orman plagues me, sometimes when I least expect it to—his hot, bourbon-laced breath on the side of my face, the way he used Dunn, the glint of satisfaction as I fall again and again into his snare.

"You need to understand how dangerous he is," Cain says, his thumb moving to rest on the soft tissue above my thumb.

I let out a sardonic laugh. "Do you really think I don't know that?"

"You let him toy with you to protect us. You knew he had all the power, and you did it anyway," Cain says, his voice darkening.

I lift my gaze from our intertwined hands to search his face. Beneath his swollen, distorted features, his eyes are fiery red. "You think you can handle him on your own, but you're wrong. You think pointing a gun at that kid was bad? Orman will use that. He's an expert at getting the upper hand."

"I'm not going to hurt innocent people to get him," I insist.

"And that's why he's going to keep winning. I'm not going to let anything stop me," he says, staring into nothing.

"Cain…" I begin, a queasy uncertainty settling in my gut. "We don't have to do anything rash. We can do it on our terms."

"Our terms?" he scoffs, looking down at me. "Alone in his office? Those terms?" He glares at me.

"What's wrong with you?" I ask, letting outrage mask the hurt.

"Orman killed my mother," Cain says, his body rigid by my side.

"He killed my family too," I counter. "And Shelby. And Dunn."

"No offense, but it's not the same."

I stiffen at his words, not sure if I should be insulted or curious. "Okay, Cain, I get that you've got a big score to settle with Orman, but you can't say something like that and—"

"Rick Orman is my father," Cain blurts.

My mind rushes the pieces together as I stare at him, mouth agape. Eli Cain is Rick Orman's son. I pull away from him, an involuntary lurch as Orman's features become clear in Cain's hard expression.

"Does he know?" I whisper.

"He never suspected. My mother escaped from the Northern Laboratories before anyone discovered the truth. She was nearly dead when Dó found her. She stayed with him for a long time—most of my childhood. Dó introduced her to the dissenters and helped her find her way to freedom through the network," he explains.

"You're absolutely certain?" I don't want to believe it.

"It took a long time to travel north after he killed my mother. By that time, I had my suspicions, and Dó gave me the rest. That's why I went to the Northern Laboratories. I needed to see him dead. I can't stand that he's my father." Cain clenches his fists.

"It's not like you had a choice," I say, resting a hand on his knee.

"I might be just like him—deep down," he suggests.

"He might be your father, but he has no stake in who you've become. Your mother raised you. And Dó, and whoever else you met along the way. You don't have to be like him."

"I hope you're right," he says, leaning his head into mine. I think the conversation is done. My racing mind has only begun to settle into the next steps when Cain adds, "But if the opportunity to kill Orman arises… I'm going to take it."

CHAPTER
FIFTY-TWO

WE DEPART WITHOUT REST, Cain's admission weighing heavy on my conscience. I sit in the passenger's seat next to Simons as we travel through the black tunnels, only our immediate path visible in the dim headlights. Jorey and Cain sit in back with Frances and Richards, nursing their wounds. I wish I could share Cain's burden with the rest of the group—that we could carry it together to some tenuous resolution until our job is done. But it isn't mine to tell, and Cain doesn't volunteer the information. There won't be any repair to the fracture in our team. It's a quiet thirteen hours.

In the moments when I'm not thinking about Orman, Cain, Jorey, or the relentless pursuit of the DDC, I think about the man who saved me. Simons is in the driver's seat again. I watch the fine motion of the tendons in his hand as he shifts the vehicle's engine down and we begin to climb, our progress slow on the mud-slicked surface. I think about how those same powerful hands cradled a little girl as his deep voice soothed and promised she would be okay. I think about it until my eyes sting, knowing I'm responsible for his broken promise.

The engine strains, and the tires slip on the steep grade. The persistent smell of exhaust fills our nostrils as the engine's combustion ticks up.

"We might not make it up this one," Simons says, shifting a final time.

"We've got to be close," I say, the thought of it causing my stomach to flip. "Maybe we should do a location check?"

"I'm already on it," Cain calls from behind us. I glance back to see he's got the map spread out across everyone's knees as he waits for the encrypted signal.

The tires slip again, and Simons makes the final call. He turns the wheels so the vehicle slips back against the tunnel wall and jams itself there. He sets the brake before turning the crank and killing the engine.

"There's an exit point ahead. We're only a few kilometers away now. We can do that overland. This area is heavily forested," Cain says. Richards marks the map with our location, and Cain shuts off the signal.

The group gathers our supplies without discussion. We're so adept at these sorts of transitions that we don't need to communicate. We pile out of the vehicle, strapping our packs and checking the charge on our pulsar guns.

"Just because it's heavily forested doesn't mean we'll be safe. This close to the Institute, there's no telling what type of security or alarms the DDC will use," I warn.

"Orman could be at the Institute. That makes it extra dangerous," Cain adds.

Simons nods, and my desire to tell him everything peaks again, but I don't dare. There will be another time.

We make our way up the steep incline of washed-out stairs toward an old service access. It appears slowly as a surface distinct from the tunnel walls. Cain takes the lead to unlock the lever, and Simons cranks the wheel until the seal gives way and the doors open. The second we step into the open, I'm transported back in time, greeted by the forests of my childhood.

Enormous trees—Sitka spruces dripping with moss, towering Douglas fir and massive Western hemlock—shade the area, making it as gloomy as dusk. My footsteps are silent on the thick, decomposing forest floor. I stop amidst a patch of familiar fungi and stoop down to take them in. Immediately, I spot a dirt-red salamander.

"Rhyacotriton olympicus," I whisper to myself as my brain immediately catalogs the new creature.

"What's that, Mason?" Richards asks, stepping toward me.

I return to my feet, putting a hand out to stop his progress so nothing gets trampled. "Nothing. Just a salamander."

"Oh. Well, that's something," he says, offering me a sympathetic smile that proves he's still thinking of yesterday's fight.

I step past him, back to the rest of the group, not wanting to settle under his compassionate gaze. The bustling forest is making me jumpy. It sounds too much like the home I'll never see again. I fight against the massive lump that threatens to take permanent residence in my throat, against the aching need to hear Hank's mocking voice. *"Rhya-schmya, why do you have to be so boring?"*

"We should head straight north unless there's a problem. The more time we spend out here, the more likely someone will find us," I announce, directing my thoughts toward Simons instead of speaking to the whole group. It's still hard to make eye contact with Jorey and Cain.

"Sounds right to me," Simons agrees. "Jorey and I will range ahead and take point."

"I'll hang back and watch our tail. I don't want anything sneaking up on us while we're out here," Cain says, unclipping his pulsar gun and moving back.

Richards gives Frances a quick glance before offering, "I'll join you. Better to have two sets of eyes anyway."

Frances gives him a peck on the cheek. "I'm going to stay with Mason. That way we're traveling in twos."

I'm immediately suspicious that Frances and Richards would split up. "Fine, but I think we should probably keep quiet."

The brush is dense, and it doesn't take long before there's a decent amount of space between the front and rear of our convoy. I glance nervously at Frances, who walks stoically beside me. The forest is wet and cold. There's a persistent drip-drip of water from the mossy tree branches. A haunting whistled bellow breaks through the idle buzz of insects, making Frances catch her breath.

"What was that?" she croaks, barely above a whisper.

"An elk, I think," I say, only partially certain I'm correct. The sound isn't exactly the same as the electronically generated one from my encyclopedia of extinct animals.

"Are they dangerous?" she asks, her eyes flitting to the side.

"They'll probably keep their distance."

She glances into the thick brush once again.

"You know, elk are supposed to be extinct," I say, unable to think of something better.

"Sure," Frances agrees, keeping her voice low as we clamor over a shallow stream.

"I'm sorry. Are you not interested?" I ask, imagining her rolling her eyes the way Hank used to.

"Oh, it's fine, Mason," she says, throwing her hands out for balance as she climbs over knotty roots. "It's just… are you sure you want to talk about elk?"

My cheeks flare with embarrassment. I've walked right into her plan.

"Did you talk to Cain?" she asks.

My heart stutters, and I worry my face will give everything away. "I did."

"Are you okay?" she presses.

I don't know how to answer. Part of me wants to tell her everything, but the other part wants to keep it close to my heart, at least for now. "I'm fine," I say.

"Ah," she says in a way that suggests that she knows exactly what sort of *fine* I'm experiencing.

"I need some time to think," I blurt.

"That's absolutely fair," she says in a tone so motherly I want to scream and wrap my arms around her at the same time.

"I don't know what I'm doing right now, and I haven't had any time to think about it. He said he loves me, but I don't know if I believe him. And I definitely don't know if I feel the same. I mean… I like him —or at least I did," I gush. A valve inside of me has been opened, and now there's nothing to stop what's pouring out.

"Figuring out love takes time," Frances says.

"What if he isn't who I thought he was? What if he isn't who he says he is?" I ask. Another elk bugles, this time farther off.

"That's why you need time," Frances confirms.

"Exactly," I say, as if this settles the matter.

We walk in silence for a minute, our feet scraping gently against the soft earth, our sleeves soaked from wiping against the persistently wet brush.

"What about Jorey?" Frances asks.

"What about him?" I ask, uncomfortable all over again.

"Are you going to talk to him?" She holds a thick branch out of our way.

"I suppose. Eventually," I say.

"You're really mad at him," Frances observes.

Her statement gives my anger permission to surface again, and it does so like a pot boiling over.

"How could he be so selfish? So… the way he was?" I wave my arm, and my hand catches against wide, wet leaves. I shake the moisture away and continue, "He's supposed to be my friend."

Frances nods, thoughtful in the wake of my anger. "The things he said and the way he acted were very childish," she agrees.

"I don't see him as a volunteer. He's a whole person. He knows that. Why wouldn't he just talk to me—"

Frances puts an arm up to stop me. My hand drops to my pulsar gun, and I look around for the threat. She waits until my eyes meet hers, her expression stern.

"Are you sure about that? That you never thought of him as a volunteer? That you never got caught up in the wicked hierarchy of the Northern Laboratories or let Simons cast too big of a shadow over him?"

Richards' statement from the side of the river comes back to me, about how we never stepped outside our roles in the Laboratories. I drop my gaze to the forest floor. "I never meant to."

"And Jorey never meant to take your friendship for granted. He didn't mean to be selfish about love," Frances says.

"It was still wrong," I protest, frustrated by the depth of pain his actions caused.

"It was," Frances agrees. "People make mistakes. Friends give each other grace."

"How do I forgive him?" I ask, trying to ignore the tears stinging at the corners of my eyes.

"By giving him a chance to make it right," Frances says. Her gaze travels north. We've nearly caught up with Jorey. He's standing still, studying a massive spruce whose branches splay out like spindly fingers covered in a stringy moss netting as though it were meant to trap us like insects in a spider's web.

As I watch him study the tree, some of the anger dissipates, replaced by a longing for the friend I've lost since the Laboratories. I step away from Frances to approach him, hoping if I reach out, it will make it easier for Jorey to find his way back. As I move toward him through the uncut woods, I notice a distinct grunting sound, increasingly audible over the forest sounds.

Jorey turns toward me, head cocked. He's been listening. *Do you hear that?* he mouths.

I nod. Simons returns, silently stepping around the massive tree with his finger pressed against his lips. We wait until Cain and Richards catch up before approaching cautiously. The grunting continues and becomes clearer as we approach a decaying redwood mass.

There's a scratching sound accompanying the grunting, but less noticeable. I pull up my pulsar gun, freeing it from the harness, and slowly raise my head above the mass to peer down.

A near-dead specimen at the end of its life is clawing at the spongy redwood, peeling layer after rotting layer as it endeavors to pull itself forward. It's the most horrific thing I've ever seen. It should be dead. The flesh is putrid and rotted to jelly in the decaying grounds that surround it. The legs are gone, composted into the ground, aided by insects and bacteria that recycle the living nutrients into something else. The thing continues to pull at the decayed log, unaware of its unwholeness. Moss and fungus have crept up the torso, creating an awful display of natural unity—it has become one with the forest.

The creature pauses and stares, motionless, into the rotted log before giving a loud shriek and a low gurgle as it catches our scent. I step up onto the log and take careful aim at the remainder of its corpse. The quick zap of the gun silences the gurgles and shrieks, leaving nothing but a scorched and rancid puddle.

"How long do you think that's been there?" Jorey asks, stepping wide over the log to avoid the mess.

"Months?" I venture, swallowing hard to resist the urge to vomit.

"They can't live that long," Frances says in direct objection to what we've all witnessed.

"They shouldn't be able to. It should have starved or died of dehydration. The organs should have failed…" I say, my database of knowledge taking over my train of thought and missing the obvious.

Cain steps around the mess, putting a booted foot on the log to avoid the gooey remains. He uses the barrel of his pulsar gun to pry a clear line away from the remains, revealing the intricate system of life support wired into the now-deceased creature.

"They're plants," Cain says, tossing the IV line away in disgust.

CHAPTER
FIFTY-THREE

THE IDEA that someone would install a patient in the forest is chilling. Even worse is the possibility the patient might be wired into the hive technology—that it could be more than just an alarm. It could literally be Orman's eyes and ears.

"We've got to run," Cain says, likely coming to the same conclusion.

The second the words fall from Cain's mouth, we hear the sound of something fast approaching from behind. We break into a run, dodging trees, roots and other obstacles as we press forward. The terrain might offer us a slight advantage depending on which direction the attack comes from.

I clamber to the top of another fallen log to find another plant below. It shrieks, reaching out for me, desperate to free itself from its rotting prison. I extinguish its cries with a quick blast, leaving it in the same decomposed puddle of sizzling ooze as the last alarm.

Wails spread across the forest, signifying more near-dead alarms being set off by our presence. Each time, the cries are doused with a hot blast of plasma as we hurry toward the energy management facility, unsure what—or who—is hunting us. We press deeper into the woods until nothing I climb over is free from a waiting plant. I progress with my finger on the trigger, anxious to destroy Orman's window into our world.

A deep rumble emanates from the woods behind us. Whatever is chasing us hasn't caught up, but there's something new. Above the sharp, cold pain of each breath, smothering out the stench of decay, is the acrid smell of smoke. I make my way through the maze of fallen trees and decaying flesh until I've reached a high point. I spare a second to glance back. The forest is melting away from us. Bright flashes of light burst into the air as something rolls through the trees, turning the land into a soup of hot flames and liquid plasma. It's the creeping plasma blast from Orman's weapons demo, and it's laying waste to the forest.

As the mass approaches, the heat becomes more oppressive.

"What is that?" Jorey screams as he zaps another plant and hops down beside the melted puddle.

"I'm not sure," Cain replies, "but whatever it is, it's worse than another hive attack."

We give up on extinguishing every planted alarm, opting to jump around their reach, leaving them to scream for our flesh as we pass. We start to gain against the creeping plasma despite the multitude of near-dead. They're as thick as two or three stationed in the same area, attached to the same, monstrous life-support. Others now stand out, unobstructed and shrieking. We're running through a garden of near-dead.

The air darkens with smoke. Every hastened step becomes more dangerous. The planted near-dead blend well with their surroundings, easy to miss in the thickening haze. Their desperate cries become our guide. I startle at the tug of something grabbing my leg. The rotten hand pulls as I jerk away, disengaging it from the host. I use the tip of my gun to pry the dismembered hand from my pant leg.

I'm staring at the disengaged appendage twitching on the forest floor when a panicked cry causes me to whirl around. Richards turns abruptly toward a mass of shrieking hands. Cain is caught as though he were hung up in a tree branch—only it's not a tree branch, it's the grasping arms of a plant.

"A little help!" Cain cries in a mixture of false humor and terror.

Richards grabs Cain's arm and fires at the plant. Its decayed skull collapses with the impact. He brushes the decomposing flesh from Cain's arm and is about to follow him out of the thick cluster of growth when another arm grabs hold of him, yanking hard. Richards loses his footing and crashes to the ground where more hands lie in wait, grabbing and pulling him into their clutches with flesh-tearing strength.

"Hang on, Richards!" Cain cries, reaching for the pulsar gun that isn't there. Too late, he sees it lying on the forest floor where he dropped it when the creature latched on.

Frances bursts past him to free Richards from the clutches of his horrific attackers. At the last second, Cain grabs her back. She strains against his grasp, screaming.

"What are you doing? We have to help him!" she wails.

"It's too late," Cain says, lifting her from the ground to pull her away from the gruesome scene.

Richards screams as the plants sink their teeth into his flesh. I freeze, too far away to act, helpless to answer his cries. Cain drags Frances away, wrapping his hand over her face to shield her from the awful spectacle. Frances flails against his grasp, thrashing to escape and move back toward Richards' tortured wails. She smacks him on the back of the head and twists to free herself.

She raises her arm to strike again, and a cadaverous hand catches her. She tries to pull herself free, but the hand has a firm grasp. Cain realizes it too late. Though he jerks with all his might, Frances is pulled from his grip as the plant sinks dead fingers into the exposed flesh where her glove should be. She pulls back against the horror, screaming. The hand tears through her flesh, cutting a deep path. Jorey extinguishes the creature with a swift blast.

Simons steps between them and the horrific display of Richards' demise. He holds his weapon in position and with one bright pulse ends the life of his first friend in the Northern Laboratories—Richards' screams are silenced. The plants continue their despicable feast in dull silence, ripping the limp body and tugging it like a rag doll. Simons turns away, his expression blank. Jorey helps Cain pull Frances from the ground. He tears a length of his shirt to create a tourniquet, wrapping her arm until the blood stops gushing with each pulse.

I'm petrified, unable to look away from the gore. Richards' glasses fall from the mangled mess, hitting the ground without sound. The blood-smeared lenses get shoved and squashed in the frenzy for flesh.

Moments ago, Richards was fine. We were all fine.

Jorey's coughing brings me back from the trance. He places his arm on my shoulder, squeezing gently. "Come on, Mason. We have to leave it. We have to go. He's gone."

"I know… I know, but…" I protest, desperate for Jorey to understand.

"You couldn't have stopped it. Please! Let's go," Jorey pleads.

There's nothing more to be done. We move quickly through the smoke as the forest smolders around us. The crackling of the sap and the hiss of the water vapor escaping the ground drowns out the awful sounds of the wailing plants. We catch up with Simons and Cain. Frances struggles to stay conscious, staring into nothing. Simons takes the burden from Cain and tosses her easily but gently over his shoulder.

The air darkens further, and the fumes from the burning foliage become intolerable. We're brought to our knees, crawling through the mire, taking turns clearing our path. Overwhelmed by the toxic air, we gasp and cough as we creep forward.

"We're not going to make it," Cain wheezes. "We're going to suffocate!"

"Keep moving," Simons rasps between coughs, dragging Frances' limp body.

I crawl on, dizzied by the lack of oxygen. There's no hope. But every time I stop, someone urges me forward. I'm so focused on making progress I don't realize there aren't any more near-dead plants. I almost miss the burning tingle creeping up my fingers as I place my hand in front of me.

The sensation surges up to my elbow, demanding my attention and making me cry out. "Stop! The force field—I've found the force field."

My voice is barely a rasp, but the others hear it. They make their way over to me as I fumble blindly in my pack. The air burns as I pull it down my throat and into my protesting lungs. I don't have time to carefully set the pinpoint blocker, but if I mess it up, we're all dead.

I press the receiver into the static mass that makes up the force field boundary, burning my fingertips and generating a pain so extreme I'm afraid I'll faint. I engage the blocker, and the hole appears. I know it's deep enough, so I don't wait to confirm.

"Go," I yell, my hand still caught in the buzz and sting of the force field.

Simons rises to his knees and forces Frances through the hole, tumbling through after her, too oxygen deprived to break his fall. Jorey tries to usher Cain through, but he waves him off, giving him a shove that causes him to topple over.

My nerves are screaming, and my head swims with oxygen deprivation and neuron misfires. I feel myself falling away from reality, unable to hold it together.

I collapse into darkness. Vaguely, I'm aware of Cain's strong embrace. His arms envelop me, and he screams as he jerks me from the force field's hold. There's a moment of relief before I'm overtaken by a coughing fit. The air is too hot to breathe. I'm suffocating. Suffocating and falling.

The ground is cold and wet. I try to open my eyes but can't. My lungs burn, and I cough so hard I vomit again and again into the cold grass.

There's a pressure against my face as Cain whispers into my ear. "You're okay now. You did it. We're safe."

I try to nod but I'm too weak.

Cain squeezes my shoulder and moves away. "I'm sorry, Mason, but this is my last chance," he says.

I don't understand what he means, and I'm too out of sorts to explore it. His hands press against the back of my leg, and my scar tingles. He's coughing loudly. My ears ring and my head spins with the effort, and somewhere off in the distance, I hear Simons shouting. I turn my head, immediately dizzied by the movement.

"Come on, Frances! You've got to breathe!" He pounds on her back, urging her response.

I give up, letting the heat transfer from my skin into the ground, taking me back to the ship's deck, where ocean winds carry me far away. I follow the current across the sea, down the cove and into the hills from my childhood. I wander those hills with a bird's-eye vantage, watching myself as I limp across the road toward the Institute —seeing Simons' truck as he picks me up, the suited volunteers sweeping us away from intake, and the pristine white-and-steel surfaces of the surgery room. My body pitches and dips in the tumult of my thoughts. I sink down until I'm level with my fourteen-year-old self—staring the screening patient down as it thrusts itself against the barrier and the door opens. The pointy-faced woman walks in to face me, smiling and saying, "Welcome to the institute, Mason. I'm Amos."

"MASON?" I open my eyes to the pointy-faced Amos from my childhood, convinced I'm hallucinating.

I squint and bring my hands up to clear the cobwebs and check for my own sanity. It's impossible that she's here. The whole world was burning around us. I'm unconscious. I'm dead…

My right arm still tingles from its encounter with the force field, my fingertips blackened from the intense energy they sourced. I look past them to Amos. She's not exactly as I remember her. Streaks of grey accent her rich brown hair as if the last year has aged her more than the four before. A tiny pair of glasses rests precariously on her pointy nose, enlarging deep-set bags under tired eyes.

I'm in a bed with crisp white sheets. A wildflower-filled vase rests on a windowsill directly overhead, making me think momentarily I've somehow been transported back to the spare bedroom at Max's facility. This room is different, though. There are three beds where there should only be one. One of those beds is occupied. There's an IV line connected to several bags of fluid. The soft buzz of electronic monitoring manages the slow drip of those fluids into the patient. The other bed is empty.

Everything rushes back, and I bolt upright. "Frances," I gasp. My voice wheezes, barely more than a squawking whisper.

"She's alive," Amos assures me.

"And the others?" I ask, my feet touching the ground as I sit up.

"All fine," Amos assures me, sitting down on the white sheets, which blend with her Institute coat.

I blink back the dry, persistent burning behind my eyes. My focus returns to Amos. "We made it."

Amos engulfs me in her arms in a gesture I never imagined her capable of. She holds me as though I'm a child. "Green sent for me as soon as she found you at the barrier."

"They'll come looking. This was the only place we could have gone," I say, worry overtaking the relief of having finally reached Amos.

"No, Mason. I'm in charge of energy management facility security. I'm here to ensure no one made it through the force fields. I'm *they*. You're safe for now," she assures me, her voice husky with emotion.

She waits patiently for me to process, smiling gently, the way she used to while she waited for me to solve complicated algorithms during instruction.

"Shelby was able to get a message to me before the Northern Laboratories went down. We knew to expect you even before you made it to your first safe house," Amos explains.

"She's gone," I croak.

"I know, Mason." Amos doesn't bother masking her sadness. "The last time we said goodbye, we assumed we'd never see each other again."

"So you know what I've brought?" I ask.

Amos' eyes glow with pleasure. "Of course I do. We've been waiting for years. You were the last piece."

"You should have told me."

"I can't tell you how many times I started to tell you, to guide you to the answers you were looking for. But you were so impetuous! Just like your father. You always jumped ahead, not waiting for a plan. I was afraid if you knew you'd rush up to the Laboratories and take things into your own hands… But I suppose you did that anyway, didn't you?" Amos scolds without losing an ounce of kindness.

"I'm just like my father, right?" I ask, shame coursing through me at the knowledge I caused this mess. My reckless experimental design, impulsive outbursts at Orman, and irresponsible side-stepping of the rules and procedures put me on the DDC watch list since the day I walked into the Institute.

"In all the best ways," Amos says, eyes glistening.

"It's amazing you wanted anything to do with me. I think I would have tossed me to the patients in my first year," I say, staring down at my bare feet.

Amos laughs. "Don't you dare think I wasn't tempted. You were such a difficult student—always too smart for your own good and too showy for anyone else's. You might not realize this, but my second option—the alternative to the cure plan—was to assign you to Garth. If it had taken another week, I might have done it out of spite."

"I'm sorry," I mumble.

"Mason," Amos says, placing a cool hand against my chapped, burning cheek, "you've done wonderfully."

"At what cost?" I ask. The image of Richards' last moments surfaces like bile in my throat.

"Some loss was inevitable. Shelby knew she'd already done all she could," Amos soothes.

"What about our families? What about Dunn and Richards?" I demand.

"I'm so sorry for what happened to Dunn, but there was nothing you could have done. In the Northern Laboratories or here, he was always slated for death in the government's eyes. The same goes for Richards and the patients."

"Do you know what he can do? With the patients?" I ask, suddenly wondering if she's aware of the extent of Orman's power.

She nods solemnly, her expression making me sick. "We've learned a lot since the Northern Laboratories were shut down."

I don't like the way she describes it—like it was a scheduled event rather than an unplanned catastrophe. "Is that what we're calling it?" I ask.

"It's what they're calling it. An easy excuse for moving things in the direction they were going anyway," she says. Then, almost regretfully, she adds, "Orman is now officially the head of research and development."

"He's going to try and find us," I say.

"He can try," Amos says, folding her hands neatly in her lap, "but you aren't here, and once we make a clean break, he'll have no means of finding you. Not before we finish manufacturing the cure, anyway."

"About the cure," I say, her words bringing up another sore spot in this disaster of a mission. "It's damaged. I've been working on it, but I haven't managed to put it back together yet."

"Whatever you have will be enough to get us started," Amos assures me. "Together, we'll make short work of fitting the final pieces where they belong."

She winks at me. It's so blatantly conspiratorial and out of character for her that it makes me giggle.

"You have too much faith in me. I think you really wanted Hank," I say. It hurts to bring him up, but it would hurt worse not to mention him.

"I'm so sorry for what happened to your family, but I'll never regret saving you," she says, stroking my disheveled braid.

She gives my head one more pat before standing. "If you're well enough, Green has prepared a small meal, and there are some things we need to discuss."

I follow Amos down the hall, amazed at the burden of my body. I knew the force field gave my nervous system a jolt, but the way my leg buzzes makes me wonder if there might have been some neurological damage. When we enter the dining room, Cain, Simons and Jorey all stand to greet me. I rush to them, trying to embrace all three at once. All thoughts of the previous day are gone now, as if the fight never occurred.

Cain is the first to break free from the huddle, moving gingerly toward the dining table. He doesn't meet my gaze when I look after him, and I suspect it's because of the terrible secret we now share. Jorey releases me next, joining Cain at the table so that Simons and I are left.

"I'm so sorry Richards is gone," I whisper into Simons' quivering chest.

Simons doesn't respond. I can only imagine his grief. He holds me until the trembling ceases, then releases me, keeping a hand on my back to usher me to the table. Once seated, he slides a steaming cup of tea in front of me. As I take it, a thickset woman enters the kitchen from the mudroom. She's average height and middle-aged with an extensively disfigured face. Her skin is dark and waxy, and her lower lip protrudes outward on the left side in a permanent grimace. Her arms are deeply scarred, and her left hand is missing several fingers. The two that remain are fused permanently together. She notices me sitting amongst her other guests and juts her right hand out at me. "You must be Kara Mason. Aubergene Green! We've been waiting for you."

I embrace her hand warmly.

Green steps back from me to observe her full table. "Since the whole crew is here, let's have some grub!"

Green opens the oven to retrieve a large, lidded pot that reminds me of my childhood. I expect it to contain some form of a rice dish, and I'm not disappointed. Much like the meals my brothers and I grew up eating, this one is made mostly from government rations. It's salty, savory, and hot. While it lacks the flavor and complexity of the dishes served by Max and Dó, it's so satisfying I keep going back for more.

While we eat, Amos brings us up to speed.

"There aren't many people left at the Institute, and even fewer dissenters. The medical wing is shut down, and the volunteers report somewhere else. There's been a lot of shuffling as the government tries to flush us out."

"Just on the inside?" Simons asks between mouthfuls.

"Everywhere," Amos corrects. She hasn't touched her meal. "Communication is down everywhere, even on the outside. Even the radio relays."

"What does that mean?" Jorey asks.

"It means we can't reach anyone outside our direct line," Amos says, her face grim.

My mind rushes over the implications. "Max and Dó?" I ask, alarm mounting.

"We don't know. We only know we can't reach them," Amos says.

My heart sinks.

"Who do we have left?" Simons asks.

"Me, of course. And Green." The list is much smaller than I expected.

"What about the DDC? Aren't they stationed here? Won't they wonder why you haven't moved on?" Cain asks. There's an edge to his voice.

"I can't manage the energy network from anywhere else. There are still DDC agents at the Institute, but most have gone mobile," Amos explains. I try to imagine the Institute, once bustling with hundreds of people minding their own tasks, devoid of its inhabitants and can't manage it.

Cain curses. "We're sitting ducks."

"It's not as bad as it sounds. Green is a skilled pilot," Amos says, making Green blush.

"Retired pilot," Green corrects.

"She's being modest," Amos says in the same whimsically conspiratorial tone as before. "She was the best pilot in the fleet."

"Until the accident, when they tucked me away here," Green adds, as if she were worried Amos might tell the story wrong.

"The accident?" Jorey asks, his eyes flitting between Amos and Green.

"The one that gave me these marks." Green indicates her face and arms. "But it wasn't an accident."

"I don't follow," Jorey admits.

Green smiles broadly, her engorged lip sticking out even farther. "You see, I was doing a routine drop—a hive I was supposed to deposit on the south bank to eliminate a certain persistent group of outsiders," she clarifies, using her fork as a prop. "And... well, I can't tell you exactly what happened, but I lost control of my hovercraft." The fork drops from her hand, hitting the edge of the table with a metallic ping before spiraling to the ground. "I lost all my cargo mid-air and crashed. The burns were severe—I spent a long time in rehabilitation at the Institute and lost most of my memory of the accident."

"I see..." Jorey says, understanding Green's original allusion. "What a terrible tragedy..."

"Indeed," Green exclaims. "The government was at a loss for what to do with me—they considered me unfit for flight but didn't want to relieve me of my services. Thanks to Amos, they tucked me away at this facility like all the other pesky scientists they don't know what to do about." She concludes her story, proud of herself.

"Do we have a hovercraft?" Cain asks, suddenly very interested.

"We have access, when it's time," Green clarifies.

"Alright, what's the plan?" he asks, fidgeting absently with the fork in his hand.

"That's what we need to discuss," Amos says, sipping from her mug.

All eyes turn to her as she returns it to the table.

"It's going to take some time before we're able to get out unnoticed," she says.

"NO," I say.

"The forest is crawling with DDC agents. They know you're nearby. Leaving too soon would be suicide," Amos explains.

"We can't wait," I repeat, unwilling to take her statement at face value.

"It's too risky. If we aren't careful, we might as well lead them right to our facility," Amos counters.

"If we stay here, Frances will die," I say, slamming my hands onto the table. Everyone stares at me in the resulting silence. "I'm not willing to let that happen if I can help it."

"You can't help it," Amos says. "She's infected."

"For all we know, so are the rest of us! Those patients were everywhere, and we're all torn up," I counter, daring her to give up on me like she intends to give up on Frances.

"That's not how it works, Mason!"

I'm at a loss. The routes of infection are so fundamental to the way we live that I haven't even considered the practicality. Not since our discussion at Max's anyway.

"The modern strains of Zoribiatus aren't hearty enough to enter through superficial wounds. All that nonsense about fluid exchange and open wounds is a remnant of the first outbreak. It takes a full viral load directly to the veins to cause infection. You don't have to worry about scratches and scrapes, but what Frances has is exactly what causes an infection."

A deep wound exposing crucial veins and arteries—like Frances' torn arm and Dunn's ripped guts—is exactly what you'd look for in a weaponized disease. Something you could control the spread of. Something you could inject…

I pry my mind away from this new piece of information, forcing myself to focus on the issue at hand. Infected or not, I'm not willing to lose Frances.

"Can we stabilize her?" I ask, cycling rapidly through our options.

"She lost a lot of blood. Simons was able to resuscitate her, but she's weak. In her state, the infection will spread fast," Amos says, pointing out everything I already know but don't want to accept.

"Does the dissenter facility have cryogenics?" I ask.

"Yes, but—"

"If we notify them ahead of time, could they be ready to stabilize her enough to go into cryo?" I press, ignoring Amos' objections.

"Yes, but nothing is guaranteed, even if we could get there. But Mason, you're not listening. We can't leave," Amos says.

All our focus is on each other. The other occupants of the room fade into the background. I don't have to worry about them. They're ready to go. They won't risk Frances.

"Agents are searching the forest outside the facility. We don't know where Orman is," Amos argues. "Even if we waited two days, or three, it's not enough time."

"What if we didn't wait at all?" I ask, a plan beginning to formulate.

"An immediate departure will set off alarms. They're probably getting ready as we speak," Amos protests.

Green leans in to gather the empty dishes, moving slowly so as not to draw attention. She moves them into the sink and begins a quick scrub—the sort of job one might do if they didn't want someone to come snooping and find evidence of a hasty departure. I grin, knowing I only have one more person to convince.

"I'm not talking about leaving later today, or tomorrow morning.

I'm talking about leaving right now, as in, we grab our bags, load up Frances and get in the hovercraft," I say, speaking slow and low.

"Green said she had access to a hovercraft, not that one is ready and waiting," Amos says.

I suppress the curse that wants to spill from my lips, not wanting her to think she's beaten me. But I don't have to overcome this particular obstacle.

"It's out back, ready to go," Green says to no one and everyone.

"That wasn't the plan!" Amos scolds.

"They won't miss it until tomorrow, right about the same time they'll start to question your report," Green retorts, making meaningful eye contact with Amos.

"If we leave right now, we'll be ahead of their alarms. They won't be able to send someone after us fast enough. It's a wide-open window," I say.

"It's a huge risk," Amos repeats her primary objection.

"We can fly in the blind. Unless someone takes off at the exact same time as us, they won't be able to track us. We can contact base through the dark line on board," Green pipes in.

"And what if someone does track us? What if Orman already knows we're here?" Cain asks, still fidgeting with his fork, not making eye contact with anyone.

"Unless they're ready to leave the second we do, it doesn't matter. I can shake just about any tail," Green brags, only I don't get the impression it's a brag as much as a statement of fact.

Cain takes this information in, weighing it with nervous energy. "We should wait," he says, as if he has some piece of the equation the rest of us are missing.

"That's what I'm advising," Amos agrees.

"If we wait, Frances dies," I remind them. "Leaving the Northern Laboratories, we were prepared to die trying. Everything went to hell, but we made it out."

"I've said before that I'm willing to risk my team on your judgment. If Richards were here, he'd tell you the same," Simons says.

His affirmation is exactly what I need to know I'm making the right decision. I turn from him to Amos, leaning across the table to put my hand on hers. They are adult hands, equal in size and ability.

"You said I couldn't save everyone. You were right. But that doesn't mean I can't try."

Amos takes in a long breath, exhaling slowly. Her shoulders relax, and she nods.

"Well, Mason, what's your plan?"

"We go," I say. Green casually rinses the last dish, as if she weren't planning to abandon this place forever.

"I'll go power things up," she says.

I offer her a grateful smile, letting it fade as I address everyone else.

"Grab your things. Nobody showers, no sleep, just up and out. I'll need help with Frances."

Simons gives Jorey a nudge. He nods, and the two of them excuse themselves to collect our missing teammate. Amos stands to follow them. "They'll need help with the medical equipment."

I'm left standing in the kitchen with Cain, who still won't look at me.

"What's going on?" I ask, nervous about his energy.

"That plasma creeper reeks of Orman's style," he seethes.

"He showed me the preliminary tech it's based on in the Laboratories," I confirm.

I take a tentative step toward him. It's like approaching a spooked animal.

"I told you how dangerous he is," he says, pulling away at the last second. He bursts from his chair with barely controlled energy.

"This is our only choice," I remind him.

He whirls around to face me, furious. "You're not listening to me! He's going to follow."

"If we're lucky, he won't be anywhere near us. That's the whole idea, remember?" I press, not daring to approach him again.

"We won't be lucky."

CHAPTER
FIFTY-SIX

THE CRAFT IS a low-ceilinged disk structure that encompasses us like a metal tomb. There's a slight echo as we exchange information from our posts. The cabin is fully loaded with little room to roam. Windows encircle the disk. The wings are set low on the body, lined with rounded, chrome-colored cells on the bottom. They wrap around to the very front of the craft, leaving just a body's width of open space where the hatch opens straight into the flight station. A wider hatch opens directly below the wings in the back—meant for cargo.

I count the handholds along the side of the craft—room for twenty-five passengers packed like sardines. Frances and the medical equipment take up most of the space. She's secured to the mattress with restraints, and the mattress is strapped to the floor. There's no threat of the disease taking over, no matter how grievous her injuries are. The real risk is to her. If we get into trouble, we don't want her thrown around the cabin.

The intensity of our focus hangs in the cool, humid air like tension in an over-stretched spring. Out the windows, we can see the earth still smoldering where the plasma creeper tore through the forest, a clean line denoting where the force field begins. Green sits at the pilot station going through a series of ready checks while Amos tinkers with the communication system so the government channels are dark. There's an electric pop before Amos cheers a brief victory.

"We're offline," she confirms. "The only open communication line is our direct connection to the dissenter base."

"We're all go here," Green adds. "Let's do this."

I reach above and steady myself as we lift suddenly from the ground. My body is heavy and unstable. We accelerate rapidly, straight up. It's like riding in an elevator that's lost control. There's a blur in the windshield as we move, then just as suddenly as we began, our ascent stops. I lose my feet from under me and fall against the side of the craft. I reach for a stability bar and, grasping it tightly, return to my feet, unsteady as I imagine the craft suspended in the atmosphere.

Green glances over her shoulder. "Sorry for the rough start. It's been a while since I've flown."

"It's not a problem," I insist. "I've actually never flown before."

Green smiles wickedly. "Well then, you're in for quite a treat."

She lurches the hovercraft forward, and we propel silently into the night sky. We're moving so quickly the clouds streak the sky. Looking out the window, I can see the current of air like a wavering sea as we slice through the troposphere.

"Whoa," Jorey breathes, leaning out right behind me.

I forget my unease, losing myself in the physics of the hovercraft. I listen carefully for the hum of the engine but hear nothing as we slice through the air, covering hundreds of meters every second.

"What's the power source?" I ask.

"Heat," Green says.

"Heat?" I ask, noting the clouds condensing in our wake.

"Like the concept of a hot air balloon," she explains. "Only much, much faster."

I ponder the idea of propulsion by superheated air. "How does it move horizontally?"

"The base cells can instantaneously heat and cool more than a hundred cubic meters of air. The craft creates its own convection cells and travels the wind currents," Green explains.

"Amazing," I whisper. "Such a simple concept of energy transfer."

"You know what they say," Green offers, settling into a stream in the upper atmosphere. "The simplest answer is the best."

I don't recognize the saying but can't argue with its logic. Like the fusion generators powering our world, this form of transportation focuses on the fundamentals of energy transfer. It's much simpler than the combustion engine vehicle we left in the tunnels.

I make my way over to where Cain leans fixedly peering out the back window. He doesn't acknowledge me when I brush my hand against his side. I grab his wrist and pull it away from the glass. "What's wrong?"

"Watching for Orman," he says, eyes scanning the horizon shimmering in our wake.

"No one followed us from the energy station. The Institute was quiet. And we're traveling dark, remember?" His body is a rigid wall, keeping me out.

"We can't be too careful," he says.

I sigh, letting go of his unyielding wrist and moving away. I asked for time, but the cold reality of our detachment from one another is hard to wrap my head around.

I leave him to his watch, uncomfortable with his intensity, to join Simons and Jorey. Settling in between them, I look out the window, following Jorey's gaze to where the sun glances off the top of thick, billowy clouds. "This is pretty cool, yeah?" I say.

"Sure is," Jorey agrees, taking his eyes away from our surroundings and meeting mine. "I never thought I'd fly."

"Before all this happened, I would've said you were right," I agree.

"Geez, Mason, I'm so sorry," he says. His words come out in a jumbled rush like words do when you've been holding them back too long, waiting for the right opportunity.

"I know." I place a hand on his arm.

He studies my expression. "You aren't mad?"

"I am—or I was. But that's okay. You'll make it right."

"I will," he promises.

I replace my hand on the side of the craft, comfortable resuming our journey in silence. Below, the landscape changes from rich forest to spotted mountain ranges. When the cloud cover breaks, I catch glimpses of rivers and lakes surrounded by the brilliant reds and oranges of mid-fall. After a while I relax, leaning against the side of the craft and listening to the hum of the convection cells.

About an hour after departure, Green announces, "We're about to travel across the southwest corner of 105-39.NSW."

We turn to the windows, eager for a glimpse of the southern-most City State. From so high up, I don't expect to see much, so I'm surprised to see the city grid with such clarity.

"Is it a different style of force field?" I ask, moving around Simons to get a better view. If I look closely, I can make out the energetic edges of the city's boundary.

"It's open air," Amos corrects.

I tear my gaze away from the window. "The force fields are spherical—a gravitational dome around the city."

She shakes her head. "That takes too much energy. They're fence boundary. It's been that way for years."

I return to the window, staring into the city with awe. At least it explains how I encountered so many extinct species before we left. Jorey leans into the window, suddenly picking up on something. "Look, fields! And those trees are all uniform—orchards?"

I study the far end of the landscape as we depart the area and know he's right. Just outside the city boundary, taking up as much space, if not more, the fields stretch out in a patchwork of greens, yellows, and browns surrounded by low buildings that could only be housing. If the people in the ruined city weren't enough evidence, we've seen it with our own eyes now.

"We're entering the barren lands separating the inhabited area from the Deadlands," Green announces.

I'm shifting again to look beyond Jorey at the approaching landscape, fascinated by the way the landscape changes, when Cain calls out, "We're being followed."

We turn to the back window as one to see another craft in hot pursuit.

"No one could trace us," I whine in disbelief.

"I told you it would happen," Cain says, returning his focus to the window.

The other craft is smaller but just as fast. I make my way to Cain on unsteady feet to watch our pursuer. Green turns on the local scanner and watches the digital tracking screen with Amos. My stomach clenches at the sight of Amos' pale face. Her brow creases.

"I'm going to try to shake him over the Deadlands," Green says. She grabs the steering bar, pausing long enough to add, "You're going to want to hang on."

I grasp a handle with all my might as Green once again propels us high into the atmosphere with stomach-churning speed. Holding on to his own bar for stability, Cain glares out the rear window, watching the other craft. We end our ascent and pitch forward with sizable speed.

"It's riding our current," Cain shouts.

"Not for long," Green says quietly as she propels us upward.

"Green!" Amos objects. "You can't keep ascending. You'll run out of atmosphere. You'll lose control of the craft!"

"If we lose control, they lose control," Green hisses through her teeth, her eyes fixed forward as she watches the altimeter climb on the dash.

"We're below 1% atmosphere," Amos warns.

"And dropping," Green confirms, ignoring Amos' concern.

The craft wobbles as it hits thinner pockets of air. I stabilize myself with a second bar and watch the pursuing craft take on the same wobble.

"We're about to lose control," Green warns us.

"You'll kill us!" Amos cries.

"Not on your life," Green growls as the hovercraft shudders and wobbles, the air beneath us too thin to support the craft.

"She's lost the other craft," Cain exclaims, his face pressed against the rear shield. The other craft spins wildly, pitching and dipping in space. The view only lasts a second before we begin our own uncontrollable spin.

CHAPTER
FIFTY-SEVEN

THE FORCE of the spin rips the stability bar from my hand, and I plunge into Simons, who braces himself and pulls me upright—or downright, depending on the spin. I grab another stability bar and hold on, my feet no longer touching the ground. We're in free fall.

Blinded by the chaos, I can hear Amos and Green arguing. I'm in awe that they still have enough sense to be angry with one another.

"What good does it do to send him into a free spin if you kill us in the process?" Amos shrieks.

"I'll pull us out of it. I guarantee they won't be able to do the same," Green insists.

My stomach turns inside out as Green engages the side-rear thrusters and halts the spin, leaving us to soar toward the earth like an arrow. The thrusters over-correct, and we're again put into a spin, only this time in the opposite direction. There's a buzz somewhere outside my head that I think might be my eardrums escaping my body. I'm about to be sick when the vehicle instantaneously pulls free of the spin with a steady, body-shattering lift, followed by a steep drop. I hit the floor hard only to be ripped from it again, connecting with the window as the craft stabilizes.

"Did we do it?" I ask, afraid to look.

"We did it," Green assures me with an enthusiastic whoop.

We've all recovered, more or less, from the ordeal. Simons walks on unsteady legs to the back of the cabin to check on Frances.

"Was the other craft destroyed?" Cain asks, not having lost any of his previous intensity.

"I can check," Green says, looking over her shoulder at Cain. The hovercraft pitches, and Green turns back to the controls to steady our flight path.

"Whoops," she sings as Amos groans.

"How far are we off our predicted flight path?" I ask, glancing nervously to where Simons kneels next to Frances.

Green fidgets with some controls, scowling.

"Considerably. We did a pretty big leap in that free fall. I'm having trouble getting a pinpoint on our exact location."

Amos leans into Green's screen, a look of concerned contemplation marking her face. "It could be the signal blocker interfering with the geosatellite connection," she suggests.

"I can't get a pinpoint location unless we land," Green laments, slamming her fist against the console.

Amos shakes her head vehemently. "It's too risky."

"If we land, I can scan for the other craft's remains. And get our location," Green says.

"I don't really want to fly more, but I don't feel great about land- ing," Jorey says, his face pale to the point of green.

"Don't worry," Green says, bringing the craft down with surprising gentleness. "The other pilot crashed."

"He's not worried about the other pilot," Cain whispers. I glance back at him. No one else seems to have heard him.

"We'll be back in the air before you know it," Green says, making some calculations to determine our landing area.

It takes three minutes to find the ground. The craft settles silently and sinks into the earth as though the ground is uncertain of its composition. As the hatch opens, a flood of stale, dry air greets us. I nearly trip over Jorey trying to get out of the hovercraft. Simons takes a few staggering steps on the dry, sandy ground before stopping. Wind rips across the surface of the earth, tugging at his clothes and beating sand into his skin. Jorey steps cautiously in the sand and watches in awe as his feet sink down like they would in unpacked snow.

Simons turns back toward the ship and addresses Cain, yelling to be heard over the gusts. "Are you coming?"

"In a minute," Cain says, walking back toward our packs.

Simons shrugs, pulling his jacket closed. "Suit yourself." He looks at us and sighs. "Something's gotten into him."

"Unless he's made of iron, it was that fall," Jorey says, shaking his whole body to rid the tension.

"Where did we land?" Simons asks, scanning the empty horizon.

The earth is red where it isn't covered in sand and devoid of growth. Off on the horizon, the sun hangs against a backdrop of steep, layered canyons. The land around us is dead and barren like the frozen tundra of the Northern Laboratories, but sand-covered and dry instead of frozen, creating an unobstructed path for the wind. As I search the landscape, taking in this new form of beauty, my eyes sting from airborne sand. Odd land masses tower in the silicate field—arches, towers, stripped cliffsides that ripple like ocean waves. The land mimics the sea, dotted with strange islands and hiding its life somewhere deep below.

"We're in the bottom half of the North American continent, just south of the southern-most city," Cain illuminates as he makes his way out of the craft with a pulsar gun in one hand and one of the flat boards that serves as a personal glider in the other. He sets it down long enough to readjust his pack before giving us a meaningful look. "Welcome to the Deadlands."

"Seems cozy," Jorey says.

In other circumstances I might laugh, but there's something sinister hanging in the heat-baked air that sucks all the humor from the situation.

"It's beautiful in its own sort of way," I acknowledge.

"It sure is," Green says. "And it should be no trouble finding the signal for the fallen hovercraft out here."

She runs her fingers over her tablet, which beeps softly as it comes to life. She raises it over her head, bracing through another gust of wind, and sweeps the area for a signal. Bringing the screen close to her nose, she squints to read the results in the glaring sun.

"Nothing," she says, surprised.

"The other craft could have crashed hundreds of miles from here," Amos says. "Falling from the upper atmosphere like that."

"True," Green says, punching coordinates into the screening program, "but I didn't land blindly. We should be close to the crash site. Give me a second. Let me recalibrate the search radius."

"How could she possibly know that?" Jorey asks, spitting at the sand stirring around us.

"Green has some very special talents," Amos explains. "She's the most valuable flight pilot the government has ever seen. It's why they refused to put her back in the air after the accident."

"That doesn't make any sense. Why didn't they put her back in the air?" Jorey lifts his hand to shield his eyes, trying to watch Green work.

Amos turns to face him, crossing her arms over her middle to keep her Institute coat closed. "Even someone half as good as she shouldn't have lost control of the craft like she did. If they could have proved she did it on purpose, she'd be dead, but that generation of carrier had some technical errors. It's what saved her life, but it couldn't save her career."

Green sweeps the air again, and this time something registers. The faint beeping turns into a buzz as the scanner locks in.

"That's it!" Green squeaks, dialing into the device to finish her location. "That's strange," she says, turning the device again. "There are two signals."

Cain moves behind me and whispers, "Mason, I need to talk to you."

I turn to study him, about to insist he explain when Green says, still working with the device, "That's odd…"

"What?" Jorey asks, dread lacing his tone.

Simons scrambles up a weathered rock stack to study the horizon. The eroded formation wobbles under his weight, but years of conditioning give him perfect balance as it sways gracefully in the wind. Cain tugs at my arm, trying to pull me away from the rest of the group while Amos peers over Green's shoulder to interpret the reading. Silence hangs in the air like so many sand particles.

I reach down for my pulsar gun, only to find I'm completely unarmed for the first time in years. I reel around to grab a weapon when Jorey emerges from the craft, arms full of weaponry. He tosses me a gun, then distributes the others to Simons and Amos.

"There are two signals, one moving toward the other," Green muses, trying to make sense of the data. Her voice is light with curiosity despite the discovery.

Cain grabs my arms, forcing me to face him. "Mason, I need you to hear me. This is a trap," he says, confirming the revelation dawning just below the surface of my conscious thoughts.

"Oh, I see now. The craft was a drone, following our signal." Green sounds as though she doesn't believe her own proclamation.

"We don't have a signal," Amos protests.

"Mason," Cain shakes me hard.

"There it is," Simons says, so quietly it's terrifying. From his vantage point, whatever he sees sends chills down my spine.

"Let's get back in the hovercraft and get out of here," I suggest, gripping my gun tightly.

"We can't," Cain says grimly.

"Why not?" Jorey asks.

"It's too late," Cain concludes as a dark shadow blocks the sun from the sky. Before now, I would have insisted net force fields were purely theoretical. I would have been wrong.

FIFTY-EIGHT

TRADITIONAL FORCE FIELDS are mostly transparent, sometimes shimmering as air diffracts around the electron-rich space, but this one is dark like storm clouds. Like the arced bubble of the ring force fields we used during the last hive attack, this one depends on deflecting energy around the area below, possibly with conductive material like my diode cloth. Whatever makes it possible, it's the noose finally tightening around our necks.

My breath catches in the back of my throat. "We were so close."

"Mason, I need you to hear me," Cain snaps, squeezing my shoulders so tightly I wince.

I finally meet his eyes, and I realize I've been avoiding it. What I see there is worse than whatever is waiting for us in the darkening horizon.

"This is my fault. I did this to you—to us," he says with a heartbreaking intensity.

"What are you talking about?" I ask, trying to reconcile what he's saying with the wild sequence of events leading to this moment.

"I didn't want to miss my chance. It was a stupid decision. If I could take it back, I would. I'm sorry," he rambles, digging into my arms so hard my fingers go numb.

"What did you do?" I ask, terrified.

Simons shields his eyes as he peers into the nothingness, his body rigid with apprehension. "There's a hive on the horizon, absolutely massive and headed our way."

Amos takes in the dark mass moving within the field barrier, watching it swell. "That can't be a hive... It's too big." Her hand tightens on the pulsar gun.

I twist my arms free from Cain's grip, taking his hands into mine. "You didn't do this. You couldn't have! Orman knew we would come. I'm the one who insisted we leave."

He pulls his hand out of mine, shoving it deep into his pocket. "You wouldn't have if you'd realized what I'd done."

"What did you do?" Jorey asks, inserting himself into our bubble. His rage is palpable on the viscous air.

Cain retrieves his hand to reveal a small, black chip he lets fall into my open palm. "I found these trackers in the cargo hold. They're from the laboratory salvage. After everything you said, I knew there had to be some sort of tracker tech in your leg. All I had to do was figure out how to activate it. I thought if Orman came to us, I'd be ready. I wouldn't have to wait." His words are drowned by a gust of wind. Sand pelts our faces, boring into our exposed skin.

I stare at him, speechless, the innocuous piece of metal and plastic resting in my palm.

"I wanted to lure Orman into a confrontation. Instead, I gave him exactly what he needed to win," Cain says, hanging his head.

"You've killed us! You've killed Mason!" Jorey screams, advancing on him.

I step between them, pushing my chest against Jorey to stop him. I can't make sense of what Cain's saying, but the two of them fighting again won't help.

"She's not dead yet, brother," Cain says over my head. Jorey tenses but doesn't advance.

"How do you plan to get her out of here then?" Simons asks, barely masking his own anger.

"It's a hive," Cain says calmly, pulling the personal glider to his side. "If there's a hive, there's a mind. Orman's in that mass."

"Cain, be reasonable. Even if you kill him, there's no escaping this one," I protest.

"There's a way out for you," he says, studying the force field-covered sky behind the hive. He locks in on something and whispers, "Got you."

He grabs Simons by the shoulder and pulls him down so we're standing together. He speaks definitively, commanding and leaving no room for objections. "Orman is in that hive. This one isn't a program. It's like the one in the labs; he's directing it. He can't control a group this big remotely. You can't escape from the flank. You're going to have to go straight through the hive. The exit is low. You have to fly right on top of it."

"You can't know for certain," Green objects.

"I can," Cain insists. "Orman doesn't do suicide missions. He always leaves an exit for himself."

"Even if there's an exit, there's no way we can make it through a hive that size. They'll bring down the craft." Green would know.

"You won't have to," Cain persists. "I'm going to pull them around the flank so you can fly through. If I'm lucky, I'll break the hive signal and they won't even care about the craft."

"It won't work. We'll have to fly through regardless to pick you up!" I object, immediately finding the flaw in his plan.

"You won't be picking me up," Cain says, the same fire lighting his eyes as earlier.

I open my mouth to object, and Cain grabs my shoulders. "You listen to me, Mason! You can't tell me how to handle this. You aren't in charge right now. I'm not leaving that hive until Orman is dead. If I die doing it, so be it. You leave this to me and get the hell out of here!"

He drops me suddenly and turns to Simons, still fueled by fury. "You've gotten her this far; don't give up now. Get her out of here. Don't let me down. Get Mason and the cure out of here."

"You sure about this?" Simons asks as the wind dies. Everything settles in a dead calm as natural atmosphere is shut out by the force field. In the stillness, Simons reaches for him. "You made a mistake, but that doesn't mean—"

Cain blocks his arm and lands a blow square across his face.

Simons brings his hand to his cheek, stunned. "I'm not deferring to your authority this time," Cain says.

He returns to me, and I almost manage to capture his hand as it brushes against the side of my face. "I love you. I'm sorry I didn't do it right."

Before anyone else can object, he launches himself off a dune and glides across the sand toward the approaching hive. We stand silently, watching.

All at once I find my voice. "Get in the craft! We need to cover him. I don't care what he said. We'll pick him up and push our way through. It's worth the risk. If Green can pull us out of that drop, she can pull Cain from that swarm."

"No, Mason." Simons puts his hands on my shoulders, exactly like he used to. "Cain's right."

"No," I yelp, turning desperately to Green. "Tell him you can do it! We've all seen how you fly."

Green shakes her head, tears building in the corners of her eyes. "I can do a lot of things, but nobody can fly low through a hive that size and survive."

"We can't leave him to die!" I insist, searching for help. "Amos, tell them!"

"We have to deliver the cure," Amos says apologetically. "You can't save everyone."

I refuse to let her be right. Not about Cain, no matter what stupid, foolish thing he did. I swallow hard to force the mounting panic back, searching frantically for a view of him. In the distance, he looks like a dark speck moving toward the hive, about to converge. I put my fist against my head, desperate for something that isn't there, gripping my gun so hard my hand aches where the handle bores into my flesh.

Frustrated, I fire three quick blasts into the shadowed sky. Each plasma pulse crackles against the electromagnetic net before being swallowed by the cover. I watch in horror when they reemerge like a delayed ricochet. We dive for cover as they return with greater strength than when they were fired. The ground divots and shudders from the impact.

In the distance, Cain pauses long enough to look back. I will him to return with all my might, closing my eyes and picturing him turning the craft so we can fight together. When I open them, he's moving toward the hive again.

"You have the cure," I say, something familiar welling up inside of me as the dust flurries around us, making it difficult to watch the horizon. In a distant part of my brain, I see my father's lips moving, mouthing that one last word. "*Don't.*"

"Leave me."

"No," Simons, Jorey and Amos say in unison.

"You don't need me anymore. You stand a better chance of getting out of here if Orman comes after me. If he knows you left me, maybe you can escape. I'll fight with Cain. Together I'm sure we can bring him down."

Cain brings the personal craft to a stop. He's stationed himself atop a distant formation. The hive begins to swarm. The echoed blast of one of the low-powered orbs indicates he's trying to herd rather than kill them. To clear a path for us. As the bodies move and swell, something rises above the hive. It's an open craft with a single figure standing in the center.

Orman.

I check my pulsar gun's charge and say in a low, firm tone, "Go. Now."

Simons reaches out toward me as Amos says, "I'm sorry, Mason, we can't do that."

I duck to escape Jorey's reach and sidestep as Green closes in. Simons grabs me before I can make my escape.

"What are you doing?" I demand, pulling at the massive arm wrapped firmly around my waist.

"Saving your life," he responds. He tosses me over his shoulder and carries me back onto the hovercraft.

The hatch closes securely before Simons drops me to the floor. I burst from the ground and jerk at the latch, using my full weight to try and pry it open. The hovercraft lifts into the air, moving toward the hive.

"We can't leave him," I scream.

I scramble over to the arms station and pull myself into position as the mounted pulsar gun charges. Spinning the seat around, I search the swarm for signs of life. "Move in," I demand. "I'll take Orman out from the air. Once the hive disperses, Cain can catch our wake and ride out with us."

We approach the hive low, just as Cain instructed. I fire into the swarm, attempting to clear a view, searching desperately for any sign of him in the mass, hoping if Orman realizes I'm on the craft, he'll leave Cain untouched. Green brings us even lower, nearly scraping along the canyons as we move around the side of the swarm, nearly level with them. Drawn by our presence, the near-dead on the outer edge of the hive turn their focus to us. I fire steadily as they approach, keeping one eye deeper in the mass, still searching for Cain.

At the center of the hive, the open craft rises, and I see Orman up close, clear for the first time since the Northern Laboratories. His lanky arms rest on the controls of the craft and on a weapon of his own. His eyes are fierce and clear, a sinister, self-satisfied smile plastered across his smug face. The sight of him urges a dark fury from inside me. I prepare my aim, making sure to target his face, noting the tendrils of unkempt silver hair blowing wildly from the base of his cap.

He's wearing the same headset he wore the day the hive took down the Laboratories. I know now it's not to stay in communication with someone in the government or DDC. It's to stay in communication with the hive.

I tighten my finger around the trigger and breathe out slowly, the same way I always do when I fire. The craft shudders, and I lose my shot. I turn toward Green. "What the hell was that?"

"They're on us," Green apologizes. "I can't shake them!"

The craft shudders again. Orman's attention, and therefore the swarm, has turned to us. Cain's distraction failed.

"I can still get Orman," I insist. "Hold it steady for one second." I return to position and search again for Orman's craft.

"I'm doing everything I can, but we've got to keep making progress or we'll be grounded," Green calls back.

The air fills with the stench of burnt flesh. Shrieks and wails drown out all other sound as near-dead from the swarm throw their bodies against the craft's energy cells and melt in the heat. There's so little air in the space between corpses that the craft shudders and churns, riding a sea of melted bodies. The swarm thrusts itself forward, using the fallen as footholds as they thrash against the craft, causing it to pitch and dip aggressively.

"Just give me one shot," I plead.

I search frantically for Orman, needing to fire before it's too late. I find him, closer than before and approaching quickly. Our craft shudders violently as it pushes its way through the hive. I decide to take my shot, steady or not. Orman is maybe fifty meters away, his face plastered with a maniacal smile. He brings a hand to his head, momentarily leaving his weapon untended. I fire just as our craft lurches and dips, riding the turbulent wave of the swarm. I miss Orman's head but clip his craft, making it spin violently.

I hold my breath and pray he falls into the swarm. Instead, he regains control. The hive moves away, repelled by his presence. He fires at us. Our craft shudders as his blow impacts the right side. I return fire without aiming. A few near-dead drop as their bodies are decimated by the powerful plasma beam. I curse, unable to land a good shot in the struggle.

"We're not going to make it," Green cries. The craft surges and swells as though climbing a wave. "I can't keep us in the air."

"Keep trying. Crank up the engine," Amos insists.

The craft shudders again, smoking from one side. It sinks into the hive with the weight of their reaching arms. When I relocate Orman in the masses, he's not alone. Cain has appeared. He jumps from his glider onto Orman's.

"Dammit, Cain, move!" I scream as he blocks my shot.

Our craft is landed by the hive, dipping and rocking in the ocean of melted flesh. The metal walls creak and moan as the swarm presses in. A steady stream of curses flows from my mouth as Cain struggles to maintain his position on Orman's craft. I watch helplessly as they struggle. The walls of our craft start to buckle under the weight of pressing bodies. Despite Cain's sacrifice, the end has come after all.

Green struggles frantically with the controls, and the craft returns to life under her persistent coaxing. "Come on, baby!"

Cain lunges at Orman, landing a blow on his temple. The headset flies from Orman's head, falling into the swarming bodies. Orman twists around on the hovercraft, reaching for the fallen headset. Cain seizes the opportunity and tackles him. The two bodies topple off the craft, disappearing into the hive below.

"No!" I scream just as our craft breaks free from the swarm.

"Got it," Green cries, turning the thrusters to full power so we move toward the low, sunlit horizon at full speed. An enormous burst of energy that could only be one of the high-powered orbs radiates outward from the focal point of the dispersing bodies, consuming a good third of them.

"Cain!" I scream. The remaining near-dead pile onto each other in the canyon, appearing smaller with each passing second as we break away from the trap and burst through the opening in the sky cover.

The craft continues to rise until even the land masses are distant.

CHAPTER
FIFTY-NINE

HE'S GONE. He's really gone. I stare at the receding Deadlands, willing myself to see him one more time. Tears streak my cheeks as I grip the mounted weapon so hard the blood drains from my hands. It happened so fast. Cain is gone like Richards and Dunn before him, but I don't feel anything.

I sit at the craft's weapon, paralyzed by the shock of what's just happened. Simons calls to me, "Come on down from there."

I hear him but don't respond. If I move, then it's really over. I don't move.

"Mason," Simons calls again from below the firing station.

If I look at him, it'll make it real. Instead, I mumble, "As soon as we land, we need to prepare a search team."

"Kara." Simons' voice is low and soft. I finally look down at him. His face is streaked with tears and dust. "He's gone." It comes out as a whisper. He puts his hand over mine and gently urges me to let go of the trigger. I slide off the seat, and my feet hit the ground with a hollow thud. The craft is quiet.

"He betrayed us," I say, reaching for anything that will make the sharp ache of loss lessen.

"I don't think he meant to hurt anyone." Simons treads carefully. I don't know if he's as angry as I am or if he feels the loss as acutely, but he knows I do.

"It doesn't matter because that's what he did," I say, wishing for indignant fury to stifle the blooming sadness.

Amos leaves her position next to Green to join us. "Where is it?"

I remember the chip Cain gave me before fleeing to his death and retrieve it from my pocket. I hand it to her, trying not to think about it being Cain's final offering. "He said the tracker is in my leg."

"If the tracker is in your leg, how did he have anything to do with it? Orman would have been able to follow us the second we left the Laboratories," Jorey says, perplexed.

"This is a pair tracker," Amos says, turning the small piece of technology over in her hands. "The chip in Mason's leg wasn't activated until Cain joined it with this one. Together they create a signal that can be followed from anywhere."

"How did he do it?" Simons asks, shaking his head.

"He found the tracker on the ship. He practically admitted his plan when he found them, but I didn't realize. By then, I'd already told him about the surgery at the Institute," I say, realizing it was my trust in him, more than anything else, that allowed this to happen.

"How do we kill the signal? Can we destroy that thing?" Jorey asks.

Bitterly, I remember telling Cain not to mess with anything he found in the supplies and him telling me he wouldn't dare without reading the manual. *He should have left us the manual…*

"That might work," Amos offers, still studying the innocuous hunk of technology.

"What do you mean, might? You said the signal is created by proximity to one another," Jorey argues, as if he could out-logic the tech.

"It depends on what sort of a chip is in Mason's leg. If it's a simple pairing unit, the signal would be broken by throwing this piece out the window," she explains. "But if she's got a full unit in there, all the pair tracker did was activate the signal."

I consider the breadth of technology at the government's disposal—the archives of weaponry developed right under our noses in the Northern Laboratories. "How soon did the DDC know I'd made it to the Institute?" I ask, setting aside my gun and unfastening my jacket.

Amos falters before admitting, "Almost immediately."

I nod, taking off my jacket and unstrapping my pants. I've always known the DDC was aware of my presence at the Institute, but the way Amos described it, I believed there had been a lull—a breath between Amos extracting me from screening and my placement in the intern program.

"We have to take it out." I reveal the scar marking my hamstring.

"Out of your leg?" Jorey balks.

Amos stares with knowing dread. I hand her the knife I keep clipped to my waist. After a long minute, she takes a knee at my thigh and places the knife at the top of the scar. "This is going to hurt."

"You're going to do it right here? With that?" Jorey's voice rises with growing panic. He steps toward Amos, and Simons grabs his forearm, pulling him back.

"We don't have much of a choice about this. We can't leave it in there and risk leading the DDC straight to dissenter headquarters," Simons rationalizes.

"What if it's a simple pair tracker?" Jorey pleads.

"What if it isn't?" Simons counters.

"It's okay, Jorey. The tissue in there is mostly synthetic. If Amos is careful with her initial incision, the bleeding should be minimal. Once we're safe, I can get some real help," I say. I need him to be on board.

Amos pulls the tip of the blade away from my leg long enough to address Green. "Keep the ship as steady as possible."

"You've got it," Green agrees. The ship slows, then stops, suspended on a thick pocket of air flowing with the atmospheric currents.

I reach out and grab Jorey's hand, giving it a vicious squeeze. He squeezes back, as if he could lessen the impending pain by sheer will.

The knife cuts deep, and I wince, bearing down on the handhold as the world dims at the edges of my vision. I try to think of anything but the red-hot fire moving down the back of my leg, but it fills my senses. I groan and stagger, unable to help my body's involuntary recoil from the assault. Simons steps in, grabbing me under my armpits and holding me up.

"Someone give me a hand," Amos demands as I slump into

Simons, trying to hold still. I wish for blissful darkness, but it doesn't come. Everything hurts too much.

Jorey pulls his hand away from mine to kneel beside Amos.

"I need pressure—here," she instructs, and then I feel the pressure as Jorey pushes.

There's a sickening tug when Amos pulls my skin back from the area, exposing a miracle network of synthetic artistry. She works quickly as I pant, amazed at my capacity to feel so much. Jorey's hands move again, applying firm pressure above the wound. Then I feel something else.

"I've got it," she cries, pulling a small, bloody chip from the works. There's a twinge in my leg so sharp I cry out. Simons eases me to the ground, wiping the pouring sweat from my brow before leaving to retrieve a med kit.

Amos brings the piece into the light, wiping the blood from it onto her sleeve. Jorey looks up from where he holds my leg. "Is it a full unit?"

"It is," she agrees, putting it with the other piece in her lab coat pocket next to her heart. Simons hands her the small white box.

"Shouldn't you destroy those?" Jorey asks, increasing the pressure on my thigh. I wince and groan again, gripping weakly for Simons' hand.

"It was part of a biological circuit. It's inactive now that it's removed from its power source," she explains, working with Jorey to stitch the open wound that was my leg. I let their activity fade from my consciousness, concerned at how easy it is to do now that the task is finished. When they're done, Jorey puts his arm around me and helps me sit up. The craft spins like it did when we fell from the upper atmosphere. Sweat pours down the back of my neck, and I swim on the edge of consciousness.

"I'm cold," I murmur, shivering as he brushes the loose hair out of my face.

"Here," he says, draping my jacket over my arms. He puts his arm around my shoulders, pulling me toward him. I rest my head against his chest, too weak for anything else.

"Let me see the tracker," Simons says, holding his hand out to Amos.

She retrieves it from her chest pocket, prying it from the one Cain relinquished. "Without a network, there isn't much to see," she says.

"I don't need to look inside of it. I need to get rid of it," Simons clarifies, taking the piece in his massive palm.

"It's inactive now," Amos argues, refraining from reaching out to retrieve the piece from his clenched fish. It strikes me how much her time at the Institute has influenced her. She doesn't consider the chip a tracker any longer. Now it's a *resource*.

"What if this one is different?" Simons asks.

Amos' eyes flit to the side, thinking. "The technology doesn't exist."

"You can't know that. There's so much we don't know," I say, fighting the involuntary convulsions. It feels like I'm back on the icy tundra, holding Jorey's hand, fighting back death.

Amos returns her focus to Simons. "What are you going to do with it?"

"I'll take it toward the communities on the outskirts of the Dead-lands. If it's still active, they might believe we'd go there next," Simons concludes.

"We can do a drop," Green suggests.

"No, it's too risky. There could be any number of scouts, more traps..." Amos protests.

"I'll go by personal glider," Simons offers.

"That could work," Amos agrees.

Simons nods.

"No," I say. I won't let him ride out on the same device Cain used to fly to his death. "You can only fly at low altitudes. You'd be exposed, an easy target."

"She has a point," Jorey pipes in.

"I'm not risking the alternative, so this is going to happen." Simons gives Jorey a look that makes him immediately back down. He turns to me. "Mason, you're going to have to trust me. I don't mean for this to be a suicide mission."

I look at the personal glider Simons intends to use. It's meant for short-range trips, not the sort of journey he intends. It certainly feels like a suicide mission. I consider all the tracking technology the government has at their disposal on top of everything we don't know about. Even if Simons flies dark, the DDC can still read his heat signal or make a visual sighting.

He takes my silence as encouragement. "I promise I'll be careful. It will be like I'm a coyote again. Invisible."

Invisible. From the depths of my shock and agony, the word arouses inspiration. "You *can* be invisible!"

I try to stand, and the world spins away from me. The sweat reappears on my brow, and I have to resist the urge to vomit. "I need my bag."

Simons complies, and with his help, it only takes a few moments to find what I'm looking for. From one pocket I pull the small sack and retrieve the thin metal ring. From the other I pull the unfinished components of the orb night-light I never bothered to finish. I take a blank cartridge and attach one end to my receiver and the other to the orb's power intake. The fiberoptic tendrils hand from the side like limp strands of something that used to be alive. The programming is so simple it only takes a few minutes. I work as I explain. "Use the orb as a personal shield. This program will reverse your heat signature into light, blending you into your surroundings so you're invisible on any thermal or visual scan."

"Absolutely genius," Amos gasps.

"You're complimenting the wrong twin again," I admonish.

"When will you realize this is you?" Amos asks.

I ignore her and finish my work. Simons is already holding the personal glider at his side. I hand him the ring and programmed cartridge, my good leg trembling even with Jorey's support. "I hate that you're going."

After the matter of breaking off what rations we have, Simons is ready for departure. He looks at us and says, "After the drop, I'll find the dissenters at the outpost. This isn't goodbye. I'll be seeing you all before long."

Jorey nods, unable to speak. I fall back against him, heart thudding in my ears. "I'm going to hold you to that."

CHAPTER
SIXTY

SIMONS IS GONE before the sun touches the horizon. We remain in position until he disappears. Amos returns to the front of the craft and sits next to Green, holding the chip Cain stole between two fingers. "There's something peculiar about this piece. I'd like to know how he held onto it for so long without cuing the signal."

"You should have sent that thing with Simons," Jorey scolds, rubbing my back as I shiver.

"It's inactive. I'd like to study the programming when we reach base. We may find something useful," she says, tucking it back into her pocket.

Green reenters our flight plan, taking off into the darkening sky. Above the clouds, early stars streak past us like meteors in a milky black sky. I turn my head away from the windows, intending to sit in silence for the remainder of the journey.

"I'm sorry," Jorey says.

"It will heal," I say, my breath ragged as I inhale through the pain.

"I'm sorry about Cain," he says, putting his chin on my head.

"Me too," I sniff.

"He was an asshole, but he didn't deserve to die," Jorey says, keeping me in his embrace.

I nod as the tears begin to flow. "He was an asshole," I agree, then add, "He's an asshole for deciding to die like that and not giving us a choice."

Jorey goes silent, holding me while I cry. After a few minutes pass, he says, "He loved you. I was wrong about that."

I squeeze his shirt as another wave of tears bursts free. I nod again, realizing it's probably true.

"Simons is going to make it," Jorey insists.

"If anyone can, it's him," I agree.

"This is what he used to do—move through the world right under the DDC's noses," he says. It's a flimsy attempt to bolster us both.

"I'm going to be so mad at him if he doesn't." The statement comes out somewhere between a laugh and a sob that I bury in Jorey's shoulder, unable to fathom the possibility.

We fly for another hour. Jorey remains in place at my side, mourning with me in his own way. I'm frozen. Time has stopped in the little bubble where Jorey and I sit. The low static on the communication receiver bursts to life. "Green 1. Green 1. Come through."

"Holy hell," Green proclaims. "It's base… We've made it through!"

"Green 1? Confirm approach," the voice calls out.

"This is Green 1. Full delivery, request clearance and permission to land," Green replies enthusiastically over the comm.

I think about how wrong she is—how far off we are from a full delivery without Simons and Cain, or Richards… Shelby, Altman and Dunn. We're refugee survivors of an impossible mission.

"You're clear to land, Green 1. Landing base 3," the voice instructs. Green banks, and the craft turns toward the landing area. As she does, the comm comes back to life, and a new voice asks, "What happened out there?"

"We'll give a full report once we've landed. I'd rather be offline. Even on this channel," Amos replies. I don't disagree with her. Right now, after everything that's happened, even a dark channel could be dangerous.

We descend to the designated area—a large building whose roof has opened to receive us. It's a simpler process than landing in the

Deadlands. The heating cells power down, and we sink gently into place on solid ground.

"We're here," Jorey says as the roof closes above us.

Slowly, it sinks in that we've made it. We're at dissenter headquarters, delivering the cure.

Green puts the craft in shutdown, and Amos opens the hatch. From where Jorey and I sit, we can see our arrival party. We're surrounded by personnel. Instead of the form-fitted suits of government workers, these people are dressed in the uniform Dó coined frontier pants. Their hair is wrapped tightly in cloth, and they're heavily armed with pulsar guns, lashing poles and artillery I recognize as modified old-world guns. I note the absence of communication devices like my glove and wonder if I should remove it so I don't look so much like our enemy.

I let go of the pulsar gun I've been absently holding and stare at my hand. My raw, heat-blistered skin is bloody and impressed with the texture of the handle. Jorey places my pack, which now only holds Shelby's cure and a few disks of my own research, onto my shoulder before standing and offering assistance. I lace my other arm through the second strap and let him help me up. The shock of my foot touching the ground sends pain up my leg and brings some life back into my body, but I'm still numb.

Jorey puts his hand on my shoulder before I collapse and squeezes. "Come on, let's get you to the medics," he says, taking the better part of my weight.

Green and Amos exit the craft to cheers and shrieks of joy from our dissenter greeting party. The chorus of voices creates a hollow echo inside the damaged craft.

"Amos, it's a pleasure to meet you in person. I'm Officer Drake." A very large woman with close-cropped hair under a khaki hat greets us as she and Green set foot on the landing area. Amos replies, but her words are lost in the swelling sounds of celebration.

"...a near miss like nothing I've ever experienced," Green says to another officer.

"You were the right pilot for the job," he replies, grasping her hand in a congratulatory shake.

We exit the craft slowly, my pack pulling at my shoulders with more weight than I remember, as though the cure has grown within it. I have to lean on Jorey for support. It's more than pain inhibiting my leg's function. Something inside is broken now. The roar of the crowd is painfully reminiscent of the wails from the swarm of near-dead.

At the bottom of the hatch, Amos pulls me from Jorey, practically vibrating with joy. "Mason, we've done it!"

Tears streak the sides of her face as Jorey takes me into his care once more and Amos ushers us toward the waiting officers. "We'll get our laboratories up and running. It won't take long once we get communication back online—"

Officer Drake cuts her off, stepping into Jorey's and my path. "Kara Mason?" she asks in a voice that booms over the roar of the crowd.

I nod, too overcome by the swirling mix of joy and devastation to find the right words for this moment. She takes my free hand in her own and gives it a solid shake. "Thank you for everything you did."

"We need a medic," Jorey says, drawing Drake's attention.

She gives him a companionable smile and a stiff nod. "We've already got a group taking your patient in. We'll get them stabilized and into cryo as quickly as possible."

Drake turns away to engage Amos, her mind already on the next order of business. "We need to talk about the comm line. Have you heard—"

"I meant for Mason," Jorey says, speaking louder than I've ever heard him speak before. His tone reminds me of Simons. He intends to be heard. "She's injured. Mason needs a medic."

Drake's eyes return to me, and she registers for the first time how incredibly pale I am. Jorey shifts, and I nearly slip from his embrace, but he doesn't let it happen. He places an arm around my middle, lifting me into his arms.

"Mason, I'm so sorry. We'll get you some help," Amos gushes, pulling the other officer away from Green. He gives her a curious look, clearly not wanting to abandon Green's rehashing of our encounter with the hive.

"We need another medic team," Amos prompts.

He looks past Amos toward me and Jorey before jogging off toward the exit.

Green says something I can't pick up to Amos, who embraces her before they both approach me.

"I hope the back end of the flight wasn't too hard on you," Green says, sympathy replacing some of the jubilee of our arrival.

"It was fine. I'll be fine," I promise.

Officer Drake gives my shoulder a hearty shake. "That's right. We've got a good medical team here. You'll be right as rain by the time we've got the labs up and running."

"What do you mean?" I ask, looking between her and Amos.

"For the cure. Once you recover from your injuries, we should be ready," she says.

"I thought the lab was ready," Jorey says, his lips pressed against my ear to keep his comment private.

All around us, dissenters mill in celebratory oblivion, their cheerful voices making it difficult to hear. Amos makes a comment about Green's plummet from high altitude, and Drake responds with a low whistle. Green gives Drake the short version of our encounter with Orman.

"Get with Ash as soon as you can. The location of that hive should help nail down the facility," Officer Drake says.

The other officer is making his way back to us now, leading two medics through the crowd. One of them is carrying a familiar bag of medical supplies. I have no doubt it was siphoned away from the Northern Laboratories' supplies, which means it contains potent pain medication. The window for explanations is closing fast.

"Tell me what's happening," I insist as the medics converge.

"Mason, I don't want you to worry about this," Amos says, stepping away from Drake and Green. She places a cool hand against my burning cheek, meeting my gaze.

Officer Drake chimes in, "We've had a few setbacks since the comms went down. This facility is old world. We were counting on a lot of what came down from the Northern Laboratories to remedy that but couldn't make it happen without communication with the inside," she begins.

"Things were supposed to be ready. If the government hadn't been so intent on recovering supplies, they might have caught up to you before you made it to the Institute. We had to make a choice," Amos finishes. Green places a supportive hand on her upper arm. Amos places her hand over it.

"So the labs aren't ready," I say, clutching the handle of my pack and trying not to let my disappointment show.

"We've got a plan," Drake insists. "We're going to finish the lab and recover the missing dissenters, and we're going to do it right under the DDC's nose."

The medics are here now, shaking my hand and urging me to sit. My legs fall out from under me as they transfer my weight from Jorey's arms. I land on the ground with a heavy thud. The impact sends a jolt through my leg. My head spins. One of the medics is investigating my leg while the other prepares a syringe. When the medic administers the shot, a numbing wave of warmth travels like a shockwave through my body, instantly dulling everything.

"We need to get her into surgery now."

"I'll carry her," Jorey says with so much certainty no one stops him. The pain is still there, but far away.

"Once the other team has your patient stabilized for cryo, they'll treat you. I've got a few rooms set up in the residence hall. I'll send Timo in with rations," Drake says, escorting our diminished team toward the medical facility. She opens the door to a narrow path through heavy tropical growth. The air is thick with humidity. Amos and Green follow.

"Someone needs to get Simons before he gets caught," I say, resting my head against Jorey's chest.

"He knows how to hide. You made him invisible," Jorey promises.

The world is dim, as though the air has texture. We're approaching a structure built low into a tropical, forested mountainside. The medics take us down a long hallway lined with metal benches. My head is so heavy I might sink through Jorey and into the earth, but he manages to hold me with surprising ease.

"Bring her this way," the medic says. I'm floating down a brightly lit hall, away from Amos and Green.

"Wait." My mouth is fuzzy, and it's hard to get words out.

Jorey stops, and I force my eyes to open. I search the faces around me, not recognizing any of them. I strain against incomprehension until I find Green.

"You need to get Simons," I say in a voice that doesn't sound like my own.

"Mason, the ship is damaged," Amos protests, placing a hand on my shoulder.

"Please."

"We can get a craft ready," Drake says.

"Please, this way." The medic is getting impatient.

I'm moving again. The voices in the hall float back, diminished by more than distance, but Jorey remains beneath me, solid.

"Make sure they get Simons. He doesn't know where we are," I plead.

"Green will get him. You focus on getting better," he says, following the medics into a small, sterile room.

"The lab isn't ready," I say, letting him have some of my disappointment.

"It will be. We'll make it ready," he says, as if my concern is inconsequential. He deposits me on the table, where an assistant makes quick work of removing my clothes, replacing them with a sterile sheet. The second medic places an IV in my forearm. Equipment beeps, transporting me back to the Institute. I remind myself I'm with the dissenters now.

"I'll be right outside," Jorey says.

The assistant grabs at the handle of my pack as Jorey makes his way toward the exit.

"Jorey, the cure!" I call after him. The room stills as Jorey returns to my side. I push the pack into his hands, forcing my eyes to stay open.

"Is that…" the assistant begins.

"The cure," a medic breathes reverently.

"Don't let go of it. We've got work to do," I say.

"I'll guard it with my life," he promises.

"Don't you dare," I scold.

The door shuts, and he's gone. I close my eyes, letting the sounds of medical equipment and astringent smells of sterilizers fall away. My last thought is of Jorey standing outside the door of the dissenter headquarters, cure in hand, waiting for me to wake up so we can begin.

ACKNOWLEDGMENTS

When I was preparing to publish Due North I said some very bold things, like, "I think I could have the whole series published by the end of 2021."

Oh to be so, incredibly wrong. To everyone who listened to my grand ideas, thank you for not laughing in my face. It turns out raising a small family, adopting puppies, weathering a pandemic, and so much else really had an impact on my publishing timeline.

A huge thank you to my fan base for always checking in and making sure I knew there was an audience waiting for this book.

To my editors, I appreciate your work so much. Thank you for being willing to hurt my feelings in such productive ways.

To my kids, who remind me daily that life is about more than productivity. And, of course, to Drew, who's still supporting me even though we both know how hard the author journey is.

ABOUT THE AUTHOR

Jill N Davies started out as a chemist working for a pharmaceutical manufacturing company. After several years working in development she moved on to become... a high school science teacher. (You see where this is going, don't you?)

Before she went full *Breaking Bad,* she took a sharp left turn at Albuquerque and decided to dedicate her working time to creating stories. She now writes in the quiet moments of her life, squeezing novels into the nooks, crannies and nap times that act like the pauses between heartbeats.

Her debut series combines much of her acquired knowledge and experiences with the fascinating dystopia of a science-driven world.

When she's not writing, you may often find her running the trails near her home, hiking the national parks, or reading the same book over and over to her two daughters.

Find more at www.jillndavies.com

ALSO BY JILL N DAVIES

Due North

The Darkling Project (Book 3) Publication Date TBD

Extinction Event (Book 4) Publication Date TBD